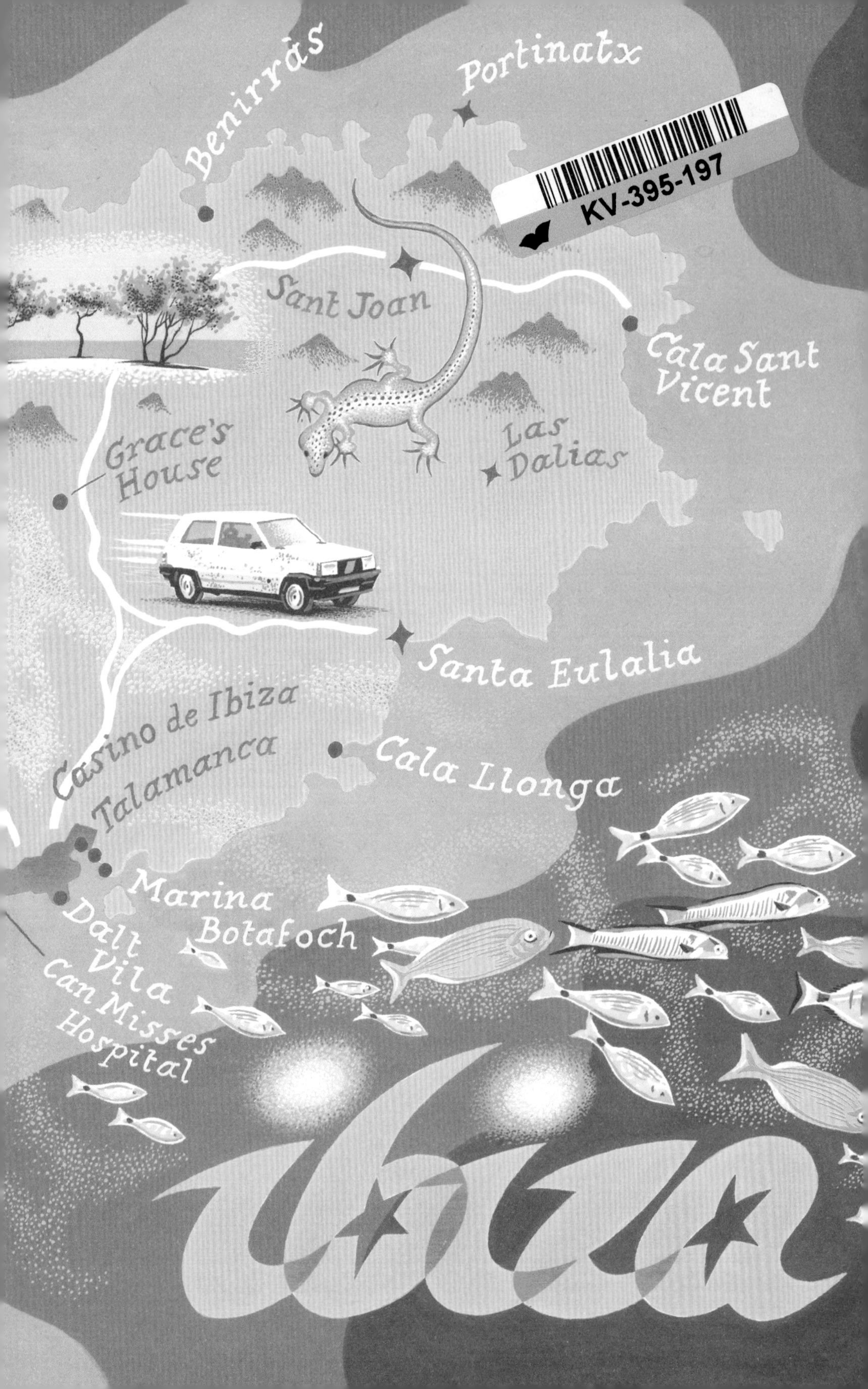
Benirràs
Portinatx
Sant Joan
Cala Sant Vicent
Grace's House
Las Dalias
Santa Eulalia
Casino de Ibiza
Talamanca
Cala Llonga
Marina Botafoch
Dalt Vila
Can Misses Hospital

THE LIFE
IMPOSSIBLE

Also by Matt Haig

The Last Family in England
The Dead Fathers Club
The Possession of Mr Cave
The Radleys
The Humans
Humans: An A–Z
Reasons to Stay Alive
How to Stop Time
Notes on a Nervous Planet
The Midnight Library
The Comfort Book

For Children

The Runaway Troll
Shadow Forest
To Be A Cat
Echo Boy
A Boy Called Christmas
The Girl Who Saved Christmas
Father Christmas and Me
The Truth Pixie
Evie and the Animals
The Truth Pixie Goes to School
Evie in the Jungle
A Mouse Called Miika

THE LIFE IMPOSSIBLE

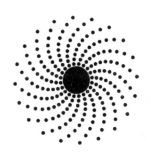

MATT HAIG

CANONGATE

First published in Great Britain in 2024 by Canongate Books Ltd,
14 High Street, Edinburgh EH1 1TE

canongate.co.uk

1

British Library Cataloguing-in-Publication Data
A catalogue record for this book is available on
request from the British Library

ISBN 978 1 83885 557 4
Export ISBN 978 1 83885 558 1

Typeset in Minion 11/14 pt by Palimpsest Book Production Ltd,
Falkirk, Stirlingshire

Printed and bound by CPI Group (UK) Ltd, Croydon CR0 4YY

MIX
Paper | Supporting
responsible forestry
FSC
www.fsc.org   FSC® C171272

To the island and people of Ibiza

Reality is not always probable, or likely.

Jorge Luis Borges

When the angels from above,
Fall down and spread their wings like doves;
As we walk, hand in hand,
Sisters, brothers, we'll make it to the promised land.

Joe Smooth, 'Promised Land'

Dear Mrs Winters,

I hope you don't mind the email.

You may remember me. You taught me mathematics at Hollybrook. I am now 22 years old and in my final year at university. I am studying mathematics, you will be pleased to hear!

I bumped into Mr Gupta in town in the Easter break and I asked after you and he told me all your news. I'm sorry to hear about the loss of your husband. Mr Gupta said you have moved to Spain. I had a grandmother who moved back to Grenada, which she hadn't visited since she was seven, and she found happiness there. I hope you are happy with your move abroad.

I too have experienced grief recently. My mum died two years ago and after that I fell into despair. I don't get on with my father and have found it hard to focus on university work. My sis (you may remember Esther) needs even more support now. I let my girlfriend down and she broke up with me. There have been other things too. At times I have found it very hard to carry on. It feels my life is already written at this young age and everything is known. I sometimes can't breathe with all the pressure.

I am in a pattern, like a number pattern, a Fibonacci sequence – 0, 1, 1, 2, 3, 5, 8, 13, 21 etc. – and like that sequence things get less surprising the further I go on. But instead of realising the next number is found by adding the two before it, you realise that everything ahead of you has already been decided. And as I get older, as I pass more numbers, the pattern becomes more predictable. And nothing can break that pattern. I used to believe in God but now I don't believe in anything. I was in love, but I messed that up. I hate myself sometimes. I mess everything up. I feel guilty all the time. I am drinking too much, and it screws up my studies and I feel guilty for that too because Mum wanted me to try hard.

I look at what is happening in the world and I see that our whole species is on a path to destruction. Like it is programmed, another pattern. And I just get fed up with being a human, being this small tiny thing that can't do anything about the world. Everything feels impossible.

I don't know why I'm telling you this. I just wanted to tell someone. And you were always kind to me. I am in the dark and I need a light. Sorry. That sounds melodramatic. I just need to be a good role model for my sister.

Please don't feel obliged to answer this. But anything you can say will be greatly valued. Sorry for the long email.

Thank you,
Maurice (Augustine)

Dear Maurice,

Thank you so much.

I am not in the habit of getting back to emails, not that I get a great many of them. I don't really 'do' the internet at all. I don't have social media. All I have is WhatsApp and I rarely even use that. But with your message I felt I must reply, and reply properly.

I am so sorry for all you have been through. I remember your mother from parents' evenings. I liked her. I remember her as serious, but with a little smile twisting the corners of her mouth when she spoke about you. You clearly cheered her up. Just being you. And that was a real achievement, especially for a teenager.

I started writing a response to you and it just grew and grew, far beyond a little email.

I have been meaning to write this all down for quite some time now, to be honest with you, and your message was the perfect prompt.

What I am about to tell you is a story even I find hard to believe. Please don't feel any obligation to take my word for anything. But know that nothing in this is made up. I have never believed in magic, and I still don't. But sometimes what looks like magic is simply a part of life we don't understand yet.

I can't promise that my story will help you believe in the impossible. But it is a tale, as true as any, of a person who felt there was no point left in her existence, and then found the greatest purpose she had ever known, and I think I have a duty to share it. I am definitely no role model, as will probably become clear. I have felt a lot of guilt in my life. And in a way this is a story about that. I hope you find some of it valuable.

Please find it attached.

Very best wishes,
Grace Winters

Sob Story

Once upon a time there was an old woman who lived the most boring life in the universe.

That woman rarely left her bungalow, except to see the doctor, help at the charity shop, or visit the cemetery. She didn't garden any more. The grass was overgrown, and the flowerbeds were full of weeds. She ordered her weekly shopping. She lived in the Midlands. Lincoln. Lincolnshire. The same orange-bricked market town that she had stayed in – apart from a stint at Hull University centuries ago – all her adult life.

You know the place.

And it wasn't so bad, but its streets were less welcoming than they used to be. It was hard to see half her fond memories covered in chipboard and ripped posters.

She sat and watched daytime TV and read the occasional book and did crosswords and Wordle to keep her brain in gear. She watched the birds in the garden, or stared at the small empty greenhouse, as the clock on the mantelpiece kept ticking. She had been an avid gardener once, but not any more. She was only seventy-two, but since her husband passed away four years before, and her Pomeranian – Bernard – shortly after, she had felt completely alone. In fact, she had felt alone for more than thirty years. Ever since April 2nd 1992, to be precise. The date she lost her entire meaning and purpose and never really found it again. But the loneliness had become a deep and literal reality in the last few years, and she felt approximately one hundred and thirty-two. She hardly knew anyone. Her friends had either died, or moved away, or retreated. She only had two contacts on her WhatsApp – Angela from the British Heart Foundation and Sophie, her sister-in-law, who had moved to Perth in Australia thirty-three years ago.

But of all the sad moments of the past, it was still that April date long ago that reverberated most profoundly. The death of her son, Daniel, had been the hardest and most devastating, and when a tragedy is as large as that it leads to other sadnesses and failures, the way a trunk leads to branches. But life went on. She and her husband Karl eventually moved into a bungalow and tried to make the best of things, but that hadn't really worked, and so they'd sat in mutual silence, watching television or listening to the radio. Her husband had always been very different to her. He had liked hard rock and real ale but had really been a fundamentally quiet soul. The trouble with tragedy is that it tars everything that comes after. On occasion they'd been comforted by the sharing of their memories, but when Karl died it became harder because the memories had nowhere to go. They just stayed, growing stale, inside her head. Which was why, whenever she saw herself in the mirror, she only saw a half-life. A slow-falling tree in an unseen forest.

She was also in a bit of a pickle with money.

Her life savings no longer existed. Ever since a scammer with a comforting Scottish accent had pretended to be a NatWest security advisor, and – with her foolish help – stole the £23,390.27 she and Karl had put away together. It was a long story, full of cunning characters and one ridiculous old fool (hello!), but much to your good luck it is not the tale being told here.

So anyway – this particular lady – she just sat there, with her aching legs, trying not to answer any emails from strangers, and letting her crumpled life drift like an empty crisp packet down the river. Her only spark of interest was the sight of a chaffinch or starling at the bird feeder in the small back garden, as she inhaled old memories and faded dreams.

Apologies

Sorry. That was a bit grand and melancholy. Talking about myself in the third person. I am just *setting the scene*. It's going to be fun, despite that introduction. And, like so many of life's fun things, it will begin with minimally invasive radiofrequency-based vein ablation surgery.

The Inability to Feel Pleasure

I was upside down when I decided to go to Ibiza.

The surgery bed I was lying on was tilted so far back I thought I was going to slip off. There was a mirror on the wall. I looked at my unkempt grey hair and tired face and hardly recognised myself. I looked like a faded person. I avoided mirrors, where possible.

They were trying to reverse the blood flow in my legs, you see. I was more covered in blue veins than a chunk of Gorgonzola and I needed to get them done. Not because of how they looked, but because they were making my calves itch and giving me sores. My aunt had died of a blood clot which broke free and achieved the lofty status of a fatal pulmonary embolism, so I wanted to get the varicose veins sorted before a clot of my own arrived with similar ambitions. I am sorry if this is too much information. I'm just determined to be as honest as possible with you, so I am starting as I mean to go on.

Truthfully.

So, as I listened to the radio, the vascular surgeon injected me multiple times with local anaesthetic along the length of my left leg – the final injection she fondly but accurately named the 'bee sting'. Then we got to the main part where, she told me, a catheter would be inserted into my calf to blast my great saphenous vein from the inside with 120°C of 'sauté-an-onion heat'.

'You should be able to feel something . . .'

And I did feel it. It wasn't pleasant, but it was something. The truth was that I hadn't really felt much for years. Just a vague lingering sadness. Anhedonia. Do you know that word? The inability to feel pleasure. An unfeeling. Well, that had been me for some time. I have known depression, and it wasn't that. It didn't have the intensity of depression. It was just a lack. I was just existing. Food was just there to fill me up. Music had become nothing more than patterned noise. I was simply, you know, *there.*

You should be able to feel something.

I mean, that's the most basic and essential form of existence, isn't it? Feeling. And to live without feeling, then what was that? What *was* that? It was like just sitting there. Like a table in a closed restaurant, waiting for ever for someone to occupy the furniture.

'Think of something nice . . .'

And for once, it wasn't very hard to think of something. And the main thing I was focusing on was a letter I had received from a solicitor's office less than two hours before.

Pineapples

The letter had been an unusual one.

It had informed me that I had been left a property in Ibiza, Spain, belonging to someone called Christina van der Berg. This Christina van der Berg had died and left me her worldly goods. Or some of them, at least. Another scam, I thought. You see, when people have stolen from you, it is hard not to see the world as a den of thieves. But even if I hadn't been scammed, it was ridiculous to imagine that someone I had never known would bequeath me a house in the Mediterranean.

It took me a while to understand that this is not exactly what had happened. Or, to put it another way, it took me a while to realise Christina van der Berg was not a stranger. Not exactly. The trouble was that the name had rung precisely zero bells. The Dutch element – van der Berg – added a kind of grandness that seemed fictional and unfamiliar, and it had thrown me off. Luckily, though, the letter from Nelson and Kemp Solicitors gave some further information, including a fleeting mention of this Christina's maiden name: Papadakis.

Now, that did ring a bell.

Christina Papadakis had been, for a very short while, a music teacher. We had worked at the same school together just before I got back with Karl. (We'd been together at university, but he had been in too much of a rush, so I'd called a hiatus.)

I must admit I didn't know her very well at all. I remember her as a very beautiful and shy young woman, with an air of glamour, which was a rarer quality back in 1979 than it is now. She had a heavy fringe and long dark hair and wore beads. She reminded me of the singer Nana Mouskouri, but without the glasses. Her father had emigrated from Greece as a young man just after the war. Apparently she had never been to Greece, but she seemed the epitome of Mediterranean sophistication to my provincial land-locked brain. And she did miss the food she had known growing up amid the Greek community in London – the first time I'd ever heard the word 'halloumi' in my life was out of her mouth. She always ate a lot of fruit. For instance, she would produce these elegantly crafted pineapple slices – not chunks – from her lunch box and that always impressed me. I once walked past her door while she was singing 'Rainy Days And Mondays' and the class were all open-mouthed in awe. Her voice was on a par with Karen Carpenter (another singer from Triassic times). The kind of voice that seems to still the air and time itself.

Anyway, one evening close to the Christmas holidays I had stayed late at school, adding tinsel to a display on trigonometry, and – on the hunt for more staples – I found her at her desk. She was sitting there, picking at her nails.

'Oh, don't do that,' I said, intrusively, as though she was a pupil rather than a colleague, 'you'll chip them.' I liked her nails. They were a warm-hued terracotta. But I felt immediately bad for saying that, especially when I saw her thousand-yard stare. I was tactless, socially. Always had been.

'Oh. I'm sorry,' I said.

'Please, don't be,' she said, suddenly looking at me and offering the most strained of smiles.

'Are you all right?'

It was then that she poured her heart out. She had been off school for a week, which I had barely noticed. She was having a crisis. She hated Christmas. Her now-vanished fiancé had proposed to her on Christmas Eve the year before. Being a relatively new arrival to the area, she didn't have any family. So I told her she could have Christmas Day with me.

And that is what happened. She came around and we watched the Queen's speech, *Goldfinger*, and Blondie on *Top of the Pops* singing 'Sunday Girl'. It was then Christina said she wanted to sing in front of crowds. We drank several bottles of Blue Nun, which was never the best mood stabiliser, and I apologised for the lack of pineapples. We talked late into the night.

She was feeling entirely unable to cope with things. A feeling I know more now than I did then. She was struggling with teaching, wondering if she was in the wrong career. I told her everyone at Hollybrook felt like that. At one point she mentioned Ibiza. We were on the very edge of a new decade and the Spanish package holiday boom was going strong and she'd heard of a new hotel over there looking for singers and musicians.

I was intrigued. I found her to be a mystery, and I probably asked her too many questions. It is a maths teacher trait. The value of the unknown variable must always be found.

'I feel like I have a life inside me that needs to be lived and I am not living it.'

Those probably weren't her exact words. But they capture it. And she said, 'I know it doesn't make any sense. I am Greek, not Spanish. There are enough Greek islands. I should go to one of them. Because I can speak the language. Kind of. And I don't know any Spanish and I really think it is good to know the language if you live somewhere.'

'You could learn Spanish. You should do it if you want to. You should.'

'It doesn't make sense.'

And then I said something very un-me. I said: 'Not everything has to make sense.'

She had a fire in her eyes at the prospect of getting a job over there, so I told her to go for it if she wanted to, and not to worry about what people thought. I am pretty sure that's what I said, because I remember giving her a necklace I'd had since I was a child – and on the pendant was St Christopher, patron saint of travellers. I was a lapsed Catholic and associated it too much with my upbringing but had never been able to throw it away. Giving it to Christina felt right.

'He'll protect you,' I said.

'Thank you, Grace. Thank you for helping me. With this decision.'

She sang 'Blackbird' at one point. She sang it solo first. Very unfestive but very beautiful. There was a bittersweet quality to her singing that made me cry. She tried to teach me. 'You just need to become the song. Be inside it. Forget that you exist. It's the easiest Beatles song to sing,' she reassured me. 'Well, after "Yesterday". And "Yellow Submarine".'

It turned out it wasn't an easy song at all to sing. But we'd had enough wine not to care.

She explained her love of music to me.

'It makes the world bigger,' she said, eyes glossed with alcohol-infused sentiment. 'I feel like I am trapped in a box sometimes and when I am playing piano or singing, I break out of that box for a while. Music to me is like a friend that comes in just when you need it. A bit like you, Grace.'

Anyway, we went for a walk. One of those cold Christmas walks where you smile at every stranger you pass. Well, you certainly did back then. And that was it. There really wasn't much more to it than that. She went back to school for a few months and then she was gone. She never came around to my place again. We did speak in the staff room, although she seemed a little embarrassed in front of me. I didn't understand it. How this lovely, talented person who wanted to sing in front of crowds was embarrassed about needing some company at Christmas. And one day – possibly the last time I saw her – she came up to me in the car park and said quietly, with tears glazing her eyes: 'Thank you. You know, for Christmas . . .'

Just that. I can't emphasise enough how much of a nothing I had thought it to be. That was all I did. Gave a person a place to be on Christmas Day decades ago.

And then, decades later, out of the blue, I get this letter. And it told me that Christina had died and that she had given me her house in Spain for 'an act of kindness long ago'. It also made clear I could sell the house, or rent it out, if moving there was too 'impractical'.

It was a surprise, to say the least. And one that left me feeling like I had lost more than I had gained. A friend I never really had from a time that felt like a distant dream. I had no plan to move there. As you get older, patterns become harder to break. And you don't want them to break. My pattern had been broken various times in the past. When I retired. When my husband keeled over in his greenhouse. Even losing our dog, Bernard, had thrown me off balance. And, of course, when Daniel got hit by a Royal Mail lorry while riding his bike.

And nowadays, while I was craving the old married pattern I'd once found too much, a new pattern had formed. Feed the birds each morning. Food delivery on Monday. A morning voluntary stint at the British Heart Foundation charity shop on Friday. Cemetery on Sunday. And eternal guilt and grief and emptiness. There were only the most minor fluctuations. I had settled into the pattern called Increasingly Elderly and I had not really thought about it.

But that was all about to change.

An Ongoing Situation

'Sorry if this is too direct,' I told the solicitor. 'But how did she die?'

'I thought you knew,' she said. Mrs Una Kemp. A voice like it had only just come out of the fridge and needed time to soften.

'No,' I said. 'It stated that she had died, in the letter, but it didn't say how. So I would like to know how she died, if possible.'

'She died at sea . . .'

This wasn't, I realised, a direct answer.

'I'm sorry. *How* did she die?'

A crackle of breath on the line. 'Oh. That is an ongoing situation.'

Ongoing situation.

'Sorry. In what sense?'

'In the sense that the Spanish authorities are still looking into the precise circumstances in which she died. They are very thorough. The only thing that we know for certain, the only thing that we have been told, is that she died at sea.'

It only occurred to me a good five minutes after the conversation had ended that this ambiguity seemed rather peculiar. Why were the facts so mysterious? According to the solicitor, her will had been recently changed to include me as a beneficiary. This, combined with the general bizarreness of it being left to me, filled my mind with questions.

And I had always been the type who couldn't see a question without pursuing an answer. Wherever it took me.

.14159

'No two legs are ever the same . . .' said the surgeon. 'Even on the same person. Even if they look identical. The veins are always a different pattern. It's like fingerprints.' And there was something about what she said that made me think of mathematics. All those examples of unpredictability sitting inside sameness. The way if you times a diameter by pi you will steadfastly always find the circumference of a circle, yet the numbers that make up pi's decimal placings follow no pattern at all.

3.14159 et cetera, for ever, with total and utter and mind-boggling randomness.

There is always an element of unpredictability in even the most predictable things. And if you lived like it wasn't there, then life would pull the rug from under you, so you might as well embrace the .14159.

I stared at the blank wall and the upside-down clock. I knew almost nothing about Ibiza. Except that it was exactly the sort of place I didn't think I would ever visit. Or want to visit.

Blondie came on the radio. Not 'Sunday Girl' but 'Heart Of Glass'. Unpredictability within a pattern. Like life.

'You're not going to be flying anywhere soon?' the surgeon asked, a few minutes later. 'Because it's a bit dangerous, with your legs.'

'Are you suggesting I go without them?'

She didn't appreciate my joke.

'No,' I said, watching the nurse slowly hitch a compression stocking up my leg. 'No. I am not flying anywhere soon.'

It had been a long time since I had knowingly told a lie.

And I felt as naughty as a retired and widowed maths teacher possibly can. Because in that second, still tilted upside down on that surgery bed, I knew I had a plan.

The plan being a simple but noncommittal one. To fly to Ibiza with an open return ticket, to have a look at the house which for some ridiculous reason I had been left, and to stay there until I hated it so much even an empty bungalow in Lincoln with a thousand memories was a better option.

But before I could begin I had something to do. I had to go to the one and only place I deemed truly important to visit. The cemetery.

Conversations with the Dead

On the way to the cemetery I passed my old boss – and your old head-teacher, Mr Gupta – leaving a coffee shop. After some small talk he asked me how I was doing, and I was feeling sad, so instead of saying that I told him another truth.

'Ibiza?' he said. Raised eyebrows, stifled smile. 'I never saw you as the Ibiza type.'

'No,' I said. 'Neither did I.'

And shortly afterwards, I continued on my way.

Later, having changed the flowers on my Daniel's grave, I sat down on a bench beneath a yew tree. I stared at the simple grey of the headstone and its spare design and engraved letters, the words made visible by shadow.

DANIEL WINTERS
A beloved boy.
March 15th 1981 – April 2nd 1992

I was there for about an hour that day.

I sat, as always, in silence. I never knew what to say to him. To his imagined presence. It wasn't that I was averse to talking to the dead in public. I spoke to Karl all the time. But with Daniel it was difficult, for many reasons. More than three decades of grief had passed – we were deep into another century and millennium – but I still felt stuck for words. I had nothing to say but sorry. As ever, I calmed myself by counting gravestones, and doing sums with them.

I don't want to weigh down this story too much with talk of sad things, but I want to tell you that he was a very special boy. I want to picture him. He was always tall for his age and narrow and would read books as he walked. He was bright and funny and even in a sullen mood he would have a small smile on his face as if he found the whole world a comedy. He loved *Choose Your Own Adventure* novels and pop music and TV that was too old for him (*Hill Street Blues*, which to my disapproval he watched repeats of with his dad when he was nine). He made himself triple-decker sandwiches with peanut butter and Marmite. He made his own comic strips about a time-travelling dog. He didn't like school very much – well, not his new one because he wasn't into sport, and didn't want to pretend. He was a very honest person, actually. Lying never really occurred to him. I think. But he was a dreamer too. If he had never gone out on his bike in the rain that day, he would have ended up doing something creative. An illustrator maybe. He loved art and was good at it. When he was eleven, he drew a beautiful picture of a bluebird and gave it to me for Mother's Day because he knew I loved birds.

He died before he became a teenager, let alone an adult, so it is hard to say who he would have turned out to be. There are two kinds of ghosts that torment you when a young person dies. The ghost of who they were, and the ghosts of who they could have been. His death created a hole right through me that could never again be filled. For years getting through a day was an Olympic event. There was a continual sense of terror at the knowledge that life dared exist without him. It was hard not to be furious. Most of all with myself. *I should never have let him out on the bike in the rain.*

I know you have known grief, Maurice, and I am so sorry to hear about your mother. For the first two years after Daniel died, I was beside myself. *Beside myself.* It's an interesting phrase, isn't it? I was there, but not there. I was watching myself in the third person. A character in a life that looked like mine but wasn't. I missed him so much, but also I felt like I was missing myself too. That's the thing with grief. The way it kind of sinks you into death as well. I mean, you are still biologically functioning obviously. You are out there breathing and seeing and talking but you aren't properly alive any more.

'I love you,' I whispered, eventually. 'I am going away for a while. I will think of you every day. Goodbye.'

And then I took one of those deep, shaky inhales I always did when I was near him, and I swallowed back the tears before they started and walked a short distance to Karl's grave. I always felt like it was a walk through time. Do you know what I mean, about cemeteries? Each row another era, onwards and onwards. Karl's headstone was marble, but black. He specifically had shared a preference for a black marble headstone.

'It's a bit more rock and roll,' he'd said. He was about as rock and roll as a cheese sandwich, but he did enjoy rock music and his favourite band was Black Sabbath so that probably explained it.

KARL WINTERS
January 20th 1952 – October 5th 2020
A devoted father and husband.

The word father was weighted with pain, I know, but the devotion was real. When we moved to the bungalow, he'd still insisted we take as much of Daniel with us as possible. His old *Star Wars* figures, toy cars, comic books, drawing pads, the works. It was like he became a kind of museum curator and I always felt bad that I found it suffocating, seeing his memory everywhere. But even after Karl died, I never took any of it to the charity shop.

'Karl, I've made a decision,' I told his headstone, as I stood there on my fresh legs.

His silence was much the same as it had been whenever I announced something he sensed he wouldn't like. I could almost see him raising his eyebrows. He had never been much of a conversationalist, and being dead had done very little to improve the situation.

'I am going to Spain. To the Balearic Islands. To . . . *Ibiza* of all places.' I flinched a little, saying that. And I spoke the italics out loud. The whole cemetery heard my distaste. 'Please don't judge me.'

Karl had been to Ibiza's large neighbour Mallorca before. He had spent three days in Palma years ago, at a civil engineering convention. It had been a career highlight, apparently. But Mallorca had a different connotation in my prejudiced mind to Ibiza. Mallorca was a balanced elder sibling with a confident smile. Ibiza, I imagined, was the loud younger mischievous one who went off the rails. Ibiza, I imagined, was *naughty*. Right down there with Las Vegas, Cancún, Rio during carnival and a full-moon party in Thailand as a place I would least likely choose to visit, even if I had the money. A place of parties for young people with reasons to celebrate. Or maybe for rich people and their yoga mats. The opposite of me. I was old and stiff with a depressing bank balance and hadn't danced in decades. And I had the very sincere belief that I had no reason to celebrate.

I was, in short, prejudiced. I had of course no real idea what Ibiza was like. It was a mere word. Synonymous with a loud kind of fun. And I had decided long ago, with a kind of self-punishing masochism, that fun of any kind was the very last thing I should be having. Or deserved.

'I don't think I'll be going to any nightclubs . . .' I reassured Karl's grave.

It was then that I cleaned the vase and placed the new foam filler inside before firmly pressing the stems of the chrysanthemums in place. I always did this, but today I was doing it with extra effort. I didn't want the flowers to blow away. I needed them to stay there as long as possible.

'So, I don't know how long it will be until I come back and see you again. But I am not selling our bungalow or anything like that. There really is no thought-out plan. I will just see how it goes. A change of scene.'

A tear formed, and the sun appeared from behind a cloud, and I felt its warmth. I wiped away the tear as I smiled at another woman, another widow, vigorously wiping clean the marble of a newer headstone. I stared down at the grass, suddenly shining and bright. When you grieve someone you see their message in everything. Even in the sunlight on a blade of grass. The whole world becomes their translator.

And then I told him what always comes so easy when it is too late.

'I love you, darling. I will see you later.' And then I added, with barely a second's thought: 'I am sorry for what I did.'

The Tall Rock

On the plane to Ibiza, I sat in front of a row of young people talking excitedly about nightclubs. It sounded like a new but half-familiar language. A kind of code. 'So . . . Ushuaïa tomorrow, Monday DC-10 for Circoloco, Amnesia on Wednesday, Ushuaïa then Hï on Friday, Pacha on Saturday . . .'

It occurred to me that I had never been young. Even at twenty-one I'd have found that schedule – dancing all night, sleeping on sun loungers all day – exhausting.

They were lovely young people, though. Dressed like rainbows and bouncy as Labradors. They had tried to tot up how much the tickets were going to cost, and I did the maths and told them, and they had a collective gasp and rethought their plans. They were gushingly grateful. When you have been a teacher, you always see the child in everyone. You imagine what they would have been like in class. Especially those who were just one step in front of that childhood.

It was a mixed crowd on the plane.

Immediately on my left was a handsome Spanish man with long hair and flip-flops and a feather tattoo on his forearm and a Zen air of calm, patiently trying to read. To my right, a boaty middle-aged woman with aggressive perfume and upturned collar was talking across the aisle to a cold-eyed person called Valerie, comparing property prices across the Balearics. 'Ibiza is silly money these days. *Silly money.* It's suddenly very chi-chi again. Posh boho. I'd pick one of the other islands. *Men*orca, not *Mal*lorca, is the place to invest. That's what Hamish says. Total buyers' market right now. I know someone who converted a finca there and quadrupled its value. *Quadrupled!*'

A trio of thirtysomething women, sat in front, were off to an agro-turismo retreat for a week of yoga and wellness but wanted to make sure they visited a hippy market and saw the sunset at a beach whose name I forgot the moment they said it. One said she was determined not to post on Instagram or look at TikTok for the entire week.

A young teenage boy was talking in very gentle tones to his mum about TikTokers, YouTubers, a rapper called 21 Savage and other emblems of a new world I couldn't even hope at that point to understand. He had a sweet relationship with his mother. I tried not to think of Daniel and just be happy for them. The mother was very youthful. They were across the aisle and I could see them clearly with a single glance. She had bobbed black hair and a T-shirt which said 'Taylor Swift: The Eras Tour' on it. The word 'eras' entered my mind and didn't leave. I thought about how you enter a new one. Not just by stepping back through rows of headstones in a cemetery but in your own living existence. How you need to create a distinct break with what has gone before. In geology it is often after an extinction, isn't it? The Mesozoic Era ended with the mass death of the dinosaurs via a meteor. I wondered if I was starting a new era or if I was taking too much with me. This is the challenge of life, isn't it? Moving forward without annihilating what has gone before. Knowing what to clasp onto and what to release without destroying yourself. Trying not to be the meteor and the dinosaur at once.

There was also, in the front aisle nearest the toilet, a couple my age who spoke in polite voices and were attentively studying a book called *Secret Walks: Ibiza and Formentera*. They were talking to each other about something they'd heard about the island on Radio 4's *Start the Week*. I felt a twist of sadness. Oh, to still have someone to share secret walks with. They looked so snug. I thought of a bittersweet nature documentary I'd once watched about Eurasian beavers, and how in order to ensure they had enough tree bark to keep themselves going they mated for life. And if one died early, the other was basically scuppered.

I wished I could squeeze Karl's hand.

My legs weren't a problem. There were no real aches, just a mild swelling of the ankles but I was used to that. I did my calf exercises and moved my feet around a bit, a slow unseen tap dance to get the blood moving. My hips were beginning to ache in the seat. I tried not to think about that. Joint pain was like grief. The more you thought about it, the more it hurt, but you couldn't *not* think about it because it bloody hurt. Vicious circle.

I felt the weight of my own silent stillness, sitting there, amid such life and noise. I stared down at the rings on my left hand. The wedding band and the ruby of the engagement ring. I remembered him proposing that second time, in the library, sheltering from the rain.

I'd said no on his first attempt, six years before in an Indian restaurant in Hull, because we were too young and someone had to be sensible.

As the pilot gave us an update of our altitude I stared deep into the red gemstone, and the memories it contained. Then I snapped out of it before I went too maudlin.

Speaking of memory triggers, there was a baby being carried up and down the aisle. The mother was kissing his head and bobbing the young chap in her arms. There had been a time when such a sight hurt. A time when I'd wanted to give up teaching simply not to be faced with so many children, alive, riding to school on bikes that never crashed into lorries. I smiled at the baby and tried to mean it. The baby began to cry.

'Sorry,' I mouthed to her mother.

She humoured me with a grin and a nod.

A flustered air steward passed by, wheeling a drinks trolley, and I got myself a gin and tonic, which was slightly out of character and probably not advisable given my leg vein situation. Not that I was exactly following doctor's orders.

I was meant to keep standing up to help my circulation, but I was quite self-conscious, so I stayed sitting down most of the time, surreptitiously doing those exercises.

There was some turbulence. The clubbers seemed to enjoy it.

The baby began to cry again.

We began our descent.

I glimpsed a rocky coastline and rugged green hills out of the porthole. Swathes of golden beaches. A landscape studded with white houses and occasional clusters of mid-rise hotels or apartment blocks. I saw an islet out in the Mediterranean. A vertiginous uninhabited rock I would soon learn to be Es Vedrà. Even then, from the distance of the plane, before everything that was going to happen, it gave me a feeling of both dread and wonder. If I had been more in tune with that feeling, I would probably never have left the airport and taken the first plane home. But back then my senses were dull, and I had absolutely no idea what I was in for.

Eventually, we landed.

As everyone stood and excitedly took their hand luggage from the overhead compartments, about to head off to their known destinations, I sat still for a moment. I took a few slow, deep breaths, just staying there. As if a part of me was still up in the clouds and I needed to wait until it reached me.

When you move a number from one side of an equation to another it is of course called a transposition. I felt like such a number. Like I had not just taken a short flight to another part of Europe, but that I had been transposed. That I had *crossed over* something unseen and that I would now, somehow, be rearranged. Revalued. And there would be a permutation of elements. I had a vague but not entirely new sense that I had upset the order of things.

The airport was impressive. It was stylish and bright and shone with clean efficiency. And as I neared the exit, passing a row of car rental kiosks, I noticed two women saying goodbye to each other. They were about thirty years old, I would have guessed. One, with her back to me, had blonde hair. The other had glasses and wild, unruly hair, and denim shorts and a T-shirt. I noticed the T-shirt because it had a picture of Einstein on it. The one with him sticking out his tongue. She looked sad. They were in love, but the blonde-haired one was going somewhere the other wasn't. And I walked slowly past them.

The dark-haired woman saw me looking at her. She smiled, instinctively, rather than be offended by my nosiness. It was a kind smile. It put me at slight ease, in that busy airport. But I had no idea that I would soon know this young person, or that we would eventually become friends. And I often think about how I saw her right there, just after I had landed. How strange it was. How it was part of a pattern that even now I can only glimpse at.

I headed outside and the air blasted me like a furnace.

I looked around, trying to get my bearings. The building had a large sign outside in big stylish letters saying *Eivissa*. That was Catalan. Ibiza is a Spanish island, and they speak Spanish, though Catalan is also an official language.

Eivissa. It was a good name. It sounded like a promise. I suppose I was about to find out what kind.

I realised how mad I was. *What was I doing?* I knew absolutely no one on this island. I hadn't been abroad in years. I couldn't speak Spanish except for 'muchas gracias', 'por favor' and 'patatas bravas'. And yet, here I was. Undoubtedly here. Undoubtedly transposed.

Abroad. Alone. And already a little bit afraid.

It Begins with A

I had a small tartan suitcase and an address and an envelope with a key inside. That was it. That was everything. A world condensed.

'What hotel?' the taxi driver asked me, smiling, as he placed my case in the boot of the gleaming white car, with a whole row of identical vehicles lined behind him. His aftershave evoked a sylvan glade and he was impressively groomed. Neat beard. Sunglasses. As much Formula 1 as taxi rank. Strong. Arms that could wrestle an ox. He slid his glasses onto the top of his head and made eye contact. His English was heavily accented but very good. I am terrible for judging people on their faces, and he had an honest face and a mother's-boy smile. I liked him. But still, I felt very abroad. The throbbing heat, the signs in Spanish and Catalan, the exotically blue sky, the number plates, the slick camel-coloured modern architecture of the airport. I stood staring up at dizzying palm trees like a baby at tall strangers. Stranded. Confused. I had no idea what I was doing. The furthest I had travelled in the last four years had been to the Tesco on Canwick Road, so being in a taxi rank amid frantic crowds and rolling luggage and beside these giant palm trees made me feel like an explorer. A Don Quixote dressed in Marks & Spencer.

'Hello. Hola. Oh, it is not a hotel. It's a house . . . casa . . . casa . . . casa . . .' I had that terrible English habit of believing the only barrier to linguistic comprehension was not repeating things enough. I handed him the address. He stared at it like it was difficult. Or as if it disturbed him a little. I told him the road even though he could read it. 'Carretera Santa Eulalia.' I was clearly pronouncing it wrong, but he was polite about it. Or at least, ignored it completely.

He kept staring at it. At the writing. A look of concern still haunted his face.

'My handwriting is awful,' I said, apologetically. But that wasn't it.

'I know this place   ' he said, quietly, his smile completely gone now. 'I have been here before . . .'

'Oh. Have you?'

He nodded and looked at the next taxi driver in the rank. An older, balder man leaning against his vehicle as he smoked a cigarette who gave us a frustrated get-a-move-on kind of look. So we got inside the vehicle.

'Is everything okay?' I asked.

There was a little pause. Then he pulled away and seemed to snap out of it.

'Sí. I think so. That house . . . It is the one a little way past the go-kart track, yes?'

'I don't know, actually. I am new here.'

'Are you visiting family?'

Family. Such a friendly but painful word. 'No. No. I'm not visiting anyone. I am just here to stay in the house. I used to know the woman who lived there.'

He seemed to have something to say about this. But decided against it.

As we drove, we passed palm trees and roadside taverns and giant sun-bleached billboards advertising nightclubs, and a cockerel walked nonchalantly onto the main road. Two old men laughed as they played chess in the heat outside a basic-looking bar with a battered ancient vending machine advertising Fanta Limón. We passed a couple of high-end designer garden centres with lots of large pots of cacti and olive trees sitting in the dazzling light of the forecourt.

The driver had his window open a little. I caught the scent of juniper and pine and faint citrus. A sweet Mediterranean perfume.

The island was greener than I expected. I don't know why but I had been imagining more arid than lush, and it was certainly hot and dry, with buildings rendered a blinding white under the sun, but as we got further away from the airport, I saw dense pine-covered hills. Nestled away from the road, situated among those trees, were beautiful villas. One was closer to us. Bright pink and magenta clusters of bougainvillea flowers spilled over walls in a proud display of beauty. I observed the twisting trunk of a carob tree.

'I know this house . . .' the driver told me again. But this time he seemed to get closer to the thing he had wanted to tell me. 'It is all on its own on the road. People went there. They went there a lot.'

'People?'

'Yes. People.'

'Ah. What kind of people?'

'All kinds. There was a man with a beard, wearing nothing but swimming trunks. An old man he was, with a beard. He was a diver. You know . . . scuba.'

'Did he know her?'

'I think so. I have taken him twice. The last time he had a woman with him. A much younger woman.'

'Were they friends with her?'

'I don't know. She must have a lot of friends. There have been whole families who came to see her. Tourists too. British, German, Spanish. A rich man – well-dressed – I picked him up from the restaurant near the Hard Rock Hotel. He had been there to eat. He told me the restaurant. It is the most expensive restaurant in the world. Do you know that? The most expensive restaurant in the world is right here in Ibiza. Not Paris. Not New York. Not Dubai. Right here.' The driver said this with a strange cocktail of pride and scorn. 'He owns hotels . . . I forget his name . . . It begins with A . . . Most recently there was a woman who was crying.'

'Crying?'

'I asked her if she was okay and she told me she would know soon, after her visit. But anyway, that wasn't the strangest thing.'

'What was that?'

'One night I saw something . . . crazy there.'

'Crazy?'

He nodded in the rear-view mirror. 'Yes. A light. A massive light. Coming from the house. From the windows . . . I was driving past . . . It . . . how do you say this? It nearly makes me not see. I nearly drove off the road . . .'

I was going to reply, but then his two-way radio went, and someone asked him something in Spanish and he answered and I didn't understand a word.

*

It was definitely not a desert island, nor a deserted one, but I could already see it was an alluring place despite my prejudices. There was something in the air. I wondered what Christina's house would be like. My house, I mean, though it is hard to feel like you own something you have never seen. And something you feel you don't deserve. Like you won a prize by mistake.

I was feeling something, though. Something fleeting but pleasant. Which was unusual. I had a faint sense of something I used to have when I travelled when I was younger. It's a silly feeling but I will share it in case you have ever had it too. The feeling is that of *the whole world happening*. It squares – no, cubes – no, quartics – the *now*. What I mean is that travel *tesseracts* experience. It explodes it to the fourth dimension. And it becomes dizzying to realise how many nows are happening all at once. To think of how many taxi drivers in every continent are talking into their radios right now. How many people are giving birth. Or eating a sandwich. Or writing a poem. Or holding the hand of someone they love. Or staring out of a window. Or talking to the dead.

'You mentioned a light . . .' I said. My voice was faint and distracted because just at that moment we passed a shop called Sal de Ibiza alone on the road. It was painted a pretty turquoise colour. But then something broke my calm. I felt a sensory heightening, like an animal that suddenly realises they could be eaten. There was a red bicycle lying on the dusty ground outside. One of the main problems of the world was the continued existence of red bicycles. Anyway, I did what I always did when I saw one, or saw anything else that so keenly reminded me of Daniel: I turned to mathematics. A road sign said *Santa Eulalia 3, Sant Joan 21, Portinatx 25*. So in my head I worked out percentages: 25 per cent of 3 is 0.75, 3 per cent of 21 is 0.63, 21 per cent of 25 is 5.25. Some people had deep breathing. Those three women on the plane had yoga. But I had mathematics. It helped distract me. It helped me forget, for a moment, there were some things that couldn't be broken down or subtracted away.

Salt

The driver had seen me looking at the bicycle and thought I was interested in the shop. He seemed to be trying to make up for his earlier awkwardness at seeing the address.

'Ibiza is an island of salt. They harvest the salt in Ses Salines. The salt . . . you know . . .' He mimed something big and flat as he searched for the English word.

'Pans?' I offered.

'Yes. The salt pans. They are beautiful. You must see. Especially when the . . . pink birds are there.'

'Flamingos?'

'Yes. Yes. You must see them. My father was a salt-miner, and his father was a salt-miner, and his father's father was a salt-miner, and father's father's father was a salt-miner . . .' I was getting it. 'You see, señora, Ibiza has been invaded by many different people in its history . . . but always the salt has stayed the best in the world. We salted the fish eaten by the emperors.'

I would later discover that the taxi drivers of Ibiza often doubled as tour guides and historians.

'And now you are invaded by tourists,' I said, calm again after my bicycle-induced wobble.

'Yes,' he laughed. 'Them too. The worst of the invasions. The hippies then the ravers then the celebrities and the hippies one more time. From everywhere. Not just Britain. Germany, France, Holland, Italy, Portugal, Sweden, and even today you have the Americans and everyone else too . . . Brazilians, Argentinians . . . No, it is a happy invasion really. We are all the same species, right?' His smile was wide and genuine. 'Ibiza is where you come to remember that. All places, all ages, all people. It's good. Apart from the golf courses. We do not like golf courses here. There is one but no more. One is enough.'

'Golf courses?' I thought of Karl. He didn't like golf.

'¡En serio! People go to the streets here if you want to make a golf course! Beach clubs not golf clubs! We like music, we like the sea, we like good food, and we like nature. But not so much the golf courses. Or the price of apartments. Or the roads in August.' And then the car and conversation took a left turn. 'We have aliens too. That's what some people say. There are a lot of . . . crazy people on this island.'

'Noted. I will try my very hardest not to open a golf course,' I said, earnestly. 'And I will look out for ET.'

And he laughed and even gave the steering wheel a pat of appreciation.

'Yes. Very good! Golf! No! Aliens! Yes!'

And I smiled on the back seat and stared out of the window, but then my thoughts darkened a little.

We like the sea.

I looked at the driver, as if he was a Rorschach inkblot that hadn't quite revealed itself. He went quiet for a little while. He frowned, in thought. And then he came out with it.

'I know that she died,' he said. 'I read about it. Christina van der Berg.' He pronounced the name carefully. As if it was something porcelain. 'I saw it in the *Diario*. The newspaper here. *Diario de Ibiza*.'

'Did they say how she died?'

'She was diving, I think.' I caught his eye in the rear-view mirror. The next question he asked very tentatively, I remember.

'Were you her friend?'

'No,' I said, for some reason. And then, 'Yes. I mean, a *long* time ago. I used to be her friend and I am coming to look after the house.' I don't know why I said it like that. *Look after*. Maybe I was self-conscious suddenly of just how odd it was to be given a house by someone you hardly knew. 'She came here years ago to be a singer, but I don't know if that was what she was still doing. She was very talented. She had a gift.'

His concerned expression was back. 'A gift?'

'Yes.'

He swallowed this like a pill. 'There are things about this island,' he said. 'Things that most people don't get to see. Things that aren't easily . . . explained . . .'

I had no real idea what he was talking about. When I was a child, I once went on holiday to the Isle of Wight, and I had made friends with an odd woman in a fudge shop in Yarmouth who believed she was a former mermaid. Maybe it was islands. Maybe they sent people insane.

Desolation

We were pulling over now. We were here. A desolate place with nothing around but traffic.

The only picture I had seen had been of the exterior, reprinted onto a letter, and, like my eyes, was not of very good quality. Just a hard blue sky and white walls. I had been picturing a villa in a hillside village.

But we arrived somewhere else, and I instantly felt like I was making a mistake.

I don't want to sound ungrateful, but it was, quite possibly, the least attractive house on the whole of Ibiza. Absolutely no bougainvillea in evidence. Or charm. And it made the bungalow in Lincoln look like a mansion in the Hollywood Hills by comparison. Maybe this was why she didn't give it to any of her real friends. *They didn't want it.*

It was a small white box, existing where it did for no real reason at all. Single-storey. Tiny windows. Standing above the roadside grit and blanched tarmac, with the paint peeling like scabs. Patches of brown cement dotted all over it. Smashed glass from a thrown beer bottle and random pieces of rubbish strewn around the outside on the tarmac. Walking distance to nowhere.

To make things worse there was a billboard across the street for a deluxe hotel. An aerial photograph of swimming pools and impressive buildings situated on a clifftop. *Open now. The latest Eighth Wonder Spa Resort Hotel, Cala Llonga, Ibiza. Visualise your dreams and make them reality.*

'Is this it?' I asked him, as I handed him twenty euros, staring at the small decrepit house.

'This is the one.' He smiled a little courteous smile. 'It was nice to meet you,' he said. And he had a look you get used to as you get older. Concern. 'My name is Pau. Like Paul. But without the l.'

'I'm Grace,' I said, opening the car door. 'Also without an l. How do you say "nice to meet you" in Spanish?'

'Mucho gusto.'

I nodded, as he got my luggage out of the boot. 'Okay. Mucho gusto.'

'And buena suerte is good luck.'

'Oh. I hadn't asked for that one.'

He nodded. 'I know. But maybe you will need it . . .'

Before I had time to ask why, he was back in the taxi.

And then he waited for a gap in the traffic, turned the car around and sped away.

The Pictures on the Wall

And there I was, on the asphalt in the sunshine. My swollen feet desperate to be released from their shoes. I wished I had worn my easy-fit sandals, but they had seemed a bit too outré this morning, when I had woken in Lincoln.

Oh well.

The noise of traffic competed with cicadas, as I stared at it.

At the house.

The rundown white box. And instead of a front door, a blue metal gate to the side of the building, leading to an impromptu patch of gravel and scrubby plants. A battered old car – a Fiat Panda – was parked outside.

'Right,' I said, to no one. A feature of my ageing process was that I was increasingly acting like I was on stage, throwing out muttered asides to an audience that wasn't listening. Or even there.

I went through the gate. I could feel my heart beating. Tingles in my legs. I wondered if it was to do with the vein surgery or to do with the fear. I fumbled around for the door key. Dropped it. My creaking knees didn't thank me as I crouched down. (Enjoy the ability to crouch down without effort, Maurice. It's one of the many gifts of youth.)

For a moment, staring at the key surrounded by grit and shining in the sunlight, I felt my own stupidity at coming out here so strongly that I wished I could be swallowed up by the universe. Get hit by a car and let my carcass nourish a wild dog.

I heard my mum's voice echo through decades. *Look at you. Grace Good-for-Nothing.*

Ridiculous, I told myself. *Pull yourself together.*

I grabbed the key and stood up, my body all quiet creaks and cracks.

There was a small, sad patch of garden. A wasteland of weeds and unwatered soil and little scraps of grass. I had never seen anything so neglected.

Inside, it was only mildly better.

The theme for the décor was battered brown. It smelled musty. And the air felt thick and stale. I saw dust hovering in the air, glowing like a tiny galaxy. A macabre thought overtook me. I wondered if there was dead skin among the dust. I wondered if I was inhaling her.

There was a hallway, where I left my luggage and shoes. My swollen feet sang with relief to be out of the loafers. And then the living room with its sofa and a hippyish throw and a rug that needed cleaning. A large fan was visibly clogged with dust and the floor tiles needed a mop. I walked around, still spooked and half expecting to bump into her corpse. I felt like I was intruding. There was something private and intimate about the space, so to be there was to trespass on memories I never knew. I was an interloper, inside a gift that already felt more like a curse.

On the walls there were framed photos. A gallery of Christina's life here.

A photo of her on a beach with her long dark hair blowing in the breeze and an equally long-haired man, with sparkling eyes, and a Mini Moke beach buggy in the background.

One of a little girl with a nervous smile, holding a teddy bear.

One of her and that same little girl, and that same man.

One of her with a microphone in hand, entertaining a hotel crowd.

One of her standing next to a man who appeared to be Freddie Mercury at some party in the eighties.

One of her in diving gear, with a different man. A man with a wilder beard than the first. He looked made for the sea. A shorter Poseidon in badly fitting Spandex. They looked more like friends than a couple.

One of her at some kind of local festival, dancing in an old-fashioned costume.

In all of them, she looked happier than she ever had as a teacher. But they seemed to be from quite a few years ago. There was nothing recent.

'Why am I here?' I asked, to that imaginary audience. I stared at the little girl and her cuddly purple bear. Was this her daughter? Why hadn't she left this house to her? Or to someone else in these photos. 'Why me?'

But there were no answers. Instead, there was just silence. And worry. And humidity. And quite a lot of dust.

The Olive Jar

I walked around the place. I was looking for answers, but I couldn't find any.

I saw a dried and probably dead potted plant in the bedroom on the chest of drawers, drooping and brown. A peace lily, I think. I noted the bed. It looked fine. It had new clean sheets. Then I headed back into the living room and clocked an old eighties hi-fi and rows of cassettes and stacks of vinyl.

And quite a few books.

I always think that the quickest way to understand someone is to look at what's on their bookshelves. Especially if they are honest bookshelves, not the fancy ornamental kind. And there was nothing fancy or ornamental about this place.

There was an assortment of books, some on shelves, some on the floor near the shelves. Some in English, some in Spanish, and one or two in Greek. Of those in English there were translations of *Siddhartha* by Hermann Hesse and a copy of the *Tao Te Ching*.

A guide to the flora and fauna of the Balearic Islands. A couple of Agatha Christies.

She had a classic that I had read and loved when I was young. *The Count of Monte Cristo* by Alexandre Dumas. (Have you ever read *The Count of Monte Cristo*? You really should. It's the best book I have ever read. It is about revenge *and* forgiveness, and it includes a prison escape. I have always loved a good prison escape. As a teen I read all of Dumas, as well as *Frankenstein* and *The Adventures of Sherlock Holmes*. You know. Proper *stories*.) There was also *Zorba the Greek*, not in Greek, and the poems of Cavafy, this time in Greek. In Spanish she had more poems (Pablo Neruda) and a Carlos Ruiz Zafón and a well-thumbed Isabel Allende.

And then I saw a jarringly out of place book on clairvoyancy called

The Ultimate Guide to Psychic Power: Volume 8. The title caused me to release a little awkward laugh. *Music teachers,* I thought to myself.

There was another book that also stood out. This was another one of those in Spanish. *La vida imposible* by Alberto Ribas. *Impossible Life.* It had a crude cover. A badly drawn illustration of the sea and a rocky islet. A view from a beach. The water had lines coming from it, like it was shining. There was a photo of the author on the back cover. A sun-leathered man with a wild beard wearing a T-shirt with an octopus design on it. He had a big smile and a missing tooth. He looked like an elderly pirate.

I had a strange feeling I had seen him before. And it was because I *had* seen him before. About a minute before, in fact, staring out from the wall.

The photo of Christina and the man with the wild beard and big smile. She knew this man. I went back to look. It was definitely him. I stared at the photos some more. I could see in one of them she was wearing the St Christopher necklace I had given her back in 1979. She had it in the other pictures too. Even at the party where she met Freddie Mercury.

There was a slight fusty smell. Not quite fetid, but far from pleasant. And perfume. Very faint. Her ghost in the air.

My stomach grumbled. I went to the little kitchen and opened the refrigerator and there was nothing except a carton of gazpacho that was out of date. In the cupboard some biscuits. There was also, strangely, an olive jar, minus olives. It was a normal modestly sized vessel – a fraction narrower than a standard jam jar – but it was full of water. I knew it was an olive jar because it had an illustration of green pimento-stuffed olives on the label, along with the words 'Olivos del Sur'. I twisted the lid and opened it up and gave it a sniff. It had a briny, mildly sulphurous scent but not the kind of brine you normally would get in an olive jar. This water had a lot going on. It had a shifting, complex look to it. Maybe it had some algae in it. I didn't know, though it didn't seem like ordinary seawater. But I was pretty sure it was of no use to me, so I walked to the front door, opened it, poured the water onto a parched piece of ground and went back inside and noticed something else.

A card on a little shelf in the hallway.

The card was a drawing of flower petals spelling out 'MUCHAS GRACIAS'.

A letter fell out of it. *Here it is,* I thought to myself. Maybe this would tell me everything.

Dear Grace,

If you are reading this you made the right decision. This house isn't much, but it is everything I own.

I wanted to thank you. Your kindness all those years ago saved my life. I know it sounds melodramatic, but I genuinely think I wouldn't have made it through that Christmas. I was at my lowest point. Your suggestion that I come to Ibiza helped release me. And now it is my turn to help you untap any unlived potential inside you. I know it won't make sense to you, why I chose to leave this place to you more than any other person I have ever known. But you have to trust me, because if I explained how I know that you are the right person you would think I was insane. And besides, you will find out in due course why you had to come here. But for now, I will just say that you are a very rare person, and I sense you will find peace here.

I know that I don't have long left. I am not afraid. I truly know this is not the end. And I feel I am heading to a better place.

I have loved living here. I would never have moved to this wonderful island without you. That conversation we had on your sofa watching Top of the Pops *all those years ago led to this moment right here. I never became Blondie. And certainly never became rich, in the conventional sense, as you can see from this modest house. But I have had a rich life, and discovered things I never could have dreamed of.*

People will tell you that it is a magical island. And you will hear some strange tales and myths too. Not all of them will be true. But there is more to life than we know. And there is more to our minds than we realise.

Whether you use this house for holidays or to live, try and visit all the beautiful places. Here are my tips:

Get lost in the narrow lanes of Dalt Vila – the old citadel of Eivissa, or Ibiza Town in English, perched high on a hillside behind fortified walls.

Take a hike from cala Sant Vicent along the old pilgrims' path to Tanit's Cave.

See the horses at the sanctuary at Es Murta.

Go to the north, surround yourself with pine trees.

See the flamingos at Ses Salines.

Head to Las Dalias hippy market – the daytime one, not the evening one when it becomes a rave – and say hello to my friend Sabine.

Hop on the boat to Formentera and take note of the lighthouse.

Drink a shot of Hierbas Ibicencas at a bar in a hilltop village.

See the drummers at Benirràs beach at sunset.

Get your shopping from the grocery store at Santa Gertrudis. They are very friendly in there.

Drive to the old stone fountain known as the Font de Peralta and catch a traditional Ibicenco 'peasant dance' – ball pagès – full of brightly dressed people leaping and twirling to the sound of castanets.

Go dancing yourself. Just once. Age matters not a bit here.

Have fun.

Oh, and most important of all: go to Atlantis Scuba at Cala d'Hort. Tell Alberto I sent you. He won't charge you. Go and see the seagrass meadow. It is the oldest living organism on Earth.

And please, when you are there, keep your mind open. Any change that happens will be for the better. Trust me.

Your loving and long lost friend,
Christina
X

PS: The white Fiat Panda parked beside the road is yours too. The keys are in the kitchen drawer.

Satisfaction

It was a lovely letter. Any letter that gives you a car in the postscript has its bonuses. But I must admit it made me feel exhausted. And troubled. And even more confused than I had been to begin with.

I don't have long left . . .

Well, that answered one thing, I realised, as my heart drummed away. She *knew* she was going to die. But she didn't mention an illness, or give any other reason, and it seemed a very long way off a suicide note.

Someone once told me the way to die happy is to die complete. To live like you eat a delicious meal. To devour and enjoy every course so that when you have finished you are full, and enjoyed every mouthful, but aren't too sad there is no more. It seemed that Christina, after a mediocre starter, may have had a satisfying main course and dessert, and left this planet content.

I reread her recommendations. I felt, somehow, they were more than recommendations. I felt they were signposts to something I wasn't yet able to understand. So, even though I was hardly in the mood to be a proper tourist, I thought I would take what she was saying – or half saying – in the letter seriously. I looked again at her advice.

A lot of the things had to be ruled out instantly. There was no way, for instance, I was going to go scuba diving. I was pretty sure it wasn't advisable to start at the age of seventy-two. And even with my new legs I very much doubted I would ever dance again. After all, I hadn't danced since 1992.

Never mind the seagrass. I felt like *I* was the oldest living organism on Earth.

The one part that really stood out was the bit about *keep your mind open.*

I suppose it was a normal thing to say. Especially after the mention of scuba diving. But that, and the reference to some of the strange tales being true, and the cosmic books around the place, made me wonder if Christina had come here and taken too many drugs and got into some mystical mumbo jumbo. She had, I distinctly remember, been into star signs.

I was being judgemental. It was a bad habit I'd got into, after festering in my bungalow for too long on my own.

I calmed myself down and went to the bedroom and unpacked my suitcase. The wardrobe, like the rest of the house, was a bit tatty. It had scratches all over the wood.

The first item I unpacked was a dressing gown. I would say it took up about 28 per cent of the entire case. It had been Karl's dressing gown. I couldn't leave it or get rid of it. I needed it, even in the heat of the Mediterranean. After he'd died I often pressed my face into it. And wearing it was the closest thing to a hug from him. Ridiculous, I know, but everything is ridiculous after a certain point in life. I'd also brought with me Daniel's drawing of a bluebird. The one he drew me for Mother's Day. We'd had it in a frame for years and I'd wanted to take one thing of his with me.

There is a comfort in unpacking, Maurice. I recommend that whenever you arrive at a new place to unpack with great care. It gives a sense of order and ritual to the new. And so I sorted my clothes as carefully as if leading a tea ceremony for a Ming emperor. I don't know why I was surprised to see Christina's clothes in the wardrobe. Maybe I felt someone would have been in to sort them out.

They were colourful and bright and the kind of things that flew off the rails at the charity shop when the students came in. It was sad, to see these kaleidoscopic outfits pressed together, a concertina of colourful ghosts. A spectrum of personalities I never knew. And then, after I placed all my clothes in there, I realised how drab they looked. All muted creams and corals and lilacs next to her indigos and yellows. It looked wrong, our clothes side by side. Like I had just put mashed potato on a fruit salad.

I then lay on the bed and tried to have a nap but couldn't. Well, actually, I think I did doze off for a couple of seconds but I soon woke up, achey, my back ill-attuned to the mattress and with my mind contemplating what she might have meant when she wrote *keep your mind open.*

Cars sped by on the main road, a kind of white noise I found soothing. And I needed soothing, as I wondered what the hell had happened to Christina and why she had chosen me.

It is hard to explain what I was feeling.

Vulnerable, I suppose. And alone.

The nightclubs and beach clubs and luxury villas and sunset bars and yoga retreats and mega hotels and Michelin-starred restaurants the island was now famous for may as well have existed in another universe.

Necessity

I needed to get out of the house. I needed to know what happened to Christina.

A Third Full

I felt uncertain. And this uncertainty was to intensify until I had to hear my own breath just to know I was real.

A part of me wondered if I was now taking part in some elaborate prank. After all, if she had thought so highly of me, why hadn't she made contact with me while she was still living?

The possibilities fanned out like vectors. I felt dizzy. And my stomach reminded me that the last food I had eaten was a bowl of Grape Nuts in Lincoln. I needed to find a meal, or at least get some groceries.

I noticed the olive jar by the door again. It was precisely where I had left it. Same jar, same position, the lid screwed on. But it still had water inside. I could have sworn I had tipped it all out. But no. There it was. A third full.

A not entirely new thought: I was losing my mind.

Old age, I sighed inwardly as I stepped outside into the afternoon sun. And I tried my hardest to think there could be no other explanation.

Mathematics

I am not great at believing in the mystical.

I think it is because I was raised a Catholic and have had a life full of unanswered prayers. I wouldn't say I am totally unreligious. But even when I was younger, years before Karl and Daniel, I grew tired of looking for answers where none could be found.

Maybe that is why I loved mathematics.

To properly know mathematics is to *know* the only thing that can be assuredly *known*. Politics and sociology and history and psychology have facts you have to *interpret*. But in mathematics facts are just facts. There is no arguing. There is no left-wing or right-wing algebra. There is no sin in geometry and no guilt in trigonometry.

Mathematics is the purity of peace. Except, of course, it is also as mysterious and enigmatic as the whole of life, and expecting it – or anything – to conform to what I wanted it to be was a mistake. And that is the most devastating thing of all. When the logical world we have sought out crumbles to dust in front of our eyes.

A New Theory of Infinity

I am telling you this for what will follow, so that you really know where I am coming from. I am not prone to far-fetched nonsense. I think the moon landings were real and that the Earth is, roughly speaking, a sphere. I am not a crystal person and nor do I have a desire to attribute every mood to one of Jupiter's moons or Mercury being in retrograde. I don't even own a candle.

And yet, I am also a person who now realises that our human understanding of the world is incredibly limited, and that there is a bias not to believe things that don't fit our worldview. *What I am saying* is that sometimes we can't accept the truth that is right in front of our eyes. And that sometimes the mad people of one era become the sages of the next.

I tell you all this because, over the course of the following pages, you may end up thinking I have lost my mind. So please consider the case of Georg Cantor.

As you are studying mathematics at university, I am sure you have heard of him.

I think I even used to talk about him in class. The guy who came up with Set Theory at the end of the nineteenth century. Anyway, when he proved that there were, technically, different sizes of infinity he was branded a heretic. He was criticised and ostracised and made a laughing stock. He couldn't take it. He fell apart because of what he had discovered. He had his own belief system questioned. To stop believing in a single infinity was to believe the impossible. He had nervous breakdown after nervous breakdown and ended his days in an asylum. But he was right. Mathematically, at least. There are different sizes of infinity. But it took a long time for everyone else to see what he was seeing.

Now, I am no Georg Cantor. But I too have had my worldview flipped on its head recently, and have felt a need to tell someone about it. I too have seen things that challenge me to my core. You emailed at just the right moment, because I think my need to tell this story has coincided with your need for answers.

So, the question is, are you ready for a new theory of infinity?

Santa Gertrudis

Christina's car was a reluctant old thing. I sat in it a while, breathed in the stale upholstery, looking for clues about her life. There was nothing in there except an empty bottle of diet lemonade and a half-eaten packet of biscuits in the glove compartment. I switched the radio on. Fast Spanish voices interspersed with jingles and then a rap song. I wondered if it was 21 Savage, the one the boy on the plane had talked about. I switched it off again, sighed and turned on the engine.

I hadn't driven abroad in my life. It was a little daunting. At first, I was all over the place. I had typed 'Santa Gertrudis supermarket' into my phone before setting off. My phone lost signal and I quickly forgot what I had seen on the map. Now I was just following signs for Santa Gertrudis, travelling over the grey tarmac, trying to remember which side of the fading white lines I was meant to be driving on.

I soon discovered that Santa Gertrudis is very pretty. Wide streets, geometrically pleasing houses, whitewashed buildings, pink bougainvillea and cafés full of laid-back people. Everything perfectly designed for the hard blue sky above. I drove around. I passed a vegan café and a Pilates studio and eventually reached a shop that looked like it sold food. A window had posters advertising beer and olive oil. I parked somewhere near the kerb at an angle that would have interested Pythagoras.

I walked the three little aisles with a basket. It was a whole new world. I felt like I was a university student again, learning how to think about the things you need to live. The autopilot had been on for decades. Since I'd been widowed, I'd hardly ever changed the weekly shop. It was quite scary to be starting afresh. I walked around. There were signs above the produce, written in chalk. *Frutas y verduras ecologicas*, for instance, above cardboard boxes of nectarines and mushrooms and the plumpest tomatoes I had ever seen. I put one of the tomatoes in the basket and continued down the aisle. I soon encountered a strange-looking machine next to a stack of empty bottles. The machine had a spiralling metal chute descending into a transparent cylinder. Beside it, there were a lot of oranges. I rolled a few down the chute and waited patiently as the trickle of juice slowly made it into the bottle I was holding. After a couple of minutes I had a bottle of (very) freshly squeezed orange juice. Then I filled the rest of my basket with a baguette and cheese and biscuits and coffee and washing-up liquid and shower gel and toilet roll and gin and tonic water. Above the humming of refrigerators and a fan, and quiet but bouncy pop music on a radio, I had a conversation with the lively checkout person, whose name badge read *Rosella*.

The shop was empty of people and Rosella was clearly in the mood for talking. Her English was great. She had lived in England – in Brighton – for a couple of years and had moved back.

'This island is a magnet,' she said, as she scanned the coffee. 'Do you know Es Vedrà?'

'Es Vedrà? No. I am new here.'

'Ah. Well, Es Vedrà is a rock. A large high rock that sticks out of the ocean. You can see it from Cala d'Hort. A beach in the south.'

I remembered the slightly ominous feeling I'd had looking at the tall rocky islet from the plane window. 'I think I saw it when I flew in.'

She nodded. 'Yes. They say it is the third most magnetic point on Earth. There is something special about it there.'

'Really?'

'Yes. There are good stories and bad stories. Years and years ago there was a hermit who lived there. In a cave. A religious man. A priest. He wrote about lights he saw in the water. Lights that lit up the whole sea. And since then, they have been seen at other times. They nearly caused a plane crash once . . . And now the rock gives off a strange vibe. It feels scary sometimes. I always feel something is there. Inside it.'

It was quite a dramatic conversation to be having in a supermarket. I tried to be polite. 'Oh well, it's an interesting island.'

The Woman Who Sold the Future

I noticed a small dark tattoo on Rosella's arm. A circle and a horizontal line that meet on the top of the vertex of a triangle. Off the horizontal line were two short upright lines on either side. Like the purest, most schematic representation of a person raising their hands.

I have never been a tattoo person. It's a generational thing, I think. Back in my day, a tattoo meant you were a convict or a sailor or just a general miscreant. Karl liked them, or pretended to, but he'd never dared go and actually get one.

She followed my gaze. I hoped I hadn't looked too judgemental. 'It is the symbol for Tanit,' she explained. 'Goddess of the moon.' I remembered the reference to Tanit's Cave in Christina's letter. I'd later learn Tanit was quite a big thing in Ibiza. The Punic goddess of the moon, yes, but also rain, fertility, dance, creation, destruction, and a thousand other things which possibly included conversations in grocery stores. 'The ancient people believed she protected the island.'

'It's very nice,' I said. Like the old person I was. I noticed some bright leaflets beside the till – flyers – advertising nightclubs.

And then she said something I wasn't expecting. The words as bold as headlights. 'You are Grace, aren't you?'

I tried to look relaxed. 'Oh yes. I am. How did you know?'

'She told me you would be coming.'

'Who?' I said, ridiculously.

'Christina.'

'Christina, right, yes.'

'Before she died.'

'Obviously,' I was so stunned I said it twice. 'Obviously.'

She stopped seeing to my shopping and looked directly into my eyes. 'She loved the water. She loved to dive. She had only started a few years ago. Such a tragic accident.'

'Actually, they don't know for certain what exactly—'

'She told me to be nice to you. She said you are special.'

'Right. Um. Well, I hadn't seen her for years. Decades. We were never really that close . . . did you know her well?'

What I really wanted to ask was: *Did you know she was going to die?* After all, I had come to the island *because she had died.* The house was left to me *because she had died.* And Christina's letter itself had implied she knew she was going to die. Yet it didn't even hint at how. If Christina knew her death was imminent, and yet the Spanish police were looking into it, then that really did raise a host of questions.

I was attempting to piece this all together in my mind to make it make sense. It was like trying to prove the Riemann Hypothesis or Goldbach's Conjecture. It boggled the brain.

'Yes. She lived on the island a long time. This is my parents' shop. When I was little, she used to come here. And before she lived here she lived in Sant Antoni, I think. San Antonio. We call it by the Catalan and the Spanish. But you Brits just call it San Antonio. She used to sing in one of the hotels. She was a good singer. She always came here. She was cool. Had an aura. But she hadn't been in so much recently. Not since she started working at the hippy market.'

'Las Dalias,' I said, remembering Christina's letter.

'Yes,' she said, scanning the freshly squeezed orange juice. 'That is where she spent a lot of the time.'

'What did she sell there?'

'El futuro.'

'Sorry?'

'The future . . .'

'I don't understand.'

Rosella laughed. 'She had . . . become a . . .' She searched for the correct way to say it in English and made an enthusiastic gesture in the air as if words were pets that could come when beckoned. 'A psychic.'

For some reason this didn't entirely surprise me. After all, I had seen that book back at her house. And she had been a music teacher. In my experience of music teachers, they are a little bit prone to eccentricity. And no doubt music teachers who moved to Ibiza at the tail-end of the seventies were more prone than most.

'Like a fortune teller?'

'Yes. A fortune teller. I think it was for tourists most of the time. Not the local people. I never asked her too much about it . . .'

'Oh. Right.' And then, without thinking, I asked something instinctively. 'Did she tell you she was going to die?'

'No!' she said, quickly. And then a sceptical expression twisted her mouth. 'No.'

'But she told you I was coming?'

'Sí. She said you were coming to stay in the house. She told me what you looked like and wanted me to be friendly.'

Old, I guessed. *She told her I was old.*

'And how did she seem, when you last saw her?'

'Okay. Quiet. But okay.'

A customer entered the shop. A woman in a floaty white dress carrying a woven straw bag.

'Hola, Camila,' Rosella said, as I started to pack my groceries. They had a brief exchange in Spanish or Catalan or both. Then she turned back to me and resumed scanning my shopping.

'Who was her husband?' I asked Rosella.

'Johan. He was just an old Dutch hippy. They divorced years ago. He moved back to Amsterdam. That is when she stopped singing, I think.' Then Rosella dropped a bombshell. 'She had a daughter back in the early nineties. With Johan. She lives in Amsterdam now.'

I remembered the picture of the little girl on the wall. The one holding a teddy bear.

Again, the same thought popped up. *Why me? Why didn't she leave the house to her daughter? Or at least to someone who knew her well enough to know she had a daughter?*

'Did she see her daughter?'

Rosella smiled as she put through the last of the shopping. I felt like I had told a joke without realising it. '*Everyone* sees her daughter.'

'Sorry, I don't understand.'

And then Rosella pointed through the shop door's window, across the street. 'Her name is Lieke. Lieke van der Berg. She is very successful. A musician. And a DJ. She still lives in Amsterdam but arrives to Ibiza every summer. She is . . . *over there*.'

She pointed again. I looked through the glass of the door to the nearest of the two visible roadside billboards. One of them featured the face of a young woman, exotically lit in blue, with a bobbed bleached haircut.

LIEKE. AMNESIA. EVERY WEDNESDAY.

'She is playing Amnesia this year.' Rosella arrived at the correct assumption that I wasn't an Amnesia type. 'It is one of the big clubs.'

I stared a little longer at the billboard. Give or take a few details, I could have been staring at Christina in 1979. Maybe the ambition to become Blondie was fulfilled, but hopped a generation. And maybe that was why the house wasn't left to her. A superstar hardly needed a road-side shack.

'Oh. Wow. So she is a big deal.'

'Sure is. But I don't think Christina thought so.'

'Oh, did Christina not get on with her?'

Rosella shrugged. 'I don't know. I think there was some pain. I think they had grown apart. When she talked about her she had tears in her eyes. She said she had tried to contact her. Families, eh?'

'Yes. Families.'

Something rose up from the depths. The day before my son's funeral. Karl with tears in his eyes slamming the kitchen cabinet. *Why did you let him out of your sight?*

'I think diving made her happy. Have you ever been?'

The question embarrassed me. I don't know why. 'No. No.'

'Christina said there was nothing so calming in the world as diving. You forget everything in the water. She thought you would love it.'

This seemed peculiar. I mean, why had Christina told someone in a supermarket – someone who spoke near-perfect English – to get me to go diving? It felt a little too much. It felt, just slightly, like a set-up. But what I was being set up for, I didn't know. Yet Rosella herself seemed warm and natural.

'I am seventy-two. I am too old. And I forget everything just by waking up.'

Rosella laughed, but in the opposite of a hurtful way.

'No!' She said some Spanish words. 'Come on. Too old? Can you swim?'

'I used to love swimming. But it has been many years.' Then I tried a bit of Spanish. 'Muchos muchos años.'

'Well, then. If you can swim and if you can breathe, you can still dive. You still look quite strong.'

I was being patronised but very gently, so I went with it. 'Do I?'

'¡Sí! ¡Está claro! Are you here on your own?'

'Yes,' I said. And the sadness leaked out. It was there on my face and in my eyes. Grief was a flood that ran through you and caused others to stand aside. Or at least wind up the conversation.

Rosella seemed to notice. She stiffened a little. My awkwardness rubbing off on her.

'That's forty-seven euros and forty-nine cents.'

I got out the purse Karl had bought me years ago, the once-bright crimson fabric now a dull pink.

'But if you go diving, don't go to Atlantis Scuba. It is where Christina went. But she is the only person who has ever said anything good about the place. It is run by a madman.'

'A madman?'

'Yes. Alberto Ribas.'

Alberto Ribas.

The smiling pirate.

The Spanish woman Rosella had chatted to was now behind me in the queue. I decided not to take up any more time.

'It was nice to meet you,' I said.

Rosella smiled. 'It was nice to meet you too. Chao.'

I walked out of the shop into the pine-scented heat of the afternoon and stared up at the vast picture of the azure-lit Dutch DJ, wondering what had happened to her mother.

The Yellow Flower

On my return to the house, I noticed a plant growing right outside the front door. It was quite tall, nearly reaching my knees, thin yellow petals, and right in the middle of the dusty path.

Though tall, the flower seemed too beautiful and delicate to be there all alone. I don't think it was a weed.

Of course, weeds don't really exist. They are only a matter of perception. If someone doesn't like a dandelion growing on their lawn, they will call it a weed out of spite, because we human beings have to draw a line between everything. Us/them. Mathematics/poetry. Weed/flower.

But what I mean is: it wasn't the kind of flower people would call a weed. It was the kind of flower people choose to plant. But why would Christina, or anyone, plant a flower on a dry path directly in front of a door? And, more pressingly, why hadn't I noticed it before?

I took a photograph and sent it via WhatsApp to my sister-in-law Sophie in Australia. Not only did she run a florist, but her partner had a degree in botany. Maybe they would be able to tell me its name. I was going to have to look after all the plants on the premises if I stuck around.

I went inside and noticed another thing.

The jar of seawater was now full. Not a third full. But *full*. There was sure to be a rational explanation. The lid was still screwed on but I still looked up for a sign of a leaky pipe. There was nothing but a dry ceiling, and it certainly hadn't been raining.

Yet there it was. An olive jar that had somehow refilled itself with seawater.

A kind of reverse evaporation, an extreme condensation that – at least according to the laws of nature I was familiar with – would be impossible. I felt, again, like someone was playing a practical joke on me.

When I was young, as I have told you, I read quite a lot of Sherlock Holmes alongside my Alexandre Dumas. The novels and the short stories. There is a famous line in the most perfect of all the novels, *The Sign of Four*, where Holmes tells Watson that when you 'have eliminated the impossible, whatever remains, however improbable, must be the truth'.

So that is what I was faced with. All the explanations as to why an olive jar would refill itself weren't possible. So I was left with only illogic and improbability. And I have to say, I didn't like that at all.

The Knock at the Door

I was hungry and in need of a drink.

I washed down some bread and cheese with a gin and tonic. I was on Christina's little sofa, half-watching a dubbed version of *Indiana Jones and the Last Crusade*. I have always liked Harrison Ford's face. It was comforting. Like an old slipper. That is the thing with movie stars. The good ones are so familiar you kind of wear them whenever you see them. They cover some lonely part of us. Make us warmer.

Daniel had loved the film before this one. *Indiana Jones and the Temple of Doom*, especially the banquet scene where there is an eyeball in the soup. That and *Return of the Jedi* were his favourites. This added a bittersweet note to watching the film. Films from the eighties may be four decades old, but also – for me – too modern.

At home I'd often stick an old movie on. Something black and white, from another world. *Roman Holiday. It Happened One Night. His Girl Friday.* Or, if I am feeling more Technicolor, *An American in Paris*. Proper classics that you are still too young to have come across, I imagine. I liked watching things from before I ever met Karl, from before I'd become a mother, sometimes even from before I was born. It was like not existing for a while. Escaping to a world before my pain began.

As I watched the movie something happened that made me jump in my seat.

There was a knock on the door.

It must have been pretty late, as it was dark outside, and this was June, remember. Long days. But I suppose this was Ibiza and Ibiza didn't really understand the concept of 'late'.

I opened the door to find a man. A large man, broad in the shoulders. Arms all muscle. Stare of a buffalo. Bleached hair and a tattoo of a crucifix or a dagger by his left eye. Had a dangerous, twitching energy to him. His skin a tapestry of scars. He could have been seven foot for all I knew. It was as though a boulder had been given sentience via a tub of creatine. He looked like he had taken considerable effort to look this intimidating. He had one hand behind his back. I wondered if it was holding a weapon.

'You're not Christina,' he said. He was British. Cockney. Or Essex.

'I'm sorry,' I said. 'No. I'm not.'

'Where is she?'

'Not here.' I didn't want to tell him she had died. I didn't want to tell him anything.

The man smiled. Quite a shy smile.

'Tell her it's Frankie. Tell her she was right. She was right about everything. Tell her thank you. And this is for her.'

He took the hand from behind his back and held it out for me. My stomach dropped, like it was going over a humpback bridge. But when I saw what was in his hand I laughed with relief. It was a giant pouch of Haribo gummy bears.

'She said sweets are her guilty pleasure,' he said, a giant smile on his face. 'Pineapple Goldbears are her favourite. There's some in there. Just a thank-you.'

'Right,' I said. And I was about to tell him the truth about Christina, but he had already turned away.

'Thank you,' I said. And I felt guilty for judging him, as the metal gate clanked shut behind him. I heard a car door shut. Then electronic music sounding like a very loud heart palpitation.

La vida imposible

I went online.

I had brought my laptop. My ten-year-old laptop with a Harley-Davidson sticker on it. It had been Karl's – the Harley-Davidson sticker to add a frisson of danger to his civil engineer life – so to upgrade it would have felt like betrayal. Not that he had ever actually owned a motorbike.

I typed 'Christina van der Berg' into Google.

I saw the piece on the *Diario de Ibiza* website which Pau the taxi driver had mentioned. When I translated it, the phrase 'disappeared presumed drowned' stood out. She had booked a midnight dive at Atlantis Scuba and had never returned. Alberto Ribas had been taken in for questioning and then let go.

I added the word 'psychic' and there was just one mention, in relation to a list of stalls at Las Dalias market, so I went back to just her name again.

A few things came up. Mainly related to her singing at a hotel called the Buenavista in Santa Eulalia, years ago. There was a photo of her at a nightclub called Ku in 1986, and a different one of her, starstruck, with Freddie Mercury – but clearly on the same night as the framed photo on the wall. This was, apparently, Freddie's forty-first birthday party at Pikes Hotel and she was one of several local acts that performed there that night. In this one she was wearing a little bowler hat, like Sally Bowles in *Cabaret*. This was the same place, I discovered, where the pop group Wham! had filmed the video for 'Club Tropicana' a few years before. It all seemed a very glamorous world.

I felt proud of her, as I kept researching. A mention of her and a friend, way back in 1981 at a nightclub called Glory's on an English Instagram page called 'Ibiza Nostalgia'.

This was very much the Christina I remembered, but with slightly more make-up and bigger hair. Then there was a photo of her looking greyer in the *Diario*. She was standing with two others holding a banner that read, in English, *NO OIL*. The article's text was in Spanish so I put it into Google Translate and it was about protests held in Ibiza Town in 2014 against a Scottish oil firm's plan to drill for oil off the coast of Ibiza. A plan that, further research told me, never happened because the protests were so strong. Ten thousand people marching through Ibiza Town. The same number that had protested against a golf course at Cala d'Hort a few years before. There was another mention of her in relation to a protest against a hotel at Cala Llonga too.

I tried something else. I typed 'Alberto Ribas'. I found a mention of him on a blog called the Roving Sceptic, in an article titled 'Scientists Who Lost the Plot':

Alberto Ribas. This once respected marine biologist was a former oceanography graduate of the University of Vigo, before teaching in the US at the University of California and then numerous Spanish and South American universities.

He was one of the first people to draw attention to the hazard of microplastics in the ocean and has authored several books, on a variety of subjects from algae to sea turtles to the ecology of coral reef systems. He was widely discredited after publishing a paper on the *Posidonia oceanica* seagrass meadows of Ibiza and Formentera. The paper concluded that the seagrass has managed to live as a single organism for over 100,000 years because of a 'peculiar and ethereal presence within the water here, occasionally manifesting as an abnormal light with unnatural properties, which bears no relation to algae and does not appear to have an earthly origin'.

Ribas's belief that some extra-terrestrial force inhabits the Mediterranean saw him kicked out of the International Society of Marine Biology back in 2016, and lost him his post at the University of the Balearic Islands, located in Palma, Majorca, when subsequent independent studies found no evidence to back his claims. Dr Ribas, however, doubled down and even self-published a book called *La vida imposible* – or *Impossible Life* in English – claiming that he had proof of many occurrences of life forms that scientists consider 'impossible' existing here on planet Earth, primarily in the Balearic Islands.

Okay, I thought. An insane person. One of those insane people the taxi driver had talked about. And maybe Christina had been mad too, and maybe that is why she left me – a virtual stranger – a house here.

The Alberto Ribas search also led me to the website of Atlantis Scuba.

I clicked on it and saw two flags – one Spanish, one British. I clicked on the British one and arrived at the English-language version of the site and a beautiful photograph of two divers swimming in crystalline waters.

'Leave your troubles on the land and explore another world,' read the text. 'Another universe of natural beauty and wonder. A place of calm . . .'

I clicked through some more pictures. Some people on a boat in diving gear. Christina was among them.

She was next to an older man with a beard. I recognised him from the piratey author photograph. Alberto himself. He still looked made for the sea. He was also smiling, widely, like Christina. But there was a possible malevolence to his gaze. I don't know why, but I had an uneasy sense just looking at him. There was some text about the importance of ocean conservation. I flicked through some more photos, with a feeling that made my mouth go dry.

A fluorescent sea creature; a diver heading into a cave; an octopus; a moray eel; another diver visiting the shipwreck of the *Don Pedro*, the text explaining that it was a boat that sank a few kilometres from the Port of Ibiza in 2007; an orange rockfish swimming through a coral reef.

And then an image of a vast plant. An underwater meadow of seagrass. In the clearest, cleanest water imaginable, with fractured sunlight breaking through the ocean and a school of small silver fish in the background. It was, quite possibly, the most beautiful photograph I had ever seen. A fleeting feeling came over me. Something different to the rising fear. Something alongside it. Wonder, I suppose. A magnetic, forceful kind.

I stared at the television a little, as the temple containing the Holy Grail collapsed around Sean Connery and Harrison Ford, then I turned back to the laptop. I clicked it open to the photo and that's when I saw something new. Something small and missable. A tiny golden object amid the seagrass.

I zoomed in.

And this is the moment it became terrifying. Being all alone in that new house, on that new island, feeling miles away from everything I'd ever known, imagining olive jars filling themselves with water, and plants appearing out of nowhere. And now *this*. Something most peculiar was definitely happening. I couldn't work out the odds, but they were seemingly many millions against. Yet there it was, sitting at the bottom of the sea. Something that I truly felt had belonged to me. The detail was sharp enough for me to see not only the colour of the necklace, but the image of St Christopher on the pendant itself.

I had not a single doubt in my mind that this was the exact same necklace I had given to Christina back in 1979, that Christmas, shining like lost hope.

Please Stay Away from Mr Ribas

The Guardia Civil officer, a man of indeterminate age, sat behind his desk in his immaculately ironed short-sleeved military-green shirt staring at Christina's letter to me. He chewed gum as he read it. There was the soft glitter of sweat on his frowning scalp.

He exuded suppressed emotion. He was a clenched fist of a man.

'I know that you are still conducting an investigation into Christina's disappearance and I thought this might help. Even though there is not much there.'

He gave the smallest of nods. Growled a little to himself. Then spoke to me in a gruff Spanglish. 'Es verdad. There is not so much there.'

'But it tells us that she knew. She knew she was going to die . . . That has to be significant. I should also tell you that there was a necklace in the water. I saw it in a photograph online. I had given it to her. It was a St Christopher.'

The policeman looked up at me. A man of few words and gestures. He had a spherical, shaven head and no beard. There was no expression in his tired eyes. 'Cuándo?'

'Sorry?'

'When?'

'I don't understand.'

I sensed his frustration. He muttered something to himself in Spanish. Then asked: 'When did you give the necklace?' He gave the question reluctantly, like coins to someone begging.

'Nineteen seventy-nine.'

He looked at me like he didn't understand.

'Forty-five years ago,' I clarified. 'I gave it to her forty-five years ago. And according to photographs she wore it ever since.'

I don't like police stations. They always make me feel guilty.

He sighed and gave the impression that I was wasting his time. Maybe he was embarrassed that they hadn't worked out precisely what had happened to Christina. I really wished I knew some Spanish so I didn't seem like such a naïve old tourist.

'Where was the picture?'

'It was on a website. Atlantis Scuba.'

Something flashed in his eyes when I said that.

'Atlantis Scuba?'

'Sí. Yes. Sí. The one owned by Alberto Ribas. I believe she knew him quite well.'

'Mmm. Alberto Ribas.' He sighed a long sigh. 'Pues. Have there been . . . other things you see . . .?'

I wasn't going to tell him about olive jars refilling with seawater or flowers appearing from nowhere. 'No.'

'Okay.'

There was a long pause. For a moment it looked like he was going to say something else. His mouth hinted at it, like an egg before it hatches, but nothing came.

'Is that it?' I wondered out loud.

The man gave me a stern look. I tried a softer approach. The way you might a grizzly bear in the woods whose lunch you interrupted. 'It's just that I am very concerned about my friend. I understand that there are still some questions about how she died and I know you are trying to get to the bottom of it . . .'

'You are a guest on this island. It is important to remember . . . This island is not easy to . . .' He searched for the English word and he decided upon '. . . see . . . I mean, you can see it. You can see . . . beaches . . . and palm trees . . . and you can pass the discos and the restaurants in your car. But you will never see it like an Ibicenco. Now. Thank you for your assistance, señora. Now, please, leave us to the investigating. You go and enjoy your holidays.'

He placed the letter to one side and went onto his computer.

'Do you still need the letter?' I asked.

'Sí.'

'Right. I see.'

I was going to ask for a copy but I felt I had reached the end of my question quota.

My time was clearly up. But as I was walking out of that humid room, hand on the door, he cleared his throat. 'Oh, and señora, please stay away from Mr Ribas.'

I turned and nodded.

And, at that point, I really was going to do precisely as he said.

Anhedonia

I tried my best to put all this detective stuff behind me, to give up being Miss Marple for a while. So I did what most British people do on a Mediterranean island.

I went out and had a holiday.

And, on the face of it, it was a rather lovely holiday.

I saw the lighthouse at Portinatx.

I went to see the salt pans at Ses Salines and walked along the beach at Es Cavallet and tried not to blink an eye at the nude sunbathers.

I did as Christina had recommended and took a hike from Cala San Vicente along the old pilgrims' path to Tanit's Cave, up the steep hill, and felt about to die. I caught up with a small tour and took a sprig of rosemary and offered it as a gift to the goddess that had been on Rosella's arm. I felt a bit silly placing it on the little shrine there, in the cave.

I traversed a sixteenth-century drawbridge to get lost amid the narrow lanes of Dalt Vila.

I saw a man on a skateboard and his dog trotting alongside. I saw colourfully clothed nightclubbers. I saw people speeding around a go-kart track. I saw hillwalkers. I saw hippies drumming at sunset.

I gazed up at palm trees.

I consumed bread and olives and aioli.

I ate a cheese-and-mint tart called a flaó.

I bought a cone full of ice cream sculpted like a flower.

I saw expensive yachts and small sailboats.

I drove around.

I saw hills, horses, beaches, orchards, churches, salt marshes, sand dunes, caves, coves, cliffs, watchtowers.

I saw an old abandoned nightclub from the seventies, now covered in plants and graffiti.

I saw the giant sundial at the deserted beach at Cala Llentia.

I absorbed the quiet amid the pines at the peak of Sa Talaia.

I spotted a kingfisher.

Everywhere was beautiful.

Most of it, anyway.

But I felt empty.

It was a common feeling, or a common unfeeling.

Anhedonia.

I was blocked.

You see, the problem was this: I sincerely believed I wasn't a good person who deserved happiness.

I had become who I believed I was. A terrible human. Believing yourself to be bad is very often a prelude to doing bad things. And I had felt that way since Daniel died. He had died on a Saturday, when I was not where I should have been. He had finished watching *Superman II* on TV and had gone out in the rain and he had wanted me to take him into town. His dad was at the pub, which was where he went every Saturday afternoon in those days. But I hadn't gone into town because it was raining, and I *couldn't be bothered.* So he went out on his bike in a bad mood and I'd stayed in, reading catalogues. I was browsing for hair dryers when my son turned onto Wragby Road and straight into a lorry.

And it was me. It was my fault. It could have so easily not happened if I'd simply said, 'Hold on, Daniel, I'll just get the umbrella, then we'll go to the shops together.' And that guilt got into my soul and convinced me I was faulty at a fundamental level. And when you believe that, you act on it. Just as Superman knows he is the person who saves people from falling over Niagara Falls, and so continues to do good deeds, I was the person who let the person I loved more than any other die.

Don't get me wrong. My capacity for guilt pre-dated Daniel. I was always prone to it, even as a child at St Cuthbert's Catholic school wearing my St Christopher. When you had a childhood surrounded by saints it was easy to feel like a sinner. A teacher once told me if prayers aren't reaching God, it was because they had been blocked by your own sin. And my parents – who had wanted a boy – always treated me like I wasn't quite enough. But Daniel's death solidified guilt as my defining feature. Something I had to carry for ever.

And so, a few years after Daniel died – but still decades ago – I had done something else. I'd been unfaithful. And I never told anyone about it, least of all Karl. And after he died the guilt just grew.

Aidan Jenkins. Mr Jenkins. The history teacher from before your time. After his divorce he had flirted with me in the staff room and in the car park and in corridors. He sensed a chaos inside me. He sensed I was in a permanent spin and could go almost anywhere with the right push. And I had flirted back. It was as thrilling as it was terrible. And the more I scolded myself for being a bad person, the closer I came. And then there was the fateful time we bumped into each other in the stock room.

This was the start of it.

We became clandestine creatures doing something unspeakable amid the piles of exercise books and rows of staplers and surplus copies of *Watership Down* and *Brave New World*. And then it happened again. He liked the drama of it. The cliché of it. The teachers' sex-in-the-stock-room fantasy made real.

(Paper would forever smell like sin.)

There are no real excuses except feelings. The Spanish poet Federico García Lorca believed the greatest punishment was to have desire and not declare it out loud. And for that brief moment in my married life I had been burning with desire. Not for Aidan Jenkins necessarily. But for escape. For *something* that wasn't grief. It felt like Karl had left me even as he stayed with me. At times he had blamed me. It was like there were ten thousand miles between us even as we sat on the same sofa. I needed air. Something. Anything that wasn't this lonely stuckness.

And Aidan was single and good-looking and when he spoke I felt his voice reverberate through me. I felt it on my skin. I felt something electric that was exciting. He was also quite heavy with his signals. I was selfish and depressed and couldn't handle the weight of things. So I acted like an idiot.

I say all this to help you.

Sometimes in order to be helpful we have to give up the desire to be liked.

So I am here to say this: I like you, you were a good pupil, you were always kind to me and the others in the class. I remember there was a mix of confidence and meekness to you. You were never afraid to raise your hand if you knew the answer. And you didn't hesitate when everyone giggled at the teacher's pet as you recited pi to the first thirty digits. But there was a humility there too. You bowed your head. You said sorry when you didn't need to. You said sorry for things you hadn't even done. I always find it interesting when people do that. It is like an admission that everyone in the world is a little to blame for everything.

Your email was heartfelt. And what I want you to know is that I like you enough that I don't need you to like me back. I want to be honest with my own mistakes to help you forgive your own.

You wrote in the email that you let your girlfriend down and she broke up with you. It was a bit vague of you, but it also told me everything. It is hard to be young and flawed, especially in a judgemental age. (Of course, every age is a judgemental age, as humans stay humans; it's just that we move the judgements around like furniture when we want the room to feel bigger.) The one good thing about having regrets is that I no longer judge others too harshly. Every single person on this planet is a context and the circumstances of that context can never be seen fully. We are all mysteries, even to ourselves. This world can brutalise us in a myriad of ways, not just the obvious ones. A person can look smart and successful, with a tie and a smile and a shining life and fancy education, yet still hear a distant father screaming abuse in their ear as they drink or gamble or screw that pain away, unable to break the cycle.

I am here to tell you that at some point everyone – and I mean *everyone* – lets someone down. They might not do it as soap-operatically as me in that stock room but there are a million other ways. But in truth I feel I am particularly guilty. I not only feel responsible for our son's death, but I was unfaithful to the only man I ever loved.

Anyway, I never really allowed myself any more pleasure after the fling. Or even during it. I'd exhausted my supply, I decided. I would close my eyes afterwards in that stock room and see Daniel's bloodied face as he lay on the tarmac, as if my soul was solving the equation, transposing a plus from one side to a minus on the other. So, for years, I had barred myself at some deep level from any kind of pleasure again. Even innocent varieties.

I suppose the difference was that it was one thing feeling no pleasure while sitting on a sofa at home and quite another while doing things where pleasure was *expected*. And I had never been to a place where pleasure was more expected than this Spanish island.

Happiness in June in Ibiza was as common as equations in algebra, but I couldn't feel any of it.

I was missing Karl. I was missing Daniel. I was missing who I had once been, decades before. The person Christina had known. The me who never wallowed.

I wondered if that me was still there. I wondered if I would ever find her.

Hippy Market

Head to the Las Dalias hippy market . . . and say hello to my friend Sabine.

That is what her letter had said. So, having nothing else to do, I did this.

The market was very busy. It was how I imagined San Francisco to have been in 1967. Lots of people with wide-eyed expressions. Incense floating in the air. Stalls selling Balinese jewellery (including 'opal healing bracelets'), Indian sarongs, white tunics, red-and-black flamenco skirts. Someone was at a stall offering Tarot readings. Someone else was playing Joni Mitchell and smoking a sizeable joint. I saw another stall full of clothes. They were the bright kind. The kind Christina owned. I stood staring at a tie-dyed swimsuit. I had failed to bring a swimsuit with me. I wondered briefly what I would look like in it. *Ridiculous, I should imagine.* But then I bought it, primarily to ask where I would find someone called Sabine.

'Over there,' said the friendly young man behind the stall.

He pointed to a woman sitting behind a table full of paintings of Ibizan landscapes. She was part-covered in shade from the fishing net that hung above her stall, but she was still striking. Wild white hair, with flowers in it, a long floaty white dress and about seventy bracelets per wrist.

Sabine spoke English with a gentle German accent, and in words so slow and considered I felt she was in a permanent state of meditation. Sometimes she even closed her eyes. I could have really done with a seat. My legs may have been free of varicose veins, but they weren't trained for detective work.

'Christina was special,' she said.

'Yes. Yes, from what I remember of her, I feel the same.'

She looked at me for a while with a slight sad smile. I felt like I was missing something.

75

'Some people, they shine,' she said, with a deep and mysterious earnestness.

'Especially in this heat.'

Fortunately for Sabine she hadn't seemed to hear my attempt at humour. 'And Christina, she shone brighter. She shone like a goddess. A Greek goddess. That was the problem.'

'Problem?' I asked.

Her eyes were wide open then, as she leaned forward and gave me her answer. 'It is dangerous to shine. It attracts the crows. And she had a gift.' There was a long, slow inhale. 'A power.' An exhale. Another inhale. It was like she had just invented breathing and was showing off about it. 'A talent.'

'Talent?'

'To help people.'

I remembered the man who called at her house. My house. Whatever. The large man with the bleached hair and face tattoo who had wanted to give Christina a packet of gummy bears.

'What do you mean by power? What power did she have? Singing? She was very good at it. I remember that.'

She inhaled and exhaled and inhaled again. Her pauses were irritating. Or maybe it was the heat. Maybe the heat was irritating, and it made everything within it irritating. Including me. 'She was a teller.'

'Teller?'

She pointed towards another corner of the market. 'She used to sit over there and tell people's futures.'

'Ah yes, for the tourists,' I said, remembering what Rosella had said.

'No. This was not some tourist trick. She truly could see the future.'

I tried not to look or sound too surprised, or too sceptical. I was aware that I was talking to someone who might herself be prone to some – I'll put it delicately – *eccentric* beliefs. But I was a maths teacher to my *core*. I needed logic and evidence and algebraic justification. I remembered seeing the book on Christina's shelf. *The Ultimate Guide to Psychic Power: Volume 8*. I remembered that strange conversation I'd had with the taxi driver on my first day. His words came back to me.

There are things about this island . . . Things that most people don't get to see. Things that aren't easily . . . explained.

I remembered his car speeding away from Christina's house, like a mosquito fleeing citronella. I also remembered the water in the jar.

The heat, Grace, I told myself, *it's just the heat. It makes you feel strange. It makes your ankles swell and it sends your brain funny.*

'She only started doing it about four years ago, but it began taking over her life quite quickly . . . I met her years ago, when we were protesting against a golf course in the nature reserve at Cala d'Hort. And then we protested a hotel . . .'

'Which one?'

'The newest Eighth Wonder hotel at Cala Llonga, with her daughter.'

'Oh yes,' I said, remembering the billboard across the street from the house. 'I saw that advertised.'

'That was the only thing they agreed on. The environment. Christina was always very into nature. She was a forest girl really. But then, things changed. *She* changed.'

'Changed how?'

'Her whole face changed. It was clenched all the time. And she would always be looking into the distance. I thought it might have been depression at first. But then she started predicting things. Things that ended up happening.'

'I see.'

'This island has quite a few tellers and psychics and Tarot readers, but none like her. That's why she made some enemies. Word got round. She ended up with a queue of people from there to there.'

She pointed somewhere else, further along the narrow row from where Christina's stall had been. To a stall selling wind chimes and strange vessels for inhaling marijuana.

'She could tell someone's future just by looking in their eyes. She told me I had to fly home and see my father. So I got back to Leipzig and had one day with my dad before he died. There was no rational explanation. But this was not the only problem.'

This was so much to take in. I left it all just sitting there in my head like left luggage as I stared at one of her paintings. A giant rock in the ocean. The one I had seen from above. In the image it looked dark and haunting.

'Es Vedrà,' she said, slowly.

'Yes.' I remembered Rosella talking about it.

'Beautiful. But cursed. They are planning to destroy it.'

'They?'

'Yes. They are planning to develop it. Build a resort on it. Destroy all its wildlife. And people are against it.'

She handed me a flyer from the pile on her desk. It was very sparely designed. Just typed Spanish words on green paper.

'It is a protest. Against those that have allowed this to happen. On Thursday. Meeting outside the Café Mar y Sol in Ibiza Town. You should come. Christina helped organise it.'

'Oh, that's . . . oh, I'm . . . yes, maybe . . . .' I blustered. Then remembered what I was here for. 'Was there another problem? With Christina, I mean?'

And I had that feeling I often get with mathematics, where the answer is there, and you know the answer is there, it is in your brain and taking shape but not fully visible.

More elaborate, slow breathing. She closed her eyes, meditatively. I wondered if she had fallen asleep.

'Alberto Ribas . . .' she said, on her third exhalation. 'That is the person to ask.'

'So you think he is responsible for her death?'

'She predicted her own death. She just didn't know who was going to kill her. The police spoke to Alberto, and nothing happened to him. But . . .' Sabine looked at me for a long while after that *but*. And then it came. 'I think he is the one person who truly knows what happened to her.'

I nodded. I said thank you. And as I walked away, I kept seeing that necklace at the bottom of the sea. I knew there was now no way I was going to leave the island without first talking to Alberto Ribas. So when I got in my car, I typed 'Atlantis Scuba' into the phone. But according to satnav no such place existed. I just had a list of other diving centres. Divestar Ibiza. OrcaSub Ibiza Diving Centre. Centro de Buceo SCUBA. Anfibios Ibiza. But absolutely no Atlantis Scuba.

So I typed instead 'Cala d'Hort' and started driving, south.

The Snake and the Goat

An hour later I was on the beach. A short arc-shaped stretch of busy sand. There was a restaurant. A fresh-fish and paella place. A rustic-looking straw-roofed boutique selling summer dresses and swimwear. The beach itself was full of people and parasols and sun loungers and a couple of pedaloes were out at sea (I remembered me and Karl arguing on one in Corfu, decades before, while Daniel kept diving off the back).

There was an incredible view of Es Vedrà, the rocky islet that rose out of the sea in a dramatic, near-vertical fashion. High limestone dotted with sparse patches of green. The one in Sabine's painting. The one that had unsettled me on the plane. The one that was meant to have magnetic properties. I strolled along the beach, my hips aching a little. It was baking. I was wearing a long skirt and a blouse, which made me the most overdressed person within a mile radius.

I walked until the sand became pebbles. I reached the beach huts. They had wooden slats for doors and most had boats or paddleboards in them. A couple had solar panels on their makeshift corrugated iron roofs. One had washing out to dry. A child sat on top of one of the roofs, reading. I wondered which hut Alberto called home. I walked up some stone steps to the terrace of a restaurant and, further, to a dusty car park. It was over the other side of the beach from where I had parked – way up the road – but I kept walking, to the red path and trees beyond, smelling pine and hearing the pulsing chirp of cicadas. And eventually, I found a small shack with a faded sign outside saying *Atlantis Scuba – Centro Buceo*. It was a concrete cube with a flimsy wooden door. The most easy-to-miss diving centre in the world.

I hesitated. I inhaled. I exhaled.

Anxiety made my whole body alert, like the early onset of a panic attack. It was a feeling I was used to. A feeling like my existence was a delicate thread that could vanish in a sudden wind.

My skin prickled.

I knocked. I listened. I heard nothing but cicadas.

This would have been a great time to turn around and walk back to my car and forget all about it. Who did I think I was? Harrison Ford? It was ridiculous. But I was sure I could hear something now. Something above the buzz of insects. So I pushed the door open.

Inside the hut I found absolutely no one at all. Or rather: no human. The air was thick with heat. I scanned around. A desk, some diving equipment, lots of old cardboard boxes on shelves, two chairs, a computer, a futon and a bed sheet, a bag of washing from a laundrette, a dolphin calendar, an old sticker protesting *GOLF, NO!* and a wooden signpost pointing to the sky, saying *Alpha Centauri 4.367 años luz*.

And a goat.

An actual goat, front half black, back half white, with wide, wide horns and a strong musky smell that was far too much in this heat.

'Oh, hello,' I said, in quiet surprise.

The goat said nothing. And went back to eating oats in a bowl.

I noticed a scruffy pile of flyers on the desk. They were the same as the one Sabine had handed me at the hippy market. Advertising the protest against developing Es Vedrà.

I remembered the words of the taxi driver. 'It begins with A.' The well-dressed rich man who had visited Christina. Was the A for Alberto?

Then I heard footsteps and a man mumbling to himself.

The man walked into the hut with his flip-flops and his denim shorts and large salt-and-pepper beard. This was not the man Pau had talked about. This man was topless, but his chest hair almost constituted an item of clothing in its own right. His skin shone from coconut-scented suntan lotion. It took me a second to confirm to myself that this indeed was the man from the author photograph. I hesitated because – and I will just come out with it – I was thrown by the fact that he was carrying a snake. It was black with yellow markings and semi-coiled around his arm. The serpent's head was now upright, its eyes staring at me. I wasn't particularly scared of pets. Or any animal. But the combination of goat, snake and hirsute human male in such a claustrophobic location was a bit much.

'What is the matter?' he asked me, in accented English, punctuated with a chuckle. 'You look like you have seen a snake!'

Alberto

He had the look not so much of a pirate but a castaway, with the unkempt hair and the beard escaping his face in every direction, and youthful eyes that shone like a sunrise through an ancient ruin. His eyes aside, it was a lot to deal with. He triggered a primal sense of disgust that I couldn't ignore.

'I think I am in the wrong place.' I don't know why I said that. Fear, I suppose.

'That makes two of you, man . . .' Alberto said, sounding almost American for a moment.

'Sorry?'

He nodded to the snake, which was now migrating to his other arm. 'Snakes! They are great company. The most intellectual of reptiles. Their minds are full of fascinating philosophical riddles. But we are not meant to have snakes! For thousands of years Ibiza had no serpents, no snakes.'

'Oh.'

He clearly thought I was here for a history lesson.

'The ancient Phoenicians first settled here because there was nothing deadly on the island. No dangerous animals. No dangerous plants. It was a blessed island. Even twenty years ago, no snakes. And now? Snakes, snakes, snakes. And it is not good. It is not good at all . . . You see, they may not hurt us. They have no veneno . . .'

'Venom?'

'Exactly,' he pointed at me as if I had just cracked the Enigma code. He spoke English more fluently than I did, but he liked to decorate his sentences with bits of Spanish as much as possible, to remind me where I was. 'But they hurt the balance of life. They are destroying the lizards. We used to have lizards everywhere. Now we still *do* have them, but they are being finished off by this one and his friends.'

The goat had gobbled the oats and was slowly heading out of the door.

'Hasta luego, Nostradamus,' Alberto said, waving a cheery goodbye to the goat. 'Don't be like that,' he said, as if he had expected the goat to say 'goodbye' right back. Then Alberto looked at me. 'He is a misanthropic soul. Common among goats. But he will be back for supper. He always is.'

'I think I am in the wrong place,' I told him again. I just wanted to leave. Or to never have arrived.

He stared at me. His eyes had a force to them. 'No. You are in the right place, I assure you. And that is why I must finish telling you about the lizards. Now they are dying. Everywhere. People do not understand how important it is. Especially the fuckers in the hills.'

There was a violence to the way he said that. He was a man with clear resentments. Sabine's words echoed in my mind. *I think he is the only person who knows what happened to her . . .*

'The people with the fancy gardens and the olive trees. The millionaires and billionaires with their yoga mats and infinity pools. I can say this to you because you are clearly not a rich woman.'

I did not like him, even before that sentence, but that sealed the deal.

'Clearly,' I said. 'Now, if you don't mind, could I—'

But I was distracted. I noticed that as he was talking his thumb was massaging the area under the snake's neck, and the reptile seemed to be slowing in its movements.

'These snakes are Montpellier snakes. They get in with the imported trees, in the . . . holes . . . the . . . They lay their eggs there . . . Their eggs are in the trees . . . And now they are here they multiply like crazy. And the whole ecological system is fucked up. Really fucking fucked. Fucked like a dolphin. And dolphins really like to fuck. Dolphins are built for pleasure. They are pleasure machines.'

I thought he was trying to shock me. So, despite my anxiety in that moment, I kept my face as still and strong as an Easter Island statue and gave him not even a flicker of the prudery he was probably expecting.

'So there are snake-catchers, and they smash their heads with rocks. But I can't do that to him. Look at him. His mind is full of questions. You can't hear them, but trust me, this is a very curious snake. I suppose because he is a transplant, like you. He is somewhere he is not designed to be . . . Don't worry, snake. Everything is fine . . . So, I will put him to sleep for a little while. Look, the dude is asleep. His eyes are still open because he is a snake. But look.' The snake slid away from his arm as he held it up. He went over to his desk and opened a drawer for it and then closed the snake away. 'I will call my friend. He works in security for a nightclub. His little girl keeps them as pets.'

I wasn't a connoisseur of conversations these days but even I knew this was an abnormal one.

'Is the snake okay?'

'Sí, sí. It's a technique I learned from an Argentinian general.' He came over and held out his hand, which I tentatively shook. He spoke English with an accent that was half Spanish and half American, probably from his time at the University of California.

'Alberto Ribas,' he said. 'Friend of the animals and the sea.'

'I'm Grace. Friend of a person who died in mysterious circumstances. I am trying to find out what happened to her.'

'Welcome to my office.' He gestured to the futon. 'And my home.'

'You live here?'

'Yes, yes. Why not? I have other options. My daughter has a lovely house in the north of the island, and she wants me to live with her, but I like it here. I get up. I bathe in the sea and dry in the sun. What could be better?'

'Plumbing?' I offered.

He ignored me.

'Please,' I tried again. 'I would like to find out what happened to my friend.'

'You said your name was Grace? Like Grace Kelly?'

It was frustrating. The way he could keep steering the conversation away from where I wanted it to go, but I humoured him.

'My mum loved her. I was born the year *High Noon* came out.' This was all true. But hardly what I came here to share.

'Did you know that she had her honeymoon in Ibiza?'

'No. And I don't think—'

'Well, she did. Look it up. People think celebrities have only started coming here. But they always have. Errol Flynn came here on his yacht.

Laurence Olivier. Elizabeth Taylor. All before we even had an airport. Later on, Joni Mitchell came here to get inspired. A young Cormac McCarthy came to write back when he was a hippy. Bob Marley came here to go dancing. I met him. He was a hero.'

I tried to guess Alberto's age. The beard and mahogany tan made it hard. He could have been anywhere between sixty and eighty. Yet despite the wear and tear on his body, he had a youthfulness to him. He was someone who had never learned to be a grown-up.

'Listen,' I said, surprisingly strict given my nerves, 'I am here to ask about an old friend of mine.'

He ignored this completely. Maybe he hadn't heard. No. He had heard. But he carried on, talking not quite *to* me, but *over* me, as if to an imaginary but adoring crowd somehow squeezed into the shack. Maybe a lecture hall of admiring students in a universe where he still had a career. 'You see, this is not a normal island. I know people say that all the time, but I really know it to be true. This island is not normal. There is something special here. It is everywhere you look, if you know what you are looking for. Take the goat . . .'

I tried to interrupt. It was like filling the gap in a number sequence that had already been filled.

'I named him after Nostradamus because the great Frenchman originally predicted Ibiza will be the last sanctuary for life on Earth. Did you know that?'

I stared down at the empty bowl of oats, trying to imagine what any of this had to do with Christina or scuba diving or anything else.

'There are goats on Es Vedrà too. They always want rid of them. Say they are "malos para el hábitat"! Humans! Saying goats are bad for the habitat! Imagine! Fucking humans, huh?'

He then made a strange sound. Like a howling wolf. God only knows why.

I felt a little scared, I admit. He was not only an insane man but also a big one. A big, wild, hairy one. And for his age – whatever that was – probably pretty fit. Even with my revamped legs I wouldn't have been able to outrun him. So I was stuck in a deserted shack, quite a long distance from the beach and even the car park. Any scream would have been drowned out by the relentless mating call of cicadas.

'It was the seagrass, wasn't it?' he asked me. His eyes had switched from child-like to ancient. The stare had a force to it. I felt it could knock me off my feet.

'Sorry?'

'It was the picture of the seagrass. That was what brought you here.'

And I had no idea what to say.

Tomorrow at Midnight

I pictured the photograph on the website. The one with the St Christopher necklace. I had a strange feeling. Like you get when you have left a door or gate open. But the door or gate was me. 'It was one of the things.'

'You have to see it,' he said, his voice suddenly quiet and serious. 'It will change your life.'

'What makes you think I want to change my life?' My voice let me down and cracked a little.

He smiled, the gap in his teeth like a little cave amid limestone. He had the look of someone about to lay down a royal flush. 'Why else would you move to Ibiza and live in a terrible house on a busy road, given to you by a virtual stranger, if you didn't want to change your life?'

This time I didn't miss a beat. I hid all surprise from my face. He probably knew about all this from Christina. That was the rational explanation. 'Curiosity,' I said.

'Ah,' he smiled. 'La curiosidad mató al gato. You know that expression? You have it in English too. Curiosity killed the cat.'

'I am not a cat.'

This made him laugh. A proper belly laugh. A pirate's laugh. A laugh that seemed too large for its prompt. Two plus two equalling seven hundred.

And then he gave me another lecture I hadn't asked for. 'Iggy Pop sings about it in a song. I played it once here. At Amnesia. You know, the nightclub. Back in 1980 when it was still a farmhouse and we still danced to everything . . .'

I don't know why he thought I wanted to know so much about him. I waited for the chance to speak like an obedient dog waiting for dinner.

'Do you have an open mind?' He stared at me with a smile.

I didn't like his stare. For a moment I wished I was tucked away in the drawer with the snake.

'I was a maths teacher,' I said, frustrated now. 'I have a mind that likes to solve things. And I really want to know what happened to my friend, Christina van der Berg. I want to know how she died. And I think you might have some answers.'

The full name hit him. He seemed to flinch at it. Sadness fell across his face like a cloud. He nodded. He waited a while. 'She knew she was going to die. She knew she was going to be killed. So she did something about it.'

'What do you mean? What did she do?'

'I wasn't here. I was with my daughter, Marta. In Madrid. She was at a conference on astrophysics and I was supporting her.' I don't know why, but I was surprised to learn he had a daughter who he attended conferences with. It was like seeing a watercolour by an orangutan. It seemed somehow beyond the limits I had put upon him. 'Marta and Christina were good friends. Well, they worked together on things. My daughter is not just an astrophysicist but she is an environmentalist. I am a very proud papá.' He took a flyer from the desk. 'She is organising a protest. On Thursday. It is against the development they are planning on Es Vedrà.'

I nodded. 'I heard about that. It sounds like a very noble cause. But I am here to find out more about Christina.'

'Christina was a very skilled diver. Sometimes she went out on her own. The police know all this. And now you do too.'

'And that is all you know?'

'No. I know a lot of things that you don't know. Things that would help you understand.'

'What kind of things?'

He stared at me a while. He was weighing something up about me. I felt assessed. He was studying my face as if it held a clue to something important. 'Yes,' he said. 'You are ready to see the truth. I see it now . . .'

'See what exactly?'

'Your potential.' He pointed at me. I had never felt the desire to break someone's finger before. I think the heat was getting to me. 'She was right about you. You are going to be great at this.'

Then I snapped a little. 'Could you stop patronising me and talking in circles and speak to me like a normal human being?'

'Talking in circles. It's an interesting phrase, no?'

'So is *cut to the chase*. Do you know that one?'

'Listen. If you want to stay a normal human being, you should leave right now. Because this won't be a normal experience . . .'

'What won't?'

'Tomorrow night is a moonless night,' he said.

What has that got to do with anything? I wondered.

He smiled as if he knew exactly what I was thinking. He pointed behind him. 'Out in the ocean, tomorrow night, between here and Formentera, is your chance to know what happened to your friend. I will take you. Have you ever dived before?'

'No. And if you think I am getting in a boat with you in the middle of the night, then you are considerably mistaken.'

Again, he seemed to ignore what I was saying. 'Can you swim?'

'Yes.'

'Then you can dive, man. Diving is just swimming. But down. There is a little more to it. But I can explain. I will meet you on the beach at midnight.'

'I am seventy-two years old. I don't do midnights. Or diving.'

'Nonsense. This is Ibiza. No one is too old for anything. There is a ninety-year-old who dances at Pacha every single night.'

'That is fascinating,' I said. Sarcasm is my nervous tic.

He began to leave. I felt a kind of tidal pull. I wanted answers and he knew it.

'Where are you going?'

He stood at the door. Turned with a smile. His teeth, even without the gap, would have been remarkable. Angled and spaced like uneven headstones. Was he a madman? Was he a murderer? Could a face tell you anything at all? Was it better to follow him, or to stay in a humid hut with no answers and an actual snake? I was thinking of every ominous thing I had heard about him, from Sabine and Rosella. And from the Guardia Civil officer whose words I clearly remembered.

Please stay away from Mr Ribas . . .

'I just want to know what happened to my friend.'

'And you will,' he said, softly. 'I promise. But some things can't be told. They have to be shown. Tomorrow. Midnight.'

Tomorrow.

Midnight.

And then he was gone. And I exhaled for what seemed like the first time in twenty minutes.

The Inescapable Loneliness of Grace Winters

It was a half-hour drive back to the house, much of it over bumpy roads.

I felt tired and worried, and my ankles were the size of volleyballs. I imagined all this stress and heat was not advisable so soon after a vein op.

I wished Karl was with me. He would have enjoyed Ibiza. He would have liked the old hippies and he was better than me in the heat. He always liked an excuse to get his legs out in the sunshine. He believed wearing shorts made him a few degrees happier. He had been one of those terminally British people who gardened in their swimming shorts in April. I pictured him in his greenhouse, tending to his tomatoes, his face as red as one from hypertension. But smiling. Always smiling. A soft, faint smile that was his default expression. Not necessarily indicative of happiness but of stoicism. It was his whole philosophy really. Smile through it. Smile through the grief and pain and loss. A smile that was, I think, for Daniel. Like he felt Daniel was watching and he didn't want Daniel to feel upset for us or uncomfortable or guilty for our grief.

It was sad, thinking about Karl and Daniel. My boys. But there was a comfort in the sadness. It is hard to explain and I don't know if you feel the same about your mum, but I sometimes *indulged* my sadness. I headed towards it. Grief felt like the only way to keep close to them. So my mind headed to sad and bittersweet thoughts – even to a walk in the woods with them both thirty-six years ago, picking dandelions and buttercups – in order to have a kind of company.

I passed the go-kart track. It was a strange place to have a go-kart track, in the middle of nowhere. But it seemed popular. There were so many Ibizas, I realised. There was the family holiday go-karting, horse-riding kind of Ibiza. The party Ibiza. The hippy Ibiza. The spa hotel Ibiza. The scuba diving and beachy Ibiza. There was the expensive, yachty, Michelin-starred Ibiza. The Leonardo DiCaprio Ibiza. The nature trail, star-gazing Ibiza. The traditional Ibiza of folk dances and villages and festivals and churches and old customs. And then of course there was the local, lived, contemporary Ibiza I had caught glimpses of in supermarkets and cafés and amid the dog walkers beside the road. There was seemingly an Ibiza for everyone, except lonely grieving widows.

A line of tourists queued up for the karts. Families and groups of young men. Karl would have liked that too. So would Daniel. I thought of all the people, laughing, in holiday spirits. It all felt so fragile. In this state of mind it was hard to see any living person and not imagine the hole they would cause if they were gone. To see everyone on Earth as someone's grief waiting to happen.

And then I was there. At the house that wasn't yet a home. A house I still didn't feel belonged to me. I opened the door and went inside and made myself a basic supper in that small brown kitchen. I drank some orange juice and ate bread and cheese and tomatoes, and it was all perfectly fine, but I couldn't really taste any of it. My senses were even more dulled than usual. Even the fresh juice was hardly noted.

I stared at the engagement ring on my hand. At the ruby embedded in it, the second ring Karl had proposed with. The first had been an emerald.

It is funny how, at my age, the sight of something always prompts a memory of something that lay further behind it. There is no such thing as a pure present in this book of life. You can always see the words from the page before, their inky shadows darkening what is in front of you. Or at least dulling it.

A few years before I had cut my ring finger while chopping an onion. The bleeding hadn't stopped so I'd had to go to the hospital and get the tip cauterised. They burnt the blood vessels to stop the bleeding. And now I couldn't feel anything on the tip of the finger. So I felt like that is what had happened to me, that grief and guilt and life had cauterised me and there was nothing new to experience. Just a wound to look at and keep prodding for a sign of feeling.

It was a fragile, ragged evening, still light outside but dark and humid in the house. I switched on the TV and watched a Spanish chat show without understanding a word. I sat there. Staring at the TV, then at

Christina's books and her stack of old vinyl records, then at the pictures on the wall. I saw Alberto's smiling gap-toothed face staring at me from the photographs.

'What do you want?' I asked his image.

There was no reply.

Time slipped away. I switched off the TV. Listened to the sporadic swooshing of traffic.

It was late. I lay in bed with my joint aches and ringing ears and heavy sorrows. I couldn't sleep.

I felt at the bottom of things. I felt that if I passed peacefully away in the night it would be fine. I had thought, foolishly, that coming to Ibiza would shake things up, dust the cobwebs, reduce the mental weight. I thought, basically, what we all want to think when we step on a plane: that I was about to escape.

But no.

The trouble with having a change of scene is that if you get there and find that you feel just the same, then you really are trapped. And that was my conclusion. The problem hadn't been Lincoln, or the bungalow, or my situation. The problem was me. There was no escape from grief and loneliness. So long as I stayed in the same ageing body with my same curdled memories, I was my own life sentence.

I wasn't going to find out what happened to Christina. All I was doing was making a fool of myself, with added humidity. I felt tears form. A kind of progress.

What am I doing here?

And, sooner than I imagined, I was going to receive an answer.

Broken Radios

Now, I have a theory about life, and I am going to be very grand and share it with you here. My theory is an old one, but it is one I have recently found to be true.

The point of desperation is often the point of truth.

When things are wrong, we need to reach rock bottom in order for change to happen. We sometimes need to feel trapped in order to find the way out. We don't meet ourselves in the light and air. We don't understand the radio when the song is playing. We sometimes need to smash the thing to see how it is made.

And those first few days in Ibiza brought everything up that I'd managed to keep suppressed. The grief, the despair, the solitude. I was crashing, and I was seeing myself. I was opened up like a broken radio. I was faced with my own faulty coils and circuits and transistors. All the flaws and the inconsistencies. And maybe that was it. Maybe it was because I was lying there, smashed up, paradoxically numb and in pain all at once, that it happened. Maybe when you scream in silence the help arrives silently too. Maybe the universe was listening. Maybe the signal was picked up.

I don't know.

But something very certainly happened.

And the timing was impeccable.

Glow

It was well after one when I got distracted by a soft glow coming in through the doorway. I must have left a light on somewhere. But that was confusing, because I was pretty sure it had been dark everywhere. I was scared for a moment. Fear puncturing the numbness. A reminder I was alive. *What if someone had broken in? What if it was Alberto?*

I shook away my stupid thoughts and I got out of bed and headed towards the light, and quickly found the source. The olive jar by the front door, lighting up the photos on the wall. The water was shining as bright as a torch, and the vector of light beamed upwards, forming a conical shape in the air. I couldn't look directly into the jar without my eyes watering, so I stared at this light beam. It seemed different from the beam of, say, a torch. It seemed to have a life of its own. Little fluctuations and shifts and movements. It felt like I was witnessing something that, although I couldn't understand it, was there to be understood. Does that make sense? It felt like a kind of message. Like I was a baby mesmerised by the moving lips of a parent.

'What the hell is happening?' I remember asking myself.

Eventually the light faded. And I went back to bed. Strangely, I felt calmer.

I also felt certain about one thing. I knew that, against all caution, at midnight tomorrow I would be on the beach at Cala d'Hort, awaiting an answer.

A Boat Called No

It was a rickety, creaky old wooden dive boat with an even more rickety engine that stopped and started like a dog growling at a mischievous squirrel. Even in the deep, moonless dark it was clear the paint was peeling like scabs, so much so that only the last two letters of its name – *Neptuno* – were visible. If I was a believer in signs from the universe, a boat called 'no' would have been a further reason not to have boarded it. But there I was.

The sea was calm. Water gently lapped the hull of the boat, a quiet and strangely disconcerting sound, as if the whole Mediterranean had quietened itself, waiting for something to happen. Lights glowed from the island we had just left behind, and one or two flickered from the other island, Formentera, that lay on the horizon.

Alberto had stayed at the helm – steadfastly staring out to sea, like a determined buccaneer – while I stripped off down to the tie-dyed swimsuit I had purchased at the hippy market. The dim light of the lantern gave my flesh an almost blue-green hue, and even with his back to me I felt self-conscious about my old exposed flesh, even with my newer, smoother legs, and he hardly an Adonis himself. I think actually that was one of the first things I resented about Alberto. The ease he had with his own form. The way he let it all hang out. The pot belly, the body hair, the open shirts, the ridiculous denim shorts. I don't know if it was because he was a man, or because he was just him, but he really didn't give a toss. Whereas, by contrast, I cared far too much. My simmering disquiet about my own existence had always found its focus in my physical form. I had spent a lifetime hating my appearance in the present and then appreciating it in retrospect. No doubt there was a ninety-year-old Grace in the future who was wondering why I didn't like the way I looked at seventy-two. If only we could always have the perspective of the future with us as we live that present.

Sure, in each moment we have never been so old, but we are of course also the youngest we will ever be. I had never liked my body very much, and even now the lumpiest veins had been removed I still felt quite ashamed of it. Being English – particularly the condensed form known as East Midlands English – was to be raised to have self-consciousness as a virtue. But it was also being old, being a woman, it was how I was conditioned to be. It is such a ridiculous thing, isn't it? The way we judge our bodies. The way, as we become increasingly invisible with age, we still clutch tight to that self-consciousness. The way we curse the thing that has kept us alive all this time. I doubt a sparrow resents its wings, even when its feathers are dried and withered.

I had often wanted to be a bird. A bluebird. Like the one Daniel had drawn for me decades ago. But there I was, more human than ever. And the thought that Alberto – already in his wetsuit – could turn around and witness me at any time added urgency as I grappled awkwardly into mine.

Grappling into a wetsuit, by the way, is one of the all-time challenges in life. It requires the strength of an ox and the limbs of a contortionist. If wetsuits had been around in ancient times Hercules would have had to get into one as part of his twelve labours. At the end, when I was mostly covered, I even had to ask Alberto to help me a bit.

'Sí, sí, of course . . . por supuesto . . .'

Then he switched the engine off and fastened an air cylinder to my back and talked me through other pieces of equipment, including the torches strapped to our heads. For a moment or two, he seemed like quite a normal diving instructor. He told me about the regulator I was going to breathe through. Another device – a kind of vest – that was to control my buoyancy underwater so that I didn't have to keep kicking my legs. A weighted belt. A mask, which he said was very important, because I needed to keep my eyes as open as possible. And fins. I didn't know whether to feel ridiculous or terrified, so I decided to feel both. He then went back to the helm and continued heading further out.

I had no idea what I was doing here. Yes, I desperately wanted to find out what had happened to Christina, but I think there was another reason I was on that boat, and it certainly had nothing to do with Alberto's animal charisma. Maybe, at some subconscious level, it was a kind of death wish. Maybe I wanted something bad to happen. Maybe, after discovering I was unable to feel anything at all towards such a beautiful island, I realised that I had nothing to lose.

Or maybe, just maybe, it was also the opposite. Maybe I had a sense that I needed to break the pattern. And by doing it I would break out of the limbo I was in. I would die. Or I would find a way to truly live. That is to say, maybe something was calling me. Either Christina. Or something else. Something to do with that strange glowing water in the olive jar.

'People say she could see into the future,' I said at one point, when the sound of the engine lowered.

'She could,' said Alberto, staring out at the dark low outline of Formentera ahead of us. 'She saw her life was in danger. But I don't know who was endangering it. Who wanted to kill her. And nor did she.'

'People don't see into the future.'

'Of course they do. People do it all the time. Meteorologists, economists . . . Well, they try to.'

He laughed. He thought he was funny. He thought it was a good place to drop a weak joke, right there after talking about Christina's death. He had an unseemly admiration for himself.

'You know exactly what I mean. You are a man of science. You must surely realise you are speaking nonsense. Clairvoyancy is an illusion, a magic trick, it has no evidence to support it,' I said.

'There are many things that people have thought were not real that turned out to be very real. Up until near the end of the nineteenth century, every marine scientist on Earth was convinced that life couldn't exist more than five hundred metres below sea level. Then they discovered it went all the way down and it was a shock. A *big* shock.'

'That's different.'

'Is it? Everything looks obvious after history has tamed it. But at the time it was like finding proof of alien life. We are never at the end of history. And we are not at the end of science.'

'You believe in alien life, don't you? You wrote a book about it.'

'Yes. Can you imagine believing in Earth if you were someone who had never been there? Can you imagine believing in the elephant, the turtle, the clownfish, the zebra shark? It would be crazy, crazy.'

'I try to believe in known reality,' I said.

'And what about the glowing seawater in the olive jar?'

I froze. I was sure I hadn't told him about that. He dug in his pocket and pulled out a miniature bottle of rum. Only it wasn't rum. It was seawater, very faintly glowing seawater. 'I carry this with me everywhere. Ever since I quit drinking. I like to be near it.'

'It? What is *it*?'

'Something you will understand very soon. Reality is merely an illusion. A very persistent one. I think that is what Einstein said. Sometimes the illusion is the reality we don't understand yet.'

'If she could see into the future, then why did she die?'

He frowned, smilingly. 'Who said she died?'

'Everyone,' I said. 'That is why I am here. She died.'

'She didn't die. She just saw she was going to. She knew if she stayed someone was going to harm her. She just went away.'

'Where?'

'I am about to show you.'

I had no idea what to say. 'I'm seventy-two years old. Isn't there a health check I need to do?'

'Are you in good health?'

'Not particularly.' I didn't feel like giving him the full list. The problematic veins, the bad hip, the swollen ankles, the tinnitus, the osteoarthritis, the erratic blood pressure, the occasional depression, the anhedonia . . . The audiobook of *War and Peace* would have been shorter.

'Well, then. That is perfect.'

'Perfect? For what?'

For blaming my death on natural causes?

'You will see,' he said. Which wasn't exactly reassuring.

Nolletia chrysocomoides

I sat on the fitted bench on the deck and waited.

The engine failed and Alberto headed to the stern and kept cursing in Spanish until he got it working again.

We headed south, past Es Vedrà. It was quite an intimidating sight, close up, in the dark. The rock seemed to go on for ever, merging into the night. Its edges frayed with vegetation. It was hard to imagine anyone living there. Even goats. I thought it was quite conveniently sized, that rock. You could do anything behind it, unseen. My nerves got worse.

I practised putting the mouthpiece in and breathing through it.

It was a relief when I heard the buzz of my phone. I scrambled around in my pile of clothes to see that I had a WhatsApp message from Sophie, Karl's sister. She was responding to the photo I had sent of the plant with yellow flowers.

It was a long message. Or a long series of messages. This was unusual. Sophie was explaining that she didn't recognise the plant at all, so she had shown it to her partner, Sarika, the botanist. Sarika had apparently had a strong reaction to the photo:

She was very VERY confused.

She thought you must have taken the picture from the internet. Some AI thing.

The plant you sent us has the fancy Latin name Nolletia chrysocomoides – (cut and pasted that!) – it is officially extinct in Europe!!! Not been anywhere near Spain for 10 yrs. And Sar knows all about this kind of stuff . . . plant nerd . . . expert on endangered and extinct plants and flowers. So – yes – very weird!!

99

She's going to send the photo (if that's OK)
to her mate at UWA (the uni here in Perth) to
see what she makes of it. Anyway, hope you
are well and enjoying life in Ibiza. I know
you can find it hard sometimes to socialise
and to throw yourself into things. But I think
Karl would want you to. Speak soon. xxxx

I clicked off WhatsApp, and even though Alberto was still talking to me, I was hardly listening. My heart was racing faster than I knew it could and my mind was darting into formerly cordoned-off areas, full of notions and ideas I'd have once dismissed as fantastical. One of the thoughts that was entering my head was this: the plant hadn't just randomly appeared in front of the door. It had appeared where I had tipped out the water. The water that had been in the olive jar. The magic water. The glowing water.

I stared up at Alberto. I needed to concentrate.

'The ocean is very much still unknown,' he was telling me. 'People talk about the universe being unknown, but our planet is the same. More people have been to the moon than to the deepest part of the ocean. The Mariana Trench, man. You have heard of it? Very hard to reach. Most of the ocean has not been seen by humans, let alone mapped. We genuinely know more about the surface of Mars. Even in shallow seas like this one, much of it is mysterious. It will help to keep that in mind . . .'

I could tell this was very much his subject. He got quite animated about it, moving his arms around as much as the tight wetsuit allowed. He talked about the things that have been discovered and how magical they are – underwater mountains, valleys bigger than the Grand Canyon, a sub-aquatic river in the Black Sea – larger than the Thames – with trees beside it. I wondered, if he was about to murder me, would he be going to this much effort to educate me on marine life?

'And then we get to the seagrass,' said Alberto. 'The most amazing thing. *Posidonia oceanica*. It goes right from Ibiza to Formentera – one single self-replicating organism that has like a special miracle been preserved for many, many, many centuries . . . Millennia, in fact.'

'So why didn't you want me to see it in the daytime? Won't it be dark down there? Even with the torches?'

He laughed. And he echoed my question. 'Won't it be dark down there? Man, quite the opposite. You'll see.'

'If this underwater meadow is everywhere, why do we need to go so far out?'

He turned away from the helm. Spoke loudly above the motor. 'Because you want the answer, right? You want to be precisely where the picture was taken. You want to see the necklace you gave her . . .'

The necklace you gave her . . .

That was a lot of information in very few words. 'You know I gave it her?'

'Sí, sí. Por supuesto! Of course, of course. She told me about it. She said you were the kindest person she ever met. Not only kind, but strong. They are the two essential qualities, Grace. They are what's needed. Mental fortitude and emotional sympathy. Let me tell you something about kindness. I was raised by my grandmother here in the village of Santa Agnès de Corona. She was an artist. But she was kind to everyone. Before I was born she helped lots of artists fleeing Germany to find a safe haven in Ibiza. Our home was small, but I had an almond tree outside the window and it reminded me when it blossomed that this is a world full of overwhelming beauty. We were poor but Ibiza was rich in other ways. In those days we were so close to nature. There were only two paved roads and hardly any electric light but there was always music and interesting conversations and the sea. Grandma took me everywhere and wanted me to enjoy life. I remember dancing as a child to jazz on the beach at Ses Figueretes I owe everything to her kindness, and when I see kindness I want to reward it. Thanks to her, I always had three things. A love of nature, strength and sympathy. She had those qualities. You have them too.'

'Your grandmother sounds like a fine person.'

'She was. So was Christina. And she saw those qualities in you.'

'But Christina didn't know me,' I said. 'Not really. We didn't stay in touch.'

'Oh, she knew *everything*.'

Alberto switched off the engine and shook his head all the way to the bow, where he lowered the anchor. I looked over at the water. Inhaled the cool briny air. And I saw something. Something glowing amid the dark depths. Just for a moment. Before the ocean went dark again.

'There is beauty in this sea unlike any other,' said Alberto, with a squinted smile. 'Yet only a few people ever get to see it. A light in the water. It is special but it can be mesmerising. Be careful. Don't swim towards it . . . It will come to you.'

I put the regulator in my mouth and stood on the small platform ready to follow Alberto into the sea.

What am I doing? What is going to happen?

Most of life, I realised, was mystery. Even mathematics is full of mystery. We can know that every even number above two is the sum of two primes, but we don't know why. There are mysteries everywhere. In the mind of every sentient creature and beneath the surface of every sea. Sometimes the only thing to do is to dive in and find things out for ourselves.

Half of me was scared. But then I thought of that empty bungalow back in Lincoln, full of its sad memories, and I lifted my leg and stepped into the water, reminding myself to keep my eyes wide open.

The Sudden Dark

Alberto swam in front, which was comforting, as I could see him with my torch beam and make sure he wasn't secretly tampering with my oxygen. We headed at a gentle angle down towards the seagrass.

He pointed over to the right and I momentarily forgot to breathe as I turned and my torch shone on an eel, purple with yellow specks, its body heading forward in a mesmerising wave of movement. After that I struggled a bit to regulate my breathing. My legs were tingling. I very much doubted any doctors would have recommended I do this. But I'd got this far, so I swam on.

As we neared the seabed, I witnessed an abundance of life in the dark. A little school of silver fish darting in formation, their shadows on the grass and the sand below, a couple more eels weaving between the green strands of the plant, seahorses, a technicoloured sea slug. An injured fish, a grouper, leaking blood into the water.

I could see the seagrass clearly in the artificial glow of the torch. It was beautiful and eerie all at once. Long thin emerald-green leaves, going on seemingly for ever in all directions. It felt deeply important in its simplicity, as if that was the key to survival. Never flower, never progress, never complicate. Same template for ever.

Then I saw Alberto pointing towards something. Something small and gold, exactly like in the photograph. I swam towards it and picked it up. A necklace I hadn't held for forty-five years. I saw the embossed figure of St Christopher, carrying the infant Christ across the river. I clenched it tight like lost treasure and looked for some clue as to how it had been left there. I looked for signs of trouble. But there was nothing else, and the seagrass didn't look disturbed or trampled or distorted from a struggle.

Then, curiously, the fish and other sea creatures that had all been travelling in different directions were now suddenly headed in just one.

They were heading quickly away from an unseen entity, as if in panic. I was trying to work out what was going on when another thing happened.

The light strapped to my forehead began to flicker.

I turned to Alberto in the stuttering light and saw that his was too. I think he was smiling, but it was hard to tell because of the diving equipment. And then, a second after that, the lights went off completely. Total darkness. Nothing at all. I looked all around.

I felt his hand on my arm.

Please stay away from Mr Ribas.

A tight grip.

A madman.

Getting tighter.

The one person that truly knows what happened to her.

Then he let go.

And everything changed.

Light

Suddenly, there was light.

The Cloud and the Sphere

The light I was now seeing was not coming from our headlamps. They were still very much off.

No, this light was coming from about a hundred metres in front of us. Phosphorescent. And the fast-moving fish I saw darting away from something were in fact doing the opposite. They were heading fast towards it.

A luminescent *thing* above the grass, a colour that seemed bright and pale all at once, that was at first in the shape of a cloud and then in the shape of a sphere. A geometrically *perfect* sphere. The kind Euclid and Archimedes wrote about thousands of years ago but which, on Earth, only exists as an abstract idea and not as a thing of nature. It fluctuated between indistinct cloud and precise sphere in a way that instantly felt alien and unearthly. It wasn't particularly big – larger than a tennis ball but smaller than a football. At least at first. The size shifted – growing, then shrinking – like the movement of a lung. And colour-wise it was blue unlike any I had ever seen before. Not the blue of the sea, not quite, though the colour shifted as much as the scale and form. The fish swam into it, into the light.

I am very sorry to be so indistinct about this, but it is hard to describe something for which there is no real earthly reference. The moment I compare it to something is the moment I realise it was nothing like that thing. I suppose describing it is like describing a difficult emotion, a contradictory emotion. You will get more of those as you get older. Like the strange small contentment that can sometimes be traced to grief or tears, living alongside the pain. Or the bittersweet knowledge that all things must pass.

It was mesmerising; I can tell you that much. It was, quite simply, the most incredible thing I had seen in my life. I turned to Alberto and saw him smiling behind his mask and mouthpiece. His headlamp was working again. And so was mine. Alberto's smile was the smile of recognition, or of pride, like a relative showing me his favourite film. And what was incredible about it was not just the sight of it but the *presence* of it, because it felt like looking at a feeling.

Yes. That was it. *It felt like looking at a feeling.*

I know that sounds ridiculous, but that is the only way I can explain it. Like somehow it was love or hope I was looking at. Or rather, an emotion we don't have a word for but which we feel at a deep level, one we keep buried, but which connects us. I was looking at something outside myself, obviously, but also somehow inside myself.

And I was possibly there looking at it for quite a time before I noticed Alberto pointing to the cloud, and then giving me, in quick succession, the thumbs-up and an okay signal and also an open-palm signal – the latter being the kind you give to a disobedient Labrador when you want them to *stay*. So, I did. I stayed there. And I watched as the luminescent sphere became a luminescent cloud once more, before slowly changing shape again, elongating almost like an arm reaching out, in a clear direction as if it wasn't random but had an intention. And that line of light approached the injured fish, the grouper, and 'touched' the wound. Then, almost as quickly, the light withdrew back into the oscillating cloud-sphere and the fish was left there, only now it was unquestionably healed. It was fully upright, its speckled skin intact as it swam away.

I turned to Alberto, who seemed much less stunned than me. He was still smiling, as casually as if he was at a café watching a sunset. By the time I turned back around it was already happening. The sphere became a cloud, and it stayed being a cloud but then part of the cloud became a long thin arm of light again. Only this time it wasn't heading for an injured fish.

It was heading for me.

Free

I wasn't able to remember all of it.

I mean, I could remember what I have told you up until now. But much of the space from that moment underwater to the moment I woke up in hospital is so strange. And because of the nature of what I am writing about, an area which traditionally has led people to either wild flights of fancy or deeply entrenched scepticism, I feel I must stick rigidly to what I actually experienced.

So, I can tell you that the blue light reached me. The *arm of light*, which was a very ragged, long, cloudy cone of light. And the moment it touched me it was as if the whole ocean had disappeared.

There were no creatures or plants around me. No Alberto. No anything. Just water, but a strange water. Water the colour of that illuminated and glowing and unnatural blue. And it was the most relaxing feeling. More than relaxing. Something else. *Freeing*. I felt free. I must have dropped the necklace at some point, but I can't remember when.

And then, a blink later, I was on what appeared to be dry land. Amid nature. But not any nature I had seen before. There were trees that weren't trees. Tall, thin, white-leaved. There was a beach that wasn't a beach. A sea that wasn't a sea. And the air was not any air I had ever known. It was so pure and sweet it made breathing feel like the purpose of life, rather than a mere prerequisite.

I saw creatures amid the trees. They were standing upright. They could have almost been human, from this distance. They were wearing some kind of clothes. Yet they seemed smudged, like figures in a watercolour, vapours leaving their bodies as they stood there. They made me feel calm. Like they were protective spirits.

The beach did have sand, but it was a burnt orange kind of colour. And the sea was blue but not an earthly blue. It was the glowing impossible blue I had seen while diving.

I know what you are thinking. You are thinking, 'Oh, this sounds like an interesting dream.' And I can't conclusively tell you that it wasn't a dream. But if it was a dream, it was like no other I had experienced in seven decades of existence. It was all so sharp. In fact, the enhancement to every sense was such that it was easier to believe that my life up until then had been a dream, and this was reality. Yes. That is what it felt like. It felt like waking up.

'Where?' I wondered aloud.

Just that one word.

Where?

I saw something lying on the orange sand. Something shining. Not a necklace but a ring. The emerald ring Karl had proposed to me with in the Indian restaurant when we were students. The one I'd said no to at the time.

And just at that moment there was an oceanic roar. Then the sound of a powerful deluge flooding through the trees. It was that glowing water again. The colour of that indescribable blue.

Everything Was Gone

Everything was gone.

Rising, Swirling, Spinning

I was washed up inside that luminescent sea, desperate for breath, and I was rising, swirling, spinning, until I was still, on my back, swathed in clean sheets in a hospital bed, blinking awake.

Knowing Someone's Name Without Knowing How

I woke up.

Still in my wetsuit but now in a clean white room, lying in bed with a pulse oximeter clipped to my left index finger.

Whatever had just happened, I was now very much in reality. A bright hospital room, complete with the scent of disinfectant and surrounded by bleeping machines. There was a thin orange stripe on the wall. And an orange chair. It's always interesting, which countries go with which colours. Spain has a big thing for orange. Orange furniture. Orange trees. Even the earth in Ibiza is orange. Tannins from the fallen pine needles.

A nurse was there, a doctor was there, Alberto Ribas was there. They were all pleased to see me wake up. Alberto was still in his wetsuit. He looked ridiculous. I felt a deep desire to slap him. Of course, I didn't quite know precisely what had occurred but here I was in hospital and whatever had happened was very probably his fault. And so the sparkle in his eyes wasn't a welcome sight. It was like seeing a lit match in a bush. It was danger.

I was informed I was at the Can Misses hospital on the outskirts of Ibiza Town, and that I had been unconscious for three hours. They had already tested my lungs and to the doctor's surprise there was no damage from the water.

'How do you feel, physically?' the doctor asked, in very good English.

'Surprisingly fine,' I said. In fact, and as far as I could tell while lying down, I felt healthier than ever. Once, decades ago, when we had taken Daniel on his one and only foreign holiday – to Corfu – we had been so happy and active, swimming, peddling pedaloes, touring olive farms – I slept better than I had ever slept in my life. And I woke every day feeling almost like a child again. And I never slept like that again, certainly not after we lost Daniel. But now I was back feeling as fresh as I had on that holiday in the eighties.

'What do you remember before you lost consciousness?'

'I saw a light,' I said, realising how pathetic that sounded. *I saw a light.* Even Alberto seemed to flinch when I said it. Especially him.

'What kind of light?'

I tried to think. 'I'm sorry, Paula, it's hard to explain. A moving light. A cloud and then a sph—'

The doctor went very still. As if I had said something wrong. 'Sorry. How do you know my name is Paula?'

'Your name badge,' I said.

She gave me a suspicious look, placed a stray strand of hair behind her ear. 'I'm not wearing a name badge.'

This flummoxed me. 'Oh, I don't know.' I must have heard them talking while I was asleep. I'd heard something on the radio about that. About how much we take in while we are asleep without realising.

Alberto was staring at me.

'Do you have a history of epilepsy?'

'No,' I told her. 'Well, my grandfather had seizures.'

She nodded. 'Migraines?'

'Yes. I have had a few of those.'

She nodded again. 'This matches the account we have been given by the gentleman.' She gestured to Alberto. 'He said that you had a kind of fit and that he had to carry you out of the water. Your blood oxygen levels are very good, but we will need to do some more tests . . .'

Spikes

Alberto was told to wait in the reception area. He had brought my clothes along to the hospital and I changed into them. They did a blood test. They tested my blood pressure, which was fine. Then they did an electroencephalogram, which looks for any unusual electric activity in the brain. The doctor stuck little sensors to my head, with a kind of paste to seal them on, and stared at squiggly moving lines on a screen. The lines were clearly more frantic than they should be.

She pointed at the screen. 'These spikes right here are very steep and close together . . .'

'So what does that mean?'

The doctor looked at me, and as she caught my eye, I felt like I knew everything about her, like she was an open window, and I could see everything in the room. I saw memories as clear as scars. I could see her carefully talking to her ill brother during his most recent episode of paranoia. I could see her in the Plaza de España in Seville, smiling and holding hands with a husband she now detested. I could see her walking her dog in winter along a deserted Ses Variades, the sunset strip in San Antonio, passing the closed Café del Mar and crying about her dying mother. I could see her on the toilet, worried about a new mole on her forearm. I could see her in her parked car, hunched over the wheel, wondering how she was going to get through another working day. Everything was there, instantaneously. I understood it all but didn't know how. It was like a feeling I'd once had at the Louvre, when I walked into the gallery of antiquities, full of Greek sculptures, with the *Venus de Milo* there at the far end of the hall. It was a sudden absorption of intensity. It was too much but also, somehow, entirely natural. Karl had a theory that art and music and everything that ever existed were somehow inside us. A good song or a good piece of sculpture was good because it spoke to something already there within us. Well, that was what it was like. Staring at that doctor's face was like walking into a gallery of thoughts. And I knew every single one of them like I knew my own.

La Presencia

I was sent for an MRI scan.

There was something about hospitals. Something that made you think of the future and the past all at once. They smelt of school, but more so. The corridors were like a maze and there were arrowed signs everywhere.

Triatge. Radiografia. Neurologia. Ultrasò. Urgències.

I sat in the reception area with Alberto in his wetsuit. He was eating crisps he had just acquired from a vending machine. *He is a good man.* I had no idea why that thought had popped in my head, and I tried to ignore it. There was another man sitting in there. A frail elderly man smartly dressed in a short-sleeve shirt tucked into belted trousers. He had a dignified smile, a trying-to-be-calm smile. I smiled back at him. The kind of fragile smile you share in hospital waiting areas.

'I have made a mistake,' Alberto said, with quiet seriousness.

'Sorry?'

'You will have to get out of here,' he was whispering to me, with bomb-disposal urgency. 'Quite soon. We both have to get out of here.'

'Why?'

He ate another crisp. 'Just trust me.'

'The last time I trusted you I nearly drowned.'

'You didn't nearly drown. Even the doctor said it. There was no water damage on your lungs. Something happened to you, but it wasn't that.'

'I nearly died. Just like Christina died. And for all I know, that was your fault too.'

He scratched his beard. Agitated. Nervous. 'She knew what was going to happen to her. Everything that happened to her was her own choice.'

'What does that mean?'

'Listen, I am sorry. Sinceramente. I tried to be as clear as possible. I said that if you want to know what happened to your old friend, then you should come with me . . .'

'I still don't know what happened to Christina.'

Again he ignored me and carried on talking. '*Mierda.* I didn't know that you would end up in hospital. That hasn't happened before, I promise. It must have liked you more than most. Or it must have had more . . . work to do.'

I humoured him. 'What did?'

'La Presencia.'

'What?'

'That's what we call it.'

'It?'

'The Presence, in English. But La Presencia is better.'

'Please.'

'The light you saw.'

'It was an aura. That's what the doctor said. You can get them with migraines or before seizures.'

'You didn't have a seizure. I was there. But I wasn't going to tell them that. It's best they don't know the details. And have you ever heard of two people seeing the same aura at the same time? No, of course not. That doesn't mean everyone can see it. It hides very easily. It is only seen by those who need to see it.'

'Jesus,' I said.

'No. Not Jesus.'

'I meant *Jesus,*' I unleashed. 'As in, the thing you say when an odd man in a wetsuit sits next to you and starts saying utterly ridiculous things.'

Alberto exhaled a little whistle. He spoke suddenly in the exaggerated tone of a tour guide. 'There is a village in Ibiza called Jesús. But we say it as hey-zeus.'

The smart old man stared at us. I smiled again. This time it wasn't reciprocated. We were clearly in danger of causing a commotion.

'You are a difficult person,' Alberto said. 'Has anyone ever told you that?'

Yes, I didn't tell him. *Many times.*

'I tend to avoid conversations as much as possible,' I said instead. 'And you are reminding me why.'

He offered me a crisp. I shook my head, even though I was hungry. Stubborn as the wind, Mum used to say.

Alberto shrugged and spoke with his mouth full. 'They're paprika. They are very good. You don't like to take pleasure when it is offered, do you?'

A minute of silence. Then he couldn't resist. 'This is normal. This is the denial phase. This happened to Christina too. Something remarkable happens when it reaches you and you put it down to a dream, because why wouldn't you? Even as a part of you knows that it wasn't. Normally, by the way, you don't need to be carried out of the water. Normally it happens very quickly. It happens in a moment. But you had a stronger interaction. That's why you need to leave here and go home. Because if you have a brain scan, they will find something abnormal.'

'That is the *point* of having a brain scan.'

'I am talking about something perhaps never seen before. It is more thorough than the last test. And it will show something that will surprise them. And who knows, they might take you away somewhere.'

I gave him a look. I thought of the extinct flower that was blooming through a crack in the dry path outside my door. I thought of the jar of seawater that had filled itself back up. I thought of all the illogical things I didn't know what to do with. And somehow, all I could think to say was: 'Don't you have a snake to see to?'

Lucky Guess

'Listen, there is currently another force on the island,' Alberto said. 'Not La Presencia but something we don't understand yet. Something Christina only caught glimpses of. Someone or something with powers working against us.' Alberto spotted someone walking down the corridor. A doctor. A tall woman with a serious, harassed face and strands of loose hair untethered from a butterfly grip. Alberto seemed distracted suddenly. 'We have to leave here now.' It was a mistake to draw such attention to ourselves. It is always a mistake. This should be secret . . .'

'I don't believe in fairy tales.'

'We need to go. Now.' Alberto had his head down. He watched the doctor's feet as she passed.

'No.'

Alberto nodded. 'Okay,' he said and pointed at the woman at reception. 'In fifteen seconds the receptionist will touch her glasses. In twenty she will pick up the phone to make a call.'

This was ridiculous. *This is not ridiculous.*

My eyes consequently darted between the smooth movement of the second hand on the clock on the wall and the fidgets of the bespectacled receptionist. Noted as she pushed her glasses up her nose, then five seconds later as she stretched her arm across the desk, standing just slightly, to pull a landline phone closer and begin to dial.

Lucky guess, I told myself. I touch my reading glasses all the time. There is probably some research out there saying that people touch their glasses at certain times. And as for the phone – well, receptionists probably make five hundred phone calls a day.

'Good point,' sighed Alberto.

'I didn't say anything.'

'Sí. Claro.'

'Okay. I will humour you. If you can predict things, why couldn't you predict that taking me to hospital was a bad idea?'

He nodded. 'Sí. Another good point. The answer is I was scared. I sincerely thought you might die.' He looked genuinely concerned. 'Most things I find impossible to know with total certainty. And yes, I can do a few party tricks when I am closely observing someone, but really my talents are very minor these days. Once upon a time I was all-powerful, but things have changed. I pick up thoughts now and then. I can see a few minutes ahead sometimes, but that's about it. Even if it chooses you, La Presencia only reaches out once. I could anchor my boat midway between Formentera and Ibiza every day and dive in that precise spot and it would never touch me. It has done with me. I only ever had the slightest brush with it. Unlike you. Your talents will be quite something when they develop. Beyond even Christina's. It is because you were so long in the water.'

'Such nonsense,' I grumbled, and really tried to mean it.

'If this is nonsense, how do you explain how you knew the doctor was called Paula?'

'Magical powers, obviously,' I said, heavy on the sarcasm. But in my head I was doing mathematics. The time, according to the wall clock, was twenty-five minutes past seven in the morning. Twenty-five multiplied by seven was one hundred and seventy-five.

'Why are you doing sums?'

'How do you know I—'

I was sliding into a new reality and I had nothing to hold on to.

He shrugged. 'Not magical powers. No magic. But powers, yes. Given to both of us by something that is extra-terrestrial. La Presencia. The presence. From Salacia.'

'Salacia?'

'The name we give to the planet where the presence came from. It's a good name, right? Roman goddess of the sea.'

'I don't believe in this kind of thing.'

'The only thing you have to believe at this point is that there is a possibility that we don't know every single thing about life in the universe. That we aren't so arrogant as to think that *this particular point in history* is the one where we know all there is to be known. Is that possible? Now, please, before it is too late. You either follow me out of here or you don't.'

And with that he stood up. And I didn't follow him. I just glanced again at the old man opposite. He was waiting for his wife. She was having a scan for a suspected tumour. He hadn't slept with worry. I knew it even as I knew I couldn't know it.

Alberto walked out of the automatic doors. I wondered what had happened to Christina. Maybe she was trapped in a military base somewhere.

I stared at my hands. Something was odd, but it took me a few seconds to realise what it was. And then I saw it: the ring. Instead of a ruby there was an emerald. In place of the engagement ring I had worn every day since Karl proposed to me in the library, there was the one I had turned down in the Raj Pavilion restaurant near Hull University all those years ago. The one I had seen on the impossible beach.

Adrenaline surged through me. I felt alert and scared.

I had the sudden urge to follow Alberto.

So I stood up, with the receptionist still on the phone, and walked briskly towards the exit. A man in a green uniform was walking through the automatic doors. It was the Guardia Civil officer I had met. The frowning, taciturn one. I avoided his gaze, but as I passed him I knew he was called Carlos Guerrero. I knew he was at the hospital because he'd had a phone call about a woman who had been brought in by Alberto Ribas after a diving accident. I knew he enjoyed watching quiz shows with a beer every evening. I knew that he had a sofa in his apartment that still had its polythene cover because he didn't like dirt. I knew that he loved FC Barcelona as much as he hated Real Madrid, but there was another level where he didn't really care at all. I knew that his inner thighs itched in the heat and that he had back pain caused by sciatica. I knew that he had a recurring dream of being urinated on by a lion, in which he would lie under it, too scared to move. Sometimes the dream had a terrifying sexual dimension that would cause him to wake up in a sweat. I knew he had spoken to Alberto and had ruled him out of his enquiries. But I also knew he had been paid a bribe by someone. I saw him in an expensive villa that wasn't his, accepting money from someone without a face. The person obviously had a face, but I couldn't see it.

'Disculpe, señora,' he said as I kept walking.

I am not who you think I am, I thought, and I thought it with such force it seemed to become his thought too, because he shook his head and carried on chewing his gum, before heading into the reception area.

The Instructions

'Listen to me,' Alberto said, dropping me off like an anxious parent. 'You will notice some changes over the next few days.'

'I am seventy-two years old. I am used to changes.'

'These changes will be surprising ones, and maybe strong ones.'

'Will I grow horns?' I wondered, half-seriously.

He shook his head but didn't smile. He was taking this seriously. 'No. No horns. No difference to your physical appearance. But you will change. It changes everyone it touches.'

He was very good at being dramatic. I would eventually discover there was an aspect to him that wasn't quite *there*, that was always detached, observing, like he was trapped inside an eternally bigger picture.

'How? How will I change?'

He shrugged. 'Quién sabe! It's hard to tell, exactly. It manifests itself differently from person to person. But you are part-Salacian now. It has given you Salacian talents, and from the way it reached you I am imagining the change will be very significant. But the important thing is this – you must not let it be known. Not right now. Not until you have this all under control. Don't tell anyone, don't show anyone, don't let it be seen. This is very important.'

I could write a whole book about what I was feeling then.

After being told I was basically half-alien and that I had some sort of paranormal capabilities. The shock. The bewilderment. But mainly, I felt denial. I didn't want to believe any of this.

It had been a long time since I had been treated like a child. I felt indignation rise up like lava. 'I nearly died because of you. Why should I listen to a word you say?'

'Because you have to. Okay? If you didn't trust me, you wouldn't have followed me out of the hospital. Now, I will come and see you tomorrow. Do you have food and drink in the house?'

I nodded and squinted in the heat. It was really hot. The kind of day you could feel your skin cooking in real time.

'Good. Stay. Just to be safe.'

'Safe from what?'

I thought he was going to enlighten me. But he didn't. He just said: 'Safe from yourself.'

'Why? What will I do to myself?'

'You have been given talents that you are not yet adjusted to. This is a dangerous time for you. Anything could happen. But I will come and see you tomorrow.'

'I don't want you to come tomorrow.'

What I really meant was: I want things to be normal. I wanted to subtract every new addition. Including Alberto. I was, in short, more than a little frightened. And my response in fear was denial.

He handed me a scrap of paper with a number scrawled over it. 'For when you change your mind.' Not *if*, but *when*.

And then he drove away, and I stared up at the billboard of the Eighth Wonder resort and the little inset photograph of an immaculate hotel room. It looked perfect, but its perfection now troubled me. I wondered why it bothered me, when I had so much else to come to terms with. But it did. Just until I turned my back to head indoors.

The Infinite Hotel

When my old maths tutor Mr Sole told me there was something bigger than infinity I laughed. Then he gave me a thought experiment which helped explain Set Theory. I probably spoke about it in maths. The one about the hotel that the long dead German genius David Hilbert came up with as a way of explaining what Cantor was on about with his transfinite numbers. The one that has blown several minds to oblivion. That is childishly simple and devilishly complex all at once. It basically proves that a true infinity can't really be grasped. It goes something like this:

Imagine a hotel of infinite rooms. Each room has a number, as hotels normally do. Room 1, Room 2, Room 3, Room 4 . . . On and on and on and *on* for ever. Imagine now that every single one of these rooms is full. That's right. It's a popular hotel. An infinite number of people have filled an infinite number of rooms. Now, someone new arrives at the hotel. Let's call her Marjorie. She is tired. She has had a long flight. Her legs hurt. Her veins are playing up. She needs a room.

Now, what does the hotel receptionist tell her? He can hardly say that the Infinite Hotel has no more rooms, can he? Marjorie could get on TripAdvisor and take the place down. CALLS ITSELF THE INFINITE HOTEL???????!!!!! MORE LIKE THE FINITE HOTEL!!!!!! WHAT A JOKE!! (One star.)

No. The receptionist budges everyone up a room. So the guy in Room 1 moves into Room 2 and the honeymooners in Room 2 hop next door to Room 3. Okay, it's not the best system, but just go with it. Anyway, the end result is that Marjorie gets her room and everyone else still has a room. So, the hotel is now infinity plus one:

$$\infty + 1 = \text{the hotel}$$

The original hotel wasn't large enough so there were limits to its infinity. But then what if more people came along? What if another infinity of people came along in an infinite aeroplane and had an infinite number of taxis pick them up to transfer them from the airport? Then we'd have:

$$\infty + \infty + 1 = \text{the hotel}$$

Bottom line: infinity comes in sets. There can be a bigger infinity. Infinity can be doubled and trebled and quadrupled and quintupled, etc. There can be an infinity of infinities. Even without any new guests at all the Infinite Hotel had different sizes of infinities. An infinite hotel surely has an infinite number of odd numbers, but it also has an infinite number of even numbers, and in any hotel the total number of rooms is larger than the total number of odd (or even) numbers on their own. You really *can* go beyond infinity. Buzz Lightyear was the secret genius in *Toy Story*.

Why do I keep talking about this? Because it is frightening how quickly a belief system can change. And because believing in extra-terrestrial life on Earth was beyond infinity for me. When you get to my age, you feel like you have nothing major left to learn. You have accumulated all the knowledge that can serve you. Your hotel is full. I had reached the limits. And I simply wasn't ready for that extra room. And it was an earthquake inside me, only comparable with grief. But grief was the death of a person, this was the death of everything I had considered reality. And when you get older, as you wrote in the letter, it becomes harder to break patterns. So I was in the rubble. I had no idea who I was or what world I was living in. I felt reborn. And like every new baby I wanted to cry. Or scream.

The Peculiarities

I wandered around the small house.

Unusually for me I didn't need to sit down every two minutes. I had energy. But though I felt reborn, I wasn't really – there were still enough dull aches and quiet creaks to make me understand I was still in my seventies – but I was more alert and alive than I had been in years.

This is a dangerous time for you.

I switched on the television to try to shake Alberto out of my mind. I found a news channel in English. The reporter was one I had never seen before but I somehow knew he was in the middle of a divorce. He was talking about forest fires thousands of miles away.

It was upsetting news, sure, but the kind I'd seen hundreds of times before, which I'd normally gawp at like another piece of bleak twenty-first-century moving wallpaper. But this time, as I stared at the yellow diggers and logs stripped of their branches, I felt an unprecedented nausea that caused me to gag. I had a strange queasy hunger sensation, and my mouth was suddenly filling with saliva. It was as if someone had just forced me to eat soap. I switched off the TV and rushed to the tiny mildew-speckled bathroom and retched over the sink.

I was actually sick.

Not from anything I had eaten but simply from watching the news, as if the devastated landscape I had just witnessed on the screen had provoked a direct internal reaction. Unlike at home, I had no mouthwash here to rinse away the taste. I brushed my teeth.

I am sorry. I should have warned you before saying all that. But after I was sick, I felt fine and healthy again.

Then another peculiarity happened. I noticed the cars going by on the road all had their own sounds. I was never into cars. My son Daniel when he was about five could differentiate between different car headlights. Even in the dark he knew the cars when we were driving back from his grandmother's house. 'Ford Cortina,' he'd mutter from the back seat, in a kind of trance. 'Vauxhall Cavalier . . . Metro . . . Ford Sierra . . .'

I couldn't identify every model in the way Daniel could have done, but I pictured every car. Just from the sound. Right down to the shape and colour.

I don't even know if it was actually from the sound. It might be best explained as a feeling of déjà vu. But in reverse.

So I looked out of the window and thought *yellow car* and sure enough the next car that passed the window would be yellow. *Blue car*. Blue car. *White taxi*. White taxi. *Large gleaming red-and-yellow bus*. Large gleaming red-and-yellow bus. It was very, very odd and very, very far beyond anything that I could explain. And then I felt a little thirsty. So I went to the fridge and pulled out the bottle of orange juice. That makes it sound like a normal thing. But this wasn't a normal thing. This was a very unusual thing. In fact, it was so unusual I think I will give it its own chapter.

The Infinite Pleasure of Orange Juice

I took a few gulps and closed my eyes, as committed as a wolf howling to the moon. I have drunk orange juice for most of my seventy-two years – and even freshly squeezed orange juice on many occasions – but I can honestly say that I have never really noticed it. Orange juice was the water of fruit juices, I used to feel. It kind of just existed. Part of that same category of food that includes vanilla ice cream and tea-and-toast that was perfectly lovely in a neutral, take-it-for-granted kind of way.

But this was different. This was the most wonderful drink I had ever tasted. The competing but perfectly balanced sweetness and bitterness was as complex as the finest Zinfandel. I savoured every mouthful. I ended up finishing the whole bottle.

The odd thing was that the last time I'd drunk it, it had been nice but perfectly forgettable orange juice. Now, it was ambrosia from the gods. It felt like the whole purpose of life was just to enjoy the experience of pouring a liquid extraction from the vesicles of a divine citrus fruit into my mouth. Immense relief and release. Even more quenching than that feeling as a child, after playing tennis with my old friend Sarah in the heat of July, of glugging a full glass of water.

That orange juice was, quite simply, the very best thing I had ever tasted.

'That was enjoyable,' I told myself, out loud, because it felt so important that it needed to be voiced.

And then I acknowledged a fact: that this was the first time I had enjoyed something – properly *enjoyed* something – in months. Years, even. Sure, I had been diverted by things – old films, Wordle, crosswords, online chess, puzzle books, the occasional documentary, and had certainly been distracting myself since arriving in Ibiza – but enjoyment was something else. My anhedonia appeared to be over, thanks to a single glass of orange juice. I followed it up with a biscuit. It wasn't as good as the orange juice, admittedly, but it was still pretty spectacular.

The Book

Richard Feynman was an erudite American physicist who wrote a lot about mathematics too. I used to read a lot of his books. They made very intimidating things like quantum mechanics feel relatively easy. Anyway, he said something that I have been thinking a lot about recently: 'Nearly everything is really interesting if you go into it deeply enough.'

Nearly everything is really interesting if you go into it deeply enough.

This is true. And this is essentially what was beginning to happen to me. I was going deeply into everything without even trying. Orange juice, the sound of traffic, the distant barking of a dog. Everything had a sudden infinite richness and complexity to it, or I had sudden access to the richness and complexity that had always been there. The dog barking was probably the most interesting thing. I closed my eyes as I heard it. And I saw the dog in my mind, a tall brown hound of no identifiable breed, barking as he was tied up beside some stables. I even saw the horse he was barking at.

I tried to switch my focus to something else.

I opened up *La vida imposible* and it felt like it wasn't a foreign language. I could read it. Not as well as I could read English, but I understood most of the words. I remembered a documentary on the radio about a man who could learn languages just by looking at them. It seemed I now had that ability. I read that the waters around the island of Ibiza had been chosen by the advanced inhabitants of some other world as their base on Earth. I went outside and looked at the flower again. The one that was meant to be extinct. I knew everything about it. I knew that the species had vanished when the last of its kind was bulldozed to make way for a hotel. I was mesmerised for a while. It was dark now, but that didn't seem to make a difference. I was just looking at it, understanding it without any effort at all. Understanding its quiet purpose. The purpose of existing for the sake of existing.

I realised the time. It was one in the morning. It was so weird, how I was suddenly acutely aware of so much, while also letting big things – like what time it was, or even what date or day it was (17th? 18th? 19th? Saturday? Sunday? Monday?) – slip right by. I inhaled. The scent of a flower was no longer just a scent to me. It was a whole language, an advertisement of life.

I got ready for bed. And then, once there, I just stared at the ceiling, listening to the traffic.

White taxi.

Night bus.

Silver hire car with an arguing couple inside.

I wasn't tired at all. This was unusual for me. I had never been an insomniac. Even in my younger years, sleep had been my default state. I'd not always had *easy* sleep, but I'd always had sleep. But now I was wide, wide awake.

I got out of bed.

I looked at the photo of younger Christina and the man with long hair. The one with the beach buggy in it. I realised I understood everything about Christina's marriage just by looking at her image on the wall. That was the man she had married. Johan. He was a hippy and frustrated musician who stubbornly acted like it was still 1967 even in 1987. He had fallen for Christina, one night, while she had sung old Carpenters and Carole King numbers for a drunken off-season crowd at the Buenavista Hotel in Santa Eulalia. She had moved into this place a month after she and Johan split up, as she didn't have the money to stay in their former place in Ibiza Town. Johan had never been rich, but he had been earning okay money as a pool maintenance man.

Johan, in that Dutch way, had been great at languages. English, Spanish, French, German, a bit of Portuguese. He had even learned Catalan, and fused it with Spanish as the locals did. They played music together. They'd had a baby together. Lieke, who would also become a polyglot and would one day achieve in music where her parents failed. The little girl in the photos with the teddy bear and the nervous smile. A world away from the strong, fierce superstar on the billboard.

Johan and Christina had both been fun on their own terms, both into music and dancing and life, but they argued a lot and they were both impulsive. There needed to be a responsible one, and neither of them fitted the bill. They both had flings with other people and even the good times were often lost in a haze of marijuana or a flood of booze. They should have divorced earlier. That was the rear-view mirror assessment, especially for Lieke, who was a fragile thirteen when they split up and went to live with her dad in Amsterdam. Johan never saw Christina again. And Lieke did, but not very much, because her mother got into strange beliefs she was embarrassed by.

People say that love is rare. I am not so sure. What is rare is something even more desirable. Understanding. There is no point in being loved if you are not understood. They are simply loving an idea of you they have in their mind. They are in love with love. They are in love with their loving. To be *understood*. And not only that, but to be understood and appreciated once understood. That is what matters. Unfortunately, Christina and Johan had none of that. They had been in love with ideas of each other, and had ideas of how their family could be, but with parenthood came reality, and reality was no match for either of them.

Fleetwood Mac

I wanted to hear music.

The old stereo from the eighties had a tape deck. I looked through Christina's tapes. Blondie (of course). The Carpenters. Bob Marley. Fleetwood Mac. I put the Fleetwood Mac one on.

I listened to 'Everywhere'.

It was the most beautiful, lush, intricate sound I had ever heard. For some reason I lay down. I lay down on the floor of the living room as the water in the olive jar glowed again. The shifting, glowing light matching the symphony of feelings, a compendium of every positive emotion I had ever felt. The music came to me as colours and as tactile feeling, like something that could be seen and felt as well as heard.

I stared at a book on the shelf. *The Mystery of the Blue Train* by Agatha Christie. White letters on a blue spine. I had a profound sense that I could move it. As in, move it without physically moving it. Or rather, I had the sense that my imagination had the power to manipulate reality. I could see the billboard for the Eighth Wonder hotel across the street through the half-open curtain. *Visualise your dreams and make them reality.* So I did. The book nudged out on the shelf, inch by inch, before falling to the ground but not reaching it, just floating, no, *held*, because I could feel its weight inside me, the kind of hidden weight you feel when you realise you said something you shouldn't have said. It made a circle in the air and it hurt my head so I let it go and it landed on the tiles as Christine McVie kept singing, her voice an exquisite ache of perfection. Complex, earthy, ethereal all at once.

My head pain subsided, and another song came on and I sat up and stared at the book on the floor and didn't know whether to laugh or cry at what had just happened and so I did both. And then the light in the glass jar faded and I went to bed again and lay awake until it was morning.

Even though it was now with the Guardia Civil officer, I remembered the letter Christina had left me, every word and punctuation mark, and found new meaning in it now. Particularly this part:

Oh, and most important of all: *go to Atlantis Scuba at Cala d'Hort. Tell Alberto I sent you. He won't charge you. Go and see the seagrass meadow. It is the oldest living organism on Earth.*

And please, when you are there, keep your mind open. Any change that happens will be for the better. Trust me.

And after repeating this for the tenth time I closed my eyes and in my mind I saw a lobster running across the sand.

Watermelon in the Sun

The next morning, I was sitting outside the vegan café in Santa Gertrudis, and still thinking about the vision of the lobster and what it might have meant.

Alberto had told me to stay indoors but I had felt a *need* to get outside. If it was me who was the danger to myself, then surely it didn't matter where I happened to be. Because I was always with my dangerous self.

And besides, I still had no idea if I could trust anything he said. What I did know was that I had the deepest and most pressing urge to explore, and to understand fully what had happened to me and what had happened to Christina. I sensed, deeply, that the answers were to be found outside. Also, and this is no small thing: I wanted to be outside. This was unusual. Ever since Karl died, I'd had zero desire to go outside or do much of anything. But now I was bursting with a curiosity so strong I could feel it like a soft motor, deep inside, purring in the depths.

And sitting there, outside in the sunshine, I knew I had made the right choice. My fruit salad arrived, and I stared at the plate of fruit the way you might stare at a painting by Matisse. I was mesmerised by every shape and every colour. The tantalising crescents of orange. The vibrant green of kiwi. The small spheres of blueberries like planets in a scattered solar system orbiting a passion fruit. Cubes of papaya. The reddish-pink triangle of a watermelon slice, dotted with black seeds, seemed particularly exquisite. Eating watermelon in the sun was such a wonderful feeling I wondered why I hadn't spent more of my life doing it. I wondered why it wasn't everyone's aspiration. I wondered why every successful businessperson on the planet continued to work and visit offices and stare at computers when they could just quit and eat watermelon in the sun for ever.

But thoughts were entering my mind. And not my own thoughts

either. The homesick thoughts of the waiter, who was missing his friends back in Murcia. The thoughts of another customer too. A local reading in the newspaper about record-breaking temperatures across the world. I sensed her worry, not just about the climate, but about her mother's ailing health. I felt that worry as if it was my own. It passed through me like a cloud. But then so did the tentative happiness of three boys, walking by, fresh from the bus stop and on their way to the nearby international school.

It was all very strange. Alberto was right. He'd said, 'the change will be very significant,' and it certainly was. My heart raced. My body trembled. It was exhilarating and terrifying, and I wondered if I might die from it.

It is hard to put this into words because words are generally made for the five senses, and not for the sixth, or seventh, or thirty-eighth, or whatever this was. I suppose it was like a deep but inexplicable *familiarity*. As if I knew the whole world and its contents as well as I knew a close relative. Like I had known everyone and everything and I only had to look at someone to know them. It was the interconnectedness of everything made visible. It is all there if you know how to see it.

One of the most interesting and sentimental of all facts, one that I have always loved, is the one that says we are all stardust. The whole universe is inside us. Every element within us was made in a star. Nitrogen, calcium, hydrogen, oxygen, phosphorous and all the other stuff. We are made of deep space and deep time and have been forged in supernovas (or supernovae, if we are being pretentious). An element, as you no doubt know, is matter that can't be broken down into a simpler substance. They are the primes of the cosmos.

We are made of elements.

We have the unbreakable and the eternal inside us.

We have the universe in our blood and bones.

And once I'd had my contact with La Presencia, it was as though I was waking from a slumber, leaving a cocoon and flying into a new kind of sentience where I wasn't just formed of everything but could see and understand it too. And it felt entirely ridiculous and perfectly logical all at once. It was, I suppose, marginally less ridiculous than being born. Coming from nothing into something is probably even more of a miracle, but when everyone has the same miracle, you start to devalue it. It is simple supply and demand.

I finished the last blueberry. I left some money on the table. And then I headed to the car, knowing that if I got to know this island completely, I could understand what I had been brought here for. Because, without question, it had been for a reason. I knew that. And as I got in the car I saw that lobster again, in my mind, and shook it away as I turned the ignition.

I Was Life

I was on a completely new planet.

It was technically the same planet, of course. The same Spanish island here on Earth. But also: it was all new.

Everything seemed infused with sudden wonder or intensity. That moment I'd had in the past only very occasionally – at the sight of a fox or a murmuration of starlings – I was now having about *everything*. Not just orange juice and watermelons (though fruit, in particular, seemed suddenly sublime in a way I'd never noticed before). But all categories of nature, even human nature.

And at far greater intensity than I had ever had before. Nothing had changed, externally. The world was the same world it had been last year and the year before. And the island was the same one I had been on yesterday.

You see, if you want to visit a new world, you don't need a spacecraft. All you need to do is change your mind.

And my mind was absolutely changed.

Everything ached with beauty.

The hard blue sky. The scent of pine. The sound of the cicadas. The heat shimmer where the road met the sky. It was all very real and very magical all at once.

I switched the radio on. There was some of that electronic music again – a lively track I knew with zero prompting was from a Brazilian DJ called Alok, someone I'd obviously never heard of before – but the signal kept cutting out so I retuned to a Spanish pop music station. I returned to a pop music station. They were playing a song I had never heard before but somehow I knew all about it. I knew it was called 'Despechá'. I knew it was by the Spanish singer Rosalìa and that it had been released in 2022. I supposed this knowledge was simply the knowledge of filling in the gaps. The way you don't need all the pieces of a jigsaw to guess the picture. But it was now like I could tell the whole thing based on a single piece. I only had to have heard *some* pop music to know everything about *all* pop music. I understood the words of this Spanish song. I heard the singer's determination to dance away her heartbreak and I felt the fun she was having. I liked the way the joy came out of her pain. I got into it right away. I may have even bounced my shoulders a little even though it was a style of music I hadn't heard before. And after that they played a song by that rapper 21 Savage and I loved it. I turned it up and nodded my head to the beat like I was someone of a different age and life and psychology.

There are patterns everywhere. Something you observed in the past – a conversation on a plane, say – arrives at you in the present, slightly distorted. A singer on a woman's T-shirt becomes a heard melody. So along came an older song by Taylor Swift called 'Mirrorball', and I was every single person who had ever enjoyed that song from every angle. It made me realise I was a mirrorball too, but inverted. The mirrors were directed inward. Instead of the world seeing me from every reflected angle the world was itself the mirrorball and I was the nucleus, and the world was shimmering at me from everywhere, all of it, simultaneously, which sounds terrifying but felt at that moment exhilarating. The track ended and there was some adverts, and adverts – like the news – had the potential to make me mildly nauseous now, so I turned to a classic rock station where they were playing 'You Shook Me All Night Long' by AC/DC. I had heard it before, because of Karl, and I had asked him to turn it down because it had given me a headache. But now I turned it up. As loud as it could be. And I sang it with the window down and it struck me as both ridiculous and sad that I had never sung in the car before. There was such a simple power to it, and I wished Karl had been there to talk to about it. It was life. AC/DC was life. I was life.

Everything can be beautiful with the right eyes and ears, Maurice. Every genre of music. Every sorrow and every pleasure. Every inhale and exhale. Every guitar solo. Every voice. Every plant beside the tarmac.

I thought of a line from Mary Shelley. From *Frankenstein*. My second-favourite book, after *The Count of Monte Cristo*. The line was this: 'There is something at work in my soul, which I do not understand.'

I turned the volume back down when I got to the whitewashed church square and saw a couple of rich old hippies, smiling, sun-leathered and wrapped from the waist down in vibrant batik clothes, lounging on wicker chairs outside a café and drinking blue smoothies. As I drove by, I felt their relaxed contentment as if it was my own; it reached my mind like an exhalation. An old man was standing in a doorway looking out at the world with a crinkled, baffled gaze. I saw him playing on that same street as a child, probably in the fifties, pushing a toy tin motorcycle and sidecar along the paving slabs under the watchful eye of a stern member of the Guardia Civil dressed like a soldier. Not a vegan café in sight.

As I drove out of Santa Gertrudis, I switched to a classical music station. Radio Clásica. They were playing Elgar's first movement from his Cello Concerto in E minor. I'd heard this before too. I often used to listen to classical music at home, but now I was feeling it with every part of me. The sound of the strings was like a rising tide, I was floating, high, groundless, untethered, nothing beneath me, carried by an emotional current without anything to hold on to but the knowledge of being alive.

I came to a small garage where two workmen were trying to squeeze a mattress into the back of a small van that really wasn't equipped for it. They were laughing and I felt their happiness ripple through me as I drove past.

Cat

There was a wild cat in the road, strutting slowly, its mind surprisingly calm and oblivious to the concept of roads. It was a beautiful, majestic, magnificent creature, and I stopped to let it by.

Lorry

Then my mood changed.

I didn't know how it happened, but sitting there as I held the steering wheel, waiting for the cat, I was having other memories that weren't mine. A whole flurry of them all at once.

The powers – 'talents' – whatever – were getting stronger. Dizzyingly so. I was feeling Christina. Not in the car but on a beach, tasting her fury as she argued with her husband, and her guilt as her little daughter building a sandcastle began to cry and swiped at the sandcastle, crumbling it to nothing.

Then, much more recently, I was seeing Christina with a woman with glasses and dark, wildly dishevelled hair. They were in this very car. They were talking about the planned hotel on Es Vedrà.

'Who is behind it?' the woman asked.

Christina didn't know. 'I can't see them. They are not there.'

'But you can see everything.'

'I can't see this.'

This led somehow to something else. I was seeing her, Christina, talk to a man. I couldn't see his face. Just as I hadn't been able to see the face of the man who bribed the Guardia Civil officer. It was the same person, though. I was sure of it.

I was so lost in the memory that it took a moment to realise that there was a lorry behind me, its horn honking like a disgruntled goose.

I drove on. I tried to get Christina out of my mind and focus on the driving, but it was hard. And it wasn't just Christina. There was knowledge all around me. I wasn't just passing cars, I was passing thoughts and feelings. Love and hate and indifference. I was submerged in the whole sea of life. I passed Guardia Civil officers searching a car for drugs and the anxious driver hoping they wouldn't check behind the air vents. I passed a dog and could sense its loneliness. I passed a tree and somehow knew it had 86,427 leaves, just as I knew there were 123,210 hairs on my head, mostly white.

But slowly, the terror I'd been feeling subsided.

Then I passed an open-top Jeep and knew the person driving. I don't know if this knowledge came from my new talents or simply because I recognised her from the billboards. But it was definitely her. Lieke. Christina's daughter. She was pulling over at a large garden centre – Eiviss Garden – so I U-turned and pulled over too before I had time to really think about what I was doing.

Lieke

I found her staring at a large selection of potted succulents.

'Hello,' I said. 'I am sorry to interrupt. But you are Lieke, aren't you?'

She was tall, taller than her mother, and wearing sunglasses and a long vest, and her bleached hair could be seen beneath a beret the weather didn't call for. A nose ring, I noticed now. And a neck tattoo of the word 'Silence', which seemed a strange word for a DJ to have written on her skin. She had her mother's eyes, but she had more steel to her. She looked tough, strong. But I also sensed it was a front. She was as fragile as everyone. Her mind, though, told the truth, and emitted bittersweet notes of defiance and sadness.

She nodded. No words.

She was used to being recognised but maybe I wasn't the usual type.

'My name is Grace. Grace Winters. I knew your mother, briefly, years ago.'

The sadness now had thorns in it. It was clear she didn't want to talk to me. I wished I hadn't approached her. But I was here now. So I said what I had to say, as quickly as I could say it.

'I was left your mother's house and I feel awkward about it. You know. It feels wrong. When she had family. That she left it to me. So I am just saying, if you ever need it, or want to stay in it, it is there. Or if you want to talk about it—'

'We didn't get on,' she interrupted, as she touched the thick, robustly perfect leaf of a jade plant. 'And I have my own place now. In the hills. It is fine. You don't have to feel guilty.'

Her accent was strange. Somewhere in the Venn diagram overlap between American and English and Dutch and Spanish and nowhere at all.

I saw her house in the hills. I could access her thought of it as she said the words. I saw her swimming in the pool, her boyfriend watching her from a hammock.

That should have been where I left it. It is certainly where the old me would have left it. But this new me suddenly cared intensely about everything. And with this new spirit of enquiry, I asked: 'Why didn't you get on?'

It was a rude and personal question, but I needed to know, and there were too many cluttered thoughts to access. If you want to get some-where, you sometimes have to take the straightest road.

'She was hard to be around.'

'She had strong beliefs?'

'It wasn't just beliefs. It wasn't just all the Moroccan she smoked. It was fucking real. She was taken over.'

'Taken over?'

She sighed. It was a stuttered breath. Like a beat. And then it all came, in a flood.

'She had an experience. In the ocean. And after that, she was consumed. She couldn't function like a normal human being any more. I couldn't speak to her without her telling me something about my future. And it was always something right and correct, which made it worse. I mean, fuck, how can you live a life if you know everything that is going to happen? But I didn't want to know. I told her to stop. I told her to live like a normal fucking human being.'

'Normal human beings are hard to find,' I told her. 'But I'm sorry. It must have been hard.'

'Our relationship had always been difficult. She was a shit mother. I paid a therapist ten thousand fucking euros to come to that conclu-sion. But I could cope with her shitness. The thing I couldn't cope with was her trying to tell me what to do all the fucking time because she knew the future, you know?

'It was like having God as a mother. And no one wants God as a mother, right?

'If you have God as a mother, then you have no choice but to be the fallen angel. It became impossible. It wasn't just her telling me she didn't like my music, or what I did for a living, or my boyfriend, it was her stealing the thing that makes life life. You know, the *unpredictability.* And when she told me she was giving the house to you I said that was fine. I told her I didn't want her shitty little house and she didn't like that at all. She told me she was helping organise a protest against some development in Es Vedrà and she was cross with me for not caring . . .' Her voice stayed steady but regret swelled inside her. 'It ended badly . . .'

Her thoughts had a red heat, despite her impassive face. I wondered, for an indulgent moment, if she could have wanted to harm her own mother. I entered her mind and all I saw was Christina slapping her at the end of the argument. It was a hard thing to imagine. Christina. Peaceful, musical Christina.

'That's hard. Was that the last time you two spoke?'

'Nope.'

'Do you think she was murdered?'

'She predicted it. But she said she had a plan. She always had a fucking plan. That was the last thing she said. She was going to disappear to a better world, and she didn't really care who she left behind. She never really worried about me. So, you know, I tried to reciprocate.'

'Did she mean heaven? The better world, I mean.'

She shook her head. 'No. She meant another planet. She reckoned she could access another planet.' She made a wide-eyed face, and I felt the thought behind it. It was a simple thought: *I know all of this is crazy.*

She turned away from me. Put a plant in her trolley. She wanted me to leave.

'I'm sorry for disturbing you.'

She softened then. It was like the sun through leaves. 'It's okay.'

And I had a solid piece of knowledge in my mind, firm as a pebble, that I knew was true. I needed to share it. 'Your mother loved you.'

'Yes. I know. And she loved you too.'

I laughed at the ridiculousness of that. 'She didn't really know me.'

'She spoke about you a lot. When I was little. She said you saved her life.'

I shook my head. 'I just gave her some company.'

Lieke smiled a smile of infinite complexity. 'That is sometimes all it takes.'

'Right. Yes. Goodbye.'

As I walked out, she spoke again. 'She didn't give you the house for nothing. She was recruiting you. It was a trap. You are her replacement. Just don't become her, okay?'

'I will try my best.'

'And I don't know if techno DJs are your thing, but if you fancy it, I can put you on the Amnesia guest list for tomorrow.' I liked the way she spoke to me as if I wasn't defined by my age and appearance. She was the rarest of things. A human devoid of prejudice. 'Carl Cox, Amelie Lens, Adam Beyer, Paco Osuna . . . They're great DJs. It will be the night of the summer. I'll give you a couple of guest spaces too. Grace Winters plus two.'

I thought of dancing. It wasn't an entirely unpleasant thought. I had no idea what people wore to Amnesia. I wondered if my M&S slacks and embroidered blouse would be okay.

And, for some unfathomable reason, I, your retired maths teacher, said: 'Oh. Thank you. That would be splendid.'

Larger Than Thought

I drove to Cala d'Hort. I parked in the dusty car park and passed a sign by a restaurant that said *PLEASE DO NOT LEAVE ANY VALUES IN THE CAR, CAN BE STOLEN.*

I reached Atlantis Scuba and looked around for Alberto but he wasn't there. There was only the black-and-white wide-horned goat, Nostradamus.

He was outside the Atlantis Scuba hut, enjoying a bowl full of oats on the ochre dirt path. Alberto had been right when he said that Nostradamus was a misanthropic soul. His misanthropy wafted towards me along with his musky scent.

It was alarming to realise I could understand him. The thoughts of a goat are difficult to translate into any kind of human language. But I will say that the note of misanthropy is not just grumpiness but a kind of humorous grumpiness. Goats are forever looking at things from an angle. Like they don't quite fit in and they are just getting on with it. Alberto had also given him the name Nostradamus, I realised, as an ironic gesture. Goats didn't care about the future. The future and the past were irrelevant to goats. They were always in a disgruntled state of nowness. I left him to his grains and walked to the beach and sat fully dressed on the sand near one of the restaurants.

Everywhere I looked I saw people and felt their thoughts and emotions. I wished Karl was here so I could tell him about all this. That is one great thing about having someone by your side. They are a shock absorber to the madness of experience. And no experience was madder than the one I was currently living.

A boy playing in the sand was wondering who would win in a fight, five hundred small cats or one single tiger. His mother was fantasising about a young man walking across the sand while her husband tried to focus on the thriller he was reading. A rogue CIA agent was in on a plan to kill the President.

I stared out at the rock of Es Vedrà, and its smaller, flatter sister islet of Es Vedranell. The larger islet loomed over the smaller like a protective parent.

I stared at the water around them.

As my mind now seemed to know almost everything, it was only the sea that wasn't instantly knowable. It still retained its mystery, and it was calming just to stare at it. It was the one thing that seemed larger than my thoughts.

Impossible Life

Sitting on the sand, I allowed myself a quiet chuckle over how ridiculously unlikely my life had become. Or maybe it had always been unlikely. Maybe that's the truly ridiculous thing, the way we don't even blink at the sheer improbability of our lives here on this rock spinning through space. The way we exist out of nothing, the way the whole universe exists out of nothing, and here we are, the impossible *something* that made existence out of the void. Impossible life. A fluke to be cherished.

The Goat Incident

I was sitting quite close to one of the restaurants, and pretty soon I was distracted by the various conversations of the diners, a babbling brook of different languages foaming into each other. I heard two elderly voices I recognised instantly from the plane. It was the old couple who had been studying their guidebook on Ibizan walks. They were eating fish stew and sitting beside a lobster tank and planning their afternoon hike to a nearby Roman settlement.

The woman read a bit from her guidebook. Even though they didn't say their names, I now knew them. They were called Olive and Michael and they were from a village in the Cotswolds. They had been together most of their lives, and Olive was trying not to think of Michael's biopsy results that would be waiting for them when they returned home to England. Michael was trying not to think of that too, but he had a bad feeling, and was trying to keep it together, and I felt the exhaustion of that. And I saw the love they had; it seemed the colour of burnt orange, a setting sun, warm and more beautiful for its decline beneath a horizon. *Maybe I'm imagining this*, I thought to myself. Yes. Maybe I had imagined it all. But if I was imagining it, then why was I also *predicting* it? Like I had done with the cars. Every next sentence. The moment the waiter would come. Picturing the waiter before turning around to see him. If it was imagination, so was the entire world.

It was quite terrifying really, to have this new sense. I tried to focus on the sea again but heard a shot. Very faint and distant, and no one else seemed to pay any attention to it. I felt a twist in my gut. I saw a boat beyond the pedaloes. To my eye it was just a white speck in the distance, beyond the rock of Es Vedrà. But I pictured it more clearly. I saw it as clearly as if I was floating right beside it. It had a small cabin and the words *Eighth Wonder* on the side. I remembered the billboard over the road from the house. For an Eighth Wonder resort at Cala Llonga, which was miles from here.

A man was on the deck of the boat. With the naked eye it was almost impossible to see him. Like isolating a strand of hair on a person's head who is a good distance away.

But I could see the man without seeing him. The way we see memories without actually seeing them. This was a memory that was happening in the present, and not to me. He was squinting under the heavy sun as he stared through the scope of his rifle, across the water, to a goat standing amid the steep limestone of that mysterious rock, Es Vedrà. The goat was a different colouring to that of Nostradamus. Brown and white, not black and white, and its horns were smaller. The man could see through the telescopic lens that the goat was staring directly towards them. The creature had just witnessed another goat die and realised what was happening.

The man was called Nicolau. He was deeply troubled. He was thinking of what his girlfriend would say. Not that his girlfriend would know. He was, after all, under the strictest of orders not to say anything to anyone.

Nicolau had heard somewhere on the internet that goats were very intelligent animals and could recognise human faces and expressions. He hoped he was far enough away for his face to be unseen. He didn't want to be doing this, but his employer paid well, and this action was sanctioned by the local government. They were to clear the whole rock of animals. It was unclear as to why, as his boss hadn't told him. But it was obviously for the development – though how a hotel could be built on such a challenging rock, he had no idea. And so, as he felt his colleague Hugo's hand on his shoulder, he knew what he was about to do.

And I too, paradoxically alone on that crowded beach, knew what he was about to do. And for some reason, I couldn't let him do it. Because as well as knowing what the man was feeling, I also knew what the goat was feeling. I felt her grief at the death of her fellow. It was like a throbbing darkness. I closed my eyes, as if about to make a wish.

And then I was inside Nicolau's mind. I was not only seeing it but swaying it.

He held his breath as he went for the trigger. He tried to press down but he couldn't. He wondered if there was something wrong with the gun. He checked to see if the safety catch was on, but no. He tried again and this time realised it wasn't the gun that was at fault.

The other man – Hugo – was laughing at him. He wanted to know what the problem was.

Hugo shook his head and took the gun now, but this was harder. I couldn't get inside his mind. There was a closed door.

Don't do it, I told him. The voice of his conscience. *Don't pull the trigger. Keep the goat alive.*

He blinked and blinked again and shook me away, out of his head, confused as to why he was suddenly having these problems. Then I got momentarily distracted. The young boy near me was starting to wail because his sister had kicked his sandcastle over.

And then the shot came. Even if I'd had the best vision in the world, I wouldn't have *seen* it, as it was on the other side of Es Vedrà. And yet I saw it, more vividly perceived in my mind than the beach and the collapsed sandcastle. The goat fell, down the side of the cliff, fast and heavy, hitting the rock two more times before making a final splash.

I felt my gut wrench again.

And Hugo just stared at the water a moment longer, lost in remorse.

The Lobsters

I sat there, cross with myself. I had tried to prevent a creature dying and had failed. And, as I stared at the collapsed sandcastle, the voices from the restaurant started to flow back to me. I heard Spanish voices, Catalan voices, English voices, Dutch voices, and also felt the thoughts and memories around them, or contained within them, like each word was a parcel around a thought that I could instantly unwrap. But there was one voice, one mind, that stood out to me. The voice was harsh, brittle, British. The thoughts were harsh too; I felt them drift to me like smoke.

'Excuse me,' said the voice, coming from a man two tables along from the Cotswolds couple. 'We discovered this in our paella.'

The waiter looked at him, confused. The man held his stare.

'It's a hair,' the man – his name I sensed was Brian – explained, holding the strand up like it was a historical artefact, like he had just plucked it from the burial crypt of Cleopatra. 'And look, it isn't any of our hair.'

Brian was not backing down, just as he didn't back down when he had pushed for redundancies at the insurance firm he worked for back home in London.

'Oh, sir, I am so sorry. I will tell the kitchen.'

The waiter he was talking to was a man called Vicente. He had a sadness to him. A kind of homesickness that was part of him even before he moved to Spain from Ecuador. An inability to feel anchored. I closed my eyes and saw a fresh memory of his, from yesterday, when he was in his kitchen in Cala Bassa on the west of the island, distant construction noise growling through the window as he stared at the letter from his landlord saying she was selling the small apartment building to a travel company and that he would have to find a new place to live. I knew all this before I even turned to see his tall skinny frame bending forward in a sort of bowing gesture, like a courtier to a tyrannical king.

'We won't be able to eat that. We won't be paying for it.'

'Of course. I am so sorry.'

'It's really not good enough, I'm afraid.'

Vicente looked blank for a moment. This infuriated Brian. His jaw clenched, he was angry, but it was a strange kind of anger, viewed like a purple cloud in my mind, a cloud of pomposity and superiority and the desire to hurt.

'Are you listening to me?'

Brian's wife had her hand on his arm as Brian waved his fork. I tried to access her mind, but it was like trying to see a person in deep shadow.

'Yes, absolutely. I will report this to the kitchen and—'

'And what?'

I felt anger inside me. It swirled in my mind, and normally such emotion has nowhere to go. It stays, it circles, it picks up dead leaves. But of course I was no longer normal. My mind now was equivalent to a body, and just as bodies can move around in physical space this mind of mine suddenly seemed able to actively roam into other places and ignore barriers the way the wind ignores traffic lights. In other words, the information I was getting wasn't just being received. It could be played with. I could pull against it. Like the energy of a wish now came with power.

And as Brian kept talking, waving his fork at the poor waiter – about seeing the manager, about health and hygiene regulations, about refusing to pay for their entire meal, about leaving a one-star review on TripAdvisor, about how Vicente should feel ashamed to work for a place like this – I felt a wish rise up.

The wish was this: *Shut up, Brian.*

It was a very consistent wish. *Shut up shut up shut up shut up shut up, Brian, just shut up.*

'I mean,' said Brian, as I saw nothing but purple in my mind, 'this just isn't on. It really isn't. To expect people to pay seventeen bloody euros for a—'

And that was it. The purple changed to ocean blue. Brian stopped talking. I can't emphasise how astounding it was. My thoughts made manifest. The internal shaping the external with such ease.

His lips were sealed closed. He was trying to talk but he couldn't. He started making a strange humming sound, as though he had a particularly severe case of constipation.

'Brian?' said his wife. 'Brian, are you okay? Brian?'

Charlotte. Her name was Charlotte. It came to me, fleetingly, amid all this commotion of my own making.

But Brian wasn't okay, because now the fork he was holding seemed to have a life of its own. He seemed to be struggling with it in the same way he was struggling to talk. Like it was a living thing. Like it was somehow against him.

I knew nothing about telekinesis at this point. I didn't know that iron is a particularly receptive material for telekinetic powers, and as stainless steel is an alloy made primarily with iron, a simple light item of cutlery like a fork is easy to manipulate. That was a surprise. The fork he'd wagged at the waiter was now being jabbed, by his own hand, into his thigh. *Oh no. Poor Brian.*

And everyone in the restaurant stopped drinking their wine and stopped dunking bread into aioli and stared.

Charlotte was a strange fusion of shock and concern and anger. 'Brian, what the hell are you doing?'

And it was then that I let go. And Brian let go too, his mouth unclenching and opening wide to howl as he stared down at the fork sticking out of his leg. 'Faaaaaaagggggghhhh,' he said.

And as he screamed in pain, I felt my own internal scream as I saw Brian as a child. He had fallen into a bed of nettles. No. No, he had been pushed. And I could see the other children laughing at him as he scrambled to get up, they were taunting him, and as I saw this the fork flew out of his leg and across the floor and Brian's wife and the waiter tried to calm him. I felt guilty. But I was also distracted by something else. A feeling of total fear and claustrophobia and anguish. And I realised it wasn't coming from me. It wasn't even coming from Brian, or the waiter.

It was coming from the lobster tank.

The terror built inside me, and my heart was racing and my

breathing was suddenly very laboured. I once heard something on the radio about how crustaceans, including lobsters, feel pain and seek out safe spaces when stressed.

The only time my body had known this much intensity as a result of my mind was when I had kneeled on the tarmac on Wragby Road, howling and praying for Daniel to still be alive.

I stood up and walked away, across the sand, towards the car, but the feeling from the creatures in the tank was becoming too much. The sensation of a lobster in a tank is panic fused with a tragic sense of interruption. They have an enzyme that protects their DNA. Telomerase, it is called. I don't know why I knew it, but I knew it. But more importantly I felt their tragedy. These are creatures that don't age. They could be immortal if we left them to it. They don't weaken naturally. They'd had their infinity stolen, and no one wants their infinity stolen. They wanted to be free. And I wanted them to be free. I felt their yearning and their powerlessness. I felt it overwhelm me now and I was turning again, towards the restaurant. I stood on the path between the dining area and the beach, staring at the creatures in the tank, in a kind of trance. I must have looked like a madwoman.

The feeling was building and building and growing and growing. Then the glass cracked and burst. A torrent of water, complete with shards of glass and a dozen hard-shelled decapods, suddenly animated, was unleashed across the tiled floor.

The diners, who had already become a bit agitated over Brian and the fork, were now in palpable shock. They stood up, some even stood on their chairs in order to escape the lobsters.

The crustaceans started walking on their spindly legs, amid the chaos, towards the beach. Their claws suddenly free from their bands, their antennae twitching wildly. They had a clear run, past the various waiters, who were occupied with pacifying Brian and various wailing children while also trying to sweep and mop some order back into their picturesque seaside restaurant. I saw one of the lobsters exactly as I had seen it in my mind, running across the sand.

What have I done? I thought as I pulled myself out of the trance.

'Too much,' came a voice behind me. I turned to see Alberto, standing right there on the walkway. Dodgy denim shorts and an old-devil smile.

'Now,' he said, staring at the lobster scuttling across the beach. 'Please. Follow me. This time, no questions.'

And I was about to ask one, but he was already walking away.

The Scent of Alberto Ribas

'This is nonsense,' I was saying. We were in the Fiat. I was following the chaotic hand flaps that passed for Alberto's directions. And yet I seemed to understand everything and could absorb the whole landscape with a single glance. Nature sang with beauty everywhere I looked, and I was absolutely terrified. 'This is nonsense.'

'And yet,' said Alberto, patting the hairy chest beneath his open shirt, 'this is not nonsense.'

'I don't want this,' I said. 'I don't want this power. Why am I feeling like this? Two days ago, I was dead inside. Empty. I couldn't feel anything. And now it is the opposite. I feel *everything*. And I didn't sleep at all last night.'

'Yes, this is a usual side-effect. I haven't slept for more than one hour a night in fifteen years. Very often I don't sleep at all. Christina used to sleep ten minutes a night. It's like we are dolphins now.'

'Dolphins?'

'Yes. Dolphins. I used to study them. The thing with dolphins is that they split their brain in two. So part of their brain sleeps while the other part stays awake. Unihemispheric slow-wave sleep. Actually, most sea mammals do this. And humans are on the sleepier side of mammals. Elephants and giraffes hardly sleep at all. But it is nothing to worry about. In real terms, you have just extended your waking life by about a third. That's good news, right?'

'Don't you think you should have told me all this? You know, before?'

'I was very clear. I did warn you. I can remember.'

And I could remember too. Of course I could. I could remember everything. His voice echoed in my mind.

If you want to stay a normal human being, you should leave right now. Because this won't be a normal experience.

I scowled. 'It was a little bloody vague. It sounded like generic marketing. You should have been specific.'

'Oh, and you would have believed that?'

I stared at the frayed edges of his denim shorts. I doubted they had ever seen a washing machine. I could smell him. Alberto Ribas came with a scent. A not-so-delicate bouquet of musk and brine and bad breath and goat and body odour with a secondary note of Hawaiian Tropic (an incongruous note too, given that his general aesthetic seemed to be halfway between unrehabilitated caveman and pirate). I tried to ignore it. Which was quite hard when your senses were literally out of this world, and you were confined to a tiny Fiat Panda with weak air conditioning.

'I don't know what I would have believed,' I said. But I knew he was right. I knew I wouldn't have believed any of it.

'It was for a reason, you know. It was all for a reason. La Presencia only comes to you for a reason. When I first encountered it, I was an old drunk. I had all kinds of issues after my wife Julia died, and it helped me. It gave me what I needed to get sober. That is why I always carry this with me.' He dug in his denim short pocket and pulled out his miniature rum bottle full of seawater. Seawater that wasn't just seawater. I could see its soft glow. 'It's from La Presencia. It's why Christina had the olive jar. She wanted to be near it, always. I want to be near it. Near La Presencia. Near those mysterious photons. It senses when I get weak. It glows and gives me strength. You see, none of this is an accident. You coming here, you coming to see me, you going in the water. La Presencia wanted you. Christina wanted you. The changes are going to help you. The talents. They're getting stronger, right? They get stronger for a few days. Eventually you will be able to control them. I told you that you would develop them. Remember? In the hospital. Now, not everyone touched by La Presencia gets the same powers in the same way, so I need to know . . . What has emerged so far? What extra-sensory talents? Telepathy? Telekinesis? Clairvoyance? Precognition?'

The words were ridiculous. The truth even more so. I thought of the lobster. The one I had seen ahead of time. 'Yes, yes, yes, and – I think – yes.'

'None of these skills by the way are unique,' said Alberto. 'Everyone on Earth has these things. You know, when someone runs into some guy on the street and says, "I was just thinking of you." La precognición . . . precognition. That happens. All the time. Or when we feel someone looking at us from a window before we see them. Telepathy. It happens all the time. Every time we have a déjà vu. Every time we are thinking of a word and someone says that word on the radio. These things happen far more than a coincidence. You know Jung?'

'The psychiatrist? Yes.'

'Well, he talked of "la coincidencia significativa – "meaningful coincidence". The psychiatric world wasn't ready to hear it, but it was there and he observed it in his patients repeatedly. La actividad paranormal es *normal*. We add the para because we are embarrassed by what we don't understand about ourselves. So what happens with La Presencia is all these abilities we have are unlocked and empowered. It makes us become ourselves.'

'Hmm,' I hummed, doubtfully. 'What about telekinesis? Are you telling me that most people move things with their mind?'

'No. Es verdad. You are right. Telekinesis is the one that is not so common. But even so, it happens, sometimes, when the wish is strong enough and the thing is small. A father wanting their weak child's birthday candle to go out actually adds the force to their blow if they think it strongly enough . . . Telekinesis . . . it is there.' He tapped the side of his skull. 'It is there in everyone. And in you, it has now come alive. The human mind is a dark ocean. A Mariana Trench. La Presencia gives it light.'

Particles of Light

Ridiculous, I thought to myself. Although of course it wasn't just a thought to myself.

'Yes, I agree,' Alberto said. 'I really do. It *is* ridiculous. Like so many things have seemed in the past. Like the Earth moving around the sun. Like animals having intelligence. But there is a science to it all.'

He began to go into some serious scientific detail.

He talked to me about a 2011 study from Cornell University that showed that precognition and telepathy is measurable in a lab setting. He talked about how humans are essentially telepathic creatures and how our silent thoughts aren't contained in our minds any more than light is contained in a lightbulb. He talked about how the scientific establishment still lives in the age of Aristotle and how it is still seen as blasphemy to question old-fashioned ideas of cause and effect, especially in relation to time. He talked about quantum physics and quantum entanglement. He talked about retro causation – the way the future interacts with the past just as the past impacts the future. He talked about photons – particles of light – which are famed for disobeying previously devised rules of space and time. About how light is fundamentally timeless. And that we have these particles in our body. Our bodies create inner light. Biophotons. And the bioluminescent photons of La Presencia interact with the bioluminescent photons within us, because light gets through and inside everything. And, via the triggering of a stunningly complex hormonal response and a kind of biological information transfer, these new photons untap our potential. And that manifests in different ways, depending on the person, but it tends to make hidden things seen. Minds, futures, pleasures and sensations that were once covered or blocked.

'And once that happens, amiga mía, a brave new world is waiting.'

His smug tone was annoying me. Or maybe it was the heat and the stifling air in the car and the fact that I didn't like having my view of reality challenged. No. I think it was him.

'You know where the phrase "brave new world" comes from?' I asked.

'Yes. Of course. Aldous Huxley. God of the hippies.'

I shook my head. 'William Shakespeare. In *The Tempest*. A play about a crazy manipulative man on a magical island who likes the sound of his own voice and causes a lot of mischief because of a chip on his shoulder.'

'Muy bien,' he said, pulling a white hair from his chest. 'Muy bien. That is me. Crazy . . . manipulative . . . I have had worse.' Then he pointed at an upcoming turning. 'There,' he said. 'A la derecha. To Es Cubells.'

'Where are we going?' I asked.

'To church,' he said, smiling. 'So you better have been a good girl.'

In my life I have only twice had the urge to slap someone's face. Both times it was Alberto Ribas's.

If I couldn't lash out at Alberto, perhaps I could find a weak spot. I kept trying to access his mind but wasn't getting very far. In fact, he was almost as unreadable as he'd been the first time I'd seen him. I still couldn't decipher his age, his loves, his fears, his memories. The only difference – and the thing that made me trust him just a little – was that I could pick up on a gentle sadness that he didn't wear on the surface. Not a guilty sadness, but something more existential. A kind of continual sense of mourning leaked out of him, appearing in my mind daubed in muted shades of grey and green, like boiled cabbage, which was in such contrast to his permanently smiling, tanned, leathery face and Zeus beard.

So, in the absence of psychic understanding, I had to ask questions. The most obvious one being: '*Why* are we going to church?'

The road was winding and narrow and quiet. We passed a solitary tapas bar with no one outside.

'Very important research. You will be able to further our understanding.'

'Of?'

'La Presencia.'

'I don't want to understand La Presencia. I don't want to stick forks into people.' I thought of the semi-solid vaporous creatures that looked like watercolours. 'I don't want to be part-Salacian. I don't want to be Heroic Champion of the Lobsters. I want to understand what happened to my friend.'

'It's the same thing. Understanding La Presencia is understanding what happened to your friend.'

'So it killed her? That thing in the ocean killed her? And you sent me down there for it to kill me too?'

Alberto sighed like a creaking door. 'I did not want to kill you, Grace. You can be a terribly annoying person, yes, but I did not want to kill you. La Presencia wasn't there to hurt you. La Presencia wants to help and La Presencia wants to be helped. It recruited you, as Christina knew it would.'

'How many other people have come into contact with it?'

'I did a lot of research . . . for the book . . . *La vida imposible* . . . Asked a lot of people . . . Read a lot of accounts . . . It is thought to be very few. Beyond me and you and Christina, only a handful that we know of. There was a fisherman called Joan Bonanova in the thirties. And as you will see, there was an encounter in the nineteenth century. And more recently, in living memory, there was an incident forty years ago, but that was different . . .'

'How was it different?'

'Well, for a start it was in daylight. The only time La Presencia has been made visible in broad daylight. And it wasn't an adult. It was a boy. An English boy. He was on holiday here. He nearly drowned. He swam too far out from the beach, and no one could get to him. His father saw him but too late. He went under. He was under for seven minutes. He was dead, effectively . . .'

I thought of Daniel. I thought of him lying still on the tarmac. I thought of the red of the bike and the blood.

'So what happened?'

'Light,' Alberto answered. 'That's what the witnesses saw. Including the boy's father. They saw a glowing circle of blue light below the water. And then after the seven minutes the boy came to the surface. He was alive.'

'And what happened to the boy?'

Alberto shrugged. 'He went back to England. And whatever talents it had given him, he kept them quiet . . . But that was a totally different situation. You were chosen, Grace. You weren't in danger.'

I sighed. 'I don't understand why we need to go to church.'

'There is a manuscript in the church. A very important manuscript. Francisco Palau's. A very important man. He was a priest and a . . .' He mimed holding a hood, as he said the word. '. . . monk . . . who came to the island, and he often spent time in a cave in Es Vedrà . . . .'

As the path became rockier, I slowed down. The tyres growled over the red dirt and stones. I remembered Rosella from the grocery store telling me about the religious hermit. *Years and years ago there was a hermit who lived there. In a cave. A religious man. A priest. He wrote about lights he saw in the water. Lights that lit up the whole sea.*

Alberto smiled. He knew I'd made the connection. The gap in his teeth like the entrance to a mysterious cave. And then we slowed to a halt and he pointed up ahead to a gorgeous white cubic church. 'Mira, Grace. We are here. Isn't it beautiful?'

Church

It was true.

The church in Es Cubells was a thing of clean geometric beauty. With neat lateral buttresses on either side of its cubic body, it was whitewashed to the point it dazzled. Utterly simple in its design, perched above the sea, it was transcendentally calming and I could have stared at it for hours in the afternoon sun.

As I got out of the car, Alberto was heading to a bush. 'I really need to, how do you say in English . . . drain the anaconda.'

I turned away from him. 'No one says that. Literally no one.'

'Water my weasel, you know?' he continued, unabashed.

He was as close to a beast as I have ever seen a man. Once he finished urinating he came to join me on the dusty path.

Before we reached the church door, I noticed a lizard by my feet. It was totally still, the way only lizards can be, and I sensed its paradoxical state of mind. Just as some languages have words others don't have, some species have emotions humans have never known. A lizard, for instance, always seems to be in a simultaneous state of constant alertness and deep relaxation, totally in tune with its surroundings, both terrified of it all and in quiet love with it all.

You are approaching, it told me, mysteriously. *You are nearly there.*

'See?' said Alberto. 'You now understand the thoughts of animals. That's a gift, yes?'

'And yet, Mr Ribas, I still don't know your thoughts. Isn't that interesting? Do you have more to hide than a reptile?'

'Man, you say that like it is an insult to be compared to a reptile. Reptiles are the truest, most noble and purest of all creatures. They are full of ancient wisdom. They understand how to be. When they tell you something they are telling you many, many, many things. Their thoughts are more precise than a haiku. They . . .'

He stood there a considerable while, there on the hot dusty ground, in that baking shadeless heat, giving me a lecture on lizards, his accent veering from Spanish to American to a kind of English to something uniquely Alberto. And no amount of extra-sensory perception could keep me focused on what he was saying. So I stared into the distance. Beyond the cliff, beyond the juniper bushes, to the sea and its mysteries. Eventually the words stopped and he started walking again.

I knew the door was locked even before I touched it. So I told him. 'It's locked.' He probably had known it too. He frowned at the door. In fact, it was more a glower. I realised, to much amusement, that he was trying – really, really trying – to open the door with his mind.

'Listen,' he bumbled, 'I used to be able to do locks quite easily. But recently, my talent's faded.' He looked sheepish about this. As if there was something he wanted to tell me. 'It makes us more powerful until it doesn't. It doesn't make us immortal.' The tiniest crack in his defences. I could almost get inside his psyche but not quite. He sighed. Snapped out of it. 'But trust me, this is the most important bit of research there is to do, and you are the only person who can do it, so we need to open the door . . .'

'So I am here to do your research?'

'Yes,' he said. Then rethought. He frowned. Cross with himself. He scrunched up his face from more than the sun. 'No. The research is important, of course. Because La Presencia is important. But there is no point me telling you what I know because I don't even know what I know.'

'But you told me I would know by now. I would know everything about what happened to Christina. That was the whole reason I met you on the beach at midnight.'

He stuck out his bottom lip. 'Oh. Really? I thought it was my magnetic charm.'

'Funnily enough: no.'

'Oh.' He looked so crestfallen I almost felt sorry for him. Almost.

'I went diving because I wanted answers. You promised answers. And all I have is "she disappeared at sea" . . .'

'I thought it was going to tell you,' he said. 'La Presencia.'

He looked at his watch. 'We need to be quick. We need to be out of there before they open the church.' He batted away a single-minded mosquito. 'Listen, yes, I am using you, Grace. I am using you. I admit this. You have an immense talent, and you can help. Christina wasn't able to access the mind of the dead, of Francisco Palau, but you might . . .'

'Is that why she died? She wasn't of use to you any more? She couldn't help you with your research?'

He looked infuriated. He had the scowl our old Pomeranian, Bernard, used to give every time we clipped him back on the lead.

'You are a very stupid person,' he grumbled.

'Yes,' I said. 'I am well aware of that. I am the stupidest woman in the world. If I wasn't, I would never have gone to you for answers.'

I was in such a huff I was walking off. Have you ever done that? Been so angry you have to start walking? And then once you start you have to carry on like you mean it, even though you really just wish you had stayed still and taken a deep breath instead? Because there was nowhere to go except the edge of a cliff or a baking hot car you were pleased to be out of?

'You are a woman of mathematics. You want answers, don't you?'

'Yes. I want real answers.'

There were stones that bled easier than Alberto bled answers. But I sensed he was getting there. So I stayed with my back to him, staring at the sea and the bushes.

'Christina disappeared in the ocean on a moonless night. Do you know who else did that? Francisco Palau . . . And there are three hundred pages full of his own handwriting in this church. And yes, I want to know about La Presencia. Of course I do. But researching La Presencia is the exact same thing as researching what happened to Christina. Now, please. If you can free lobsters, you can turn locks. Let's get inside.'

The Belief in More

Inside, the air was cool. The floor was shining tiles. Squares tilted forty-five degrees into diamonds. Neat pews well-spaced apart along the nave with a wide middle aisle. There was a tranquillity that made me wish I'd been to church more in recent years.

I think I had been playing hard to get. With God, I mean. I wanted Him to come to me. To prove He was there. But now I realised it doesn't work like that. We make our own faith just as we make our own stories. We believe in what we want to believe, but it takes effort.

'I came here as a boy,' said Alberto. 'My mother was a very religious woman. I have sat through a service in every church on the island. But mainly we went to the church in Santa Agnès de Corona. Our village. We lived across the road from it. I used to have a pet toad. A speckled Balearic green toad. I called him El Capitán. I used to take him with me. In my pocket.'

'Poor toad,' I said.

'Sí. Es verdad. I have spoken with toads since and they have little time for sermons. Or pockets.'

'Are you religious?' I asked him.

'I think so. But I believe if there is a god you don't get to them by a church. You get there by the ocean or the forest. I learned more from the toad.'

I tutted at him, on behalf of my Catholic upbringing. 'I like churches,' I said. 'They are still and silent and serious. You could learn something from them.'

Aside from a large elaborate portrait of Christ above the altar, the church was simple, minimal, so it didn't take us long to locate the manuscript. It was in a glass cabinet beside the font of holy water not far from the entrance. It was the only thing on display in the cabinet. Needless to say, it was locked, but as with the door I opened it with alarming ease. I felt the latch in my mind, and I only had to confidently imagine it moving for it to move. And then I opened the cabinet and held this yellowed manuscript, bound with ribbons pulled through needle holes along the sides of the pages. The manuscript that Francisco Palau had written, according to the date at the top of the first page, in October 1855.

'Put your fingers on the words,' Alberto said. 'Read them but put your fingers on them too. That is how you do it . . . It is called psychometry. The ability to understand a mind of someone just by touching something they touched. It is a very deep and intense kind of mind-reading that can even cross the line between the living and the dead. You don't just read the person's mind – it involves many senses – you almost *are* them. At that place in time. It is time travel, effectively . . .'

'Could you,' I said, 'just please be quiet?'

'Stare at the words,' Alberto whispered.

'Shh.'

So anyway, I stared at the words. The old priest's account, written in an old-fashioned Catalan, of his arrival in Ibiza from the mainland. His exile here.

His writing was elegant, the letters leaning slightly backwards, windswept, struggling with the speed of his pen. As if he knew he was on borrowed time.

'No,' said Alberto. 'Not this part. Flick to the end. Flick to his final trip to Es Vedrà.'

I ran my finger over the words with my fingertips, waiting for the psychometry to begin, or – more scientifically – for my biophotonic-induced capabilities to be activated.

As I closed my eyes I could hear, faintly, the sound of the sea. It was hard to know if this was the actual sea, the one very close by, lapping onto the beach at the foot of the cliff. Or if it was the memory of the sea. The sea always sounds like the sea, after all.

'Can you hear the sea?' I asked Alberto.

'No,' he told me. 'I can't hear it at all. The actual sea is too quiet to hear. So you are hearing something else. You are hearing somewhere *not here*. I am right beside you, but you will leave me for a while. You will encounter another person in another time. Just for a little while. Buen viaje!'

His words faded into nothing.

The sea became rough. I could hear it crashing against rocks, and I realised I was letting go of the fixtures of time and identity, moving into the fluidity of pure and all-encompassing life. I had a moment of brief release, like taking off a tight helmet, and then I was somewhere and someone else entirely.

Mansions

So, Maurice, of all the things that happened to me up until this point, I believe this was the most peculiar. And because of that, I think it is also the hardest to convey to you. I suppose, like all the talents I had, it was an extreme exaggeration of something I had already experienced in my normal life. For instance, whenever I read an autobiography – Maya Angelou or Anne Frank or Richard Feynman or *whomever* – I feel a kind of empathy, where a tiny part of me becomes for a short while the person I am reading about.

I suppose that is one of the purposes of all reading. It helps you live lives beyond the one you are inside. It turns our single-room mental shack into a mansion.

All reading, in short, is telepathy and all reading is time travel. It connects us to everyone and everywhere and every time and every imagined dream.

Now imagine a dial, like a volume dial, but an empathy one. And if the experience of reading a normal book turns that empathy dial up from a one to a two or a three, then the experience for me of looking at and touching Francisco Palau's handwritten manuscript was the shifting of the dial to ten. It was a complete and utter immersion.

I wasn't just experiencing the words written. I was experiencing the life around them. The words were just seeds that grew a sudden full-sensory experience. The church I was standing in disappeared completely. I was back – if back is really the word – in 1855. I felt the hot wind on my face. I heard the sea.

The Third Person

I was gone.
   I was him.
   I was he.
   I was the third person.

The Falling Moon

I was Francisco Palau. Of course, *I* was technically still Grace Winters, and *I* was standing in a church, but in this psychometric trance I could feel everything he felt. I had no agency, I couldn't change this past experience I was observing, but at the same time I felt like more than just a witness. I felt like I was fully inside his mind and time, sitting in a rowing boat between Cala d'Hort and Es Vedrà. But it was still easy to tell that this was not the Cala d'Hort of the twenty-first century. There were no buildings on the coastline. No huts along the beach. No restaurant. No other boats. No Atlantis Scuba. Just beach and rocks and nature.

The ferryman that he was facing was a tough-faced, alcohol-scented, godless man called Miquel. He had refused to row so late in the day, but Francisco had offered him three reales to make it worthwhile.

'I am not like you, Father,' Miquel told the priest, in Catalan. 'I am a sinner. God doesn't offer me the same protection. I could not stay there on that rock one single night and see morning.'

'What is your meaning?'

'There are things around Ibiza and Es Vedrà that are not in nature. Outside of God.'

'There is nothing outside of God.'

'Well, if these things are inside God, then God is to be feared.'

'Feared, yes. But fear is just another route to Him. Another route to His love. It is there in the Book of Matthew. "So have no fear of them, for nothing is covered that will not be revealed, or hidden that will not be known . . . And do not fear those who kill the body but cannot kill the soul. Rather fear him who can destroy both soul and body in hell."'

Miquel absorbed this, deeply, as he dipped the oars back in the dark and softly swelling water. 'Now I have another fear on top of the first one, Father.'

And Francisco had laughed, tightly, and said nothing more. Miquel was right. He wasn't like him. He was lost, thought the priest, like so many were. A slave to fears, and all other impulses, an unholy jumble of varying superstitions still infecting them from the days of the Phoenicians, coupled with folkish credulities.

He contemplated that, of all the superstitious people on the island, the boatmen were the most resolute. Maybe it was that strangely concocted herb liqueur they all drank, a cask of which Miquel had at his feet. Maybe that fusion of alcohol and fennel and juniper and whatever else they put in it loaned them hallucinatory visions and feverish imaginings.

It seemed that the people of the Balearic Islands (he had been to Mallorca too, to work with the monks there) inhabited a reverse world, where the more fantastical a story, the more likely it was to be believed. But the native Ibicencos were particularly prone to such deliriums, and even had many festivals where various superstitions were fervently celebrated and honoured and featured a type of dancing around wells where men in red berets leaped into the air around bejewelled women to a cacophony of drums, flutes and castanets. He had a deep distaste of such ungodly things, which he tried his best to hide when in front of the locals.

But then: *something.*

The ferryman saw something in the water. Then Francisco saw it too. A glowing light. Some kind of reflection.

'I thought there was no moon tonight,' the priest said, sounding a little nervous.

He looked up and saw it in the sky. Some light object heading towards them. At first it was just a line of light, but then as it came closer to Earth it broadened into a bright sphere.

'I think it is falling from the sky,' said Miquel, dumbstruck. 'The moon. I think the moon is falling from the sky.'

'That is not the moon. It is too blue for a moon. That is something else. Its shape is changing.'

The light grew closer and closer. A glowing blueish white, a sphere narrowing into a thin, impossibly long rod of light that hit the water with barely an impact. And then suddenly it was gone. Into the water. But a moment later there was light again, deep underwater. A cloud of light, becoming a sphere, becoming a cloud again.

Miquel drank from his cask and then offered the drink to the priest, who gulped it back without hesitation.

1855

'I felt you feel it.' This was Alberto's voice, shaking me out of the trance.

I was suddenly back in the church.

'That was it arriving,' he blurted, way louder than you are meant to speak in a church. 'That was La Presencia reaching here. He saw it. He saw it in the sky. He didn't write that he saw it arrive . . . He just wrote about lights in the water . . . Not them *arriving*.' He was incredibly excited. 'But he was there when it landed. He was there. It arrived here in 1855. This is *incredible detail*. This is a real breakthrough. I thought it might have arrived before then. I thought it might have been here since the time of the Phoenicians. But no. 1855. Eighteen. Fifty. Five . . . Do you know what that means?'

'It means that I am your frustrated research assistant?'

'*No. No. No.* It means it came for a reason. Like we thought. It came here just as our planet was going fucking loco, man. Wars, empires, railways, and the real start of this, you know, destruction for the environment.' When he got animated his Spanish accent and grammar became more apparent. It was almost charming. 'The 1850s was when the number of extinct species went . . .' His hand became a rocket. He made the sound. 'Four times as many species went extinct as the decade previous. It was the beginning of the end. The air was full of smoke in cities. Everyone coughing. You know. Human beings in this crisis. So you get all the great writers writing their great stuff because everything is turning to shit. Dickens and Flaubert and soon after our very own Mr Galdós. It was the start of the conservation movement. And then La Presencia arrives. A healing force . . . Why then? Is it not possible that it came to help us? That it came from Salacia – was sent by the Salacians – because they saw life in danger and wanted to preserve life? Go on . . . on . . . get to his other trips to Es Vedrà . . .'

And so I placed my fingers back on the text and I slipped once more into the past. Francisco Palau was visiting Es Vedrà again, climbing up towards his cave as the day began to die.

Salvation

Francisco must have been climbing on this steep path for well over an hour now, but he knew he wasn't far from the cave. So he stopped there for a little while and absorbed the view and took his flask and sipped some water.

The sky was awash with colour.

Pink, purple, orange and gold decorating thin parallel streaks of cloud, like the ridges and furrows of some heavenly field. He clutched the beads of his rosary and silently offered a prayer of gratitude. He had been all over Spain, far beyond his native Catalonia. He had moved from place to place, due to war or hunger or persecution. He had known a lot of sky in his life, and many of his prayers were sent towards it. But nothing compared to this.

As a child on the farm, years before he was banished from the mainland, he would stare in wonder at the sun setting beside the small square church at Aitona, feeling a proximity to the One and Only Father Himself. Yet here the sky was something else. The beauty was overwhelming. The closeness to God had an intimacy that he could feel inside his chest. No cathedral had ever offered him such a feeling. It helped him breathe and gave him strength and made this journey possible. It would help sustain him through three days of meditation and observation and writing in the cave. It was almost enough to make him forget all the terror he had witnessed.

Looking out across the water, beyond the lower rock of Es Vedranell towards the cove he'd just travelled from, he caught sight of a low-flying cormorant. He loved cormorants and wished he had a better view. A striking, majestic, shining black wonder of a bird. He could just about see in the near-faded light the brown speck of the ferryman's rowing boat too, safely moored on the sand beside the rocks at Cala d'Hort.

It was now that the priest noticed something moving by his feet.

A lizard.

Nothing unusual about that. It was the common black-and-green speckled kind he had often seen in Ibiza. The lizard paused for a moment, before scuttling away towards one of the rare hardy shrubs that clung to the rock.

But then there was another. Precisely the same. And another, and another. He tried to count them but lost track at eight. They were all heading in the same direction. Down. Away from where the priest was heading.

The last time he had been here he had spotted two goats. Maybe they had startled them. But he couldn't see the goats now.

For a moment he felt an irrational twinge of fear.

It was doubly irrational, as one of the blessings of Ibiza, and presumably this adjacent islet too, was that there were no fearsome or deadly animals. No poisonous plants. No native snakes. God had made it a sanctuary of peace. A protected place.

The priest inwardly shook away his concern, let his flask hang by his side once more, and continued his journey towards the cave. He kept on looking for more signs of lizards, but they were nowhere to be seen. He did, however, see a falcon flying in circles overhead in the dying light.

By the time he was almost at the cave, halfway between the sea and the top of the islet, the sky was deep in darkness, a totally moonless night, and the path was narrow and the drop to his right a vertical cliff.

He stood in front of the opening and again stared out. From here, Es Vedrà seemed quiet to every sense. The sound of the sea was too far below to be heard. Nothing. Just the peace of God.

But then he saw something, far below.

It was a light again. Exactly like the one he had seen fall into the ocean. This light seemed to be emanating from deep below the surface, closer to Es Vedrà than it was to the beach at Cala d'Hort.

A kind of brilliant glowing transparent phosphorescence. Tonight it was almost the ultramarine-blue of the Virgin Mother's shawl but glowing, moving, pulsing, like a giant shapeshifting impossibly beautiful jellyfish.

The priest was struck with awe, mesmerised. The sunset had been one thing, but this was something else entirely. He remembered John 1:5 and whispered it, hardly thinking.

'The light shines in the darkness, and the darkness has not overcome it.'

And he realised the lizards were heading towards it.

Francisco felt a strange but blissful dissolving, as though he was no longer Francisco Palau, no longer the priest and former friar and occasional hermit, no longer the founder of the School of Virtue in Barcelona, no longer a person, or exile, or a self in time, or an identity with memories of his fellow friars burning to death in a monastery at the hands of the Spanish army. He was, in that ecstatic instant, beyond himself. There was no line between the man and the universe, between flesh and infinity.

He was the past, the present and the future.

He was, simply, life itself.

But then something happened. He lost his footing on the thin path. And then he fell, tumbling roughly down the limestone on his fall, with a pain and force so intense he lost consciousness before he splashed into the water, and the sea itself filled entirely with light from Ibiza to Es Vedrà. And when his consciousness returned he was in that ocean amid the light, winded and stunned but alive. Strangely no longer in pain. In front of him was the sphere-cloud and he swam straight towards it, imagining it was God or salvation. And then when he reached it the sphere held its form and expanded and a hole appeared in it, and he swam through until he was suddenly somewhere else entirely. He was on a beach with orange sand and a forest full of trees with white leaves and beside a different sea, one whose luminescence never faded, and he breathed in that sweet air, and he saw creatures, of flesh and of vapour, the likes of which he had never seen before, including one who came to him and communicated a message.

You are safe here. You will be forever protected.

And, with every atom and fibre of his being, he knew those words to be true. He cried with gratitude and warmth and stepped towards those creatures – angels, he was sure – ready for salvation.

The View from the Church Floor

I woke up on the church tiles. I felt weak. Mildly delirious. My head was aching. And I stared up to see Alberto's face, contorted with intense emotion, crying.

'It's all right,' I said. 'I'm fine. It's just a potential head wound.'

'Oh, don't worry. I'm not crying for you.'

'Of course not. Thank you. Then why are you crying?'

And the tears were now accompanied by a smile as open as his shirt. 'Because Christina was right. It's not just a presence. It's a portal.'

'A portal?'

He nodded like an eager cockerel. 'Yes. It's a portal back to where it came from. To Salacia. And you know what that means, don't you?'

'I very much don't, actually.'

'It means that she made it!'

'Made it?'

And then he laughed and cried some more, right there with the altar and a painted Jesus descending from the cross.

'She didn't die!' His exclamation echoed through the church like a reverberating bell. 'She got where she wanted to go! She made it to Salacia!'

An Equation Without a Solution

Now, I have no doubt you are as confused by all this as I was. Don't worry, confusion has its uses.

Indeed, the willingness to be confused, I now realise, is a prerequisite for a good life. Wanting things to be simple can become a kind of prison, it really can, because you end up staying trapped inside how you want things to be rather than embracing how they *could be*. You end up closed. You end up shutting doors to so many possibilities. I was drawn to mathematics because of its certainties, because I wanted closed doors, and simplicity, but life isn't like that. And nor, in fact, is mathematics. You can't ever fully unweave the rainbow, because mathematics and science and essential truth aren't deprived of magic and mystery. They *are* magic and mystery. So don't think that I was on some journey away from mathematics towards the mystical. Because that is not the journey I was on. I wasn't abandoning mathematical truth, I was discovering it at a deeper level.

As you know, in conventional mathematics, there is a tendency to simplify. We formulate algorithms and patterns and formulas based on everything else staying fixed; a more intricate mathematics understands that, in an ever-changing universe, very little is fixed or simple.

You may be aware of 'complexity science'. That hybrid of science and mathematics that tries to tackle the tricky stuff. Not rocket science. Rocket science is pretty straightforward, which is why conventional mathematics is enough for most engineering problems. No, complexity science involves understanding – for instance – the mathematics of nature, the intricacy of organisms as they grow, of predicting the course of climate change, of how atoms interact. And there is a concept within complexity science that is literally called 'universality', which tells us that even within the complexity of life there are universal similarities and patterns across different systems. And so the real magic is a mathematical one. It is the one that doesn't posit simplicity and complexity against each other, but one which finds the truer order within the complexity. Within the mess. The beautiful, spiralling, entropic mess we call life.

Wanting to look over life as if it is a test paper, and wanting a narrow neatness, order, cleanliness and control, is the basis for mental despair. Because it is a delusion. We are in this world. We *are* the test paper. We are a moving agent in an unfixed world in an ever-expanding cosmos.

It seems to me that if you want truth, if you want to lead a full and aware life, you should head towards possibility, towards mystery and movement, towards travel or change, because when you find the universality within that, you find yourself. Your ever-moving self. You arrive in the act of leaving. Of staying open, always, to the possibility that the simple things we tell ourselves may all be wrong.

So I am going to give you some answers here that are of a different kind. Answers that are also questions. I will tell you everything I learned after I lifted myself off those cold church tiles. And again: you don't have to believe any of this, if you choose not to do so. Being open to possibility is being open to pain, failure, disappointment, so the temptation is to curl ourselves up like armadillos. And it is perfectly understandable. Sometimes it is easier to press our metaphorical noses into our metaphorical backsides than to look out into the universe. To be human is to be scared of our own innate ridiculousness, so we do anything to reduce that ridicule. We clothe our bodies, we procreate behind closed doors, we hide every bodily function, we don't cry in the post office, or sing in the street, and we try to keep our own ideas in line with what we are told we should think.

But life is mess and confusion and full of awkward, shameful realities.

Of course, we all make our own beliefs in this world and sometimes to shift them is a frightening thing. If you really want to make wonderful discoveries, as any good armadillo knows, you eventually have to remove your head from your bottom and look out at the bright, confusing day. Into the hidden glory, into the deeper mathematics, into the ultimate reality. Into life.

Wormhole

We were back in the car. Windows open. Not actually driving.

'The theory,' said Alberto, slowly, as if I was seven, 'is that La Presencia is a very real presence full of powerful photons but also a wormhole. A wormhole is a connection between two places in the spacetime fabric. In my research for La Presencia I heard from relatives of Joan Bonanova. The fisherman who was saved by La Presencia. He told his daughter that he was going away, to another world, and he wouldn't be able to come back. He saw his own future in Salacia. And he disappeared one night, when he was old and ill, and he headed down towards La Presencia and he never came back. So, as far as we know, you can go through La Presencia but not back. And if Christina has gone to Salacia, it was via a one-way ticket.'

It was, to be fair, a lot to take in. My mind was more boggled than it had been when it had first encountered advanced calculus. But the main thing was this: Christina was probably – or at least *very possibly* – still alive on another planet.

And of course I had no idea if I should trust Alberto Ribas. But I needed him. He was the only person in the world who knew what I had become.

'I want to show you something,' he said.

He pulled out his phone from his denim shorts and played a video. I saw a woman on a boat. It took me a moment to realise that the boat was Alberto's. And that the woman I was staring at – this grey-haired, graceful, slightly bewitching woman – was Christina herself.

What Christina Said on the Boat as
the Wind Gently Blew Her Hair

Hello, Grace. Long time, no see. This is your old friend, Christina. I guess I look a little different from how you remember me. I even have a tattoo. See! Of the sun. What could be better than the sun?

By the time you see this, a month from now – on the 26th of June, in the car with Alberto – I will no longer be here. No. I don't mean I will be dead. Even though I can see my own death, I hope to avoid it. Someone is trying to kill me, but I don't know who. I know this sounds quite dramatic, but so has been my life in recent times. I will, hopefully, be in Salacia. I can see much of the future, but I can't see that for sure. So I need to have faith. Like you, I had a tiny glimpse of it when it first reached out to me. The beach, the trees, the sweet air. It is meant to be a bountiful paradise. You get to live a very long time there, in health and peace. Maybe for ever. The Salacians care. That is why they sent La Presencia here. I sometimes place the olive jar beside my bed. Right next to my head. If you do that, it tells you things in your dreams. Things you need to hear. The dreams are the most vivid you have ever known. And they are filled with the kind of truth that heals.

The theory is that if you dive down and swim directly towards La Presencia, straight as an arrow, rather than wait for it to come to you, then you are basically telling it you want to escape. And I don't *want* to escape. I *need* to. Because otherwise I will be killed.

And who my killer is, as I said, I'm not sure. Like you, I can't see the minds of everyone. Some people are harder to reach. And I know what you are thinking. You are thinking it could be Alberto. That he could be the one who wants to kill me. After all, you struggle to reach his mind. But no. Take it from someone who knew him before he pulled up the drawbridge. It is not Alberto. He is many, many, many things – at least half of which are enraging – but he is not a killer.

Now, I know I left you a letter, but I couldn't tell you everything there because it would have endangered you. You must be discreet. Indeed, I sense that if I hadn't been so public, if I'd never set up a stall at the market, then I would not have been a target. So I will say here what I couldn't write in the letter.

You are a special person. I always knew you were special. I knew it when I was at my loneliest and you gave me company. But I didn't know precisely *how* special. When La Presencia first came to me in the ocean, it gave me certain talents, but it has given you more. I have known lots of people in my life, both in England and in Spain, but you are the only one La Presencia would have gifted with so much. Believe me, I know this. You were the one it wanted. The one it was calling, through me. The only block you will face is yourself. Let La Presencia heal you.

The real talent it has given you is an appreciation of life. It is hard to explain, at least in English, what this truly means. But there is a word in Spanish, 'duende'. One connotation of the word comes from the Spanish poet Lorca. It describes that feeling when someone truly connects with the sublime essence of life, its tragedy and beauty, whether in art or flamenco or in nature. You know, like if you have ever been in a gallery and seen a painting that made you feel terrified or ecstatic, but now it won't just be art or a sunset that can make you feel that. It will be anything and everything. It could be a warm breeze, the simple scent of pine on this island of pines.

I know you have felt emptiness. But you will feel fullness. Maybe for the first time since you were a young child. Now you get to live. You will taste every experience entirely. You will be present here. This presence is better than any drug on Earth, and believe me I have tried a few of them in my time. It is the most alive it is possible to be.

In understanding the present so deeply, you will also understand the future, the way that a shark can predict a hurricane by sensing changes in water pressure.

This may not feel like a gift right now, but you have been gifted, I promise you. The talents are a gift. Alberto has them but his are fading. I had them but I am gone. There have been others that La Presencia has touched. But with you, the change will be among the most dramatic.

I know by nature you are a sceptical person, and so I have had to lay a trail of breadcrumbs for you to get to this position. That is why I left you the house. And the note. And that is also why I spoke to Rosella, the girl in the shop at Santa Gertrudis, about you. And why I told you to talk to Sabine at the hippy market, who absolutely hates poor Alberto, because I knew she would get you suspicious. And of course there is this, what I am holding in my hand. The gift you gave me. The necklace with the pendant of St Christopher.

This has been the key, Grace. This is how I knew. *Psychometry.* This gave me the knowledge about you. Holding this. Remembering you. Then gaining the knowledge of how strong you could be. How you could have the talents as strong as *anyone.* How you could save the island, animals, the sea, and even people, from destruction. How you would be a gift to nature.

I am right now going to drop it in the ocean. And on the dive in a few minutes Alberto's daughter Marta will photograph it and upload it to the Atlantis Scuba website. You see, when you saw the photo of your necklace you thought the chances were many millions against one, but it wasn't. Because we wanted you to see it. And we predicted you would visit the website after seeing Rosella and once your suspicions started to rise. And that will have been enough for you to go and find Alberto. And the rest . . . well, you know the rest.

You see, now you are a protector. Because it is impossible to feel life so deeply and not want to protect it. You will find yourself needing to help people – and animals.

I have been a protector too. I have tried to protect animals. The environment. I have tried to protect people from the future from my stall at the hippy market. I have dressed this science up as fortune-telling mysticism and the authorities have left me alone. But I have obviously stepped on someone's toes somewhere. I think I have helped people, or tried to. My daughter might disagree. But I think you will be able to help even more.

Of course, a gift is often also a curse. And you must be aware these talents come with dangers, as I now know too well. But I had to choose you, Grace. I had to choose someone to continue my work. You don't have to tell people their futures like I did. But you will find yourself protecting life, protecting nature, protecting this beautiful island.

Back in the thirties, there was a fisherman called Joan Bonanova, who was saved by La Presencia. Alberto has told you about him by now. He had such a pure soul, free from guilt and sin, that the talents he developed were powerful. One night, amid the invasion by Franco's fascists, he sent a signal to every animal on the island to help, and soon there were reports of goats and other creatures attacking Nationalist soldiers. I genuinely believe, if you really want to, you can be like Joan Bonanova. You will be able to have talents beyond anything anyone has known for decades.

And I really want you to find my would-be killer. Not for me. I will be safe, I am sure of it. But for others. They are still out there. I want you to stop them, because others are in danger. But mostly, I brought you here to save not other people's lives but your own. I want you to live, Grace. I want you to let go of your past and *live*. You need to do this. For the good of everything. Do you hear me?

Goodbye, my friend.

Grace Good-for-Nothing

'Oh God,' I said, once the video ended. I didn't like this. I felt like I was being scammed again. I felt like someone had placed a watch in my hand that I didn't want, and I was now expected to pay for it.

I felt like I was having a panic attack and, as I often had done in my life, I compulsively tried to do sums and see patterns for comfort.

The video was three minutes, twenty-two seconds long. *3 into 22 is 7.33. The square root of 3 is 1.73 . . .*

Alberto put the phone away. The heat in the car wasn't making things better. I stared out at the sea. Of all the strange stuff I had just heard, the absolute madness of it, the thing that was left ringing in my ears was the phrase 'my friend'. If I was such a friend, why had she never made contact with me in more than four decades? When Daniel died, when I lost Karl, when I needed a friend, where was she? I kept thinking of Lieke in the garden centre.

She didn't give you the house for nothing. She was recruiting you. It was a trap. You are her replacement.

'Oh,' I said. 'This is too much. I didn't choose this. Why do I need this gift?'

'All I know is that it is rare to be chosen. And it is a lucky thing that you were . . . Christina knew it had to be you. She had seen the future.'

That was it. That was the moment. That was when the scales tipped. That was when I completely forgot about the enhanced taste of orange juice or the new wonders around me. That was when I realised Christina's act wasn't just selfless generosity.

'It's like a cult,' I said. 'It's like a sinister cult.'

'Well, look, I didn't necessarily approve of Christina's methods—'

'They were your methods too. You could have spelled it out to me.'

'It would have been the easiest thing in the world to send you away. I warned you. But you wanted to know the truth. I told you this would change you. The truth is, it wasn't Christina who chose you, or me, it was La Presencia itself. She just saw it. Out of the thousands of people Christina knew in her life, you were the only one it wanted. My powers are weak next to yours. They were weak next to Christina's. They were once strong but they have faded. They have retreated like a low tide. But you are special. See what you managed to do, just there in the church . . .'

'I am not special,' I said. Those were the easiest four words I had ever said. The voice of a feeling I'd had for seventy-two years. A deep awareness of my own mediocrity. 'Why would I be special? I am a crotchety old Brit. I am a retired maths teacher from the middle of nowhere. I am a big nothing, is who I am. A big nada. No, not even that. I am not a zero, I am a minus. I am a mediocrity who has never had any impact on the world. Except occasionally for the worse. My sweet little son Daniel died because I let him out on his bike in the pouring rain while I read a bloody catalogue because I apparently thought that was more interesting than going into town with him. He died beneath the wheels of a Royal Mail van. I am the person who never made it. The one who lets people down at the last hurdle. The one who lets bad things happen. The one who settles for less because that is what she deserves. Who never got the job she wanted at the university. Who became a middle-of-the-road teacher who probably put more people off the subject. The one who was unfaithful to her husband. I have been useless over and over again. I can't do this. It's a mistake. I am not free of guilt and sin like Joan bloody Bonanova. I am a bad person. I will never be any good at this. I will never be able to send a magic signal to all the animals. And I don't think I want to.' My heart was racing. 'I. Am. Not. Special.'

'Quite the opposite,' said Alberto, as smug as ever. 'Christina tried to think of everyone she knew. And everyone she had *ever* known. And she knew a *lot* of people. She could predict every scenario, every possibility. There were others who La Presencia would have come to, but none would have had the same response. That is why you went unconscious in the water. And the fact that you have been able to travel back to 1855 and break lobster tanks and stab forks in the legs of men with your own mind just confirms it. This is all unusual – muy, *muy* raro . . .'

'I shouldn't have stuck a fork in that man's leg,' I said, remorsefully. 'He wasn't all bad.'

'No. Maybe not. But what if someone really was *all bad*? What if they were a murderer? What if they had planned to murder your friend? What if you could prevent them murdering—'

'I hardly knew Christina,' I snapped. 'She wasn't my friend!'

And Alberto nodded. He looked like I actually *had* slapped him. 'Well, maybe. But she was *my* friend. She was a good person. Complicated? Yes. A poor mother? Maybe. But good. A rare person.'

And I thought for a second he might cry, and to my shame that seemed to make me more rather than less angry.

'I am not special.' I said it again, like a maniac. 'I am a selfish person. I failed at the one thing a mother should be able to do. I am Grace Good-for-Nothing. I don't save people. I let people die. Like I let my own darling Daniel die. I have never done a single brave thing in my life. Apart from move to Ibiza. Which I now realise was the biggest of all my mistakes.'

'You were a teacher. What is better than being a teacher?' Alberto wasn't giving up. His slappable face kept talking. 'It saw something in you. Not who you have been but who you could be. La Presencia isn't concerned with surfaces. It is concerned with depths.'

'I'm in my seventies. I'm too old for sentimental fridge-magnet theories and *way* too old for who I *could* be.'

Alberto tutted, doubtfully. 'Well, I am seventy-nine. And I don't own a fridge. And I *love* sentimental theories. I am a sentimental man. And I am booked in for my first samba class next Tuesday. Then I am going to Cova Santa to dance in a cave and drink lemonade. This is Ibiza. Age is nothing.'

'This may be Ibiza. But this is not me. I don't belong here.'

'I sometimes think people who don't like sentimentality actually don't like feeling anything at all. They prefer to look at the whole world with scorn.'

'Well, I don't care what you think. I was very fine not feeling anything at all. I don't *want* to feel a single thing. And you had no right to make me.'

It had all been a trap. The house. The photo of the necklace. Every word that had come out of Alberto's mouth.

And besides, I would not be able to save anyone. I would only make things worse. That was my way.

'I've had enough of this,' I said, starting the car. 'I'm going home. I can help people with the talents at home. I'm going to drive to the airport—'

'My research suggests that the further away from La Presencia you are, the less power—'

'I don't care.'

'Shall we wait till tomorrow when you've had time to digest?'

I didn't want a tomorrow of this. I wanted to go back. I would rather never have tasted the infinite new joy of orange juice than have all *this*. I didn't want to dance in a cave. I wanted to sit on my sofa and numb myself in front of a quiz show. Allowing myself to feel infinite joy would ultimately lead me to feel infinite pain. And I had felt that and I didn't want to go back there. I craved, suddenly, uneventful, familiar emptiness. I was actually missing anhedonia.

'No. I am going *home. Home. Home.*'

The word gave me comfort. It felt solid. Like a rock in the ocean.

'But the island needs you. The people and animals here need you. You will be able to do good. Not just for . . . lobsters . . . but in general. And there is still a potential killer out there. Someone human or something else. And you could stop them. And you won't be able to do that at home. The further away you are, the fewer talents you have.'

I ignored him. I tried to block out his words the way I block out tinnitus. I drove with one single feeling.

I can't wait to leave this island.

Horse

It was a twenty-minute drive to the airport, but I was trying to make it in ten. Alberto was coming with me. The only reason he was coming with me was because I couldn't leave him in the middle of nowhere at Es Cubells. Well, that and he wanted to come with me. And someone would have to have Christina's car.

We drove inland and passed a man whizzing along the road on an e-bike, smiling in the sun. The bike was red. I ran through the first numbers in the Fibonacci sequence.

0, 1, 1, 2, 3, 5, 8, 13, 21, 34 . . .

I realised that is what my time on the island had been like. A continuing rising up of everything that preceded it, incident added onto incident, things rocketing skyward into madness.

As we drove on, we passed a giant billboard with Lieke's face on it. It was like looking at an illusion. I remembered her pain, her inner fragility and outer fury, and there she was dominating the skyline like something stronger than feelings.

I looked at her face and saw her mother's eyes.

I kept driving. I ignored Alberto. I drove ahead underneath that cloudless blue sky, clenching the steering wheel so tight I caught another memory of Christina's.

She was outside a hotel. There were a group of protesters at a building site. I saw a sign in my mind. *Eighth Wonder, Cala Llonga, Coming Soon.* Christina was with a woman with messy dark hair and glasses. I knew this woman. She had been in a vision. The woman sitting in this very car with Christina. And now I realised I had seen her before. At the airport. She was the first person I had ever seen on this island. The woman with the Einstein T-shirt who had smiled at me. But just as I recognised her the vision shifted.

The day became a night and the air became a flood.

She was now in the sea.

Christina, I mean.

She was swimming down and down, through dark water, towards the glowing sphere that didn't become a cloud but this time held and even expanded, and a hole emerged right through it. A widening aperture. Right through the sphere. It became a tunnel, even brighter than the sphere, a silvery and impossible brightness. And she swam through it, through the portal, thinking of her daughter and hoping she would be safe.

And when I came out of this micro-trance Alberto's hand was on my arm. He was shouting my name as loud as my father used to. There was a large chestnut horse and rider up ahead. I nearly hit them but swerved in time. The mare reared, but the rider stayed in the saddle, her feet pressing hard into the stirrups. I felt the animal's panic beat through me like a drum.

'It's okay,' said Alberto, his voice fading like a wave as I focused on the road. 'It's okay, it's okay, it's okay . . .'

Airport

'The next available flight to anywhere in England,' I told the woman with the strained smile behind the flight desk. Her name badge told me she was called Gabriela, but it didn't tell me she was feeling a bit bloated and crampy and wishing she had more peppermint tablets. Or that she was six and a half hours into her shift. I really wished I knew no more than her name badge.

'There is a flight to Gatwick this evening. It leaves at seven-fifty p.m. I can check if there is any availability.'

'Perfect, yes. That'll be fine.'

I had no real plan. I would return to the bungalow. I would sell Christina's house remotely. I would donate the money to charity. But that was it. That condition hadn't been in the lawyer's letter. These 'talents' weren't really talents. They would just cause more harm. As Gabriela busied herself at the computer I thought of that poor horse and rider I had nearly run into. I thought of a fork sticking out of a leg. Christina had made a mistake. I wouldn't be a help here, I'd be a harm. Just as I'd always been.

I looked around, wondering if Alberto had left yet. He said he was going to wait in the car park for a little while 'just in case'. I felt a tinge of sadness. A tiny grief. Some strange part of me wanted to still be sitting next to him. *Snap out of it, Grace. This is the right thing to do.*

There was a mother with a tired toddler in her arms and a small suitcase as hand luggage. The mother kissed the child's forehead. I saw a love coloured like indigo. I moved my gaze swiftly away, as I didn't want to know too much about them and certainly didn't want to feel what they were feeling. I wanted to feel nothing. I cursed Christina and this *fullness* she had given me. This *duende*. I wanted to feel no attachment to anything.

There were minds everywhere, their thoughts scattered through the air like pollen. There was a young woman on her own, looking forward to seeing her family. I so wished I had Karl to go home to. To give me a hug at Gatwick. To tell me he had missed me and that everything was going to be okay.

My eyes fell on a digital image I recognised, as it was almost identical to the billboard over the road from the house. The hotel, complete with the inset photo of a luxury bedroom.

Open now. The latest Eighth Wonder Spa Resort Hotel, Cala Llonga, Ibiza. Visualise your dreams and make them reality.

This triggered a thought. A memory of things that had been said to me. The taxi driver. Sabine. Things began to fall into place. I thought of Christina and Marta, side by side. I thought of the protest. The advert almost seemed like a warning.

Others are in danger . . .

A man was looking at the advert. I sensed his pride. He was standing next to a suitcase and wearing a linen suit. He had greased-back hair. He was quite young. Under forty. But then, everyone was quite young. (When you hit your seventies the whole world is basically one big crèche and everyone in it an abandoned toddler.) It wasn't the clothes or hair or face or youthfulness that interested me. Or even his tired and flustered mind, full of jagged airport thoughts and distractions. It was one of the magazines he was holding. *DJ* magazine. On the cover was a picture of Lieke. 'The New Queen of Ibiza Takes the Throne'.

'Just checking the seating availability now,' said Gabriela, with friendly efficiency.

And as I saw her face focus and her eyes squint towards the computer screen, I saw her hugging her children in her apartment building in Santa Eulalia. She hardly looked older than she did now, save for a strand or two of grey hair. She was trying to reassure the children it was going to be okay.

'Stop,' I told myself.

'Are you okay?' Gabriela asked me, her face and mind full of concern.

'Yes. Sorry. Yes. I'm just a nervous flyer.'

'Oh,' said Gabriela now, 'I am sorry to hear that. But it is actually the safest form of transport. Now, we do have some availability on that flight to Gatwick. Would you like to be near the aisle or the window?'

I was hardly listening. 'You can't marry him.'

'Sorry?'

'In two months you will leave your children with your father and you will go to London and you will fall in love with a man – a banker who is about to retire at the age of forty-two – and he will come with you to Ibiza, and you will end up marrying him. You can't marry this man. Please. Trust me. You will think he is good for you, but he will not be . . .'

She stared at me with a confused smile. 'How do you know I am going to London?'

'Please. Just trust me.'

And I saw her in a different future now, happy, at the go-kart track with her children, and I understood why Christina had wanted to help people the way she had. If you had the ability to help people, then maybe there was also an obligation to do just that. Just because I hadn't asked for something didn't mean I could walk away from it.

Just then I caught sight of a woman I vaguely recognised, heading over to arrivals. A tall woman with a solemn face and ruffled hair like a half-blown dandelion. It was the doctor. The one Alberto had become agitated around, suddenly wanting to leave. She was sipping a coffee and here to pick up her mother, who was flying in from Bilbao. And then it came. The image of her with Alberto. In a small side room at the hospital, in the oncology department, a month ago. Telling him 'El cáncer es agresivo' and running through treatment options and Alberto just staring at her, dumbfounded. Then the doctor disappeared out of view.

'Hello, señora?' Gabriela said, aware I was in a kind of trance. 'Señora? Do you still want this flight?'

I smiled at Gabriela. Then grabbed the handle of my case. 'I'm . . . I've got to go . . .'

It was no good. I knew I was staying.

Protection

I kept thinking of what Christina said. *It is impossible to feel life so deeply and not want to protect it . . .* There was no denying the change inside me. In understanding previously hidden things – thoughts, futures – I was now unable to kid myself with the sad but comforting illusion that the world was done with me. That I could retreat and fade away and it would make no difference.

You can't stay still in a moving universe. Change had happened. The shelter of grief and self-pity had been lifted. I couldn't protect myself by doing nothing. Protection is something we can only give, not something we can always receive. And I was going to do what I could to help what needed to be helped.

The Closed Door

I climbed into the car, which was parked a short walk from the terminal.

Alberto had the radio on. He was bobbing his head as Spanish voices rapped to a hip-swaying beat.

'Reggaeton,' explained Alberto, as if I had returned for a lesson in musical genres. 'It's been around for ever but people are into it like never before . . . It has a sensual energy to it, no?'

'Just so long as you keep that sensual energy to yourself,' I told him, in a clipped way.

Alberto looked at his watch and shrugged.

'What?' I asked him.

'It's just interesting,' he said, remarking on my decision to walk out of the airport. 'I thought you would be twenty minutes earlier.'

'I really was going to go, you know.'

'Then why did you come back?'

But then he caught a glimpse of it. In my thoughts. So I helped him on his way. 'I saw someone in there who I recognised from the hospital. A doctor. An oncologist.'

He looked like he had been punched. Winded. He switched the music off. We stayed parked even as cars circled us, looking for a spot.

'I'm sorry,' I said. 'I don't mean to pry.'

He bit his lip. Agitated. Distraught.

'It's just I supposedly have extra-sensory powers beyond anyone,' I went on, 'and yet I can't access a single thing about you. You are a closed door. I can't see anything. I can understand a lobster or a lizard or a horse more than I can understand you. Why don't you let me inside? I want to help. If something is wrong with you, I want to be there. As a . . . as a . . . as a *friend*. And I know there is more danger. Others will need to be protected. So I am staying. But I won't be able to help if I don't know who to trust. And I need to trust you.'

He sat there for a moment. He seemed to be weighing something up. A car beeped at us. Alberto leaned out the window and swore at the driver.

'Okay,' he said, calming down. 'Before we see Marta I need to tell you something. I know a little roadside café on the way. A quiet place . . . They serve the most beautiful orange juice. Freshly squeezed.'

Unsipped Juice

We sat inside a basic roadside café, next to a broken pinball machine.

The wall was lined with posters for old club nights from the last century, the text in a hybrid of Spanish and English.

Ku presents Fantasy. Domingo 17 de julio de 1980.

Flower Power at Pacha. Fiesta de cierre, 1988.

Moondance at Space. Every Wednesday/Todos los miércoles, 1992.

I thought of all the wild parties that had taken place while me and Karl had been raising Daniel, in our tight little enclosed family world. When you have a child, the world slips away for a while. You become your own satellite planet and forget that other things exist unless you make an effort to look. That other lives, as important as your own, are happening all over the place. Some of them happening glamorously in Ibizan nightclubs.

Alberto, too, was staring at the posters.

'Good times,' he said, as we waited for our orange juice. 'There was Pacha, of course. Basically a disco in a farmhouse. To this day it is still essentially a casa payesa. That was the place the jet set went to right from the start, when it was no more than a finca with a disco in the seventies. Then there was Ku. Which was pure excess. You know, when Freddie Mercury and Montserrat Caballé filmed their video for the song "Barcelona", they did it at Ku because Ku was on an operatic scale. Ku was the place to be. Polysexual, glamorous, eclectic. David Bowie, Grace Jones, Mick Jagger . . . you name them, they were there. It was a beacon for every wild soul, every creative crackpot out there. This giant avant-garde disco in the hills in the middle of the island. Did you know these places used to be open-air? Ku was a kind of outdoor Studio 54. Amnesia was a little wilder, a little . . . looser. Just dancing under the stars right through the night. Hippies, film stars, Indian gurus, artists, slackers, musicians, writers, elegant people, scruffy people, those first ravers, gay and straight and everything in between before it all became such an industry . . . We used to go and drink and smoke some pot and take the magic mushrooms and dance next to the palm trees . . .'

'You may not know this about me,' I told him, surprised by my own impatience, 'and I don't mean to offend you, but I am not particularly interested in the detailed history of Ibizan nightclubs.'

Our orange juices arrived.

I knew it would taste ecstatic, so I decided not to sip it until Alberto actually got to the reason we were here. Maybe that is what I had been doing for too long. Choosing not to enjoy, denying myself a pleasurable life.

'What about whales?' he asked.

I wondered if he was ever going to talk about the vision of him and the doctor I had seen at the airport. The one that had kept me here. 'Sorry?'

'Yes. You are not interested in wild parties. So what about whales? Are you interested in them?'

And then I asked the question everyone probably asked him at some point in a conversation. 'What are you on about, Alberto?'

The 52-Hertz Whale

'There is a whale in the ocean,' he told me, after a gulp of his juice.

'There are lots of whales in the ocean.'

He nodded. 'This whale is different. This whale is a very lonely whale.'

'Oh. Poor whale.'

'Do you know why he is lonely?'

I shrugged. 'He hasn't got an internet connection?'

He smiled his wide and wonky smile. 'Kind of. It's the sound of its call. Whales are big communicators. They call all the time, but it has to be the right frequency. But this whale uses a very unusual high frequency to make his calls. Fifty-two hertz. It is the world's loneliest whale because no other whale understands calls at that frequency. It is a blue whale, and blue whales are much lower. Blue whales are the Barry White of marine mammals. Deep, deep, deep. So the poor high-pitched creature has to swim through the ocean all alone, finding it impossible to make friends and with no one to hear his call.'

He was smiling, but his eyes were glazed with sadness. 'I was that whale. I was writing about incredible things, and no one was on my wavelength. No one understood me. They thought I was a joke. Like a high-pitched whale. Even my daughter Marta didn't understand me for a while. But I stayed doing what I believed in. And this was before I even came into contact with La Presencia. I just knew. I was open-minded . . .'

I shook my head. 'So what happened?'

'What?'

'To close your mind?'

He was insulted by this. He shrank back on his chair. He muttered something rude in Catalan that he forgot I could understand. 'My mind is open. I accept the existence of more species than—'

'I am not talking about that. I am not talking about species. I am talking about thoughts. I am talking about the wall you have built around yourself. Why have you shut yourself away?'

He knew what I was talking about. He knew that all I got was that grey-green sadness and his wide smiles of denial.

I pointed to a young couple getting off a hired moped at the petrol station across the road, heading to the cash machine outside the neighbouring CaixaBank.

'I can read their minds as easy as anything. They both spent the day on luxurious loungers on the pale sands of Es Cavallet beach and ate grilled calamari and salted sea bass at El Chiringuito restaurant, where they both surreptitiously held eye contact with attractive strangers. Their relationship will dissolve two weeks after they return to Berlin. And they are a good hundred metres away. Yet you. You are right in front of me, and I don't know anything.'

My words were just midges in the air. He was elsewhere.

There was music playing faintly in the background. 'Do you like this song?' he asked, reverting to one of his favourite subjects. Music. 'Listen. It is called "The Last Day Of Summer". It is by The Cure. I wasn't really the goth era. I was the Rolling Stones era. I was protest music. Soul and Dylan and Joan Baez and Sam Cooke and Gil Scott-Heron. Imagine me in eyeliner! But I've always tried to keep my mind open to later music. It is such a beautiful song. Julia – my wife – she loved The Cure. We saw them at the Palau Sant Jordi in Barcelona. She liked this song a lot too. It is so underrated. It is a bit sad and not my normal thing. But listen. Listen to those guitars, how they create shapes, like a forest. Then his voice comes in and it is as natural as a shadow.' He paused. 'This song is exquisite.'

He reminded me a little of Karl in that moment. The way he talked about music as a kind of shield, so he could talk about emotion without talking about *his* emotion. I was going to get him back on topic, but then I realised this *was* the topic. In feeling the music, in feeling its memories and melancholy, he was letting it open himself up.

And when he began to open, I sensed he was hurting. 'I'm sorry,' I said. 'It's just, you know, I just thought it would be great to know a bit more about you.' I was going to ask directly if he was ill, but it felt too indelicate so instead I said: 'For instance, it would be lovely to know what you thought of Christina.'

He sighed. It was a slow, mournful sigh. 'She was special. She made me feel like I wasn't a fifty-two-hertz whale. She was on my wavelength.'

I raised an eyebrow. 'Interesting.'

'No,' he said. 'It was never like that.' He reconsidered while staring philosophically at his juice. 'Well, okay, it was a *little* like that. We had a great time. There was a romantic connection at the start. She had recently divorced, and Julia had died not long before. Christina was very good to me, and Marta liked her. For a few weeks that became something else. Why are you asking all this?' He raised a presumptuous eyebrow. 'It's because I am more magnetic than Es Vedrà, right?'

I stared at the smile adorning his sun-battered, bearded face. There was something about him, I supposed. Something wild and pure and out of time. A kind of infuriating but attractive stubbornness that suggested he wasn't just the metaphoric lonely whale but also that he *wanted* to be so.

He was reading me. 'If you fit in, you disappear, right?'

'I don't know. I have always tried to fit in. I don't want to go against the grain. It gives you splinters.'

'Well, you are different now, Grace. And trust me, it isn't so bad to be unique. You always know you are there. You know which one you are.'

Then I locked eyes with him for a moment and I felt something shifting inside him. As if suddenly he was opening the book of himself for me to read. He held my hand as it rested on the small table. It wasn't strange. It was the gesture of a pure friend.

I decided this was the time. 'That day at the hospital. You said the reason we had to get out was because we had to keep things secret.'

'Yes . . .'

'Yes, but you suddenly wanted to get out. And that made no sense. I mean, you never hide your beliefs. You have written books on them. People at hippy markets and grocery stores know about you and your "mad theories". So why did we need to get out of the hospital?'

He hesitated. 'I saw someone. Someone I know.'

'The doctor. The one I saw at the airport?'

The pause was long. 'Yes. Dr Pérez. The oncologist. I had to get out of there. I am sorry. I didn't want you to know. Or anyone to know. Especially Marta. I am sorry. I should have been honest but—'

'Will it be okay?'

'I've had all the tests on my pancreas. The blood tests, ultrasound, everything . . . And she thinks I should have treatment, but she doesn't realise I can see the outcome. I can see my own future. Whatever I do, it only changes the date by a week or so. Three weeks at most. We see the future that exists if we do nothing. That is true. But sometimes there is nothing we *can* do. At the moment I am fine, but eventually . . .'

I had no idea what to say. I held his hand again. Squeezed it. The wall was down. I saw everything now. He only had about two months. At most. His decline would be steep in his last days. He had no idea if he was going to follow Christina into that other world. I felt his sadness flow into me. But it wasn't just sadness now. In fact, the sadness was fading. It was gratitude, relief and a kind of calm contemplation.

'I haven't wanted to upset anyone.'

'But La Presencia,' I said. 'It heals things. Can't it heal you?'

He shook his head. 'It only comes to you once. Now, Salacia might be different. If I choose to try and take that one-way ticket, I may have a chance of being healed. Who knows? I imagine it's possible. It might give me years. But it can't make me or anyone immortal here. Earthlings aren't meant to be immortal, Grace.'

I remembered his reaction to the discovery that Francisco had made it to Salacia. That was why it was so important to him. It could be a way out.

I tried not to cry.

'The air is sweet there,' I told him. 'The sea is marvellous. Can you imagine the creatures that live there?'

He smiled now, and the smile seemed entirely real. 'But for now, I am here. And the air and the sea here are beautiful too, and so I am staying . . . And I have never felt more alive.'

I entered his mind completely now.

It was wide open.

Like a meadow.

I went to him, inside his mind, and I was with him, and we just stayed there and we didn't have to say anything. We were just together.

In a state of understanding.

On the same frequency.

It was lovely.

We sipped orange juice together.

Marta and the Second Law of Thermodynamics

Marta lived on a finca in the north of the island. It was a calming but slightly chaotic place, with fig trees in the garden and cats roaming in and out of the house. If I'd been Alberto, I would have definitely taken her offer of the spare room. It was a definite step up from an old goat-bitten futon on the floor of his scuba office.

'She has no extra-sensory talents,' Alberto had told me, in a quiet and secretive and sensitive way. 'La Presencia never came to her. But she is super-intelligent.' Marta had studied at the University of Navarra and tutored there remotely and part-time. 'The best university,' Alberto said, with a pride that even I had to admit was charming, seeing that he had such a ferocious gripe with academia in general. 'It breeds geniuses, Spanish prime ministers, polar explorers, film directors and the very best scientists. Everyone likes her. And she has an investigative mind. She is a brilliant astrophysicist and finds logic where no one else can. If we want to find who was after Christina, we need her. She is better at this than me.'

'But she doesn't know?'

'No. I will tell her,' Alberto said. 'About my illness. I promise. But not today.'

I sighed. It was his decision. I got out of the car. The early evening sun, if anything, burned even hotter here, and it seemed to radiate from the hills all around the pine-coated valley.

'Hola, Grace, welcome. It is lovely to meet you.'

She was quite different to her father – less out-there and gregarious, more introverted. No. Not introverted. It is wrong to call the most successful environmentalist in Ibiza's history introverted. Someone who, I would soon discover, could stand in front of thousands of people and talk about the perils of ecological destruction – her passion for the environment was an offshoot of her astrophysicist's curiosity for the universe – and make them act to change it. But what I mean is there was a quietness to her. She had no need to make unnecessary noise. When she spoke, and she spoke quite a bit, it was for a reason. She had his wide smile as she looked up at us from the large cardboard sign she was in the middle of painting.

I had seen Marta before. The woman with glasses and wild hair that I had seen at the airport wearing the Einstein T-shirt. And in the visions with Christina. She was wearing cut-off denim shorts, like her father, and a faded T-shirt that said *Space* on it. Space was the name of a former nightclub but also apt for an astrophysicist. Marta had a lot of great T-shirts, I would discover. She also had a partner – an architect from Switzerland called Lina – but she was away. It was the woman she had been saying goodbye to the first time I saw her.

'I think I saw you,' I said, 'at the airport . . .'

Marta gave me a curious smile. 'Really?'

It was probably still too early to tell her I had also seen her in visions given to me by touching a steering wheel.

There was a three-legged cat who seemed to like me. He rubbed his head against my calves and thought warm feline thoughts.

Marta was easier to mind-read than her father. Every smile was an open door. It was a very intricate mind, an overgrown mental garden backlit by golden warmth, but there was a nervousness, a sense of incompleteness. No. That's not quite it. You see, people are like pieces of music. We don't hear their songs because very few people play them out loud. But minds play their own notes, and Marta felt stuck in a minor key. There was a theme to her, as there is a theme to everyone. My theme had always been guilt. Hers was of being overlooked, *unchosen*. Something underlined to her by the fact that La Presencia had never come to her, despite diving so often near it and spending much research time on it. But Alberto looked at her with pride whenever she spoke, seeing nothing but pure magic in his daughter.

We sat in the small garden beneath the shade of one of those fig trees. Marta brought out a jug of red wine. Music from the radio travelled to us from the kitchen window. 'Mr Tambourine Man'. I stared at the words on the sign she was painting: *NOS ALZAMOS COMO EL OCÉANO. We rise like the ocean.* There was an attentively painted picture of a globe on it.

'Bob Dylan lived in Formentera for a couple of years,' Alberto told me. 'He lived in the lighthouse . . .'

'Papá, I don't think Grace wants to talk about Bob Dylan.' Her voice was soft but firm enough. 'Tell us, Grace – how are you feeling? I have heard everything. You have had quite the time.'

'I don't know,' I said, honestly. 'Overwhelmed, I suppose. I like your sign.'

'Ahh, muchas gracias. I am a bit of a messy artist. There is going to be a protest.'

'Yes. I've heard.'

Her mind fell into shadow. 'Christina had wanted to be there. It will feel lonely without her. But she is in Salacia now. I truly believe that. And now you are here.'

'Yes.'

I sipped the wine, tasting sunshine and earth.

'I have found it a bit of a challenge,' I told her. 'The whole "being given alien powers" thing. I very nearly went home. Back to England.'

'What stopped you?'

Before I had time to answer the cat jumped onto my knee.

'That's Sancho,' Marta said. 'He doesn't normally like strangers. You are honoured.'

I felt the love emanating from the creature. I know there is a common misconception that cats are somehow less loving than dogs. This is nonsense. The love a cat can give you is sudden and warm. It is just that a cat's love comes completely free of any moral or ethical principles. It is love for the hell of it. It is an entirely recreational love. In-the-moment love. But it is still, somehow, love.

'The protest is about the hotel they are building in Es Vedrà, right?'

'Yes.'

Marta went back to painting her sign. She was working on her second globe. 'On the subject of aliens . . . are you familiar with the concept of "dissipation-driven adaptation"?' Her English was, if anything, even better than her dad's.

I shook my head. It was very possibly in my head somewhere. The way everything was now. But some things still took effort. And astrophysics seemed to be her safe space, just as mathematics was mine, and I liked to hear her talk about it.

'Well, basically, it explains how life is inevitable. You see, traditionally people believed life was a general impossibility and Earth was the exception to the rule. Humans were flukes. The Second Law of Thermodynamics said disorder increases in any system.'

'I worked in a school,' I said, staring at a fresh fig hanging from the tree. Bulbous and purple and beautiful. 'I have seen that play out.'

I turned back to Marta. She smiled and pushed her glasses up her nose. There was a tiny dab of green paint on her chin. 'And life was seen as unlikely because it requires the opposite of disorder. Life is order out of chaos. Life is cold becoming warmth. So alien life was seen as scientifically unlikely. But then came a new hypothesis that says no, actually, as heat is added to groups of atoms those atoms *organise* to receive that energy. Order, not disorder, happens. So what that means is life is the order of things. Life eventually happens. Life is now seen as the logical thing. It used to be that idiots believed in aliens and intellectuals dismissed it. Now it is the other way around. You see? Life is inescapable if this process occurs many millions of times over. And La Presencia is basically an intergalactic activist. It is here to protect things. It also has organised itself. Just as we need to. That is what the protest against this stupid hotel will be. People organising themselves like atoms for the sake of life.'

'Like atoms,' mumbled Alberto.

His daughter stared at him, a little worry floating across her face. 'You have been wearing the sunscreen I brought you?

Yes. Yes. I wear it every day. I am not a lotion person, Grace. I have never had a beauty routine. The sea is my bath. But Marta worries about me. And I wear it because I like the smell of coconuts.'

This satisfied her.

'We are in a galaxy with roughly a hundred billion stars, each with at least one planet orbiting it, so there are a *lot* of planets out there,' she said. She was getting animated now. I could feel her emotion. I focused on her face and I saw a memory of hers, of being laughed at in school for reading a book on UFOs.

'And ten billion of those stars are like our sun, and two billion have exoplanets on which the conditions for life are pretty much like ours. Two *billion*.' Alberto looked at his daughter now with not just pride but something else. Sadness glistened in his eyes. 'Papá,' Marta said. '¿Estás bien?'

'Yes. Yes. I am fine. It is nothing.'

Alberto's voice scratched with emotion. He stood up and twisted a fig from the tree. The one I had been staring at. 'La vida imposible is not so impossible. Aliens are everywhere. And many on Earth have seen them with their own eyes. But they are never believed.'

He handed me the fig. I stared at it.

'Give it a try,' he said.

And so I did.

A Fig

There is nothing like tasting a fig straight from the tree, sun-warmed and tender. You can eat the whole of it. The whole thing. The skin, the purple flesh, the seeds. Divine. Eat the whole fig, that's my advice. And take it from the tree, right in that moment, when you get the chance.

Elvis Presley and the Broken Glass

After savouring the fig, I remembered something I'd heard about on the radio.

'The Goldilocks zone,' I said.

'Yes,' Marta nodded quickly, placing her paintbrush down and picking up her wine.

I had an ominous feeling.

I didn't have any understanding of the feeling except that it was bad.

It was an alertness. That something was suddenly wrong. Alberto's eyes widened. I wasn't quite sure if he was feeling it, or if he was feeling me feel it.

'Not too hot, not too cold . . .' Marta continued, oblivious. 'Just like how Goldilocks liked her porridge. And two billion planets in the Goldilocks zone is a *lot*. It would, rationally, be far harder to believe we are the only one in two billion and it . . .'

It was then that something strange happened. To the glass in her hand. Cracks emerged, like an evolving spider web. At first I thought Marta might be squeezing the glass too tight.

'Careful. The glass.'

But that wasn't it.

If she was holding the glass too tight, it would have instantaneously broken. This was something different. This was a *display* of cracked glass. This was *theatre*. It was like it wanted to be noticed as something unnatural, and Marta was so mesmerised and confused by the sight she didn't place the glass down but just stared at it. And then, just at the point that Marta came to her senses, it smashed completely and the red wine dropped like blood onto the placard, seeping into the cardboard.

She was startled. '¿Qué mierda?'

The placard was ruined. The Earth was now as red as Mars.

'Are you okay?' Alberto and I asked, simultaneously, in separate languages.

'What just happened?' Marta asked.

Alberto looked around. To see if someone was there, amid the bushes or fig trees.

And then something else.

The radio.

The radio stopped playing Bob Dylan and became a loud hiss of static.

And then the static slowly shaped itself into music. Another song. 'Heartbreak Hotel' by Elvis Presley. But straight into the middle of it. His curled lip of a voice floating over the warm air with a sinister menace.

Marta went to switch off the radio. She came back with a cloth and a dustpan and brush as I started to pick up pieces of glass.

Alberto stared at the wine-soaked cardboard.

'It's a warning. It's whoever wanted to kill Christina.' He stared at his daughter with frowning concern. 'It wants you to stop. You can't do the protest, Marta.'

'Papá, don't be stupid,' his daughter told him. Not for the first time, I sensed.

Others are in danger . . .

That is what Christina had said.

I wasn't scared. In fact, I was pleased I hadn't got on the plane right then. I felt like I was needed here.

I stroked Sancho as a thought circled my mind. 'Christina wanted to take part in the protest, didn't she?'

Marta swept up the glass. 'She did. She helped come up with the idea.'

'And you protested together before, right?'

'Many times.'

'And you don't know exactly who you are protesting against this time? You don't know who the hotel company is?'

'No. It's all been very secret. We just know the plan has been approved by the local government.'

'Eighth Wonder,' I said.

'What about it?'

'You protested against one of their hotels. In Cala Llonga.'

Marta looked at me. Alberto looked at me. It was a collective realisation.

'You know about the goats, don't you?' I asked them both. 'The goats that were shot on Es Vedrà for the hotel?'

Alberto nodded, his face dappled in shade. 'Yes. I felt it the moment I saw you. After the lobsters.'

This troubled Marta more than the glass. 'Why didn't they just move them?'

'Because the person who gave the orders didn't care,' I said. It was a hypothesis. I couldn't know for sure, but it seemed increasingly the case. 'In fact, I think they quite relished the idea.'

'Where is this going?' Alberto wondered.

'Well, the thing is, the people who shot them were on a boat. The boat had a tiny logo on it, but I could see it in my head.'

Marta shook her head. 'The local government are stupid. But they are not that stupid. Not after all the trouble with Cala Llonga. Eighth Wonder is the very worst company ever to set foot here. They would never have given the permission to . . .'

Her voice faltered. She was holding the dustpan full of broken glass. Shade from the branches of the fig tree decorated her face.

'There was a man who visited Christina,' I said. 'There were lots of people but one was a rich hotelier. The taxi driver told me on the first night I was here. He said his name began with an A. Originally I thought the A might be for Alberto but he said he was well dressed.'

'Very nice,' grumbled Alberto, looking down at his tatty shorts.

'He had just been to the most expensive restaurant. I have tried to access Christina's memories of him but can't. There is a block.'

Marta's thoughts were a bubbling cauldron. 'The world's most expensive restaurant. That place by the Hard Rock. Where you wear virtual-reality goggles. It's a gimmick. For rich tourists and flash DJs . . . for people with more money than sense.'

I thought of Karl. How he would have tutted at the idea. I remembered how he turned his nose up at a pizza chain after they had put big holes in the middle of some of their pizzas and branded them diet options. ('How stupid do they think people are?') Complaining about restaurants had been one of his hobbies. A recreational grouchiness.

'Submarine,' said Alberto. 'That's the name of the restaurant.'

'No,' corrected Marta. 'There is no restaurant in Ibiza called Submarine. It's called Sublimotion.'

'Well, it should be called Submarine. What kind of a name is Sublimotion?'

Marta's whole mind eye-rolled. 'Papá, por favor. Focus.'

Alberto sighed. 'Look, we need to be careful we don't jump to conclusions. A lot of people were interested in her because she told the future. Almost every day she changed lives. From her stall at Las Dalias. Or, sometimes, from her house. I always thought it was a bad idea, but it was a way she could help people . . .'

I shook my head. 'Whoever wanted to kill poor Christina was very sure of the future. That was why they wanted to kill her. She was going to stop them doing what they wanted to do. And what did she want to stop? The destruction of nature on Ibiza.'

'Yes,' said Marta. 'And the worst developer is Eighth Wonder. Run by Art Butler.'

'A is Art,' muttered Alberto.

Marta nodded. 'Eco retreats, offering those who can afford it meditation and cryotherapy and biohacking and charcoal smoothies. They are these hypocritical green hotels complete with responsibly sourced restaurants that somehow always exist in former nature reserves. They preach sustainability then illegally dump raw sewage in the Mediterranean.'

Marta was kneeling, but upright, meaning business. In her flow. She tucked a stray strand of hair behind her ear. 'He has a couple in the States. Last year he opened one in Bali . . . But Ibiza is where he started. He now has seven here. This was always his testing ground. You see, Ibiza has been an aspirational place. What works here becomes cloned elsewhere, taking the heart out of it. It's always been that way. Discos, beach clubs, agroturismo, wellness retreats, whatever . . . Take paradise, package it, and make people very rich.'

Alberto nodded, wondering why he hadn't made the connection. Wondering what force had been stopping him realising the most obvious thing – that the person Christina had protested against had been the person who endangered her. And he hadn't made the connection, he surmised, because Art Butler hadn't let him. 'The bigshot Brit,' he mumbled to himself. Then something else. 'We should stop this . . . we should stop . . .'

Marta didn't hear him. 'On Ibiza he has messed up the sea with sewage, he has helped make plants and birds extinct, he has damaged the ecosystem, he has screwed over workers. He cares nothing about nature, but pretends to.'

'But does this really mean he planned to do away with Christina? It is a leap.'

'He has a lot of influence,' Marta said, ominously. 'And a lot of money. He has overcome obstacles that no one else would be able to overcome. Protected areas suddenly stop being so protected, and he always promises to preserve species and habitats, but as soon as the planning goes through everything is destroyed. As far as we know he is a human, but if he was human, then Christina would have been able to know he was going to kill her and she didn't. She said there was a block on seeing the person. They had no face.'

I thought of my vision of a faceless person and the Guardia Civil officer with money in his hand. I sensed Marta's mood darken further.

'There was a politician here,' she said, 'Ricardo Martínez, who died mysteriously after blocking the application of an Eighth Wonder resort beside the wetlands at Ses Feixes.'

'That is terrible,' I said. 'But correlation is not—'

That was the last time I would use reality-centred logic in this conversation. Because that was the precise moment reality as I knew it disintegrated entirely and any further logic would have to encompass the preternatural. Because that was when Marta's phone buzzed in her pocket.

It was a text message. It simply said, in English: *To live, stop.*

There was an eerie quiet. A collective holding of breath. The air around us seemed to tighten. Marta's hand was trembling.

'Holy shit,' she exhaled.

'It's him,' Alberto said, in a panic, twitching his head around as if Art Butler was hiding behind a fig tree.

'How?'

'I don't know. But there is something else going on with him. Something *other*.'

'He means the protest. He wants me to stop the protest.'

'Then you should stop the protest,' Alberto suggested, still panicking, his voice no more than gently sculpted air. 'It is what I am saying. We must stop. He can probably do anything he wants to from anywhere on the island. I think it would be wise to stop the protest.'

I had to agree. 'Stop the protest. Yes, Marta, I think your father is right on this.'

'Papá, you know that is not possible.'

'Not possible is always possible. What number was the text from?' Alberto asked, joining his daughter and craning his neck to look. 'It looks weird. Two, seven, one, eight, two, eight, one—'

'Wait!' I stopped him from finishing. 'That's not a normal number. I know that number. Two-point-seven-one-eight-two-eight-one-eight-two, et cetera, for ever.'

'I know it too,' said Marta. She was a physicist. She knew her maths.

I nodded. 'Euler's number. The number e. The base of natural logarithms. Every businessperson's favourite number. It is used to calculate how they can grow their wealth exponentially by compound interest. If you wanted one mathematical number that helped explain why the rich get richer, then it's this one. It's another sign. He knows we will know that isn't a real phone number . . . He is telling us to be very careful.'

Marta stared at the wet placard as Alberto picked it up off the ground. 'Exponential growth. That is all he is about. That is him.'

My mind was whirring. 'Who gave permission? I mean, for the Es Vedrà development.'

'Oh, um, well that was Sofía Torres. She's the most powerful politician on the island . . .'

Alberto was trying to shake wine off the destroyed placard. 'Everyone knows her. She eats in the same fish restaurant every night.'

'Which fish restaurant?'

'El Pescador. In the Old Town.'

Being a maths teacher, I knew that if you want to solve a problem you have to do it in the right order. And if there is an unknown element and a given quantity, you have to begin with the given quantity. Not the unknown element, because it is, well, *unknown*. And the known element was Sofía Torres, so it made sense to start with her.

'We should go there,' I said, feeling urgent and adventurous and ridiculous. The Marks & Spencer Don Quixote once more. 'We should go there tonight.'

Mindfishing

I drove us all to Ibiza Town. In the distance we could see the fortified old town of Dalt Vila on top of a hill. Clustered buildings perched behind walls and neatly angular bastions, under a sky slowly fading towards night.

Alberto and Marta argued all the way in Spanish, and I could understand every word they spoke and every word they didn't but wanted to. I was now as fluent in Spanish as if I had been born here.

Alberto was shaking his head, over and over again. 'Tomorrow can't happen.'

'It's happening. It's arranged.'

'Phone your people,' he said, his voice strained with worry. 'Please, Marta, phone Adriá and the others and tell them it can't happen. Post it on the internet. Tell them not to come. Whatever Art Butler is, we are no match for him.'

'Because that is how you deal with murderers and ecocidal terrorists, is it? You give in to their demands? No, Papá, I am doing this.'

'I am your father. And it is my job to protect you.'

'And I am a human, and it is my job to protect the planet.'

'You're impossible.'

'No. You're impossible.'

You get the picture. It was a family squabble. Their minds were full of love and concern for each other. This was one advantage of telepathy, I realised. It made the subtext text. It made the unseen seen. It showed love and kindness could sometimes be wrapped in rage and scorn. Marta really wasn't scared.

'Let's have a good time,' she said, defiantly. 'It's a nice evening. Come on, Grace, let's have an adventure. Let's go and save the world.'

'An adventure?' I said, and nothing else. Almost like I was offering myself an invitation.

Anyway, Maurice, we parked in a car park on the edge of the new town. I reverse parked, the way Karl had always recommended, and I imagined his satisfaction.

The plan was to head to El Pescador, but we deliberately parked far away. We wanted a long walk. We wanted to pass a lot of people.

Marta frowned. 'Why are we parking here?'

'We need to go mindfishing,' Alberto told her. 'Well, Grace does. I'll do what I can. And Ibiza Town is the place for it. Someone here besides Sofía Torres must know something about Art Butler's plans or where we can find him.'

It was a busy evening, which was great for our purposes.

As we walked past people, I caught their thoughts like butterflies. And, like butterflies, some were prettier than others.

'Be on guard for anything suspicious,' added Alberto. 'The information we need could come from any mind . . .'

The crowds began to swell as we got closer to the centre.

There was a woman staring at a bright yellow summer dress in a window, imagining herself in it, wondering if she could stretch her credit limit some more.

There was a child who was tired and wondering why her parents wouldn't let her have a rabbit.

There was a man who was worried his belly was too soft.

There was another man who was thinking ahead to a night in a casino, to winning his money back from the same guy who took it the night before.

There was a woman remembering an orgasm with a more attentive lover than the one whose hand she held.

There was a nauseous tourist who regretted ordering the mussels.

There was a man who felt desperate despite his smile.

There was a teenager, staring at their phone, wishing they looked like the person dancing in the video.

There was a young couple both simultaneously wishing their Airbnb was closer to town.

There was a bartender wiping an outside table, dreaming of an old flame who moved back to Argentina and married a lawyer. Marta knew him and she said hi.

'¡Hasta mañana!' he said and told her he was looking forward to the protest.

'Yes. See you tomorrow.'

There was a dog trying to tell its owner it was thirsty.

There was a cockroach scuttling along the flagstones beside a bar, up fresh and early for a night of foraging, its mind full of almost-human levels of fear and lust and hunger.

There was a deeply anxious person who was petrified about dying but whose life was so available to read I knew they wouldn't in fact die for another fifty-three years. And it would be painless, in their sleep, in a luxury hotel in Kyoto.

There were three young men wanting to get high, one of them secretly wishing he could tell his friend he was in love with him.

There was a woman who had a carrier bag full of apples and bread, who was worried she didn't have enough rent money.

I passed someone who was feeling guilty for being on holiday while their mother was ill in hospital. I knew this guilt. The guilt of having *fun*.

I passed someone my exact age. A Spanish woman who was in a deep depression. Who wanted to be nothing.

I thought of the days after Karl's funeral, when all I wanted to do was not exist. I became fascinated with zero, as a concept and a number. The ancient Egyptians had a hieroglyphic symbol for zero. It was interchangeable with the one for beauty. That appealed to my state of mind at the time. Beauty was nothing. As soon as there was something there was trouble. And pain.

I owed it to the world to feel awful; that had been my logic. And if I didn't owe it to the world, at the very least I owed it to my dead husband and my dead child.

I had believed that I was simply not *meant* to be happy. It was such a relief to feel differently. But even there, even walking through Ibiza Town, a faint guilt remained. Like a stain on cardboard that no sunlight could ever quite take away.

Heartbreaks and Hangovers

We kept walking. I knew everything that could be discerned from everything that was ever encountered, the way that with enough understanding a grain of sand could speak of the entire universe.

We walked the longest possible way to the Old Town, passing the butter-yellow facade of the Gran Hotel Montesol, which I not only *knew* was the island's oldest hotel, but could also feel, as I walked past its curved multistorey Art Deco corner where a sophisticated and international evening crowd sat under canopies watching people. Watching them but, unlike me, not understanding them.

Because I felt as if I was strolling through a crackling cloud of indulgence and experience, where the memories literally leaked from the buildings and bodies. We took a detour by the waterfront, past the Pacha shop and restaurants slowly filling up and people strolling with large ice creams and small dogs. We passed heartbreaks and hangovers, boredom and stimulation. We passed love and loss, regret and shame, hope and despair, stress and indigestion, piety and pornography, aspiration and acceptance. We passed thoughts about money and music and grief and pet-sitters and painful teeth and weak bladders and bad backs and tinnitus and someone clenching their abdominal muscles. We passed the simple enjoyment of aioli and rye bread and local vino de la tierra. We passed a Swedish woman who was wondering if humans will survive the AI revolution. We passed snippets of songs and adverts and viral videos and unwanted conversations that were stuck in people's minds like gum on shoes. We passed tourists thinking of their beach reads and flight times. We passed a man who was once told he looked like Keanu Reeves scrolling through selfies for one where he actually did. We passed a ballerina from Paris who was overthinking how to blink. We passed a native Ibicenco beside a lamppost, playing online chess, taking a queen. We passed a man who was imagining he was a DJ at

Ushuaïa, playing for a rapturous crowd dancing around the hotel pool. We passed an actual DJ booked to play at the Hï club that night and also – twenty-four hours later – a luxurious place called Club Chinois, his jewellery dazzling but his mind dull from jetlag after a layover flight from Singapore. He missed his twenty-year-old daughter back home in Chicago, and thought of when to FaceTime her as he sat alone on a bench and consumed an inconsequential Burger King veggie burger, listening to the beautiful voice of a busker singing a song I now knew was by a singer called Olivia Rodrigo.

We passed thoughts in every language and emotions of every colour.

I know how bizarre this all sounds. But really, it was beginning to feel remarkably normal. Or if not normal, then at least natural. It had only been two days, yet it already felt like for ever.

The difference between a gift and a curse was sometimes just a question of perspective.

Islands Don't Exist

I had been an island. And yet now, thanks to Christina and La Presencia, I realised that there are no islands. If you go far enough down, everything is connected. Ibiza and Lincoln are joined to the same earth. Our minds swell into each other like a million currents at sea. We merge, we converge. Everyone flows into everyone else without even realising. Even cockroaches play their part. We aren't just a person, we aren't just a gender, we aren't just an age, we aren't just a nationality, we aren't even just a species. The walls between us are imaginary. The thoughts we have that are ours are gloriously unique but also gloriously in the same continuing spectrum. Love, fear, grief, guilt, forgiveness. These are the standards in the repertoire. These are the cover versions we get to play. We think we are lonely because we are often blind to the connections. But to be alive is to be a life. To be life. We are *life*. The same ever-evolving life. We need each other. We are here for each other. The point of life is life. All life. We need to look after each other. And when it feels like we are truly, deeply alone, that is the moment when we most need to do something in order to remember how we connect.

That is why we take the invite to Ibiza or send the email to the lonely old maths teacher or share the ridiculous truth of ourselves. We can't just sit for ever in our lonely shells, making no sound.

To swim in the ocean, we sometimes have to make a splash.

El Pescador

We passed more restaurants and more tourists and more dog walkers before arriving at the narrowest alley of all. The one with the small but upscale fish restaurant. El Pescador.

A row of small white wooden tables was perched outside on the uneven ground and Sofía Torres and her husband – whose name was Jorge, I discerned – were seated at the one furthest up the sloping path.

Marta was on her phone, with her sunglasses on and her back to Sofía in case she was recognised. She was chatting to a friend and planning things for the protest. I stared at her and tried to access her future, but it wouldn't come to me, which seemed unusual for someone's mind I could enter. It was quite unusual that I couldn't see *anything* about her future. Did it mean that Marta's fate was wide open? Multiple futures hanging in equal balance? That could be both good and bad news, I supposed.

'What now?' Alberto asked me. I liked that I was now in charge.

I saw a bar further up the street with an empty table and three chairs. 'There,' I said. 'We'll sit and watch her, and I'll have a rummage.'

'A rummage!' said Alberto. 'Man, that is a good and peculiar English word.' And I thought about it and realised he was right. *Rummage*. It really was quite special. 'It is almost as good as "fungus",' added Alberto. 'Or "queue". I love "queue". Who would be as mad as to put those letters right next to each other in the same five-letter word? Only the English . . .'

'And only the Spanish would turn their exclamation marks upside down,' I countered.

'And question marks,' added Alberto, agreeably. 'What can I say? The whole of Spain likes to party. Even the punctuation. And we have la madrugada . . . another one you have no word for . . . The time before dawn but after midnight. A very important and magical time. Yet you need a lot of words for it in English . . . In fact, it is . . .'

As Alberto kept talking, it began to happen. I took surreptitious

227

glances at Sofía Torres and started to catch sight of her. It was like being a child, feeling an unwrapped present, gradually knowing what it was before I saw it. Every word she spoke, every mouthful of food she ate, every sip of wine, every gesture: each was the smoke trail leading me to the fire inside. Most of us reveal every single aspect of ourselves in every single moment, but very few people are able to understand these tells. They just exist as never-understood signifiers, which may partly explain the loneliness that hangs around so many of us humans, the loneliness of foreign words looking for meaning.

Anyway: we sat for an hour in that narrow alley, drinking pale beer and harpooning olives and observing the politician as she chatted to her husband.

Luckily she was all there, before me. She was facing our direction, but she didn't see me because I was lost in shadow and she was lost in concern.

Marta had already told me she was the highest-profile politician on the island, who had originally been a bridge between left and right but had since abandoned all pretence of environmentalism. I knew more than I had been told, though, just by looking at her. It was as simple to understand her mind as it was to notice her white linen suit, bouffantish hair and her smile carved in stone. I knew, even though I was too far away to see it, that she wasn't concentrating on her pomegranate salad or the sea bass.

Despite the smile, she was deep in worry.

Now, worry is incredibly common. Even more common than we imagine. That is one of the first things telepathy had taught me. Along with loneliness it is the polluted air that most minds live in, the thing that deprives us of the present moment, trapping us in the past and future all at once. But her worry had a depth and immediacy that almost burned. Her worry was predominantly about what would happen tomorrow. At the protest. For a flickering moment she even thought of Marta Ribas, someone she'd heard quite a bit about. Marta, she knew, had been one of the main initiators of the Cala Llonga protest and the Talamanca one before that. An astrophysicist and Ibiza native, she was a serious person, who spoke well and had good principles. A politician's nightmare. But this was set to be far bigger than that. If only she could have a word with her.

I smiled a little.

'She'd like a word with you,' I whispered to Marta, who had just put down her phone.

'She knows I am here?'

'No. But she would like a word. She sent you an email but there has been no response.'

Marta stood up. But then reconsidered. 'If I go over there right now, that is all she will be thinking about.'

'Exactly,' I said. 'It will ripple the waters. And that is bad for fishing.'

'We have to play a clever game,' added Alberto. 'Let Grace observe her. She will be able to tell us everything. If you go over there, you are placing yourself in more danger. There is nothing you can say to her that will get her to stop . . . You will just draw attention to yourself . . . The protest is your way of speaking to her.'

So we all stayed there. Marta kept her head low and posted online about the protest and I ate olives and read Sofía's mind.

Sofía was now stewing on a meeting she'd had last year with Art Butler. His plans for a hotel on Es Vedrà were going to be revealed to the press and public tomorrow, at the Eighth Wonder in Talamanca, while the protest was taking place.

A luxury hotel on Es Vedrà was a sick joke, thought Sofía. Yet it was one she had agreed to. Indeed, she had been the one to sign off the agreement. She, and her colleagues in Mallorca, had clearly been idealistic in thinking the protection of a nature reserve could be outsourced to a profit-minded corporate entity such as Art Butler Worldwide.

The protest was already all over Instagram and TikTok; the club crowd were getting involved. And she remembered the protests from the nineties, when the islanders had stood together. And she had been there, shoulder to shoulder with the environmentalists. How she had cheered when the area around Cala d'Hort became a protected nature reserve and not a golf course. Now look at her. What a hypocrite they would think she was.

Between gaps in the conversation with Jorge, her mind returned to a villa amid the wooded hills near Cala Jondal. One she hadn't visited for many months.

A ridiculously opulent, twenty-million-euro villa.

Large and white and cuboid and generically luxurious, with the walls made primarily of windows.

Once upon a time it had been a finca, with a small farm full of pigs and rabbits, but no traces of that were left. An infinity pool merged almost seamlessly with the distant Mediterranean beyond.

'Are you seeing the villa?' I asked Alberto, as he chewed on an olive.

'No. I can't see anything,' he said, feeling a bit diminished. 'I am too far away. I can't really read her at all. I could read you reading her but that might cause some mental interference.'

'It's Art Butler. She is thinking about Art Butler. He really is the one planning to build the hotel on Es Vedrà . . .'

'There,' said Marta. 'Ahi lo tienes! We were right.'

Alberto's eyes were as intense and curious as an owl's. 'Where is he? Does she know where he is?'

'I don't know. Let me focus . . .'

Art Butler

So there I was, inside Sofía's mind. Inside the particular corner of it that was housed in a villa belonging to the head of Eighth Wonder Resorts. He had actually given her the chance of meeting him at his yacht, permanently moored at the Marina Botafoch, a short walk away from his favourite hangout, the casino beside the Ibiza Gran Hotel. But somehow, she hadn't been prepared to do that. She had felt more comfortable meeting him on dry land. At the villa she was now remembering, and the one I was observing. It wasn't the precise villa. It was an observation of a memory of a villa. A villa twice removed. Every few seconds a detail changed. A vase shifted position, a chair disappeared and then reappeared. But the core details of it remained solid. This was eight months earlier. And I was looking at him – at Mr Art Butler – now. Looking at him simultaneously through my own *and* Sofía's mind.

Sofía had always thought that he was peculiar-looking, even by the eccentric standards of British men. A short man. As jowly as a Basset Hound. Haunted eyes. Greying stubble and wayward curly hair that he liked to touch. Blue shirt and chinos and flip-flops. And he had a kind of puffy and overbaked look about him. He was, she supposed, around fifty but there was something fundamentally childish about him. She couldn't say she had disliked him, before this meeting. There had been something endearing about him. Like a lost little boy pretending he wasn't lost at all and that everything was perfectly fine.

'We are going to have to say no to your plans,' she was telling him, gently, as though delivering the news of a dead relative. 'It is, I am afraid, impossible even to contemplate a development on Es Vedrà. The protests would be too strong. It's a changing time.'

He said nothing for a little while. He smiled a soft smile. 'Ah, but Sofía, this is the *new* Ibiza. This is exactly what you are after . . .'

'The new Ibiza? What's the old Ibiza?'

Art had laughed a hollow laugh. 'Everything you have tried to get rid of. You know: the drugs, the drunks, the loud music, the chaos, the cheap package holidays, all the sunburnt hordes . . . the *trash*.'

Sofía smiled a little too. The kind of smile that disguised a wince. *Trash*. He so casually disregarded people. '*That* is the old Ibiza? I don't know.' She thought maybe the Phoenicians and the Carthaginians would have something to say about that. Not to mention the Romans and the Arabs and the pirates. Or every single person born here. 'You are very British. The Ibiza you are talking about has only ever been a perception . . .'

Art's phone rang. He picked it up. 'Raj, I'll call you back . . . Yeah. Yeah. The Brazilians gave us a ballpark on it but it's still too much. We'll get back on this tomorrow . . .'

Sofía hadn't wanted to be there. She had a load of issues that were piling up – the problem of the homeless people having to live in tents near the marina, the anger around people parking where they shouldn't in Playa d'en Bossa, and the speech she was going to give next Tuesday on the discrepancy between health funding for Mallorca and Ibiza, which would surely enrage the president of the Balearic government. The last thing she needed right now was Art Butler, but still, she had to undo the mess she had made. The protests would end up costing her her job. She had to reverse the Es Vedrà decision.

Art's call ended. He turned back to Sofía. He seemed a little more tense now, she noted.

'We are talking *vision*,' he said, with big and dominating arm gestures, like a conductor reaching the end of the symphony. 'Not just the perception of how things are, but how they could be. Ibiza is being transformed. The world is being transformed. And people like us are the ones transforming it.'

'We are not Dubai,' Sofía told him. I felt her frustration and distaste and mild fear. 'We are not Las Vegas. Ibiza is a natural place. It cannot be *transformed* on the whim of a developer. Even you.'

'I have brought new ideas. I have added life to the place.'

'With respect, nothing you have ever brought here has been new. People have been staying in hotels here since the Montesol opened in the thirties. People have come here to heal and do yoga for even longer than that . . . You can't build an environmentally friendly future by building over protected areas.'

Art clenched his jaw. 'You need to unprotect the area, Sofía. Es Vedrà and its sister rock and the ocean between it and Cala d'Hort. I know it can be done. This will be good for the people, for the economy . . . You see, this is just the beginning. This will be the template. The success story that can be replicated elsewhere.'

'What are you talking about?'

'The protection of precious land.'

'Protection?' she laughed. 'My English is not as good as yours, but did you say "protection"?'

'Es Vedrà is a symbol of a sacred and natural place. And once I have it, I will make it even more special. And then I will be able to present it everywhere, to governments, and I will say, "Your land will be safe with me. I will look after it."'

'What is your obsession with buying up nature?'

'Are you, a politician, seriously going to lecture me on how to look after the environment? You had your chance. And the future will be for those with real vision. Resorts amid nature, with tourists helping to pay to protect that nature. Once I have Es Vedrà, I will do this everywhere, on every continent. I will take the most precious of the precious and make it accessible to people while also protecting the land. This is the future. Capitalism and ecology, side by side. I already have permission to develop in the deepest area of the Amazon . . . And do you know how I got it? I told them that this was happening, here in Spain. And that you had agreed. You had agreed?'

'Yes. It is true. I had verbally agreed. But I hadn't predicted all the issues. Why can't you go to developed areas like other hoteliers do? Why do you have to take something pure and destroy it?'

'Destroy is a strong word.'

Sofía sighed as she leaned forward on a large, well-cushioned chair that switched between wicker and plastic, depending on the moment inside the memory. 'Mr Butler . . . There is a species of flower – the *Nolletia chrysocomoides* – that was last seen on Earth here in Ibiza, but it was made extinct when you opened your first hotel at Cala Bassa and poured cement over the wildflower meadow there. And that is not the only story like that. You go to delicate places and disfigure them.'

'My father was a botanist,' he said, wistfully and so softly Sofía almost didn't hear him. Sadness passed over his features like a shadow.

'You have done nothing but be an environmental hazard. Es Vedrà is a very special place. People are very attached to it. And you can't simply ferry tourists from Cala d'Hort to there all day long. Think of the pollution. That is the most special patch of water. The seagrass there is—'

He rolled his eyes. 'One hundred thousand years old. Yes. I know. The oldest plant on Earth. The most important habitat in the Mediterranean. Blah blah blah. And we will run water taxis above it all day long from Cala d'Hort to Es Vedranell and have a bridge connecting that smaller island to Es Vedrà and humans – actual humans, not your precious fish and seaweed – will get to enjoy it.'

'You don't understand, Mr Butler. The water there is *very* special. The Posidonia seagrass is already hurt by tourism. To mess about with that area any more you will be asking for trouble.'

Art put down his coffee next to a statue of Tanit. 'You would be surprised. I am aware of the stories. I know them better than most.'

That was the moment, for Sofía, when the conversation changed completely. There was something fierce and commanding now about his expression.

He stared at her like a dog eyeing a rabbit. 'Look what I did to Cala Llonga. That was a tired old place before we came in. And now look at it. Ibiza is a place where people come and spend money. And we are getting better people, spending better money. The protests faded. Everyone forgot them as soon as we opened.'

'You don't understand the Ibizan people. For what you are suggesting, the protests won't ever end . . . This new tourism. The super-rich. They are not helping. We have big yachts blocking sunsets and yet we have people unable to afford to pay their rent. And look at the shape of Es Vedrà. How are you going to build a hotel there? You don't need us. You have hotels everywhere. You can leave us now.'

'Rock blasting. We'll make a nice flat shelf in the rock. We did it before, in Mallorca.'

'But there are birds that nest there. Cormorants.'

'Do you seriously care more about cormorants than the local economy?'

'I thought *you* cared,' she said, in a testing kind of tone. 'Wasn't that the idea? Ecology and capitalism working together? And you talk about the economy! Tell that to the people living in tents in car parks. It was a mistake ever to grant this. I underestimated public opinion. You will face a revolution. Christina van der Berg, for one, has a lot of influence.'

The name bothered him. It was like a wasp passing his face. But then he made a dismissive gesture. 'The sheep won't follow without the shepherds.'

'What does that mean?'

'You take them away and everything fizzles out. The people with the power to stop this will themselves be stopped . . .'

Sofía studied his cold expression. 'Take them away? How do you take people away?'

She thought of her colleague, Ricardo Martínez. The one who had died two days after blocking the application of an Eighth Wonder resort beside the wetlands at Ses Feixes. The inquest concluded his death was accidental. His heart had given up. An undetected issue with his aortic valve.

'Yes,' he said, as if reading her mind. 'Don't block progress, Sofía. It won't do you or your family any good.'

'There are laws. There is the police. This is Spain. You can't just plough in here and threaten people.'

He raised a finger, held it in the air, pointing towards Sofía but still two metres away from her. And yet she felt something – she was sure of it – she felt that finger touch her neck without actually touching it. Just a small sense of it pressing in, towards her larynx, and she reached at it, at this invisible thing pressing into her. But there was nothing to hold on to, and then his finger – still that same distance away – stopped pointing, and she felt nothing at all.

She tried to steady her breathing. 'What are you?'

The smile was suppressed but still there. 'The last thought in Ricardo Martínez's head.'

'You . . .' Sofía couldn't find the word.

'Just think of me as the future,' said Art, with an expression that seemed more sad than intimidating. A gaze of deep, if distant, pain. 'Inevitable as the setting sun.'

And then I lost the memory. And the mind. It was gone. I was suddenly back, fully inside my own self again, wondering what I had just witnessed.

Uncertain Quantities

'He threatened Sofía,' I said, out of my trance, after having a sip of beer to acclimatise me back in my own mind. In the present, Sofía had gone to the bathroom, I discovered, hence the broken memory.

And my report came out of me in a stream of whispers. 'He killed someone. A politician. Maybe more than one person. And he was going to kill Christina. He has the Guardia Civil in his pocket. And the politicians. That is how the Es Vedrà plan is happening. And the plan is just the start of his new phase. He wants to develop in the most protected areas of the world. So he is starting with the most protected area here. He wants to stain every last place of beauty on Earth, I think.'

'Why?' wondered Alberto.

'Maybe he likes the sick challenge of it,' said Marta. 'Seeing it as a game. Pretending to care about the environment while destroying it.'

'Sometimes people don't know why they do things,' I said, thinking of myself and Aidan Jenkins and that school stock room. 'They are just driven to harm because they think that is what they are there for. It's a pattern they become trapped inside if they don't know how to love, properly.' I snapped out of it. 'And he has powers. That is how he has killed people. They have agreed to give him not just the rock but the sea around it. And there is something very much not human about him. That is why Christina couldn't see him. Maybe he had the talents . . . Maybe he had come into contact with La Presencia.'

Alberto shook his head. 'La Presencia only helps the good. It would never have helped someone capable of harm.'

'Aren't we all capable of harm?' I wondered.

Marta pinched her own hand, then looked at the imprint the nails had made and smiled with satisfaction. There was something just slightly masochistic about her. 'No,' she said. 'Not on his scale. But you are right about the politicians. He must have threatened others in the parliament. He must have. There is no way they would have bowed easily.'

I shared something else I had garnered from Sofía's mind. 'They announce the hotel is happening tomorrow.'

'The day of the protest?' said Marta, in disbelief. 'Is he insane?'

'Maybe,' sighed Alberto. 'But so are you if you think that protest can still happen. We are the sharks feeling the hurricane before it hits.'

The bar was a hub of activity, a friendly fusion of tourists and locals.

Marta nodded. 'Yes. But unlike sharks, we can actually stop this hurricane.'

A couple of women walked by, leaving flyers for Lieke at Amnesia on people's tables. (Alberto had told me that flyers, though still around, were the 'old-fashioned social media of Ibiza, before TikTok'. In the old days, that is how everyone found out what was happening.)

They spotted Marta. 'Hola, Marta.'

Marta was pleased to see them. 'Hey, guys. Do you know about the protest tomorrow? To stop the development on Es Vedrà? We are meeting outside the Mar y Sol.'

'Ahh, sorry, we would love to,' said one of them. 'But my brother is playing at a pool party over near Cala Comte and I'd said I'd go.'

Marta's smile was closer to a grimace. 'No importa . . . chao . . .'

Once they had walked away Alberto looked tenderly at his daughter and shrugged. 'Look, it's going to make no difference. And the stakes are too high. Just call off the protest.'

'Papá, please. I know you are only trying to keep me safe, but Art Butler getting Es Vedrà wouldn't be keeping anyone safe. It would just make him stronger. We have to stand up now. Come on . . . You always say the thing you love about goats is that they stubbornly resist and do the thing that is right for them. Be like a goat, Papá. You always have been. Don't weaken now.'

Alberto's eyes glistened with sadness. He so wanted to tell her about his diagnosis. He was going to. He was right on the cusp of telling her he had a cancer that would eventually kill him. He was going to tell her it was the reason his talents had faded.

He realised he had to be on her side. He was trying to keep everyone safe because he couldn't keep himself safe. His daughter was about to be thirty. He had to let her be the adult she was. He couldn't try to keep her safe by telling her not to be herself. She knew every risk and she was still prepared to stand up. He was as proud as a father could be. She had always wanted to be chosen by La Presencia but never had been. This was her chance to have the power to make things better, and he wasn't going to stop that.

It was quite something, feeling that change inside him. It was like when the breeze stops and there is just the sunlight and you realise the day is warm.

'Tienes razón, mi vida. Let's make our friend Nostradamus proud. Let's be goats.'

And Marta turned to her father, with the most complex of smiles. One that contained hope and fear and defiance and love.

'Thank you, Papá.'

I confess in that moment to feeling a twinge of jealousy at their bond. It wasn't just the usual pang of grief about Daniel, but a craving for family. For belonging. For not being lonely old Grace.

But also I was in deep admiration of Marta's courage as she took her cue and stood up and walked over the cobblestones to the restaurant.

'Mierda,' cursed Alberto, then followed his daughter. 'She is crazy.' And I followed him.

When we got to Marta she was apologising to Jorge and Sofía for interrupting but then plunged straight in.

'The protest is happening tomorrow,' she told them, in Spanish, standing there as the diners around fell silent.

Sofía offered Marta a calm smile. Her face and her mind, I realised, were two entirely different entities. Maybe that was an essential part of being a politician. To have a face that bore no trace of the mind inside. 'It won't make a difference,' she said. 'There is no way there would ever be enough people on the streets to stop this.'

'When people know Art Butler is behind it, they will be there,' Marta told them. Especially after he messed up Cala Llonga. 'Es Vedrà is special. The waters around it are special too. It's not just an environmental issue, it's a symbolic one. It is the soul of the island. No one wants Art Butler to steal that soul. Ibiza is not for sale.'

I felt Sofía's panic. This was the reason why they'd had to withhold that information. To avoid giving the protesters a lightning rod for their energy.

'Respectfully, Miss Ribas, you don't quite know what you are dealing with. I strongly advise you to go onto the relevant social media channels and call the whole thing off. For your own good. There is a cross-party consensus that this is going to go ahead.'

Alberto sighed. 'But you have the influence. On this issue you are the strongest influence. Without your support, this wouldn't happen. The balance would tip. You are the deputy of the majority party, Sofía, – you are the chief – you could stop this.'

Marta's left leg bounced with adrenaline. She now had an audience. As Alberto and I were now flanking her, we *all* had an audience. The whole restaurant was staring at us.

'How many?' asked Marta.

'*What?*'

'You said there is no way there would ever be enough people on the streets to stop the hotel in Es Vedrà. I just wondered how many would be enough.'

Sofía's husband tried to intervene. He opened his mouth to speak, to put Marta in her place. *Shut up, Jorge*, ordered my mind. And that is what happened. It was a Brian situation all over again. His mouth was clamped like a tightly closed oyster, and his eyes were wondering what the hell had happened.

Sofía's smile was almost breaking, but not quite. 'What are you talking about?'

Marta was steadfast. 'You just said there is no way there would ever be enough people on the streets to stop the hotel in Es Vedrà. So I was wondering what *enough* was?'

This is when Alberto interrupted from behind her shoulder. 'Ten thousand? That was the number in 1999. Can you remember that, Sofía? We were both there, weren't we? You were young then, weren't you? You gave a fuck. And we stopped it. That January. We stopped them from turning wilderness into a golf course and instead set it up as a reserve. You remember? Cala d'Hort. "Golf! No!" Everyone had those bumper stickers. So is that what it would take? Ten thousand people?'

Sofía laughed a little. But inside she was suddenly fragile. A cracking egg. 'There is no way you would get ten thousand people to march in the streets. But even if you did, no, it is impossible.'

'What about twenty thousand?' Alberto said, like the world's worst negotiator.

'Papá.' Marta gently pressed an elbow into his stomach. I knew what she was thinking. She was thinking: there is no way on Earth twenty thousand people will turn up to the protest. At that moment she was hoping for one thousand people, and even that was pushing it.

Sofía's laugh was almost genuine now. 'Twenty thousand? Twenty thousand people. That is way over ten per cent of the entire population. You seriously think that you will have twenty thousand people? I have seen the social media accounts. No one cares. This isn't January. This is June. Everyone just wants a good time.'

Alberto was now firm. I saw where his daughter got it from. 'But what if we did? Would you stop it? You'd have to, right? You listen to the people, right? That's why you were elected, right?'

'And in this hypothetical scenario you would pay the legal fees?'

Alberto nodded. 'Forty thousand euros. I know how much those things cost to undo.'

'More like eighty thousand.' Sofía smiled. She knew Marta and Alberto wouldn't have that sort of money lying around. She noticed another diner was now recording this whole thing on their iPhone. 'So, yes. Of course. I am someone who listens. I will say it in front of all these witnesses. If you can cover the legal costs that would otherwise come from people's taxes and if you can get twenty thousand people at your protest tomorrow afternoon, then you have a deal . . . Then I will withdraw my support.'

'Well, we can do it,' said Alberto. 'We can get the people and we can get the money.'

Sofía's smile didn't waver. 'Very good. And I am a woman of my word. If you manage that, I will honour my promise.'

As we walked away, and Alberto dropped his last ten-euro note onto the table outside the bar, Marta looked at her father.

'What were you thinking?'

He tried to chuckle it off. 'Don't worry. We can do this. I have some clever ideas.'

All the Clever Ideas Presently in Alberto's Head

Flyer

As we walked past the bar table, I saw the flyer.

'How popular is Amnesia?' I asked.

Marta pondered as we passed a busker singing a folk song in Catalan. 'Around five thousand people every night of the week during summer.'

Alberto shook his head. 'Five thousand isn't twenty thousand.'

'Thanks for the mathematical update,' I said.

'Wait, she's right,' Marta was thinking aloud. 'Amnesia on Wednesdays has more locals than tourists. They actually care about things like Es Vedrà. And they know people. There is this thing called social media, Papá.'

Alberto smirked. He even enjoyed his daughter when she mocked him. Especially then. 'So you are saying you want to go to Amnesia?'

I nodded. 'Yes.' And then I did my best Alberto impression to cheer Marta up. 'This is Ibiza. No one is too old for anything. There is a ninety-year-old who dances at Pacha every single night . . .'

'Okay. You are right. You are not too old. I am not too old. And Marta most definitely isn't too old. We will go to Amnesia.'

He undid a button of his shirt as if in anticipation. His daughter frowned at him. 'Too much?' he asked her. 'Should I save it for my OnlyFans?'

Marta was confused for two reasons. First, the horror of wondering how her father knew what OnlyFans was. And second, she had no idea what I was intending to do.

'But what is the plan?' she asked me.

'Lieke,' I said. 'Lieke is the plan.'

Alberto yawned. I caught it too. Yawn telepathy. 'It will be a long night. We should get a disco nap. We don't need much sleep a day. But we *do* need sleep. Or the talents won't work.'

Marta nodded. 'Yes. A disco nap. We need a disco nap.'

'A disco nap?' I asked.

'A nap,' Marta said, with the smiling innocence of a kindergarten teacher, 'before the disco. Lieke is the headliner so she will be on around two a.m. At the earliest.'

'What kind of night doesn't get going until two a.m.?' I asked.

'An Ibizan one,' laughed Alberto. 'Come on. Embrace la madrugada . . . It's time to feel alive, Grace.'

A Purpose

So there I was. Back where I had started. Back at my new tiny house on Carretera Santa Eulalia, with cars swooshing by. It was two minutes past ten. The traffic wasn't even peaking yet. Something felt different about it now, though, Maurice. I no longer hated it. In fact, it was starting to feel like home.

I don't know what it was that made the house feel homely. Nothing had really changed about it, except for the beautiful flower on the path obviously. There was still the claustrophobic hallway, the small living room, the old sofa and tattily bohemian throw. The rug still needed cleaning, the large fan in the living room was still visibly clogged with dust, and to my shame I hadn't yet mopped the floor tiles. The piano near the window filled half the room. The old hi-fi and rows of records and cassettes had the feel of a museum piece. The air remained thick and humid and stiff. But it was different now. It felt, somehow, like a relief to be there.

Home needs a reason. And there was now a reason, a purpose, for my being there. Again I felt what I had felt back at the airport. I understood why Christina had wanted to help people. And now I was, to use Christina's phrase, a *protector*. I had to protect the people and the place around me. Wasn't that the ultimate reason? After so many years of feeling unnecessary to the universe, I felt truly needed.

And it's nice to be needed. It really is.

The Signal

I appreciated the gallery on the wall now. The one filled with images of my lost friend. Her smile was sisterly, I felt. And I never had a sister, so I liked that.

I looked at the photo of a very young Lieke holding her teddy bear.

'You loved her,' I said. I didn't really know who I was addressing – Lieke or Christina. Maybe both of them.

A sudden but familiar twinge of mental pain came to me. I thought of my son, back in the eighties, playing with his Luke Skywalker and Han Solo figures. Making light-saber noises. It was a kind of mind cramp, that sort of memory. Because it could never just arrive in a neutral way, but always filtered through the lens of my own shame and self-loathing. So, yes, the place felt different, and I felt different, but I wasn't *completely* so.

Even my newfound appreciation of the house came with the guilt that Karl wasn't there. That was my problem. Guilt arrived with happiness, or trailed closely in its wake.

I stared at the photo of Christina with Freddie Mercury at Pikes Hotel, to try to feel good again. She'd been part of the entertainment that night. I could feel, faintly, the excitement Christina had felt. And the crushing and lonely day that followed. She had been an emotional rollercoaster in those days, either dipping or soaring, but then La Presencia came and saw her potential.

Before bed, I went over to the books and picked up *La vida imposible* by Alberto Ribas. *Impossible Life*. Or *The Life Impossible*. Let's go with the latter word-for-word translation, because it fitted Alberto quite well. It was ridiculously grand and sentimental and sounded like it dreamed big.

I stared at the illustration on the cover. The sea and Es Vedrà as seen from Cala d'Hort, I realised now. The lines coming from the water were clearly meant to represent La Presencia.

I opened it at page 153 and translated the Spanish automatically:

And even when the evidence was insurmountable, such as with the Manises incident, verified by multiple first-hand witnesses and in now-declassified documents from the Spanish Air Force, people chose not to believe because it is easier to dismiss things than risk a radical shift in worldview . . .

I flicked on a little further:

Since its arrival, there has been evidence of La Presencia acting in peculiar ways in order to save Ibiza's natural environment. For instance, there were reports from a fisherman who was saved by 'a light in the ocean' and who consequently developed paranormal capabilities, that during an air raid from Franco's forces in 1936 he felt protected as his capabilities grew stronger. This fisherman was called Joan Bonanova. He reported seeing blue light run through his veins, and also recounted to a journalist how he felt connected to every animal on Ibiza and managed to send them a signal. And others corroborated this report, saying they had seen animals act in a strange manner that night. How creatures of all species that night had acted as one, heading inland, away from the bombardment experienced in Ibiza Town and along the coast. There was even a report – recounted a decade later – of a herd of goats attacking a soldier to his death outside the Església de la Mare de Déu de Jesús, though Franco's government dismissed this as 'anti-Nationalist propaganda'.

I put the book down.

A signal, I thought to myself. The kind that Christina had hinted about in her message to me. Now, that was interesting. I dared to wonder if such a power was inside me, and what it would take to unleash it. A power to speak to animals beyond a Dr Dolittle or a Tarzan. To communicate with thousands of them, simultaneously. To bring nature together for the sake of nature. It was, I realised, an interesting work. I was warming to Alberto, but I didn't want to take him to bed with me, even in book form. So I picked up *The Count of Monte*

Cristo. As I said earlier, I had read it and loved it when I was younger. I realised I didn't actually need to reread it. I knew it completely. A week ago I wouldn't have been able to quote a single phrase. Now, I could have given you the audiobook. I could pluck any line as easy as I could pluck a hair from my head.

'There is neither happiness nor misery in the world; there is only the comparison of one state with another, nothing more. He who has felt the deepest grief is best able to experience supreme happiness . . .'

I have found that to be true, Maurice. Everything is comparative. In mathematics, numbers take their value from being higher or lower than their neighbours, while in art Leonardo da Vinci needs the contrasting darkness all around to make the light on John the Baptist appear holy. Chiaroscuro, as Italians and art aficionados say. (I had always known the word, from watching a programme on the Renaissance years ago, but I hadn't known I had known it until La Presencia brought it out of me.) The contrast of light and shade. Life is all chiaroscuro. Its meaning is derived from relative difference.

Anyway, I put Mr Dumas back and picked up one I definitely hadn't read. *The Ultimate Guide to Psychic Power: Volume 8*.

I randomly opened a page. Or maybe it wasn't so random. Because the page I landed on had the chapter title 'GUILT AND INTERFERENCE'.

I read a sentence: 'To truly enhance your abilities, and reach the next level, your mind must be free of mental pollution. And nothing pollutes and clogs a mind as thoroughly as guilt . . .'

And that was all I read, but it was enough. Because it prompted me to think of what Christina had said about the olive jar. *I sometimes place the olive jar beside my bed. Right next to my head. If you do that, it tells you things in your dreams. Things you need to hear. The dreams are the most vivid you have ever known. And they are filled with the kind of truth that heals . . .*

It was that last bit. It spoke loudly to me. *The kind of truth that heals.* That was precisely what I needed. If I was to help everyone be safe, if I was to help protect Es Vedrà and Ibiza from life-destroyers like Art Butler, I would need to do what I had never been able to. I would need to tackle my guilt head-on.

It was time to face the truth.

Disco Nap

I took the jar full of La Presencia extract, unscrewed the lid and placed it on the small chest of drawers. But before I did so, I tipped a tiny amount of the water into the pot plant, the wilted peace lily, and then I got under the sheets and, despite having so much to think about, I found myself falling asleep.

It came suddenly, the dream.

I was in the ocean again. I was *really there*, in the cold water, but no diving suit this time. And I saw what I had first seen with Alberto. The arm of light from La Presencia. It shot through barracudas, enlivening them, their thoughts a collective groan of release, and reached me, surrounding me with shifting blue luminescence.

It hooked around my ankles and pulled me across the water at speed towards the glowing, pulsing cloud-sphere, until I was inside it. But the moment I was inside it, I was somewhere else. Somewhere I had been before. The orange beach that wasn't a beach, beside the glowing sea that wasn't a sea, and those white-leaved trees. And now I could breathe, or I felt like I could breathe, and the air was pure and sweet.

But in this dream, this vivid too-real dream, I felt my body weakening second by second. I could feel an encroaching physical numbness as my mental pain increased in line with the incessant voice of guilt. The one I'd lived with for too long.

I am a bad person. I have done bad things. I am a bad person. I have done bad things. I am a bad person . . .

Someone I Recognised

A moment later – somehow – I was amid the trees. The trees were as tall as sequoias, but with smooth trunks, and there were yellow flowers amid their white leaves. In the distance I saw the unfocused, cloudish outline of two Salacian children playing an unfamiliar game and laughing.

Then I saw a table. Very much an Earth table. And someone sitting there. Long hair, gentle smile, eyes shining like coins in a well. Someone I instantly recognised, as fresh as yesterday.

It was Christina.

The Best Person I Ever Knew

This was the young Christina. Carly Simon via Nana Mouskouri. Christina Papadakis, not the Christina van der Berg she would become. The one who sang 'Rainy Days And Mondays' to open-mouthed school kids.

Still with that air of glamour, and still wearing a beaded necklace. She was sat at the table, tapping her terracotta-coloured nails against the wood. The table was right there in the forest, surrounded by the trees with the children playing beyond.

I noticed a lamp on the table, with a porcelain pineapple base. A half-full bottle of Blue Nun was there too.

'Hi, Grace.'

My feet in the sand that felt as real as anything. I walked, exhausted, to the table and slumped down on a chair opposite my old friend. 'Christina? Is this happening? Are you here?'

'Yes,' she said. 'And no.'

I was weak and confused. 'What do you mean?'

'This is Salacia. You are seeing Salacia and there are Salacians here. And they have been kind and they look after me. I am in this world. I made it through. I won't be immortal, but I will be as healthy as I could possibly be for as long as I could possibly be. It is beautiful here. The inhabitants live in a place beyond those trees. And they look after the arrivals so well. They are so good, Grace. They care for the entire universe, the way you once cared for me . . .'

I was hardly able to speak. 'I am on another planet?'

'No. You are not here. But it doesn't matter. What you are seeing is truth. La Presencia is giving you that gift. This is not a dream, Grace, in any normal sense of the word. This is *truth*.'

'So why is it happening? What is this truth for?'

'La Presencia wanted you to come to Ibiza because it knew what you are capable of. It knew that you could be vital in preserving the living things here. I knew too. That is why I chose you. I knew you could save lives and I knew you could help save the island. And this is how you do it. This is how you become a protector. You do it by freeing yourself first.'

Christina had a bowl now. A bowl full of pineapple slices. I was trying in my confusion to work out if it had just appeared.

She pointed at the translucent, glowing sea.

'Freeing yourself of doubt. Of guilt. Free of what you have done. You need to be as clear as that sea. You have been good at solving things, Grace. The one thing you really need to solve now is yourself. You are still stuck in your own past.'

'But—'

'You understand mathematics, Grace. Negativity has more power than positivity. When you multiply a positive by a negative the product is always negative. You must see things differently. You must make a plus out of the minus.'

'That is impossible.'

'So many things you thought of as impossible have become possible. This is the last one.'

'It's not just about Daniel,' I muttered. 'I was a bad wife as well as a bad mother.'

'You were a good wife. And an even better mother.' She laughed a little. It had a soft melody to it. She delicately pierced a slice of pineapple with a fork. 'I could have chosen anyone. But I chose you. You are the best person I ever knew.'

'You didn't know me.'

'I knew you better than you think. I saw you whole. I saw your future. I saw what you could be.'

'I am seventy-two. I have so little left.'

'Wrong. You have been sad and lonely for a long time, Grace. But it doesn't have to be like that.'

I thought of my life back in England. The one no one saw, the one where I hardly existed. The one where I was the unheard tree falling in the forest.

'I am a flawed person.'

'For fuck's sake, Grace. Everyone is a flawed person. That's what being a person is.'

'Not everyone,' I said.

'Yes,' she said, without even a beat. 'Everyone. Todo. El. Mundo.'

And then she pressed something into my hand. The St Christopher necklace. 'It's time to give this back for good.'

And I looked at it.

And when I looked up again, there was no bowl of pineapple. And no Christina. And on the table was a menu for a restaurant called the Raj Pavilion. The restaurant me and Karl went to when we were students in Hull. The one where he proposed for the first time.

Perfect Imperfection

The table was laid now for two people, with the cutlery on napkins, restaurant-style.

I looked at the menu, lying on the tablecloth. And when I looked up he was sitting right there. Karl. The young Karl. The one who loved Jimi Hendrix and wanted to play lead guitar in Black Sabbath. The one with the black hair and the sideburns and the skinny frame and Tiggerish energy that kept him moving in his seat, his head slightly bobbing around as if he was knitting with his nose.

'The onion bhajis are good, aren't they?' he said, picking up the menu.

A waiter appeared from nowhere. 'Are you ready to order or would you like a moment?'

'We would like a moment,' I said, as an indigo-feathered sky creature flew over our heads and the two Salacian children kept playing in the background. I was basically seeing the reality of Salacia overlaid with the reality of my own memory and psychology. All bonded together around the force of truth, imbued into my dream-that-wasn't-a-dream via the photonic forces in the olive jar. It was, in short, *disorientating*. And yet my focus was on Karl. I was told once, years ago, after a trip to the Goose Fair and the waltzers in Nottingham that the way to stop feeling dizzy was to stare at a fixed point in front of you. Karl was my fixed point. I focused on him and everything else stilled.

'Moments are important,' Karl agreed. He smiled the kind of romantic smile that used to exist in our early years, his eyes shining like Paul Newman's. 'They go so quick we don't always see them.'

'I was not good for you, Karl.'

He looked at the ring on my finger. A tiny emerald stud on a narrow silver band.

'Do you know how they tell if an emerald is authentic?' he asked.

'The imperfections,' I said.

'Yes. Exactly. That's what the woman said in the jeweller's. It is the opposite of other jewels. With an emerald, the more inclusions, the more cracks and defects, the more beautiful it can be. An authentic emerald is beautiful for its flaws. They call it *perfect imperfection*. Only a fake emerald can be conventionally perfect.'

'There can be too many imperfections,' I said.

'What do you mean, love?'

'I mean, what happens when that is all you can see? When you can't see the jewel but just the inclusions?' He stared at me blankly, so I put it as clearly as I could. 'You were very good for me. But I wasn't good for you.'

'What are you talking about? Is this about Daniel? It wasn't your fault he was on his bike outside.'

'I could have gone with him into town. Like he wanted. I was too busy reading a catalogue.'

'So could I. But I was in the pub. Too busy drinking a pint of bitter.'

'It was raining. I shouldn't have let him go.'

'Have you never seen anyone on their bike in the rain? He loved that bike. You couldn't keep him off it.'

His words didn't quite sink in. There was a part of me that wanted or needed to stay guilty. So I said: 'I am talking about Aidan Jenkins.'

'Your colleague?'

'Yes. I had sex with him in the stock room. I really enjoyed it. But I haven't enjoyed much since. Because I love you. And I could never have loved him.'

He nodded, nonchalantly. 'Oh, yes. I know about that.'

'What?'

'He phoned once.'

'*Phoned?*'

'Drunk.'

'*Drunk?*'

'It made me feel better, to be honest.'

'*Better? How?*'

'You remember Deborah? The girl I introduced you to at the union bar?'

I vaguely did. Somehow the memory was still there after decades. Blonde, heavy-fringed, sly smile. 'Yeah.'

'Well, I was shagging her every Tuesday. And every Thursday.'

This took a second. 'What? But you proposed to me.'

'Yes. It is odd, I agree. Bloody bonkers really. I think it is the guilt. It does funny things. Anyway, I am a bit of a bastard at the moment in this shared past of ours, Grace. I have gone round her digs while you think I'm at the pub, and we share a bottle of ropey wine and we smoke because this is the seventies, and nine times out of ten we shag. All while you meet up with Claudette. One day you nearly caught us at it, remember?'

'Why are you telling me this?'

'Because it is the truth. The flawed truth of our love, perfect in its broken symmetry. I love you, Grace Winters, and the mistakes we made don't make the love matter any less.'

'Karl—'

'You have to move on. Listen. Look at me. Look at this young me. An older version of me marries you. And we love each other, and there are really good times and really bad times and really middle-of-the-road times. And we try and fail to have children until we eventually have one, and I become a bit inattentive and irritable and resent my job and drink too much and start snoring really loudly. And you have your job, which is at least as stressful as mine, and yet I still somehow silently expect you to do most of the child-rearing and you do. And you do it well. And we pretend we are happy until we lose him. *We*, Grace. *We*. Neither of us were with him. He died. It was a tragedy, but it was also an accident the way most things are. And I am bad at grief. I shout sometimes and I hit the wall and I storm out. And I neglected you and you did something stupid. And sooner or later, everyone does something stupid . . . And no amount of guilt will ever undo that. And it won't bring me back either. I am gone. And I want you to live. I want you to live.'

'Where's Daniel?' I asked him. And then I said it louder, hoping Christina would hear. 'Where's Daniel? Can I talk to Daniel the way I talked to you? I know it wouldn't actually be him. Just as you are not actually you. But it would be the truth of him. I need the truth. I need to see his face. Is he here?'

Karl shook his head. 'He can't be seen. You are still too . . . *sad*. That part of the truth is the hardest to reach. But the truth of me is I always loved you for who you were. All of you. Mistakes and all.'

Those words were powerful. I felt them quake inside me.

'And I always loved you,' I said, managing not to cry.

He clasped his hands together, almost in prayer. 'I always knew, Grace. You told me everything. Even when you didn't. But I am here to say I wasn't perfect either. And I lived with my mistakes and forgave myself and you must too. You are needed. I love you, Grace. I always have and always will. Love doesn't just disappear. It's like light. It keeps travelling. But you need to move on. You don't remember me. Your guilt always clouds your vision. To remember us, to remember the good, you have to let go, Grace. You have to live.'

'I love you, Karl.'

'Then, please, let go . . . You are not here to be perfect. None of us are. You are here to live. So let me go . . .'

'Before I do, I just want to say I should have let you play your music louder. It was really great. I should have tried listening to it.'

And he smiled, broadly. His eyes shone like distant suns. It had been good to see him, but now I knew what to do. And he did too. 'Go now. Go.'

It was time.

The Waking Child

La Presencia brought things back. It healed wounds and reversed extinctions. And that was what was happening. I was flowering through the cracks. I was coming back.

And just at that moment I felt water lapping at my feet. I looked down. It was glowing that indescribable blue, and rising quickly, beyond any tide.

And when I looked back up everything was gone. The table. The beach. The trees. The people. All except me. Who was carried up inside that pure luminescence, up and up, until I was out in the air. Upright, awake in my bed. Ready, just about, to live and help live.

The Brightness

It was one a.m., and I awoke from my nap as alive as a puppy.

The jar, I observed, was glowing like never before.

The whole room was bright. The kind of brightness you normally would have to turn away from, but somehow I didn't need to. Granted, there was a lot of peril. Art Butler was still out there. We were all, possibly, in some kind of danger from a man who may not have been a man at all. But I'll tell you this. I can weather any external storm compared to that internal weather that fogs your whole view. And that fog had lifted now. I asked myself a rhetorical question: what could really be better than a home full of heart, left to you by a distant friend, on the most exciting island in the world?

It took me a second or two to notice, amid the brightness, that the peace lily beside the bed was no longer drab and dying. Its leaves were a deep, succulent green. I felt its existence. Not *thoughts*, exactly. Plants don't have thoughts in the way we have thoughts.

The most remarkable thing, though, was the item I was clutching. The necklace and its pendant of St Christopher, right there in the palm of my hand. The gift I had given, returned. I felt the embossed figure of St Christopher carrying the infant Christ across the river. I clenched it tight like the lost treasure it was and turned to the olive jar and said, 'Thank you.'

And then I had a shower, put on the necklace and chose some clothes. Some smart pleated trousers and a chiffon blouse. I looked in the mirror and I felt ready.

'Come on, Grace,' I told myself. 'It's time to live.'

Grace Winters Plus Two

The isle was full of noises.

The Amnesia nightclub was just off the main road that connects Ibiza Town in the east to San Antonio in the west. It was, like so many of the nightclubs here, ridiculously massive. The scale of a cathedral or an aircraft hangar. And I must admit it was a little exciting.

I hadn't been to a nightclub since 1980 – Roxy's in Lincoln, where a drunk woman had vomited on my shoes to the sound of Kool & the Gang.

A lot of the clubbers lining up were wearing striking outfits. If there was a dress code, it was a difficult one to crack. There was a woman in a bright-green bikini accompanied by bright-green running shoes. And another wearing a long red dress that was pure elegance. There was a young man in a black net top carrying a handbag. There was a slick couple dressed in black, who were holding hands in the queue and wondering if this was their last night together. There were lots of not-strictly-necessary sunglasses. There were more colours than a flowerbed full of hydrangeas. Alberto was wearing his ripped shorts and flip-flops and an open Hawaiian shirt which did little to conceal his forest of unseemly chest hair. His daughter was wearing one of her clever T-shirts – a white one with a tiny blue Earth in the middle of it. *Pale Blue Dot* was the slogan, in English. I knew – because these days I knew almost everything – it was a reference to a Carl Sagan speech in which he referenced the distant image of Earth taken from the *Voyager 1* space probe.

She was wearing yellow plimsolls and green-and-white trousers striped like the leaves of a spider plant. She literally sparkled, thanks to the eco-friendly biodegradable body glitter on her cheeks. And her hair was curled and so fantastically wild that if you squinted she could have passed for a kinder Medusa. In short, she looked great. And rather than feel what I would normally feel next to a fashionable person less than half my age, I didn't feel at all self-conscious or frumpy. I just felt she looked cool, and that was that.

I followed Marta and her father past the long queue of clubbers standing in front of the building – which was illuminated by moving multicoloured spotlights and the daffodil-yellow Amnesia sign – to the largest of the security guards. He made the iPad in his hands look like a postage stamp.

'Rafael!'

And the security guard smiled, his face glowing blue from the lighting. 'Hey, Alberto!'

Rafael hugged Alberto.

'Papá used to DJ here,' Marta explained in my ear. 'In ancient times. Rafael's known him all his life. He taught him to dive. It's a small island.'

'Thank you for the snake,' Rafael told him. 'My daughter was grateful.'

'Ah, my pleasure. That particular snake is a very philosophical, thoughtful creature and wanted good company . . .'

Rafael humoured him. It was good to know the snake had left the drawer and had a better home. But the guard wasn't standing aside. He stayed standing in front of us like a closed door.

Alberto's smile now had a side-serving of perplexity. 'So . . . are you going to let us through?'

'No,' he said, in contrast to his friendly expression.

Marta swore in creative ways that I understood but will not repeat. I wondered if Alberto was going to use his talents. I wondered if I should. But then I realised there was absolutely no need.

I gave a little polite English wave to Rafael.

He tried to not look too amused by my presence and general appearance, which was kind of him. 'Sí, señora?'

'Hello, there, I believe I am on the guest list.'

He looked at me, confused. So did Alberto and Marta, to be fair.

'Yes. I bumped into Lieke in a garden centre and she kindly said she would put my name down. It's Grace Winters. Plus two.'

He had a peruse of his iPad. Then he nodded. 'Yeah. You are right here.' And then we were beckoned through. 'Have a great night.'

Alberto was a little put out and mumbled stunned English polite-nesses – 'Oh. I see. Yes. Very good.' – which were quickly drowned out by the wall of sound we were walking towards.

The Workshop of the Forgetful Ones

We walked over terracotta tiles, through the mainly Spanish crowd gathered near the entrance. People shouting in each other's ears to be heard. Sweating bodies. Thoughts flying around full of jagged, frenetic joy and yearning. I felt at least two centuries too old to be there, though Alberto was obviously reading my mind because he pointed to an old man in a marijuana-leaf T-shirt. 'That's Diego. He's an old guy from the mainland who came in the big summer of eighty-eight and has been here ever since. He's older than either of us.'

I briefly accessed Diego's mind but it was a strange psychedelic fog full of abstract thoughts swirling like cows in a cyclone, and so I quickly moved on.

The club was basically two vast rooms. One cavernous, dark room and a lighter – larger – room with glass windows in the roof and a more outdoorsy feel called La Terraza. Lieke was going to be on in half an hour, but first we headed to a relatively quiet area.

'Like I said, this all used to be totally open-air.' Alberto pointed to the glass roof while Marta stood at the bar. 'It was wild. It was like a Fellini movie . . . a farmhouse where people danced to everything . . . The Rolling Stones, jazz, hip-hop, mystic rock, Manuel Göttsching, Prince, Art of Noise, Chicago house, reggae, new wave, old Argentine tango, Fleetwood Mac, Kate Bush, Cyndi Lauper, Talk Talk. I love Talk Talk.' He then got quite excited and started to sing 'It's My Life'. He had tears in his eyes. 'Anything and everything. The Balearic beat. Todo vale was the concept. Anything goes. No boundaries. No boundaries between music or people. Finding the shared rhythm. Every class and culture and identity and sexuality. No narrow genres. No dividing things up. No cliques. It was natural and pure and fun. Just finding the universal in it all. Even the theme from *Hill Street Blues*.'

'The theme from *Hill Street Blues*?' I thought of Daniel asking to stay up late to watch a repeat of it. How he had loved that theme tune. How he sat forward on the sofa. And how that joy had been real, and stayed real, and was stored somewhere in the memory of the universe.

Alberto nodded. 'Yes. The cop show. My friend – the legendary Alfredo from Argentina – used to play it a lot at the end of the night. There is nothing more Balearic than the theme to *Hill Street Blues* . . .'

Now Alberto's mind was open to me, I could see it all. He had arrived back on this island in 1976, less than a year after Franco died. He had dropped out of his studies, become a pacifist. He had planned to return to marine biology, but he just wanted a good time. He caught me reading him. So he gave me some footnotes. 'A philosopher from Madrid had decided to turn an old finca in the middle of the countryside into an outdoor discotheque. He called it El Taller de los Olvidadizos – The Workshop of the Forgetful Ones. It was a bit too long, so it became just, simply, Amnesia. Always go with the shorter way! Everyone who went there had something to forget. It felt like the whole world had been traumatised. Franco or Vietnam or the prospect of a nuclear bomb destroying us all. Dancing was better . . . Dancing was not just dancing. It was a symbol of freedom . . . Whoever you were, you could be safe on the dance floor.'

Marta came back with the drinks in glasses, as mesmerising hexagons of light flashed behind her. 'Nada de plástico. No plastic. Plastic is the devil. It destroys the Earth before and after its existence. Evil little microplastics. Fucking up the fish. And us.' I had the sense that Marta would go to actual war for the fish. 'Anyway. Here are your orange juices.'

It was nearly two a.m., so we weaved through the crowds to the terrace room. I passed the girls I had seen on the plane. They were dancing and loving life, their minds luminescent with pleasure. Unlike some in the room, they hadn't even taken any artificial stimulants. They had slept before coming out and were now dancing their cares away, closing their eyes and jerking their bodies as if part of a wonderful collective exorcism.

Although it was indisputably hot, loud and congested – three things I traditionally wasn't a fan of – I was really quite enjoying myself. My legs weren't aching, my hips weren't entirely stiff, and if my ears were ringing I wouldn't have been able to hear them. And I was so caught up in the collective energy that I almost forgot what I was there for.

The Joy of Counting Without Counting

Marta elbowed me. And pointed up towards the DJ booth. And there she was. The untouchable goddess from the billboards. The distraught daughter from the garden centre. In the vast booth, with people looking up at her like they would an emperor at the Colosseum.

She was chatting to the preceding DJ while fiddling around with the technology, music filling the room like a pounding herd of invisible beasts. My view was blocked by a large young man with lots of tattoos of different animals. Snake. Cheetah. Turtle. He was called Stefano and he was an Italian tourist from Bologna who was training to be a vet and healing after a messy break-up. *Move left, move left, move left, move left . . .*

A few seconds later he took a few steps to the left and continued dancing and left me to study Lieke. But there was so much between me and her, so much space, so many people, so many thoughts and emotions and sensations cluttering the air, it was like trying to isolate a single bee amid a swarm.

It turned out that I really liked the music Lieke played. Techno, apparently.

Which was remarkable, as I normally hated electronic music. Well, I had liked 'Good Vibrations' by the Beach Boys in my younger years, and that had contained a theremin, and that is technically an electronic instrument. But you know what I mean. Music that sounds like a robot having a panic attack. Bleep-bleep music. But it turned out I had been missing out.

It had a mathematical beauty to it. I stood at the side of the dance floor as thousands of bodies moved as if they were merely reactive entities, subordinate to the music's force.

Unusually I understood this music instantly, and felt the collective love for it, golden and pure. Beneath the sound of keyboards there was a repetitive bass drum that kept perfect time. *Doof doof doof doof.* Heartbeat pacing. And then there was another beat, lighter, above it, twice as fast. And another even fainter one precisely twice as fast as that. Four beats per measure. A perfect ratio, dividing ranges of time into equal parts within each section. Euclid's algorithm come to life.

It is often said about music that it is the joy people feel when they are counting without realising they are counting. So that is what I realised I was witnessing, as I bobbed my head and scanned the crowd – the collective euphoria of experiencing mathematical harmony in an imperfect world.

Euclid would have loved dancing at Amnesia, I was sure of it. And I loved it too. I loved being amid these dancing people, their bodies breaking free. I loved the two men in love and tenderly kissing each other by the bar. I loved the people on stilts. I loved this space where it seemed everybody could be their true amorphous selves, experimenting with their clothes and hair and bodies, and sex drives, resisting rules and circadian rhythms. I loved the quieter people hanging around the bars all around the room watching the spectacle. I loved the lights and the lasers and even the sudden blasts of cloud from the dry-ice cannons.

I looked up at the balconies that sprawled the perimeter of the room, the VIP area, which had a slightly sad psychic fog hanging over it, as people stood by their tables, self-consciously bopping around their ice buckets and empty bottles of champagne.

Then I stared up at the DJ booth again. And I managed, just about, to catch hold of something. A tender darkness. Grief, maybe. I walked a little closer towards her, through the crowd, trying to avoid all the elbows and enthusiasm. I saw her in the light of day, driving back to her rented apartment in the marina. She was listening to music, but not the kind of music she played. Spanish guitars strumming soft melodies.

Then suddenly, there in the present moment in the club, she looked up from the booth to the crowd and caught sight of me. In fairness, I was probably sticking out like a hamster at a cattery, but she gave me a smile of recognition. And in return I gave her a thought. A memory, to be more accurate. It was the memory contained in Christina's photograph of her, holding the teddy bear. Her seventh birthday. Love and warmth. Light in the dark.

No. Again I am getting this wrong. I wasn't giving it her. I was revealing what was already there. And it was as easy as anything. As easy as getting a man to stick a fork in his leg. And once one memory was revealed others followed, branching and branching, and as she was about to transition into the next track she felt a growing need to do something. A need to fulfil her mother's wish for her to use her platform for good. So instead she selected a different track. Something called 'Memories Of Green' by Vangelis, from the *Blade Runner* soundtrack, which her parents used to play when she was a child.

And then she asked for a microphone, and before anyone knew it she was speaking over the track. Alberto gave me a look. 'It's happening . . .'

I nodded.

It most certainly was.

'Hello, everybody,' she said to the bewildered clubbers, in her strangely accented English. 'I don't normally do this. I don't normally talk over the music. I don't want to interrupt your dancing. But it is just that I have something important to tell you. A month ago my mother died . . .'

This clearly wasn't the night out people had been expecting. Most of the people now had their phones out, filming every word she was saying.

'I didn't always get on with her . . . But she was a good person . . . She cared about this planet of ours . . . And she believed Ibiza was something to protect . . . And Es Vedrà . . . . You know Es Vedrà, right? It's that cool rock you fly in over . . . Well, it's important . . .'

A wild whoop of affirmation filled the room.

'It is a sacred place . . . It is part of the island's mythology . . . It's been untouched for all eternity . . . And now they want to build on it and destroy all the life on that island . . . And they want to own everything from there to Cala d'Hort . . . The whole sea . . . Including the oldest organism in the world . . . Seagrass that has been there for thousands and thousands of years . . . Seagrass that protects the ocean and protects the coast and protects the air we breathe, and they will destroy it . . .'

It was impressive. She was making a speech about a marine carbon sink that sounded energising. '. . . But that isn't going to happen, guys . . . Because tomorrow we are going to protest . . . We are going to keep Es Vedrà free . . . My mother was special in lots of ways – ways you wouldn't believe – but her real superpower was that she cared about people and nature and life . . . Things that are precious . . . We must protect what is precious . . . We will meet at Café Mar y Sol at three p.m. tomorrow afternoon, and we will march through the streets and we will keep them from destroying every piece of land here . . . So who is going to be there with me? Who is going to spread the word on their socials? Who is going to help make my mother's dream come true?'

Another enthusiastic roar. Lieke smiled at me.

'And tell everyone you know! See you tomorrow!' And she seamlessly blended the music into something faster, and the pounding beat started back again. The track was called 'Meteorite'. 'This one is for my mother's friend who is here tonight.' And she pointed right at me. 'Let's show our appreciation for Grace Winters!'

'Wow!' said Marta, patting my shoulder as the whole club gave me some raucous applause. The girls I'd seen on the plane recognised me and clapped their hands above their heads and roared loudest of all.

And Alberto gave me a proud congratulatory smile.

'Now!' bellowed Lieke into the microphone. 'Let's dance like there *is* a tomorrow!'

And so that's what we did, Maurice. We danced. *I* danced. Right there in my chiffon blouse in the middle of Amnesia. I moved my not-so-tired arms and legs to the music with my two new friends.

And, quite honestly, it had been a very long time since I'd had such fun.

Hermana

Marta and Alberto were convivial people. Alberto danced with the energised chaos of a gorilla who had been shot in the bottom, complete with hairy chest on flamboyant show, while his daughter was gifted with an equal lack of self-consciousness but considerably more rhythm. She was lovely, by the way. When you get into your seventies younger people either ignore you or patronise you. Marta had neither instinct. She treated me like a true friend, and it had been quite a while since I'd had one of them.

We danced for a little while longer, but our work was done. Well, half our work was done. We couldn't have done more to spread the word about the protest, but there was something else we needed. Not just twenty thousand people, but eighty thousand euros. And by tomorrow. Well, it was already tomorrow. It was half past three in the morning. A time of day I only ever saw if I needed a wee in the night.

But I had a plan. You may remember I was one of those teachers who would do almost anything to get Year Nines to see the thrill of the world's greatest subject. And so I used to do a lesson on the mathematics of card games. Pyramid solitaire, fraction war, using the order-of-operations rule to get as close to a certain number with four cards, and – of course – every mathematician's favourite, blackjack (or twenty-one, but even a number fan like me would wonder why anyone would call it that when it can be called blackjack).

'Ibiza has a casino, doesn't it?' I said to Alberto and Marta, as we headed towards the taxis. There was a cool breeze in the air, which was wonderful. The perfect weather in Ibiza in summer happens at half past three in the morning.

'It does,' said Marta, a little weary, and wary of the question. 'At the marina in Ibiza Town. I went there once and lost my entire pay cheque from the university.'

'But you didn't have me with you. We have to do this.'

Alberto stared at me as if I was a new species he had never encountered. 'To make *eighty thousand* euros?'

I let his question hang in the air a while. I noticed, in the relative quiet, that my tinnitus was louder than ever. But I didn't mind it. Tinnitus from a night of joyful music was an entirely different thing to tinnitus that just existed for no reason. A negative with no cause is a source of deep misery. So if you can give a negative an equal-value positive cause you can turn it into a zero.

After eight seconds, I answered Alberto.

'Mmm. Yes. I know under normal circumstances it wouldn't be entirely ethical to use the talents in this way. But there is very little about these circumstances that are normal. But you two, you go home . . . It's very late and tomorrow is going to be a big day.'

Marta shook her head and stifled a burp. She was a little tipsy and had a piece of confetti stuck to her forehead. I peeled it off for her. 'Gracias, hermana,' she said. ('Thanks, sister' – I liked that idea.) 'I had my nap earlier. That is all I need. I may never have experienced a blessing from La Presencia but I was born in Ibiza. My circadian rhythms are negotiable.'

So, as we clambered into the taxi, Marta gave the instruction.

'Hello, taxi driver,' she said, pretending to be English for my amusement. 'Casino de Ibiza, please, sir.' And then we were off, with a worldly total of forty-seven euros between us.

Laurel

The Casino de Ibiza was in the affluent district known as the golden mile. I inhaled the balmy air and gazed around at expensive modern apartments and even more expensive modern yachts, with evenly spaced palm trees lining the road and well-manicured flowerbeds and patches of perfectly mown grass.

After we paid the taxi a cat stepped out from beneath a hedge and came up to Alberto. A stray, dappled white and black and orange. A cat full of questions and philosophy and curiosity. Animals loved Alberto. He was a magnet for them. He crouched down with a flinch on account of his old knees and stroked the creature and conversed with her a little while.

Marta, as ever, had a spirit of humoured frustration with him. 'Papá, now is not the time to be Dr Dolittle.'

'She is telling me about the pleasure of watching headlights. She enjoys watching the moving lights of cars and the caress of the breeze . . .' But then he said his goodbyes and wished the creature good luck with her mouse-hunting.

I had once thought him mad, but now I realised he had just been understanding things that others didn't. Maybe that was what madness was: the loneliness of understanding what others can't.

The casino itself was very much in keeping with the billion-euro aesthetic. Modernist design. A potted laurel tree outside so immaculately clipped it looked like it had just won a topiary contest. The exterior of the building was weathered steel, with an artfully rusted appearance. You couldn't see inside, but it was spotlit in such a way that it looked like some kind of decadent heaven was situated within.

I had never been to a casino in my life. I had been to a bingo hall once, with Angela from the charity shop, but that was very different. The doorman – slicked-back hair, sharp suit, infinity symbol tattooed on his wrist – told us we couldn't come in.

'I am sorry, but we are full,' he said. 'And you are all too casual.' He looked at Marta and the glitter on her face. Then he pointed to Alberto, and his ripped shorts and flip-flops and his open Hawaiian shirt and his forest of unseemly chest hair. 'Especially you. This is a sophisticated place.'

Marta began speaking to him in Spanish, earnestly and with considerable hand gestures, but the conversation wasn't going well.

'Change his mind,' Alberto whispered to me. 'I'm finding it too hard. He is clenched like a . . .' He searched for the perfect poetic simile. '. . . a rabbit's anus.'

So I tried to, well, *unclench* the doorman's mind. It was actually considerably easier to enter than the casino.

He was called Javier. He was originally from Cádiz. He liked swimming and watching MMA fights and eating pork and Padrón peppers. He had recently been unfaithful to his wife with a Scottish tourist he had met on the beach at Playa d'en Bossa. The tourist was called Alice.

So I now pretended he was someone I knew but had only just recognised. 'Javier!' I said. 'Wow. It *is* Javier, isn't it?'

He eyed me suspiciously. His mind an orange desert of confusion. 'Um. Yes.'

'So great to meet you! I'm Helen!'

Javier frowned. 'Helen? I don't know any Helens. Now, please, step aside . . .'

'Alice's mum.' And then, feeling cocky: 'La madre de Alice.'

It was like I had slapped him. He was speechless.

'She has shown me the picture of you and her together,' I said, doing my best clueless mum impression. 'The one of you two at a jolly nice daytime disco. Oh, and that one of you drinking caipirinhas together at a busy café by the sea in San Antonio. Café Mambo. She said you were a lovely man. Had her best interests at heart.'

Javier was flustered. His colleague, a squat fellow with a sardonic, grizzled vibe, was looking on with interest.

'I don't know what you are talking about, lady.'

'Poor Alice,' I went on, enjoying myself now. 'She is quite besotted with you. She wants to tell the whole world.' I leaned in, to pat his chest and give him a conspiratorial whisper. 'But I have told her that *just maybe* you might not want the whole world to know. Especially a *certain person.*'

He gulped. He nodded. He understood. 'What do you want?'

I took a breath and said in my most reasonable tone: 'I would really like for me and my two friends here to be able to play a game of poker.'

Javier looked defeated. I had only seen the expression once before. In the eyes of our recently castrated Pomeranian.

The poor chap then proceeded to beckon us through.

Marta elbowed me, stifling a giggle. Her sleepy mind suddenly as vibrant as a sky full of fireworks. 'Look at us,' she said, 'Ocean's Three.'

'Okay, be cool,' said Alberto, about as cool as a sauna. 'Let's get to work.'

Roulette

There was a quiet solemnity inside. The kind you might find in a church. People seated at tables or leaning over roulette wheels, sending silent prayers.

We passed the blackjack table and Marta made a questioning face, but I shook my head. There was no point trying to win money playing blackjack, because anyone with determination and basic addition and subtraction skills can learn to cheat at blackjack by counting cards. You give dealt cards lower than seven a +1 and cards higher than seven a -1 and you can work out the probability of the next card being high or low. Casinos are always on the lookout for people who do this. The roulette wheel was safer. So that is where we went.

Everyone was betting safely on black or red or multiple rows but that was no good to us. A bet on a colour would only double our money, whereas a bet on a single number would give us a pay-out of 35–1. And 35 x 47 would give us €1,645, and 1,645 is a handsome number. So I was feeling confident as we took our seats at the wheel.

We watched for a while, and Alberto realised he could predict the outcome only after the wheel was turning, whereas I was able to see the winning number two, three or even four turns ahead. So it was down to me. To considerable bemusement, I placed the chips down – all of them – on the number I saw, which was thirty-three.

'It's my birthday!' Marta told the small crowd, in Spanish, excitedly celebrating her made-up birthday as she hugged me. 'Tengo thirty-three años.'

'That's right,' I added. 'And she is my lucky friend! So thirty-three it is!'

And the wheel was turned, and the ball began to spin and I wasn't even nervous. I knew a minute into the future as well as I knew a minute into the past.

So that is what happened. The ball landed on thirty-three. Good old stubborn thirty-three.

We had another go, but I knew if I placed it on an individual number people would get suspicious. After all, the odds of winning once was a realistic one in thirty-seven. But to get two numbers right in a row the odds are a lot higher because:

$$1/37^2 = 1/1369$$

The beautiful thing about roulette is the choice on offer. You can go for a single number, or two adjoining numbers, or three horizontal numbers as laid out on the felt, or a whole column, or twelve numbers at once, or do the first or second half, or all the reds or all the blacks. It is tantalising in its variety. As with life, you can weigh up the inherent risks and rewards and act accordingly. It appeals to the conservative-minded as much as the daring.

So, on Alberto's prompting, I went for a couple of colour bets rather than individual numbers. Then, as Marta left for the bathroom, I placed a deliberate wrong bet for a lower amount on two adjoining numbers. Then bet big on the first twelve numbers. By that point we had more than fifteen thousand in winnings and had become very visible.

'We must be more like cuttlefish, not clownfish,' mumbled Alberto. 'Everyone can see us.'

But then I thought again about the man I had passed in Ibiza Town. He'd not only lost the night before – when I tried to see who he'd lost to, the man he was playing had looked remarkably like Art Butler.

'Poker,' I whispered to Alberto.

And right on cue Marta came back from the bathroom looking like she had seen a ghost. I looked at her. Alberto looked at her. We both knew straight away.

She had just seen Art Butler. He was in the casino. He was in the poker room.

The Turn and the River

We took our chips and headed to the inner sanctum that was the poker room.

'Wait,' I said, before we entered.

Marta tilted her head. 'Wait *what*?'

'You shouldn't go in there.'

Alberto backed me up. 'Grace has a point. Elvis Presley. The radio. The wine glass. It was a warning to you. You must stay back . . .'

'And you must stay with her,' I told him, as a distant roar of applause came from the baccarat table. 'You need to make sure she's going to be okay.'

Marta didn't like this. 'But we can't let you go in there alone.'

'I'm a big girl. I'll be all right.'

Alberto made a reluctant groan and gave me his chips. Then his daughter did the same. 'Okay,' he sighed. 'But we will not be far away.'

And with that, I walked towards the tense quiet of the poker room and the terrifying mystery of Art Butler.

Art was sitting with the other players, wearing a crumpled linen shirt and a frown to match. He was staring at his cards with a fixed focus. But beyond that, there wasn't much I could sense at all. It was like trying to see the image of something in a painting by Jackson Pollock. It was too tangled and hummed with prohibitive force.

This was why Christina had never known who wanted to kill her. It was because he was almost unknowable. His mind was Fort Knox.

A woman with a tangerine fan leaned on his shoulder, but he hardly seemed to notice her. He looked tired as a melted candle, but he was also clearly driven to win the game he was playing. And he did.

I took a seat and put the buy-in, a black chip worth a hundred euros, onto the green felt of the table.

Art looked at me. I still had no idea what he was thinking but he certainly acted as though nothing was up.

My plan was to win some money *and* try to get into Art's mind.

Two birds, one stone.

Now, before I continue, I should say that I had never played a game of poker in my life. It was never part of my Year Nine card game lessons, and I had never been to a casino. And yet I suddenly knew I could play it. I had seen enough films and read enough books that had featured poker in some capacity that – with my enhanced mental capacities – I now knew how to play, even without having to mind-read anyone.

So.

Texas hold 'em.

Aside from me and Art Butler, there were six other players.

There was: the rich fifty-year-old Anglo-American music industry lawyer and online wellness advocate Melissa, who was currently high on cocaine. The eighty-one-year-old restaurateur José. The newly divorced German former billionaire called Dietmar, who had inherited a pharmaceutical company and had a short walk back to his yacht. The mildly drunk, sentimentally-minded American guy from Atlanta called Benjamin, who was staying on a work freebie at Art Butler's spa hotel, and had just been dancing at nearby Pacha but was missing his dogs and his mother and his boyfriend in Milan. The insomniac Parisian called Anne, who worked in asset management and wrote erotic poems no one ever saw and who hadn't been able to concentrate on her novel in bed at the hotel next door and didn't want to lie awake depressed next to her husband. And an Italian art dealer called Flavio, who had triceps sculpted by Michelangelo. This was the man I had passed earlier. The one who had lost to Art last night and was back for more. And then of course there was Art Butler himself.

Right there and totally distant all at once.

The first round I had nothing and folded early. The second round went mostly the same way, and Art won big thanks to a flush of spades. I tried to read him again but there was nothing. No information, no emotion, no psychic text or context. I knew I had to beat him, because I had a strong sense that vulnerability was the way in, and there was no evident vulnerability – or anything at all – at this point.

The third round was where it got interesting.

After the flop, I had a pair of sixes. Then the fourth and fifth cards were revealed to the table. The turn and the river (I knew not only the rules of poker, but the rather poetic terms too). I now had two kings as well.

A fairly strong hand.

I sensed the rest of the table.

Melissa had a pair of threes. Dietmar had a strong hand – a straight – and was feeling pretty confident putting a nice pile of chips forward to raise the bet. We were playing for one thousand, four hundred euros. If I didn't at least match Dietmar's raise, I would have to fold. So I matched it. Anne and Benjamin and José had nothing, and all of them folded. Flavio had an eight in his hand to match the eight on the table. He mulled it a moment, then folded too. Art raised. Melissa matched it.

It was time to place a doubt in Dietmar's mind. Which was easy. His mind was the softest and most malleable I had entered since poor Brian's at the beach restaurant. And the doubt I pressed into him was a simple one: *Something feels wrong.*

He was suddenly so nervous he folded, to his own confusion.

'Why did I do that?' he asked, in English.

So now it was just Melissa and Art and me.

Melissa was already starting to feel paranoid and antsy of her own accord, because she was on a cocaine downswing and vowing to do a full week of ashtanga yoga and vegetable juice after the holiday, so she bailed. And now it was just me and Art. He looked at me. I met his eyes. And for the first time since I had sat down at the table, I caught an opening, a tiny rip in his mental fabric. I didn't waste the moment. I sneaked straight in like a burglar through a window.

He had a similar hand to mine, I realised, as he sipped his whisky. Two pairs. Two fours and, like me, two sixes. The difference was my two kings trumped his lower pair. But it wasn't just the cards I wanted to read. So I took my chance to go deep.

Contradictions

Art Butler's mind was a forest of contradictions. There was nothing particularly good in it, but it did contain a lot of oppositional forces.

He was full of pride and shame, ego and insecurity, cold and heat, fear and determination, apathy and passion, reservation and impulsivity, everything and nothing. He was a sitting paradox. A terminally flawed lifeform. He was, in short, a human.

But. *But.* There was something else going on. There was more to his mind than I could reach. Something there but not there. An unseen element, something that blurred darkness and light, a mysterious *penumbra* lurking in the cave of his psyche. Something hurt and sad and soft.

I don't want to make him sound too enigmatic or charismatic. He was a killer. He had killed the politician Ricardo Martinez. Maybe others. And he would have killed Christina. And he was prepared to kill Marta. But to know is to conquer. And I wanted to know him.

Another note that struck me was that he was filled with a kind of mental yearning. I pictured it as a hole that kept collapsing the more he tried to fill it. He was in it. In the hole. Freefalling for ever. He was worth £889 million and ached to make it to a billion. He had a very big yacht. He travelled everywhere and drank and consumed expensively. But really, I sensed he wasn't living. He had replaced the idea of life with something else, with the kind of hunger that can't be sated.

He laid down his cards and I laid down mine. He took the defeat as he took everything – personally. I gathered the chips and his anger grew. I could feel him in my thoughts like shade across a lawn.

We played again. I won again. The six became five as Melissa left the game. Then four as Dietmar yawned out of the room, defeated.

Because I could mentally read everyone's cards, I knew when to play and when to bail. I felt I had cracked the whole key to life. Knowing which hands to play and which hands to give up on. And which bad hands I could play with and still win. I wasn't even trying to play it safe. I wanted to weaken him, make him vulnerable. There was a risk he would get angry, but there was a bigger risk in leaving him. So I continued.

But I must be honest here.

I was *enjoying myself*. And that was no small thing.

Joy!

Me. The person who had never even indulged in a lottery ticket. I know it is probably terrible of a former teacher to tell their former student about the joy of playing poker at five in the morning, but it wasn't the gambling. It was the sense of doing something old widows aren't supposed to do. It felt like Caesar coming back and crossing the Rubicon. *The turn and the river.* As though I had this night taken risks and left an old version of myself behind and expanded the territory of who I was. Sometimes the rules of who we are supposed to be need to be broken. Sometimes we need to obey something deeper. I wondered if Karl would approve or disapprove of me being in Ibiza, using my newfound paranormal gifts to play poker with a psychopath, and then realised that was irrelevant. I was done with the diktats of ghosts. It was sometimes good to be naughty, especially when the naughty thing was actually a good thing in disguise. Within an hour at the table, I had accumulated, together with the earlier winnings elsewhere in the casino, fifty-six thousand euros. In other words, I had more than half the amount I needed. I felt like I was not only dominating the game but dominating the mysterious Art Butler too.

The dealer – a tall man with mother issues – was smiling at me. He didn't like Art Butler very much. And Art just stayed there, not saying a word. And we had quite a crowd now.

It was all going well.

But then, after losing that final round, I saw Art smile at me. And as he smiled I felt a sudden terror, a feeling like I had walked into a trap that I didn't know existed.

'It's funny,' he said, speaking for the first time as he stared at me across the table. 'The thing with poker is you have to discover every player's weakness. The thing that will distract them. I think I have discovered yours. She is standing in the other room.'

Then his face changed, and he looked towards the exit with an intense glower. Even the other players noticed. But they obviously didn't realise what was happening.

And there, right on cue, was the moment.

Because that was when I heard the rising hubbub from the other room. There was a scream. And I felt the force of fear emanating from Alberto's mind. It came to me as clearly as a sight or scent, a siren of panic.

And then his distant voice.

'Marta!'

A Lot to Take In

Just because something happened, you are under no obligation to believe it. All I will do is lay out the facts as I remember them and leave it to you to interpret them how you wish. The only thing I ask is that you leave a door open in your mind to possibility. We are never at the finish line of understanding. There is always something about life and the universe that we are still to discover. That has been the ultimate lesson for me. That at any moment along the line of our existence it can branch off. We get so used to it going in a straight line that we believe that is all life is, and then, suddenly, it twists or turns or takes a sudden right angle.

So.

Here goes.

Here is what happened as I remember it.

I left the poker table and headed to the main room.

When I got there I saw Marta was lying on her back on the diamond-patterned carpet, in her jolly striped trousers and her blue dot T-shirt, struggling for breath. A small crowd loomed over her. I pushed my way through. A faint purple hue was on her cheeks, her wild hair even wilder than usual, as if she'd been in some kind of struggle. A crowd was gathered. Alberto was on his knees beside her. He looked up with boyish fear. Eyes wide.

'Grace, he's got a hold of her . . . Do something . . . I tried . . . He's too strong . . .'

'Marta?'

She clutched her own neck. I could sense her tightened windpipe. People were getting staff to come over. One member of staff, still at the blackjack table, was phoning for an ambulance. But then, suddenly, she wasn't. The phone appeared to become piping hot in her hands and she instinctively let it go with a sudden jerk of her arm. The device then smashed and burned and incinerated.

It was him. He was there, still sitting at the poker table and using his mental abilities to do whatever he wanted. It was terrifying. To face that kind of murderous power. Smiling nonchalance. To see how freely evil could roam, if the usual fences of law and reality didn't exist.

I knelt down.

'Marta, it's okay, it's okay . . .' An absolutely ridiculous thing to say, given the circumstances. But if my mind could make grown men stick forks in their legs and burst lobster tanks wide open, I was pretty sure it could do something on a smaller and closer scale, such as expand the airway of a restricted trachea literally centimetres away. I knew I had to act fast. I knew that if she was taken away in an ambulance she may never return.

I had a choice. I either went back into the poker room, to deal with Art and nullify him, or stay with Marta. Push or pull. The fire or the burn. I stayed with Marta.

I know what I told you earlier. About how my mind now was equivalent to a body, and just as bodies can move around in physical space my mind suddenly seemed able to actively roam into other places and ignore barriers and how I felt like the energy of a wish now came with power. Well, that was still true.

But it was tough. It was tougher than anything. I was wishing as hard as anyone could wish for Marta to breathe freely, but it was like mentally pushing against a wall. No. Wrong analogy. It was more like a tug-of-war. Little bits of progress – gasps of breath – followed by feeling too weak to help her.

Because of course there was a counterforce pressing against every wish, pushing in the opposite direction.

It was at this point that the whole room went quiet. There were no more voices and no more thoughts crowding the air. Because everyone in the room was now collapsed on the floor. They weren't struggling to breathe like Marta. They had just had their consciousness temporarily disabled. You know, like a hypnotist putting someone to sleep. Only, en masse, and without the talk. The only exception was Alberto, who – with the talents inside him – was a little harder to control. But he was still being pushed back away from Marta as if being pressed by a hurricane, until he was pinned against a slot machine.

'He's got me,' Marta managed to say, her hand clutching mine, then weakening again. Her voice no more than a rasp. Her fingers falling open like petals. His plan was clear. He was going to kill Marta and he was going to get away with it. I could not let it happen.

I changed tactic. Instead of focusing on expanding her airways, I stared over to the poker room and focused on pushing Art away. But he wasn't in the poker room.

He was standing right there, above the crowd of collapsed bodies. He was cradling his tumbler of whisky as his smile curled like a cat's tail.

'Hello, Grace,' he said. 'How are you doing?'

The Miniature Bottle

Marta's breath was fading beside me. Alberto was still pinned against the fruit machine, his expression pained as he tried to wrestle with the force of Art's power.

'You made a big mistake,' Art said, with a voice of almost sincere concern as he stared at me. 'You should never have come to Ibiza. You should have just stayed where you were, old lady. On your sofa.'

I stayed fixed on him. I was burrowing into him now. Seeing the truth. The politicians and protesters he had threatened and harmed and killed. His obliviousness to life every time he chose a new plot of land. But also, I was seeing pain. A jagged, open wound. A gleaming invisibility. A memory that wouldn't leave him. His dead father, as he found him in the garage.

I remembered what Alberto had said.

The only time La Presencia has been made visible in broad daylight. And it wasn't an adult. It was a boy. An English boy. He was on holiday here. He nearly drowned. He swam too far out from the beach, and no one could get to him. His father saw him but too late. He went under. He was under for seven minutes. He was dead, effectively . . .

I pictured Art as a child on the beach. He was Arthur, then. Artie. The beach was Cala d'Hort. His mother was reading a novel and his father was reading *The Times* and he was bored of digging holes to catch the waves. So he went out to swim.

I saw him as he swam further and further out, imagining he could make it to Es Vedrà. I saw him as he looked around and realised he was way out of his depth, the currents too strong to swim back. I felt the weight in his young arms that could hardly make another stroke. I felt him wrestle in panic, as his chin slipped below the waterline, calling for his parents . . . His father eventually saw him. His head sprung up and he pressed his palm into the sand and ran into the water. A desperate front crawl to him but he never got there. Artie never forgave his father for not looking sooner. 'I would be dead if it was up to you.' And his father couldn't cope with what nearly happened, and what had happened. He felt he had gone mad. He turned to drink and eventually hanged himself, and Artie had felt a pain so deep that he used to carry a box of matches with him so he could light a flame under his palm to distract himself.

As I observed Art sipping his whisky, I thought this couldn't be so. La Presencia would not bestow gifts on someone who would so drastically use them for harm.

'That's where you're wrong,' Art said, still leaning over me in that casino as Marta slipped into unconsciousness. He said it with his mouth but I could feel him in my mind. 'You see, I know you think you were the special one, Grace. I know what they told you. That your talents are the best there have been since at least Joan Bonanova. But it's a fabrication. It isn't true. You see, next to mine, your talents are sadly rather mediocre. La Presencia came to me *as a child*. I was with it for seven whole minutes while my parents thought I was dead. The whole ocean glowed with the effort. I have it in me. It chose me. My parents didn't protect me, but La Presencia did. It saved me because it saw my potential. It saw what I could be. I make money for this place. I give back. I give beautiful experiences . . .'

'No,' I said, seeing everything in his mind as I was saying it. Seeing it all light up like a dark sea. 'You take life. That is what you do. You want to kill Marta because you know tomorrow she is going to stop the Es Vedrà resort at the protest. Just like you knew Christina would have stopped it. You killed Ricardo Martínez after he blocked the application for one of your resorts. You use this power that the ocean gave you and you do terrible things with it. You choose the most controversial locations and the most sensitive habitats because it makes you feel in control. It makes you feel what you didn't feel when your parents weren't there to save you.'

'And you would know all about neglectful parenting, Grace . . .'

Marta had stopped breathing. She was still. That terrifying stillness I knew too well.

'Don't cry for her. She was nothing special. Even La Presencia knew that. Poor, unchosen Marta . . .'

He wanted me to say something. He wanted me to communicate with him. Hate wants hate. But I realised I didn't need to. I didn't need to talk with hate. Because I understood what Alberto had in his hand. The rum bottle. I remembered that first encounter with Alberto, when he had shown me his miniature rum bottle. I remembered him explaining how it helped him become sober after his wife died. He had it now. He had been reaching for it. He couldn't move his hand for me to see it, because Art had him rigidly held in place. But that was okay. Because I could see the glowing light coming through his fingers. I knew what it was. Extract of La Presencia.

So I didn't focus on Art, and I didn't focus on Marta, I focused on the thick, aged, sun-weathered fingers of Alberto. And I opened them. And the bottle dropped, and it didn't smash on the carpet, but Art had heard or noticed, and his attention was gone for a second. So I smashed the glass with my mind and then it was free. La Presencia was there, a small glowing puddle that refused to be absorbed, and it was moving now, towards Marta.

'Stop,' commanded Art. '*Stop!*'

But it wasn't stopping. It was crawling like a legless and luminescent watery creature, gleaming brighter and brighter, and then when it reached Marta it rose through her hair and across her skin and into her mouth, and, a moment later, she coughed and her eyes opened. She was very much alive.

And those eyes stared at Art, just as I stared at Art, and just as Alberto over by the fruit machine stared at Art. And there we were. All now gifted with whatever talents La Presencia had chosen to give us.

And then something even more incredible. Marta's body *glowed*. Not massively, but undoubtedly, and not for a long time but for long enough. Flickering, and blue, with little specks of light moving through her veins like headlights in a city. Or like a thousand lanternfish in the deep ocean, as Alberto later put it.

And then I felt something strange inside me. A feeling of total *calm*. Which was ridiculous, given that I was surrounded by a load of collapsed bodies in the middle of a casino facing off against a murderous psychopath with inhuman powers. And the calm came with a feeling of internal warmth and togetherness. I felt like something had been missing and now it wasn't. And I looked at my hand and saw tiny lights shoot through the veins there too. The same with Alberto. He was staring at his hands in disbelief and laughing.

'It's working together . . . it's connecting us!'

Marta remembered the words on her placard and stood up, La Presencia's light still travelling like fireflies through her body. 'Nos alzamos como el océano.'

Art was a mix of confusion and consternation. Then he stared down at his own hands and was relieved to see the moving lights there too. 'You can't touch me!'

But still, he was worried. He sensed this was not the time to strike. And the worry was strong enough for him to retreat. He walked away, as La Presencia faded in all of us.

'Tomorrow,' he said and pointed at us, as if the word contained the terror of fate itself. 'Tomorrow will be the end.'

Everyone else in the casino was waking from their unconscious state, bleary-eyed and confused, and getting to their feet. There was a general bubble of commotion in the room again, this time infused with gasps of wonder and muttered questions.

Alberto frowned at his daughter. 'We can't just let him go. He just tried to kill you . . . He is a killer.'

'We can stop the hotel,' Marta said. 'There will be enough people. And we can get the money, we don't need much more. We can get it. The casino doesn't close . . .'

As Art Butler reached the door he glanced around at all the humans staring at him. He was about to say something else. I sensed a big monologue, half-formed, waiting unhatched behind his twitching lips. But he thought twice about it, and then he simply walked away, out into the foyer, beyond the security guards, into the emerging day.

We watched him leave, doing absolutely nothing about it because of all the witnesses. I then returned to the poker room to collect my chips, thinking, *That was a little too easy.*

Because, of course, it was.

The Gathering

Marta was speaking beside a lake, in the shimmering heat. Sun scattered light across the water like a thousand jewels.

The lake was a small one, in the Parc de la Pau, where we and all the protesters had arrived following a slow and noisy thronging through the streets of Ibiza Town.

The *Diario de Ibiza* would later say that more than twenty thousand protesters came to the streets of Ibiza Town that particular Thursday afternoon. Indeed, the actual figure was twenty-seven thousand, four hundred and fifty-two.

There was every type of person you can find in Ibiza there. The old and the young. Hippies and business owners. Locals and foreigners. Rich and poor. Clubbers and yogis. Modernists and traditionalists. Radicals and reactionaries. The hyper-healthy and the eternally hungover. The shouters and the silent. Winners and losers. Families and friends and loners. And drummers. Lots of drummers. I could have done without the drummers, I have to be honest.

I will give you a roughly translated extract of Marta's speech:

'When me and my friend Christina went online and asked for people to protest against the development on Es Vedrà, I expected about a hundred people. To see all of us here is truly remarkable. Ibiza is a special place. And I wish Christina could be here today. She would have loved to see this sight. She would have wanted to thank you all for coming. Today is the day we make a stand and tell the people with power that nature is something we want to protect . . . Because when they destroy nature, they destroy a part of us. Today is the day we tell Sofía Torres we don't want flowers to go extinct. We don't want goats to be shot. We don't want any more agreements to destroy the most precious parts of this island. We don't want any more of Art Butler and his Eighth Wonder Resorts stamping all over this island. Because what is good for this island is good for us too. We will keep protecting what makes this place special. We will keep rising like the sea . . . And we have risen. And we will walk to Sofía Torres and Art Butler and make sure she fulfils the promise, that if we turned up before the start of her press conference with more than twenty thousand people and eighty thousand euros she would withdraw her support for the Es Vedrà deal. Which would mean her party would too. Which would mean there would be no deal at all. So that is what we will do! We will walk to the Eighth Wonder hotel in Talamanca, beside Talamanca beach, and we . . .'

She was good at this. She walked back and forth, pumping her fists like a rock star. The crowd cheered at the right moments. Everything was going well. And we had eighty-one thousand euros, in cash, in my beach bag.

Again, I was enjoying myself. People think of a protest as something angry, or something earnestly hopeful, but it can also be something quite meditative and healing. It is about being part of something bigger. A kind of selflessness, in the true sense of the word. The way a herring must feel swimming in a school with her fellows.

All we had to do was walk the crowd down to the hotel in Talamanca before the start of the Eighth Wonder press conference at five p.m., show the money and the people to Sofía Torres, and she would uphold her bargain, or face the wrath of the whole island.

But something was wrong. There was a note of discord within the plan.

Something I only picked up on because I was standing near to a journalist – Rosa Piera, thirty-eight years old, hypochondriac, recently divorced, mind like a hectic funfair in the rain – and she had just received a WhatsApp message from a colleague telling her the press conference would be taking place at Cala d'hort in half an hour. On the actual beach.

Alberto realised. 'We have to tell everyone.'

'No. Think about it. It's a twenty-minute drive. If everyone here heads there, we'll never make it. The roads will be blocked. And what if Art does something to them? It's too big a risk. Let's wait for Marta and go.'

Alberto sighed. I knew what he was thinking. He'd heard Marta's speech and it was *long*.

'We need to go *now*. Right this minute. Let's leave Marta here. We can handle this. More than twenty thousand people already turned up to the protest, so that part is done. We just need to show Sofía the money and film us doing so, and if Art is a problem, we will deal with it. ¡Vamos! ¡A la playa!'

A Bag of Sand

The press conference was about to start.

There was a small stage set up on the beach, with journalists sat in chairs on the sand and a little aisle between them. Like a wedding. Or a funeral. Es Vedrà loomed large in the background, dark and powerful and beautiful, like a shadowy and inescapable truth.

Sofía Torres and Art Butler were seated on the stage, behind a table garnished with papers and water bottles, with Art Butler's PR person ready to do the compering. Sofía was looking at her watch.

Alberto was striding across the sand, shouting in a cocktail of Spanish and Catalan and English and Alberto for them to stop the press conference.

Art Butler's PR, a brittle-minded person called Alison, just looked over to a hired security guard on the back row and clicked her fingers. 'Paco?'

'I am not going to cause any trouble,' continued Alberto, as I tried to keep up with him across the sand. 'I just have something important to tell Sofía Torres. There is a video of her on the internet agreeing to prevent the development of Es Vedrà if we managed to get her twenty thousand protesters and eighty thousand euros. Well, I can confirm that there are many more people than that currently walking the streets of Ibiza Town. And in my good friend's bag we have eighty-one thousand euros in cash, which—'

Sofía was deeply uncomfortable. She undid her water bottle. 'We will discuss this after.'

'No,' Alberto said, stepping forward. '*We will discuss this now.* You made a promise.'

The smattering of journalists were looking at us. I felt their focus on me the way a flower feels a press, but I stayed firm. I looked around. There was no one else on the beach, I realised. The beach boutique was empty. Even the restaurant was empty. I noticed a new tank now. And new lobsters. Alberto's boat was there, though. The rickety old *Neptuno*. Bobbing in the waters. And his even older rowing boat, once his grandmother's, perched high up the beach in the distance.

Sofía turned to Art. 'I'm sorry about this.'

Art smiled. The smile disconcerted me. I couldn't understand it. It had taken me an hour to get inside his mind last night. But I was pretty sure the smile was genuine. I remembered him leaving the casino voluntarily the previous night. Too easily. This was all a trap. 'It's over, Mrs Winters.'

That did it. I stormed over and put my bag on their table. I opened it and showed them the cash. 'It's all there.'

'It's too late,' said Sofía, her hand cupped over her microphone. 'The deal has been signed.'

'No,' said Alberto, backing me up. Putting another useless 'no' into the air. 'We have the money. We *have the money*, Sofía.'

'Unfortunately, you don't,' said Sofía.

'What?'

'The casino wants it back. They believe it was won unfairly. Several witnesses reported seeing you bring your own cards to the poker table.'

I shook my head. 'That's a lie. Art is making them think that. That's what's happening.'

Sofía shrugged. 'I'm sorry. But you have to go now.'

Alberto stayed staring at her. 'You don't know this, but I am from the north of this island too. We are from the same village, Sofía. Santa Agnès de Corona. I was already an adult before you were born, but I was there. In the little house opposite the church. The house with the almond tree outside the window.'

'I know the one . . .'

I wondered momentarily what Alberto was doing. But then I saw her memory. She was a child, watching as they carried the coffin of Alberto's grandmother across the street to the church.

'I am of this island as you are,' he was saying. 'And like you, and unlike *that man there*, I want what is best for it. I remember when travelling from the north to the south took half a day, not half an hour. I liked that. You had to respect the shape of the land. The topography.

You had to respect the hills. The pines and the soil. All of it. And it helped to keep ourselves whole too. If you destroy the nature around you, you destroy the nature inside you soon enough.'

'We are in a different time,' Sofía said, softly, as she looked across the beach towards a Guardia Civil officer. The frowning, difficult one I had spoken to, walking over the sand towards me. Carlos Guerrero. The one who had the recurring dream of being urinated on by a lion.

'Cheating at a casino is illegal,' Art was saying. 'They treat it very seriously here in Ibiza. Quite rightly so.'

I felt terrible, weak and useless, standing there in that heat.

Alberto looked more upset than angry, standing on the beach and staring out to the sea beyond Art. '*Hijo de puta.*'

'I will tell the truth,' I told Art, with a fearless defiance I'd never experienced. 'I will tell the police. And I will tell everyone else. Over and over. Until I am believed. And I can make them believe.'

Art ignored these words and stayed in his chair, staring up at me. 'You look ill,' he said. 'You look tired. Do you want to sit down?'

He was doing something. I knew he was doing something. I realised every time we had felt we had the upper hand over him – like last night at the casino – was only because he *wanted us to feel we had the upper hand.*

'Grace?' Alberto's voice spun around my head.

Sofía stood up. I heard her voice, as she came towards me. 'Are you okay? Do you want to sit down?'

'I'm . . .'

Everything suddenly felt very heavy, as if the sky began at my shoulders and had a real weight, and then things began to spin and I staggered forward, trying to balance, my eyes on Art's stare, following the slope of the beach until I was almost at the sea. And that is when I collapsed.

Salacia

I was between the tall trees and the glowing sea, trapped in that other world.

The Beach of Truth

'Why am I back here?'

I was so weak it took me a moment to notice the red bicycle leaning against the sand. I knew this bicycle. I even knew the model. It was the only bicycle in the world I knew this well. An old red BMX from the eighties.

And then I noticed the footprints in the sand.

Leading away from the bike, towards the trees.

I followed the footprints into the forest, each step a growing struggle, but I kept going. I wanted the truth that Christina had promised.

Eventually, I reached him. A boy sitting cross-legged on the ground. He was in shadow. When I trod closer I could see he was wearing his paisley shirt that he had made in textiles class and the skin on his face shone with dark blood. His hair was matted with it. But he was smiling when he saw me.

It was him. I could finally see him. The truth of him. He wasn't in Salacia. But he was in this Salacian vision, which like all my Salacian visions was trying to show me the reality of something long denied.

Our son. Our beautiful, darling boy.

'Daniel.'

I ran over and hugged him.

'Don't cry, Mummy. Please don't cry.'

It was his voice. It was his exact voice. Right there, as if nothing had happened for thirty-two years.

'Daniel, I'm sorry. It was my fault. I should have looked after you. I shouldn't have let you out on the bike in that rain.'

'It wasn't your fault, Mum. It was no one's fault. I was angry for no reason at all . . .'

'You wanted to go to the shops with me and I didn't go. Because it was raining.'

He shook his head. Adamant. 'No. No. I didn't want you. I wanted to be on my own. I took off on my own. I'm sorry, Mum, but you cramped my style.'

'I . . . I . . .' Guilt is hard to let go of. So I stuttered for a while. 'I still shouldn't have let you go out in that downpour.'

'You didn't have a chance to tell me not to go out. I was already headed down Wragby Road by the time you even knew I wasn't there.'

This was true. This was all true. But for some reason it was never part of the memory.

'You had a whole life ahead of you. It was a waste. I think of you every single day, Daniel.'

'It doesn't have to be like this. You have nothing to feel guilty about. No more than anyone else.'

'I miss you so much.'

He scrunched up his nose. 'You miss me but don't see me. You just see your own guilt. You just see versions of me as a grown-up that would probably never have existed.'

I had nothing to say to that, because it was true. Of course it was. There was only truth here.

'You're needed, Mum. You can be happy again. You don't have to let things turn to sand. You were so happy, once upon a time. You can be that way again.'

Once upon a time.

'It is deep inside me. The guilt. I was your mother. I should have protected you.'

'I don't want to be your guilt. I want to be your son. Please . . . it's time . . .'

'Yes,' I said. 'It really is.'

And then the blood started to disappear.

His large eyes and smiling face, the one that was always ready to change at any mood alteration, the one that crumpled like a spoon-smashed egg every time he cried. He looked as happy and healthy as he had done in the last school photograph.

'You will remember me like this now. Not as a moment, but a

person. You will know it wasn't your fault. Now, please, go. You are pure now. You can be the signal that you heard about. You can save yourself and you can save others. They need you.'

And then he ran away, into the trees, and I stood there a second longer, as a solitary bluebird flew and danced in the air.

The Signal Can Happen Now

I opened my eyes. The tide was lapping at my hair.

I saw Sofía standing in Art's way. She was talking to him.

Art looked distressed. Yes, that is the word. *Distressed.* Not angry, not cold, not villainous.

'I'm . . .'

He never finished that sentence. The unsaid word an eternal mystery. But there was no time to ponder as he switched and stared with burrowing eyes at Sofía. He was about to do her harm. He knew that without her interference I would be dead by now.

She spoke with confidence. 'This was all a mistake. *I* made a mistake. This island doesn't want you.' I saw her as a child helping her arthritic grandfather get out of a chair.

Art was about to hurt her. I couldn't let it happen.

Alberto was beside me. 'Grace, you are stronger now. It came to you. While you lay there. The signal can happen now. You can send it. You just have to realise how connected you are to all of it. To everything. You can do it, Grace.'

I remembered the paragraph he had written in *La vida imposible.*

This fisherman was called Joan Bonanova . . . He recounted to a journalist how he felt connected to every animal on Ibiza and managed to send them a signal. And others corroborated this report, saying they had seen animals act in a strange manner that night. How creatures of all species had acted as one . . .

'Look, Grace . . . Look at the sea . . . It healed you.'

So I looked at the sea. In fact, everyone was now looking at the sea. Because once you saw it, it was impossible *not* to look at it.

It was glowing that impossible blue. Brighter and broader than ever. Pretty much all the way from the beach to Es Vedrà. And as with the first time I saw La Presencia's glow, it was like staring at a feeling. But this time that feeling was stronger than ever. It was a hope so strong it became certainty.

'I've seen this before,' said Art, aghast. He was remembering the day La Presencia saved him and carried him back to this very beach. For a moment, he felt like he was eleven again.

I got to my feet, and I realised everything was different. I thought of Joan Bonanova himself. The fisherman saved by La Presencia. The one who wasn't just in Alberto's book but also Christina's message. The one she had described as having had 'such a pure soul, *free from guilt and sin*'. The one who sent a signal to every animal on the island to fight the fascist soldiers.

Without guilt and grief and pain to imprison me, I realised I was everywhere. I was we. I was the sum of infinities. I was in every mind. I was in every grain of sand. I was in every drop of water. The isolated fortress of me no longer existed. I was still me, but also I was everyone else. The way a one is still an entity to itself yet there in every other number. I was wide, wide open. There were no lines between myself and others, or between humans and animals, or animals and plants. Everything was just a connecting thread in life's tapestry. I had an infinite power in that moment. A power granted to me by the ocean, by La Presencia. I wasn't there to *save the planet*. I *was the planet*. Just as we are all the planet. The difference was that I was allowed right there to really feel it. It was like I had a telephone line to every creature on Earth.

And I was calling for help. I was indeed sending a signal.

'What the *fuck*?' Art wondered aloud.

And now of course he wasn't talking about La Presencia's light. He was talking about something that looked sublime and ridiculous all at once, the way miracles are inclined to do. He was talking about the sky full of birds.

I didn't have to follow his stare, like everyone else did. I knew about the cormorants flying towards him, responding to my silent hope, their shining black wings beating with urgency, their long necks all forward at the same angle.

'Cormorants,' gasped Art, remembering his conversation with Sofía about how they nested on Es Vedrà.

But it wasn't just them in the sky.

There were gulls too. A couple of kestrels, a lone falcon, and now – remarkably – a flamboyance of pink flamingos, who had only just recently migrated to the salt lakes in nearby Ses Salines for the summer. Their wings were even bigger than the cormorants', beating hard in the sky, angled back like arrowheads.

I remembered the taxi driver telling me about them on my first day on the island. *You must see them.*

'I'm seeing them, Pau,' I whispered. 'I'm seeing them.'

Art began to walk backwards. He tripped on a rock and landed on his backside, causing his attention to turn to the sky.

And then, back at beach level, there were other creatures. Including a goat. Coming from beyond the car park, from the shade beside Atlantis Scuba and the disappointingly empty bowl. It was Nostradamus, hobbling on his cloven hooves across the sand, a sense of determination and even hope flavouring his usual misanthropy. Indeed, every animal within a mile radius was rallying together like white blood cells to an infection, heading towards the hotelier currently scrabbling to his feet.

Lobsters again burst out of their new tank in the restaurant and scuttled towards the beach.

A bottlenose dolphin jumped out of the water and dived back into the sea, heading fast towards us.

Rabbits hopped across the sand, travelling in the same direction as geckos, lizards, snakes.

Moths and butterflies fluttered and danced their way towards the shoreline, the air between them specked with mosquitos and a loose cloud of cicadas. Every animal heading steadfastly towards Art, like iron filings to a magnet.

Sofía tried to address the crowd, telling them to leave the beach for their own safety, but no one listened to her. Well, no one apart from the Guardia Civil officer, whose fear of wild creatures was causing him to retreat back to the car park.

Alberto gave me a knowing look. 'You did it, Grace. You sent the signal.'

And I turned to see Art trying to run across the sand, but the first cormorant had reached him, pecking at him, attacking him with the intent to push him back towards the ocean. Art stayed steady, and pushed the creature away with his mind, breaking the poor bird's neck. The dead bird fell heavily to the sand. He then kicked a rabbit and stamped on a variety of insects. 'Die,' he said, trying to comfort himself with the word as well as using it as a command. 'Die, die, die, die, die . . .' It was a marked departure from the speech about sustainability and responsible tourism that he'd planned to give the assembled journalists and travel vloggers, who were still generally in a state of stunned silence as animals walked and ran and slid and flew around them.

But it was too late for Art now. A Montpellier snake similar to the one Alberto had given to the doorman at Amnesia was now biting his ankle. The light La Presencia had given him was now being taken back. It was leaking out from the wound the snake had given him, visibly diffusing into the water.

'No!' said Art, his voice loud but broken and fragile. 'Come back! Come back! Come *back!*'

He waded further into the sea in his linen suit. He cupped saltwater in his hands and gulped it down, as if he could somehow scoop La Presencia's light back inside him.

The whole beach by this time was so full of animals it was like looking at an army. A strange, eclectic animal army.

But in the end, it wasn't the land animals that proved to be the problem for Art. It was in fact a Portuguese man o' war jellyfish, a type that hadn't been seen in Ibiza's waters for more than seven years, whose long tentacles with nematocysts containing unusual levels of poison wrapped around Art and stung him multiple times on his calf and his inner thigh.

'I was better!' Art howled, his mind filled with a distant and maybe even mournful memory of torturing a woodlouse, before the pain became too much and he fell into the water.

I was better. It was an ambiguous statement. It could have meant and referenced many things, and his emotional state, fused as it was with fear and fury and a tinge of regret, certainly didn't give a clear insight into his meaning. His mouth then made another sound before his whole body went into shock and he collapsed face down in the water.

The body was brought back onto the beach by the humans. I and Alberto joined the effort. I didn't want Art to die. I promise you that.

Even though he would have tried to surreptitiously kill Marta and anyone else who got in his way if he'd stayed alive, I didn't want to be the cause of any more death. Alberto even made an attempt to resuscitate him. But it turned out that nature had other ideas. And, within a minute, his vital organs stopped functioning. I tried to read his mind in the last few moments, but it was impossible. It was like trying to read freshly inked words blurred in the rain.

And all the creatures – apart from the human ones, who stood there in bewildered silence – went back to their usual indifference towards humanity. The glow of La Presencia that had spread across the entire sea between the beach and Es Vedrà retreated until there was just a faint throb of light above the spot where I had first encountered it. And then it disappeared completely, back to the cloud-sphere hovering just above the seagrass, awaiting its next necessary intervention, and the surface of the sea looked as though nothing had happened. Just calm waves and the ordinary glisten of a reflected sun.

The sky soon cleared of birds, no more cicadas could be seen in the air, and the snakes slithered away across the sand. The dead cormorant stayed there, its pitch-black feathers contrasting starkly with the golden sand, its neck twisted at an unnatural angle, its head pointing towards the sea, towards Es Vedrà, towards La Presencia.

Only the goat, Nostradamus, seemed to show any real interest.

He stood there for a few seconds, staring at the dead human with a sense of something I interpreted as curiosity and relief. But then his general air of misanthropy returned, and he walked away from the commotion and the humans, to find some peace.

Alive

Of course, you knew I didn't die. That was always a spoiler. How could I have ever written this if I had?

I love that word 'spoiler', don't you? The idea that if we know what is about to happen, it takes the enjoyment from it.

It's so strange that we don't want spoilers in our stories but we seek them in our lives. We want to know we will fall in love, or be healthy, or finish the degree in style, get the good job or the comfortable pension. We want the solution. We want it all mapped out. We want to know everything ends well. We want it all *spoiled*, with as little mystery as possible. But where is the fun in that? And take it from someone with gifts of precognition beyond all the world's population: there are no real spoilers. There is always an observer effect. There is always an unknown variable, and that unknown variable is often yourself. Embrace the mystery would be my advice.

Embrace the impossibility of it all.

Enjoy the not-knowing.

Don't rush to the wedding or the death or the amen.

But yes, of course, it is no ghost writing this manuscript. I am very much still here and very much still alive. In fact, I am more alive than I have ever been.

The Fate We Make

So it was that Es Vedrà remained precisely as nature intended. No further goats were killed. No limestone was blasted out of shape. No habitats were destroyed. No busy route of water taxis was allowed above the Posidonia seagrass.

Sofía Torres went back to the regional parliament in Palma and, after declaring the deal with Eighth Wonder was no longer in effect following the event of Art Butler's death, she remarkably backed a vote to proceed with a bipartisan bill stating that no future agreements would be made for hotel developments in areas of 'ecological or cultural significance'. The bill passed.

The casino decided to drop all charges against us, as the former witnesses now said that they never saw any cheating and wondered why they had said that. The legal fees were considerably less than expected, and we donated more than half of the remaining money to the Ibiza Preservation Fund – though I kept a little of it for my shopping budget.

And, interestingly, of the journalists who had attended the press conference only one accurately reported what they had seen – but they were soon dismissed from their job and recommended psychiatric help on account of 'delusional thinking'. A couple of journalists had managed, despite their shock, to record everything on their phones, including a sky and beach full of determined creatures. But internet users later said that the footage was an example of how clever AI-generated imagery had become.

The official version of the story soon became that the famed British hotelier Art Butler had experienced some kind of mental breakdown and had wandered into the sea, where he had been stung by a jellyfish. La Presencia or the glowing sea was never mentioned. Alberto said this is how extra-terrestrial experiences were always treated. 'They start with a whole loaf of truth and reduce it to one edible crumb.'

Anyway, I should tell you one little thing more about that afternoon on the beach.

Marta arrived after Art's body had been taken away. Her newfound talents – as strong as mine, I think – had told her exactly what was happening, and so as soon as she could get away she'd headed to Cala d'Hort.

'It happened, didn't it?' she said, once she found us. The beach looked normal again, with only a few extra lizards and shell-shocked journalists hanging around. 'The signal.'

'Yes,' I said. 'Yes. I think it did. But I . . . I didn't want him to die.'

Alberto shook his head. 'No. No, you didn't. And you didn't kill him. A man o' war jellyfish did. Or La Presencia did. And, yes, La Presencia is in you as it is in me and Marta, but it acted through you to save the island. You helped save Es Vedrà, and you saved the future of Ibiza too. He was a killer, Grace. And if he had stayed around, he would have probably killed us too.' Alberto put his arm around Marta. 'It was a good speech today,' he told her.

'Thanks, Papá.'

Alberto smiled his big, bushy smile. 'What a family, eh?'

I smiled too, watching the lights fade in the ocean. 'Yes, you are.'

Alberto shook his head. 'Grace, for a mind-reader you really are bad at picking up things. I meant us. We are all family now. Me, you, Marta, the ocean. Even Nostradamus.' He looked over to the dusty red beach path, where the goat was waiting for his oats. 'We're a team.'

And for the first time in a long while I had the feeling, the very clear and hopeful feeling, that everything was precisely how it was meant to be. It was, however, short-lived. Because this was also the moment Alberto's mood shifted. He turned to Marta, and he was smiling but he was also frowning, and he scooped up some sand and looked at it as it slid through his fingers.

'Papá, what is it?' Marta asked. But she saw it all before he had even said a word. Just like I had seen it all. The gift of La Presencia was also its curse. Her first emotion was the easiest one to find in the face of pain. Anger.

'Papá, you didn't tell me. How could you not tell me? You can't be dying. You can't be . . .'

I understood her disbelief. People you love deeply become elemental. To hear they won't be there any more is like hearing the air or ocean won't be. It feels like a fatal disruption to the universe.

Alberto grimaced, as if taking glass out of a wound. 'Lo siento mucho, cielo. I didn't want you to look at me with pity. While I am here, I want to be alive in front of you. But you deserved to know.'

'I love you, Papá.'

'Whatever is awaiting me is awaiting me. For now, let's live.'

And Marta sobbed for a while. And he sobbed too. And I went away and sat on a wall and looked out at the sea, and for some reason I thought of a very young Daniel on a walk in the woods so many years ago, blowing the seeds off a dandelion and laughing in the sun.

This Is Life

We were on the *Neptuno*, out at sea. It was early in the morning. Ibiza looked like a dream of green and white in the distance. Alberto was in his full diving gear, but didn't have his goggles pulled down or the regulator's mouthpiece in yet because he was staring into his daughter's phone as she recorded him. He still had some days of life in him, but this felt like the last moment he would be strong enough to dive. This was, in short, his last chance.

'Is it on?'

She nodded. Marta was sat on an icebox, pointing the camera up at him.

'Right now?'

'Yes.'

He did his best to conjure a smile. He spoke his message first in Spanish, then in English, to make sure as many people as possible understood.

'My name is Alberto Ribas,' he said. I could feel his sadness as I sat on the deck. But it wasn't really there in his voice. He was sounding quite official, in fact, almost like he was giving a lecture. But there was a weakness, a tiredness, to him. Which may not have been entirely attributable to his illness. 'I am a marine biologist and author of *La vida imposible*. It is my strong belief that intelligent life exists elsewhere in the universe. I also contend that first-hand proof of such occurrences on the island of Ibiza has been overlooked. I believe this strongly, and it is a belief that cost me my job and my academic reputation.' He paused. Took a breath. His voice cracked a little now. 'Currently, I am dying. But below me, in the Mediterranean, is an extra-terrestrial entity which arrived into the ocean in the nineteenth century. We call it La Presencia.' He waited a moment as a plane flew overhead. 'La Presencia is a benevolent and life-preserving force sent from a planet we have termed Salacia, after the Roman goddess of the sea. It came to the sea because that is where life is. Ninety-nine per cent of the living area on this planet, in terms of cubic metres, is found in the ocean. That is why we must look after it. And that is why La Presencia is here. To help us protect life. Just as the seagrass beneath, it protects life. All life. Although humans tend to imagine the existence of alien life as a predatory threat, that has more to do with our own predatory nature reflecting back at us than the reality of unrecognised life we have encountered.'

He paused and looked across the ocean towards Ibiza and the golden sand of Cala d'Hort and the tree-lined slopes beyond.

'I am recording this because I want there to be no mystery about my disappearance. It is my belief that, as well as being here to help us protect our world, La Presencia's photonic forces also act as a portal. Crossing through that portal to Salacia is the only way I can be healed and have a chance of staying alive in some form, and so I have decided to . . .'

He paused again. A more substantial one this time.

'Papá?' Marta peered at him from behind her phone.

She could already sense it. I could too. The change.

'Actually, no,' he said, shaking his head, arguing with himself. 'No. No. I'm not saying this. I'm not doing this. It's bullshit.'

'Papá? What is going on?'

He took a breath. He closed his eyes to appreciate the air. Then, when he opened them again, he just stared at the large vertiginous rock behind us. He was no longer interested in the camera.

'Look at it. Look at Es Vedrà. It is precisely as it should be. We did that. We kept it. How it should be. Look at its shape. That outline. It is so complete. It is not too big and not too small. That is what my life has been. Complete. That is what you have helped it be, Marta. And so did your mother. You too, Grace. You have been a part of it too. I have no desire to have more than I was given, because I have been given so much. My life has been a strange shape, but I am pleased with it. It is the shape it needed to be. I know Salacia could be beautiful. But I am not a Salacian. I belong here. On Earth. And I am lucky to have roamed around this beautiful planet. I am a human. I don't want to be the snake egg in the olive tree that goes to a different ecosystem that wasn't made for him.'

Marta didn't know what to say.

'But maybe if you go to Salacia there will be a chance we could see you again,' I said. 'When our time comes. You can leave possibility open. Where there is life, there is possibility.'

He laughed a little at me then. 'Now who sounds like a magnet on a refrigerator, Grace?'

'Well, I have come round to fridge magnets. Just as you are proud to be a sentimental man, I am now happy to be a sentimental woman.' And then I remembered something I should tell him. 'Christina says she is well looked after. She says she is as healthy as she can possibly be. You could have that too.'

He smiled at me like I was missing the point. 'This is where we belong. Not out there in another galaxy. Christina was right to leave for Salacia. She had no idea of who or what was after her. Her natural life was about to be cut short by many years. She had more inside her. That is not me. I don't need to exile myself. Everything is done. I have danced and dived and loved more than most ever do. I have been true to myself. The next few weeks will be hard. But I need to stay here. I need to stay and be with you both. And enjoy whatever I have left. I would rather a single day on Earth than a lifetime elsewhere. This has been my paradise.'

And there was a finality to how he said that. Something solid. That couldn't be argued with. Like limestone rising out of the ocean.

He sat down. Tired. He looked over at Marta's icebox. 'Now. Por favor, cielo. I really fancy a lemonade.'

Vive Por Mí

Ten days later we were in the hospital. Marta held his hand as he died. He was in pain on that last day but at the very end he smiled his familiar gap-toothed smile. And he meant it. Every part of him was smiling, and the gratitude he felt filled the room.

They said they loved one another.

He had also managed to ask me to check in on Marta, if I was staying in Ibiza. I told him I would.

'Vive por mí,' he told his daughter. He then looked at me and said it again. That was his last wish to us. *Live for me.*

Marta cried. Her partner, Lina, was back in Ibiza now, and they hugged for minutes as Marta sobbed into her shoulder. And then I was beckoned into the hug too, and so I joined them, and I felt Marta's pain so sharp and real as her body convulsed. She felt it all. She didn't flinch from the pain. She howled like a wolf under the moon in that sterile hospital, strangely echoing her father's howl the first time I met him. Tender animals. And I silently underlined the promise I had just made to Alberto. *I will be here for you, Marta. I will do everything I can.* And we stayed there and just let her cry. Which is sometimes all you have to do.

Ashes

We scattered his ashes at sea, after dark. The water glowed a little. A soft throb of light coming from the seabed. I allowed myself an indulgent thought, that maybe La Presencia was taking him to Salacia anyway. Whether he liked it or not. Reconfiguring his atoms and sending him through the wormhole. Or maybe it was just saying goodbye, like we were.

We stayed in the boat a while. Marta had brought a little stereo and had made a playlist of songs that meant a lot to him. There was Bob Marley's 'Redemption Song', an absolutely gorgeous old Catalan song called 'Per Una Cançó' by Maria del Mar Bonet, 'It's My Life' by Talk Talk, The Cure's 'The Last Day of Summer', Fleetwood Mac's 'Landslide', José Padilla's 'Adios Ayer', the Rolling Stones' 'Beast Of Burden' and a dance song called 'Promised Land', which Marta and Lina bopped to on the boat.

They both pulled me up onto my feet.

'Come on, Grace,' said Marta, her mind a whole universe of emotion. 'Let's dance.'

And we danced. The water was calm enough for me to keep my balance. And after the song ended, she turned to me and said: 'I don't want to forget him.'

'You won't,' I told her. 'I miss my son and my husband every day, but I see them clearer than ever. I remember the good times and I am grateful to have lived them.'

'I love you, Grace. Thank you.'

And we hugged, and I felt a childhood memory of her father sailing her and her mother to Formentera, singing to her.

'You should go,' she said, knowing what my mind was seeing. 'To Formentera. You would love it.'

I Happen

Marta and I have agreed to take it in turns to feed Nostradamus. Every other morning I get in the Fiat Panda and go and pour a load of oats into his bowl and he is as grateful as a goat can be. Which isn't much, but it is something.

On my way there one morning I noticed something as I stepped out of the door. Not only that the plant – the *Nolletia chrysocomoides* – had grown and was in full bloom with the most exquisite yellow, heart-shaped flowers. But that there was another one further away, on the patio, which had grown through cracks in the tiles. And one a short way from that. And another, and another. Nine in total.

It had been a Tuesday.

Every Tuesday, by the way, I get the boat from Ibiza Town to Formentera and spend the day there, just as Marta recommended. Just to get away. The journey is less than half an hour so I have plenty of time even after feeding a goat. And nothing happens on Formentera. That is the whole point of it. Well, I mean, nothing too annoying happens. Of course, really, it is as happening as everywhere else. Air happens. Solitary cafés happen. Juniper bushes happen. Wheatfields happen. Sand dunes happen. Salt pans happen. Sheep happen. Lagoons happen. I happen.

Alberto wanted us all to live. And I am pleased to report, for good and bad, I feel alive. Here, a lucky guest on this fascinating and varied small island. It's bittersweet, to be so present when so many people I care about are absent, including Alberto (even the scent of Hawaiian Tropic makes me think of him). But that is how we beat death. We beat death by living while we are here. Death may be infinite, but, as we know, infinity is a relative concept. We can create a bigger infinity out of life. By *feeling*. And every day I feel. I feel deeply and intensely and what I feel is gratitude. To Ibiza, to Spain, to the world, to people, to nature, to life, to the hidden forces of the universe, and it makes me want to carry on helping to protect and cherish every natural thing.

Bluebird

You said in your email that you were in the dark and you need light. Well, don't rush it. It will come. Sometimes the light is there and we don't realise it. People sail over La Presencia and its photonic forces every single day and never know. What feels impossible now won't always be. But don't think of the bad times as unrelated to the good. The dark is how we see the light. We need the contrast. We don't see all the stars in the day, do we?

Speaking of stars, I had an interesting conversation with Marta yesterday.

She came round to help me with the garden. There is only a small patch of earth, but it is starting to look lovely. The once-extinct flowers were just the starting point. Marta wanted to help me. She said there was nothing more healing than gardening, and I think she is right. There is something about putting hands in the earth and trying to cultivate life that makes you feel elementally connected to everything. Marta had brought with her a few plants. A small hibiscus bush full of pink-red flowers she had bought from the garden centre, along with some lavender and potted herbs – parsley, mint, basil, rosemary. All are doing wonderfully with a little help from some agua de La Presencia from the olive jar.

They smell divine.

Anyway, we were talking about mathematics. We'd started off talking about the Fibonacci sequence and how its spirals are visible in the leaves and petals of plants and flowers. She said that, like me, she has always found comfort in mathematics – one of the things that led her to a career in astrophysics – but it was only recently that she understood *why* the subject was such therapy for her. It is because, in mathematics, you realise that balance and symmetry is actually in everything, even when it feels like chaos or pain.

'The ancient Greeks worshipped mathematics because they saw it as representing ideals,' she said, in roughly those words. 'And that it was always tied to religion because it was seen as something purer than normal life. That is why Pythagoras was a kind of spiritual leader. But I think La Presencia has given us the understanding that mathematical purity is everywhere. We are inside it. Nothing is random. Not life, not death. Not even randomness. Not even us two here making this dirt into a garden. All of it connects. Everything is part of this whole. This beautiful fabric. Heaven isn't somewhere else. Nor is everyone we have lost. We are tied to them. The strings are in us. Am I making sense?'

'Yes,' I said. 'You are making total sense.' And I meant it, because I had to say what I meant in front of her, because she could read my mind just as I could read hers.

Anyway, even after she left, I looked at this modest but lovely garden and I felt – more than any of the weird things that had happened – that this was the true change that had happened. I was gardening again.

But it wasn't just the garden. It was the inside too. I fixed up the house. I went back to the hippy market at Las Dalias and bought the painting of Es Vedrà from Sabine. I also acquired a picture of fruit. I now have a giant orange hanging in the bedroom. I bought some other bits and bobs too – some brighter clothes – with winnings I gained from a second little trip to the casino.

I didn't want to entirely rid the place of Christina's memory, though, so I thought I would cherish it instead.

I went to the dry cleaner's in Ibiza Town and had Christina's bohemian throw and rug given a makeover. They emerged bright and pretty, and I dusted the large fan in the living room and mopped the floor tiles. The old piano near the window still filled half the room, but I didn't want to get rid of it, so I did something else. I started to *play it*.

Yes, I can play the piano now. It comes easy to me. And the thing I like playing most is 'Blackbird'. I still can't sing, though. La Presencia is powerful, but not *that* powerful.

One other thing to tell you. I once found tattoos distasteful. But I have changed my mind. I recently went to the tattoo parlour in Playa d'en Bossa. I took with me Daniel's picture of the bluebird he'd given me for Mother's Day and asked for a version of it on my wrist. So now, whenever I see a red bicycle, I just look down at my wrist and remember the good.

It's really quite lovely. It flies with me everywhere.

Blaze

It rained yesterday.

I was in Santa Gertrudis. I'd just been food shopping. I stepped outside and it was raining. It fell hard and it comforted me. My car was parked a little way along the road, so I walked along, beneath the fading poster for Lieke at Amnesia, and a moment later I passed a villa with over-flowing pink and magenta bougainvillea flowers and a swimming pool visible through a gate. I stopped and watched the drops bounce and dance in the water. A kind of percussive music. I was mesmerised for a moment. I looked up to the sky and opened my mouth a little and enjoyed the rain's mineral taste. I am trying to do this now. Let moments get the best of me, however mad it looks to passers-by.

You see, shortly before he died I had sat on the beach with Alberto. We ate watermelon together. He was looking older and weaker and was in some pain. But he also looked quite calm and wise and handsome in the dying light, more philosopher than pirate, as we sat and watched the most glorious and complex sunset.

I told him I felt a responsibility. That I should go to the Amazon rainforest or to the Antarctic or equatorial Africa or somewhere else where I could use the talents I'd been given, but that I knew my talents would be stronger here, near La Presencia.

'It wants you to be here,' he said.

'I know. I think I will stay.'

He paused then. We sat in silence as he gazed at the sky above the water and Es Vedrà.

'It looks like a miracle,' he said, after a while. 'Every day Ibiza has sunsets like this, and I have taken them for granted. Does that make sense?'

It made sense. 'Galileo called mathematics the language of the book of nature. And we are trapped inside that book. We are words in that language. So it is hard to read and absorb and appreciate what we are inside, what we are familiar with. Just as Marta said, there are patterns everywhere.'

'Patterns, yes. You sound like Marta. I suppose that is a pattern.'

I contemplated this. The recurring mathematics of the natural world. The Fibonacci spirals found in whirlpools and pine cones and created by humpback whales in Antarctica to capture prey. Our blood vessels patterned like fork lightning and the twisting branches of trees. The fabric of the cosmos is woven with fractals and so are we. We are not alone in the universe, and we are not alone on Earth. We are connected not just to each other and not just to primates but to *everything*. To a goat, to a lobster, to the seeds of a dandelion. You said you felt you are in a pattern. A sequence. And you are. But it is vast and magnificent, this sequence. It connects you to every single thing in the universe. And one day it will surprise you in its expanse.

The light was still there in the sky, just a trace of it, as we sat on the beach. A strange deep red bleeding into the dark.

'The sky looks so still,' I said. 'Even though it is going to be night soon.'

Alberto tutted at me. 'Don't think about the night, Grace. Not just yet.'

And I looked at the red sky. And I felt its wonder so powerfully. Like it was dangerous just to inhale because I might dissolve into the universe.

'Yes,' I agreed. 'A miracle.'

I want you to understand these moments. They are all around us on this familiar, alien planet of ours. In every raindrop and scattered particle of light. Life sings and blazes. Even when we are numb to it, when we hide from it, when it is too loud and painful to experience, when we aren't equipped to feel it – it is there, waiting, to be cherished and protected, ready to give us at least one more blast of beauty before the night.

Dear Maurice,

I know I only clicked send ten minutes ago, and I know you won't have read the manuscript yet, but I wanted to say one more thing about it.

I describe a lot of things we are taught to believe are fantastical and even impossible. Paranormal powers. Protective forces beneath the ocean. I have experienced all these things, but not a single one of them is more or less remarkable or ridiculous than everything already here.

The taste of fresh orange juice. A fig. The sight of a flower. The sound of music. A slab of sunlight on floorboards. Cats and dogs and goats and lizards and dolphins. Harrison Ford's face. Imagine if you were from a planet with none of those things. Imagine how full of wonder everything would seem. How unjaded we would be by everything in front of us. How a picture of a sunset would never seem corny again. How a simple walk in an orchard would be utopia. How a cool breeze on a hot day would be a lottery win. How each and every bird song would be a symphony.

We should see ourselves as aliens, Maurice, because to the rest of the universe that is who we are.

Also – I should have said – if you want to visit, please tell me. It would be lovely to see you. I wish you well. I wish you everything. I sense your life will work out fine.

Your friend and teacher,
Grace Winters

PS: There is a bungalow in Lincoln I no longer need. I am sure you could get a good price for it. You didn't mention your financial worries – you just wrote 'there are other things too' – but I know the struggles you are having, in the same way I know all sorts of things that no one tells me. I hope this can help you solve them. It contains too many memories, and

I would like to give it to you. You see, I was once left a house in Spain, and it was a gesture that changed my life. So I would like to offer you a similar one. After all, knowing what I can now do in a casino, I no longer have to worry about money.

THE LIFE IMPOSSIBLE

Dear Grace,

I know I have told you this many times, but I still can't begin to express my deep appreciation for the bungalow. I thought you would like to know that a sale was agreed yesterday. It truly was a life-changing gesture and I will be able to help my sis a lot with it too.

But also, I want to thank you for your story. I shouldn't have believed any of it, and yet I somehow believed all of it. You have helped me break the pattern. Or at least switch to a better one. And so I am coming to Ibiza. I am going to have an adventure and get a train all the way to Dénia and get the ferry. I hear it is best to arrive by boat. I will be there the second week of September. I have a good feeling about it. Maybe you could say a premonition. Last night I dreamed of the sea. It glowed. Maybe it calls me the way it called you.

See you soon, I hope.

An infinite thank you.

Maurice
x

Acknowledgements

All books are a team effort. This one especially. I have quite a lot of people to thank.

First, my brilliant editor Francis Bickmore, who I have worked with on every book since *The Radleys* fifteen years ago, and who always knows how to help me best tease out the story and gives me licence to embrace my weirder ideas. Also, I was very lucky at an early stage to have input from my international publishers, including invaluable comments from the shining minds of Patrick Nolan, Doris Janhsen and Iris Tupholme.

I'm equally grateful for my agent, Clare Conville, a literary legend who thankfully got into this idea right from the start and understood what I was trying to do.

I want to thank, as ever, Jamie Byng and everyone at Canongate Books. Thanks to the brilliant and indispensable team of Jenny Fry, Alice Shortland, Lucy Zhou, Jessica Neale, Charlie Tooke, Vicki Rutherford, Jo Lord and Sasha Cox.

My snippets of Spanish were helped by having the wonderful Silvie Varela kindly cast her eyes over the dialogue.

And, as always, I must thank Andrea Semple. My first reader, my first editor, my best friend – and not to mention the person who was there through the highs and lows of our early Ibiza years. And to Pearl and Lucas, for putting up with me trying to interest them with facts about seagrass and Spanish history.

This book is self-evidently shaped by my love of Ibiza, and I want to thank everyone I know and have known on that island. From when I first lived and worked there in the nineties, to rediscovering my love for the place and in recent years. I am grateful to the numerous old and new friends I have met there, and to the place itself. That magical, mystical, multifarious island in the Mediterranean which always defies any preconceived perceptions.

And I would like to acknowledge the people who do a lot of work in protecting the ecology of the island. In particular I'd like to mention Ibiza Preservation (ibizapreservation.org), which for nearly two decades has been working to protect the habitat of the island, with key projects to protect the island's lizard population, to reduce plastic pollution on Ibiza and Formentera, and to preserve the endangered but vital Posidonia seagrass meadows against pollution, damage from boats and coastal urbanisation.

Last but not least, I want to thank you, the reader. I am very lucky to have you to share my stories with. I had stepped away from writing for a few years. But support from readers helped bring this story into being. I hope you liked it. Cheers. Gracias por todo.

Santa Agnès
de Corona

Santa
Gertrudis

San Rafael

San Antonio

Cala Bassa

Cala Comte

Amnesia

EIVISSA

Sa
Talaia

Cala
d'Hort

Cala
Jondal

Es Vedrà

Es Cubells

Playa
d'en
Bossa

Es Cavallet

Ses Salines

Formentera